Anita Sivakumaran was born in Madras and has lived in the UK since 2004. Her historical novel, *The Queen*, based on real events, has been made into a major television series. *Cold Sun* is her first novel in the DI Patel detective series.

Also by Anita Sivakumaran

The Queen
The Birth of Kali
Sips that Make a Poison Woman

COLD
SUN

Anita Sivakumaran

dialogue
books

DIALOGUE BOOKS

First published in Great Britain in 2021 by Dialogue Books

10 9 8 7 6 5 4 3 2 1

A CIP catalogue record for this book
is available from the British Library.

ISBN 978-0-349-70156-1

Typeset in Berling by M Rules
Printed and bound in Great Britain by Clays Ltd, Elcograf S.p.A.

Papers used by Dialogue Books are from well-managed forests
and other responsible sources.

MIX
Paper from
responsible sources
FSC® C104740

Dialogue Books
An imprint of
Little, Brown Book Group
Carmelite House
50 Victoria Embankment
London EC4Y 0DZ

An Hachette UK Company
www.hachette.co.uk

www.littlebrown.co.uk

For Harry

'His cold righteous heart burnt the women in red.'

Chapter XIV, Verse IX , Book 2,
The Resurrection of Manu

Sparks flew from the welding gun. Spots danced in the boy's unprotected eyes. He blinked them away, placed the gun on the tamped earth, stood, stretched. Waiting for the metal to cool, he watched the mechanic kneeling in the dirt, blue coveralls filthy, reattaching a rusty bumper to an old Ambassador. The mechanic glanced up, his eyes meeting the boy's and flitting away like a butterfly. He nearly dropped the bumper.

It wasn't often that the boy allowed his eyes to meet another's. Crouching now, he steadied the cylinder at his feet, checked if the joint had sufficiently hardened. Tugged at it to make sure. Then he lifted the cylinder into his backpack. Without a word or nod to the mechanic, he lifted the pack to his shoulder and left.

Outside, he paused to blink a few times. The sun hung low over the strip of wasteland on which the concrete and corrugated-iron motor-repair shack perched. Scrub grass, hard brown earth. Torn plastic bags flapped in the dusty breeze. A faint stink of decaying offal and human faeces. The rough concrete walls and curtained rear doorways of a row of butcher shops stretched in either direction. The boy walked slowly, eyes lowered.

A street dog nosed at a mound of rubbish. Her teats stretched low, pink and white patches on them. One eye glistened pearly in blindness. Ignoring the angry buzz of displaced bottle flies, the boy knelt beside the dog. He brought some stale bread from his pocket. The dog wagged her tail. Intent, the boy watched her gobble it down from his open palm. He let her lick his fingers, lifted them to his nostrils, smelt the stench of rotting meat and butcher's bones in her saliva.

Soon the dog grew restless. She cocked her ears at some far off sound, prepared to move on. The boy reached for his backpack, slid the zip open. The dog wagged her tail again with renewed enthusiasm. He tugged at the metal ball one more time. The joint had hardened well. He fitted it into the tube.

The dog's tail drooped to cup her anus as the boy positioned the tube's mouth to her forehead, his knee propped under her jaw. Inured to the city's noise, she barely flinched when he pulled the lever and the sudden boom filled the air.

The tail wagged on for a few moments, even after the one good eye had glazed over. A smile curled the boy's lips. He gazed slowly around the empty wasteland. Then he packed up and left.

Soon, a blanket of bottle flies covered the carcass.

Part One

Chapter One

'Patel!' Sergeant Jackson hollered across the heads of fourteen detectives busy at their desks. 'Skinner's looking for you. Hop to it, baby.'

Patel ignored the sniggers. He took the blue pencil to the report in his hand, marked a missing apostrophe to the word 'its'. He threw the pencil into an open drawer, where it was swallowed by clutter, and ran a hand through his hair.

'Sadly, I already left,' he said to Jackson, who just shrugged.

He closed the file, tucked it under an arm, slung his jacket over one shoulder and jogged to the stairs. His hair bounced and flopped over his forehead, overdue a cut. Boyish locks did not suit a homicide detective. Even if, as Sarah put it when she felt friendly, combined with his smoky brown eyes they made him look like a Bollywood hero.

By the time he'd passed the IT help desk and rounded the conference block, he was out of breath. Those years of athletic training were long gone, together with his cricketing career. Mostly now he ran to catch the Piccadilly Line and lifted pints of lager.

He slowed outside the row of senior management's private cubicles, glanced through windows overlooking the Thames. Bitter rain streaked the glass, transforming London's dust into slime. Through the worm-runs of water, he saw the traffic lights flash dully on Westminster Bridge. Orange, then red.

Perfectly miserable weather. Perfect for a jaunt down the road for a pint of London Pride. But really, he ought to be heading home to pack. The flight was at five a.m. and he hadn't so much as laid out a pair of swimming trunks. In fact, where *were* his trunks? He'd last seen them in September, when they'd booked a holiday at some posh hotel in Cornwall. He and Sarah. Booked and cancelled last minute for emergency root-canal treatment. The very thought of it made his jaw ache.

He pushed Inspector Rima's door open.

She looked up from her computer, swept her hair off her shoulder, said, 'Don't you knock?'

'I was going to leave this on your desk.'

She held her hand out for the report, eyes twinkling. 'So you're off, then? Sunny Tenerife?'

'Yeah.' He grimaced, breathless and sweaty, feeling a little foolish to be having this conversation. 'Nearly got cancelled again.'

'Oh yeah?'

'This case came up.' He indicated the file, the cover of which Rima was flicking open. 'Skinner assigned me.'

Rima raised her eyebrows. She wasn't unaware of Superintendent Skinner's feelings about Patel.

'You got lucky?'

'I guess.'

'How?'

'Deceased is a forty-one-year-old homeless male. Name: John Snow.'

'No kidding.'

'Anyway, another homeless fella comes down off his four-day bender under some bridge in West Margate, half frozen to death. Looks down, sees the blood all over his bony hands, his rags. Runs himself and his bony arse straight to Station WB10 South Precinct and 'fesses.'

Rima, flicking through the report, didn't appear to be listening.

'You'd think the devil got hold of the poor bugger.'

Rima closed the report, opened it again, studied the top sheet. She frowned, put her finger on it.

'Why no copy for the FLO?'

'Homeless man doesn't rate a Family Liaison Officer.'

She made a face. 'Of course. We've to make "savings" –' she used air quotes '– of thirty million by the end of the year.'

'You sound just like Skinner.'

She smiled. 'If we had the resources, we'd track his family down. Even a bum has family, somewhere.'

It was unlike her to display Samaritan urges.

'Homeless murder,' said Patel. 'Cold pavement to cold slab.'

'Poor bugger,' she said. She stared at him. 'Come here.'

A shiver up his spine. 'Got to go pack, Inspector.'

She came around the desk and put a finger on his shirt button. 'How about something to remember me by in Tenerife?'

Fighting the urge to back away and run, he said, 'Sarah wants to—'

A knock on the door. Without pause, it opened.

'There you are, Sergeant. Been looking everywhere for you.' The smarmy voice of Detective Inspector Bingham.

Rima's hand was back by her side. 'Dave,' said Patel. 'Not down the pub yet?'

'About to, then I got asked to run an errand.' Bingham chuckled, then guffawed.

Patel smelled beef stroganoff from the canteen lunch. He waited. He thought there was a joke brewing.

Bingham guffawed and chuckled some more before saying, 'Super wants you.'

'When? Tomorrow?'

'Now, cupcake. He's got an assignment for you.'

'He knows I booked the week off.'

'Yeah, he might have mentioned something like that. All the homicide detectives tied up, you know? After the New Year's Eve spike in cases and all.'

'You're the SIO?'

'Nothing to do with me. I'm going to Thailand tomorrow. Did I tell you? Warm up me old cobblers.'

Patel just looked at Bingham.

'Don't keep the man waiting. Ta, love.' A quick ferrety glance at Rima and Bingham went away, strutting and chuckling his head off.

Patel raised his eyebrows at Rima.

She twitched her lips in a smile. 'Go and get some, Sergeant.'

'Have a seat, Patel.'

Superintendent Skinner gestured to the faded leather chair across his desk. Patel cautiously lowered himself into it, knowing it creaked madly. Although the smile on his face and his salt and pepper bouffant hair gave Skinner an avuncular air, his steel-grey eyes emanated hate.

'You've closed the homeless case.'

'Yes, sir.'

'You'd think that in these times of austerity we wouldn't have the resources to go after every teenage drug overdose, every homeless man pissing himself to death.'

'It was murder, sir.'

Skinner's smile vanished. 'Murder of one fuck-head bum by another.'

'Report's been submitted, sir. Second-degree manslaughter.'

'Justice for the poor homeless man. Could go on a recruitment poster: "We serve with ... care in the community."'

'Just doing my job, sir.'

'Twice the patriot, aren't you? Playing cricket for the country, and now righting the wrongs done to your countrymen, be they royals or the great unwashed.'

Patel felt a prickle of wariness.

'Our poster boy.' Skinner's tone implied he was a highly unlikely one, and on that point, at least, Patel had to concur.

'You've been with us three years, have you not?'

Patel nodded. Baiting, taunting, and now the trip down memory lane.

'You certainly caused a storm in Yorkshire.'

Patel stared at Skinner, keeping any emotion off his face.

'The Dales Ripper.' Skinner smacked his lips. 'Some of us can only dream of netting such a high-profile criminal.'

Skinner leaned forward.

'Tell me. What did it feel like, the eureka moment?'

'Eureka moment, sir?'

The whites of Skinner's eyes shone like a dirty enamel sink that'd had a good scrubbing.

Patel breathed deeply and thought of things he wished he could forget. Someone had seen a girl in the area, alone, a stranger. She matched the description from the latest missing case. Patel, covering for his mate, did a few extra knocks on the door in his lunch break. Beautiful, picturesque Thirsk. Sheep bleating, apples on trees. Sunny autumn day. Last cottage in a lane overlooking some pasture. A lone man in his seventies lived there. What had triggered his suspicions? Apart from the jibe about Patel's tan, he'd been such a sweet old man. Put the kettle on. Rooted out the chocolate biscuits. Did the chitchat. *Lovely autumn weather, isn't it ... ?* Patel had sat down. What harm in one cup of tea, he'd thought. The old man rattled teacups with shaky hands, reminding him of his dada-ji. He could see the door to the living room through the passageway, shut. An under-stairs half-cellar, the door ajar. The old man had placed the cup of tea in front of Patel with a bright smile. Poor thing was desperate for some company, he'd thought. The man sat down and smacked his lips, glancing ever so briefly at the clock above the passageway before pushing the sugar bowl towards the middle of the table. Patel also turned to look at the clock, then his eyes lowered to the passageway, and the partly open cellar door. It was then that he'd seen in his mind's eye the grille in the ground by the front door as he'd stood pressing the doorbell, and whilst waiting, heard what he'd put down to a little scurrying creature in the underground joists.

'It's not rats, is it?' he'd said to the old man, whose smile faded, and in its place appeared an expression that froze Patel's blood. Part glee, part relief at not having to pretend any more, to be this doddery, kindly grandpa.

Now Skinner pressed: 'You know, you've never given me the details. How many times have I asked you?'

'Details are in the case file, sir.'

Skinner shook his head. 'I want to know how you knew, Patel. What you felt.'

Like he'd been hit with a twenty-ton truck. Like the great maw of hell had opened beneath him in the middle of a sleepy Yorkshire village.

'Did you feel –' Skinner sprayed spit '– like you'd hit the jackpot?'

'Like the goddess Luck had given me a good going over, sir.' Patel said, thinking, Asshole.

Skinner sighed. His face shut down. He tapped a finger on the file in front of him. 'How do you find London, working with us?'

'Quiet after Yorkshire, sir.'

Skinner didn't smile.

London. He liked the anonymity London offered. He blended in better, after rural Yorkshire. No one gave him a second glance in London – although he did get some surprised looks when he told people he was a police officer. But when they asked him how he came to be a murder cop, he felt at a loss to explain. It felt lame to admit he'd drifted into it, after the cricket didn't pan out. Did he always want to be a homicide detective, people asked? All he could say was, he'd loved reading Sherlock Holmes as a kid. Still, the past three years, his work had felt like treading water. Open and shut cases. Manslaughter rather than premeditated. Doper A kills doper B. Teenagers without passports knifing each other for sport. Domestics. A hell of a lot of domestics. Usually, man kills woman. Occasionally, woman kills man. Gruesome, sure, but at least within the purview of humanity. A policeman's humanity, he'd come to feel, was linked to the humanity of the criminal. He opened and closed files, wrote up reports; made few friends and no enemies. And then, a year ago, Skinner'd given him a case, his first as senior investigating officer: Skinner's army colonel friend's son's high-profile death. Accidental erotic asphyxiation, Patel and a bunch of experts concluded. The dad had wanted it to be murder, so he could fix his rage on someone. Or so he could rewrite his son's homosexual history. He remembered Skinner's words. *At least entertain the possibility for a few days. Look for someone, just to give the man some relief.* Patel wouldn't, couldn't.

'Let's move on,' Skinner said now.

Hallelujah.

'I'm sending you to India to help with an investigation.'

'Sir?' Patel wasn't sure he'd heard right.

'You fit the bill, Patel. You have the record. They need a goddamn genius. It's a Category A+. Well-connected victims.'

Patel's nostrils twitched. Did he say victims, as in plural?

'Why are we involved, sir?'

'Foreign minister pushed buttons. So the Home Office—'

'Ours or theirs?'

'What?'

'Foreign minister?'

'Oh, ours. His ex-wife, an Indian national, is the latest victim. There may be a British connection.'

Patel remembered. It had been a 'most read' item on the Beeb's news website. Sabah Khan, socialite, ex-wife of Foreign Minister Alex Goldblum, girlfriend of tennis ace Freddie Bhatt, found 'Murdered', found 'Slaughtered by Psychopath'. Prominent Indian women up in arms 'Demanding Psycho's Capture. A March for Safety. Candlelight Vigil'.

'Wasn't that a week ago?'

'The Indians are competent to handle it. It is their turf, after all. However, they've agreed to be guided by some old-fashioned Scotland Yard expertise.' Skinner cracked a smile in support of his pronouncement.

'Sir, I'm hardly qualified to lead such an . . .'

'You're not there to lead, Patel. You're there to liaise.'

'So I'm not SIO?'

'They have an SIO. Some feller called –' Skinner squinted at the screen '– Sub-ra-man-i-um. Can't pronounce the name. You'll play consulting detective.'

'Ah, like Sherlock Holmes.'

'Eh?' Skinner looked blank, frowned. 'Listen carefully, Patel. Don't muddy the waters. They don't need hand holding. Serve up some of your famous instinct. It's not a question of if, but when, they catch the killer. Always the same, these situations. Sooner or later, psychos make mistakes, start showing off.'

Sooner or later? What was he, a goddamned clairvoyant?

'Officially you are a Scotland Yard consultant. They take credit if they catch him, they take the blame if they fail.

'Here's the file.' Skinner lobbed the green folder over. 'Indians faxed most of the material they have. You'll have time on the flight to review.'

'Flight, sir?'

'You leave at noon tomorrow. An expedited visa will await you at the airport.'

'Sir.'

'No time for modesty, Patel. This is deadly serious. You're the best man for the job. Now go tell your wife and pack.'

'Fiancée, sir. We're off to Tenerife tomorrow.'

Skinner looked at him for a moment, expressionless. 'Guess not,' he said. He turned to his computer screen and peered long-sightedly through his bifocals.

Patel got up.

'Oh, and another thing, Patel.'

'Sir?'

'First thing tomorrow, go see Minister Goldblum. His office is expecting you.'

The bouncer came flying. Hook it to the boundary or take it on the chin.

'Yes, sir.'

Patel fumbled for the key with one hand, checked his breath with the other. Gently unlocked the door. Cautiously entered. Slipped his shoes off and padded down the hallway. Peeped around the living-room door frame.

Sarah was curled on the sofa, reading a book. He peered at the cover. Erin Sarkof's sculptures. A white-haired woman leaned against a plaster-cast bald head wearing giant sunglasses.

Her white linen dress was bright against deep-brown arms suffused with that golden glow denied the skin of South Asians. Golden light of southern France. He thought of the rain-awful pitch-black night he'd trudged through after five rushed pints at the pub.

'Hey, honey.'

Sarah looked up. 'Hey.'

He took off his jacket, flung it on the back of the sofa, before remembering to kiss the cheek she'd turned up for him. He flicked at a bit of plaster dust on her chin.

'Still working on the orgy scene?'

She laughed in an exasperated but friendly sort of way. 'It's not —'

'I know, I know.' He waggled his eyebrows. 'You show me three women, naked, fiddling . . .'

'It's not about—'

'It is to the punter. You say female sexual expression. I say, *wahey*!'

She shook her head. This wasn't one of the times she found him funny.

'I'm sorry, Sarah.'

'It's not like you planned this.'

'Skinner's orders.'

'You already apologised.'

He'd called from the pub, after a fortifying pint. She'd been reasonable, given the circumstances. Still, he was filled with guilt.

'I know you wanted to discuss . . .' He made vaguely circular gestures with his hands.

Sarah blushed. In that instant she looked fetching: girlish, with her long dark hair in a ponytail, no make-up on her winter-pale, freckled face.

He sat next to her and put a hand on her knee.

She took an audible breath. 'Could they not find someone else? There are, what, hundreds of homicide detectives?'

'Twenty-four, actually. Skinner said I was the best man for the job.' He felt himself wince, saying it.

'Best man, or the man with the right colouring?'

'Hmm, I honestly don't know. My grandparents are from Gujarat. My parents are from Uganda. I'm not exactly an old India hand.'

'India hand? What does that mean?'

'It's from colonial times, you know. Someone with experience in dealing with the natives.'

Sarah laughed a little. 'You've been there before, no?'

'To play cricket. Once. It was all a blur. Airport to hotel to nets to gym to team talks to stadium. Didn't catch a breath. Just overwhelming, you know. And then that's where ...'

'Oh, it happened there?'

'Yeah. The Chepauk stadium in Madras. Or is it called something else now? Channa?'

'Chennai.'

'Yeah, there.'

His hand still lay on her knee. She rubbed the top of his wrist, the injured wrist (it was fine now, but he still thought of it that way, as if it, and him, still needed succour).

Sarah said: 'Why don't you change and shower? I'll whip up some pasta thing.'

'There's some bacon from yesterday.'

'That was from last week. I chucked it.'

'Oh.'

He left her on the sofa and went into the bedroom.

Two suitcases were propped open on the bed, full of neatly folded clothes – shorts and summer dresses, sunglasses and sun cream. He poked through his things. She'd even found his swimming trunks. Passports and tickets in his green wallet that she liked to keep in her handbag when abroad.

He began to get out of his clothes. He picked up a towel from on top of her packed suitcase. The one in the bathroom was rank. He saw a wispy bit of black satin. She'd packed her sexy lingerie, black with little red bows on the stockings. She had worn it often in their first year together. Years since it'd made an appearance.

An incoherent sound escaped him. He sat down beside the suitcase, put his head in his hands. He admitted to himself he was relieved to be going somewhere, anywhere, that wasn't Tenerife with Sarah. Even India, to the middle of a homicide operation to catch a psychopath.

And he admitted to himself, finally, that the root-canal treatment in September could have waited till they'd got back from Cornwall.

The smell of frying garlic reached him from the kitchen.

'Ten minutes.' Sarah's voice pierced the bedroom.

Shaking off the beastly feelings, he got up and padded to the shower, towel slung over one shoulder.

Five minutes later, suitably broiled, he heard two slight taps on the door – Sarah's version of a knock.

'Yeah?'

'Your phone beeped.'

'What's it say?'

Since he'd begun having his doubts about their future, he liked to make overtures of openness with Sarah, as though showing her he had nothing to hide, like some feinting poker genius. He dried his toes and hung the towel on the rail. There was a longer pause than usual for reading a text. Then a cold fist landed in his stomach. He'd texted Rima from the pub. Oh

God, he hadn't checked if she'd replied yet. He'd regretted the text as soon as he'd pressed send.

Sarah's voice cut through the wooden door, cold and level. 'It's from Inspector Rima Seth. She says, "Sounds like a lucky escape, then. Perhaps you can start making the baby on Skype. LOL."'

He closed his eyes.

'Would you like to dictate a reply?'

Chapter Two

Yawning, Patel read from the *Whole Earth Guide to Everywhere*, 'Karnataka is an intoxicating cocktail that is quintessential India.' He was sure the words together had meaning, but it eluded him. Booze, guilt, insomnia, the cold-shouldered good-bye from Sarah – deserved – and a frustrating morning chasing the minister, undeserved.

The tannoy overhead shrieked, 'Flight BA 134 to Bengaluru has commenced boarding.' Has commenced, he said under his breath. Why use a simple word when ...?

A manic toddler crashed against his left leg. He picked it up and stood it on its feet. It gurgled at him. Its mother raised sleep-deprived eyes by way of apology as she dragged the squealing bundle away towards some unsuspecting aircraft. Patel shut the *Whole Earth* guide, put it back on the shelf, picked a Lonely Planet. He looked over at the till queue, wondering if there was time to dash to Boots for some Eno.

'There he is.'

He turned. A man, arm extended, pointed at Patel. Blue epaulettes on a white shirt, crackling walkie-talkie. Airport security. What now? Then he saw the hassled, puffing toff behind. Flanking him were two men in dark suits with shades and earpieces.

'Minister,' said Patel, 'I couldn't see you this morning.'

Foreign Minister Alex Goldblum put his hands up. 'Tried my best. Couldn't get away. Thought I'd catch you here.' His phone beeped. He glanced at it, raised a finger. 'Just got to take this, sorry.'

Patel swallowed his irritation and took the guidebook to the till. He had turned up at Goldblum's office at eight a.m. sharp, to be informed that the minister was at a G7 organisational committee meeting at the other end of town. The secretary rang the minister on his mobile and Patel was sent to catch him a few minutes before Goldblum's nine a.m. He had to cadge a squad car and be blue-lighted through the lovely London traffic. Wading through hundreds of woolly-hatted, rainbow-trousered protestors, he entered the building where the minister and his foreign colleagues had been holed up since the previous evening. It was the eve of the G7 summit.

Nine a.m. came and went. Patel spent an hour and a half in the noisy lobby – communing with slippery, bright sofas and pop art prints. Svelte, hard-looking female secretaries rushed past him with printouts, and keen bespectacled young men, investors of the hedge fund variety no doubt, peacocked back and forth. Surely Goldblum wasn't going to save capitalism single-handed that morning. A homicide investigation, any right-minded individual would say, took precedence over whatever nefarious deal he was running. Especially since it was Goldblum who wanted the Yard's involvement in the first place. But the minister didn't appear, so Patel left to catch his flight.

Now, in the departure lounge WH Smith, Patel reached the front of the queue. Goldblum stood beside him, mumbling on the phone. Pocketing his change and guidebook, Patel turned to the minister, who put his phone away. 'Can you walk and talk?'

It was a long slog to the C gates. They should have a bit of time. Just. They passed Accessorize and a Costa.

'Do you know . . . ' began Goldblum as Patel noticed a Boots, and remembered his need for Eno. He dropped his hand luggage, a heavy Billingham full of files on the Indian investigation, made eye contact with one of Goldblum's spooks, pointed to his bag and headed across the floor into Boots. Goldblum continued talking by his elbow, as if they were taking an evening stroll. 'I'd wanted an experienced officer, one who's conducted major homicide operations, to fly to India and take over the whole investigation. Damned well threw a fit in front of the home secretary. Still, I owe her my left ball for green lighting this at all.'

Patel digested this as he looked high and low for the Eno. 'You must be disappointed.'

Goldblum gave a small laugh. 'Skinner convinced me we needed to send you, just the one officer, just you, *Sergeant* Patel. Told me you shit gold.' He shook his head.

The insides of Patel's stomach began to burn. He looked for a shop assistant. He could not claim to understand the politics involved.

'There's one.' Goldblum waved.

Patel had to spell out 'Eno' three times, then google it on his phone and present a picture. The pimpled teenager in charge of the pharmacy said they didn't stock that product.

'You do.'

'We don't.'

'I've bought it from you before.'

The child morosely shook his head.

His stomach felt like it was being stoked for the fires of hell, the one place he wanted to hurl Skinner. The bastard had grasped the Indian crown of thorns and laid it on Patel's head. Not an inspector, not a team. Just him.

Outside, one of the spooks was leaning against the shop's automatic doors, probably in contravention of several health and safety laws, the Billingham's strap under his fake-Prada shoe.

Patel jerked his bag off the floor, causing the spook to stumble back, and strode on, aware of the clock tick-tocking.

'Sir, just a few pertinent questions as we walk. When was the last time you saw Sabah Khan?'

Alex Goldblum clutched the handrail and cleared his throat, momentarily disorientated by the movement of the walkway.

'A mutual friend's wedding ceremony ... well, renewal of vows, actually, in Florida. Last summer.'

'Could you tell me a bit about her? A general picture.'

'She was ... You've seen the gossip rags? She was provocative, feisty. Not cut out to play the politician's wife.' A faint smile crossed the man's ruddy face. An old joke, perhaps.

'Did she have enemies?'

'Good God, no. She was into saving the world. Board of a dozen charities. In the soup kitchen Christmas mornings. She even—'

The tannoy shrilled, 'Mr Vijay Patel, your flight is about to depart. Please come to Gate Fifty-seven immediately.'

Patel glanced behind him. The airport security officer had disappeared and only the two spooks remained. He walked faster.

'The Indians have promised co-operation,' Alex Goldblum said. 'Which could equally mean non-co-operation. Make sure you're on top of them. If you don't ask, they won't tell.' His cheeks grew redder by the second as he struggled to keep up.

'I'll do my best.' Patel thought Goldblum sounded like his dad, nagging him on the first day of secondary school. At least the minister hadn't made reference to him being 'one of them', on account of his skin. It was refreshing to be treated as the Englishman he was.

They didn't speak until they reached the shuttle stop. Patel looked up at the black screen with glowing orange letters. Next shuttle in three minutes.

'First time to India?'

'Yes, sir. Actually, no, sir. I've been there briefly, once, to play cricket.'

'Of course! You're *that* Patel! How's the wrist?'

Patel's mouth turned down as he said, 'It'll never be the same, sir.' He hated being asked about his wrist.

Goldblum made a noise like grunting. Patel assumed it was sympathy.

'Don't expect the bureaucracy to be as efficient as it is here.'

It took a moment for Patel to realise Goldblum was in earnest.

'Thing is, Patel,' he said, 'I've been dealing with the Indians, professionally and otherwise, nearly all my life. You really have to go with the flow there, but never ever give them the wheel. At the end of the day, they love a man who likes to run the show.'

Some foreign minister, thought Patel. Next thing he'd be calling them piccaninnies. 'I thought I was going there to liaise, sir, not to lead.'

'Well, we can't trust the natives not to bodge the investigation. I'm told you're the man with the leadership skills.'

Told by Skinner. And it was Skinner who'd instructed Patel not to stir the pot. He wondered what the Indians had been told.

'It will be a challenge to run an investigation with my hands tied, sir.'

Not to mention, Patel silently added, the lack of a fully equipped homicide team. He had no illusions about Indian resources.

'You think your trip a waste of time?'

Patel couldn't read Goldblum's tone.

'I'll certainly do my best to be an asset to the Indians, sir.'

'The murderer might well be British.'

Tosh, thought Patel. From his rapid perusal of the case files faxed over from India, Patel saw no reason whatsoever to suspect

British involvement. Khan had given up her British residency a year ago and moved to Bengaluru. At the time of her death, she'd been dating an Indian tennis star.

'The files suggest an Indian, sir.'

The minister shook his head emphatically from side to side, like a child.

'She had loads of British expat connections there. I wouldn't take the Indians' assumptions as bona fide. It isn't likely Sabah was taken in by a stranger. You don't know her like I do. Like I did.'

The minister's eyes were wide and shiny. The shuttle approached.

'Why d'you think it wasn't a stranger?'

The shuttle stopped. Before Goldblum could answer, the doors opened.

Patel stepped in, the minister, his spooks and two other passengers following. Goldblum shifted from one foot to the other. He clasped his hands together, then had to unclasp them and grab a handrail as the shuttle shot forward with a whoosh.

As they stepped out of the shuttle, the minister rasped in Patel's ear, 'We must have been married for about a year or so when we were invited to Balmoral.'

'The *castle*, sir?'

Goldblum nodded reverently. 'They'd organised a stag hunt the following morning. Sabah forbade me to go. I still remember now, she was standing by the window, furious, in her long black dress. The window had spectacular views of the Scottish mountains, but my eyes were only on her. Beautiful when angry – brown and flashing . . . '

The minister trailed off, his eyes fixed hauntedly on a digital noticeboard. Patel waited.

'There were all these people there. The Duke of Wellington,

the prince, Sven Hitchem, Vanessa Murdoch. So I said, "Babes. No way I can't go." The marriage was probably doomed from that minute. You know what she did? She crept downstairs in the night, slipped past the guards and whatnot, put a padlock on the shotgun-room door. They had to replace the door.'

Wow. That item didn't turn up in any of the gossip rags. The minister must have done a hell of a mop-up job.

As gently as he could manage, Patel said, 'You know there are two other victims before Ms Khan, sir. All three women unrelated to each other. It is unlikely there's a personal connection between Ms Khan and her killer.'

Of course, Patel knew Goldblum was insisting on the British connection so Scotland Yard could get involved.

'She was a black belt in karate, brown in tae kwon do. She nobbled two muggers in King's Cross when she was barely eighteen. I cannot believe she'd let a stranger . . . ' Goldblum's breath caught in his throat. 'For this to happen to her.'

His politician's swagger gone, Alex Goldblum looked a picture of loss.

Patel lifted his heavy bag, nodding towards the wildly gesturing stewardess at the boarding desk.

Goldblum cried: 'She deserved to live. Of all the people I know. If I could only swap . . . '

Patel put his bag down, took a moment he didn't have to shake the minister's hand. 'I'll do my very best, sir.'

Chapter Three

Mayor Hariharan's driver blew the horn over and over, then switched on the siren. The crowd – five thousand strong, passionately, chaotically, chanting peace messages – refused to part. Two police constables jammed in the front seat leaped out, scrabbling at the various items on their belts. Hariharan sighed.

He rolled down his window. 'Don't use your lathis,' he called to the policemen's backs. 'These people have every right to be here, same as me.'

Just in time. Both cops re-holstered their batons. Instead, they began pushing people from the car's path, with at least some show of moderation for their boss. Hariharan checked his watch. Nearly five. He'd be late, damn it.

At last, they pulled up before the canopy of the thousand-year-old banyan tree, under which the prostrate form of the fasting Mahatma Sankara lay, frankly melodramatically, on a raised dais. Mendicants and other assorted hangers-on ringed him.

Hariharan emerged from the car into the early-evening cool. A faint stink of sewage reached his nostrils from the nearby river. He edged along in front of the crowd. Many fell silent as they saw who it was. A man carrying a placard stumbled against the rope. The placard's corner nearly took out Hariharan's eye. For a moment, he was held by the images inches from his face:

the pixelated-inkjet corpses of the four Dalits and six Muslims lynched or burned by mobs in the last month.

He climbed the steps and knelt beside the great Gandhian, mindful of his trousers catching a stain from the filthy makeshift plankboard stage. Gently, he lifted the shaggy head, the hair white and fluffy like cotton candy. A young woman handed him a glass of orange juice. He held the glass out to the crowds. For a wild moment, he thought of the Christian Jesus, of the Holy Grail. What was the story?

The withered old husk that was the nobly fasting saint gasped, barely conscious. A doctor hovered, stethoscope held high like a vulture's beak.

'And with a sip of this juice,' Hariharan announced to the crowd, 'Swami Sankara ends his ten-day hunger strike.'

The crowd drew breath together. Palms came together. He poured a little liquid between lips so cracked they resembled more an old lava flow than a man's mouth. Gently enough, he placed the Neta's head back upon the pillow and shook his stiff arm. His eyes ranged over the clacking placards.

I am Dalit, Dalit is me …

Muslims are our brothers

Cows are God! Cows are food! Cows are an Excuse!!!

Such dark comedy. He caught the sympathetic eyes of the great-niece who'd delivered the juice into his hands, and smiled dutifully at her. She'd been instrumental in persuading the Mahatma to accept Hariharan's deal.

His smile soured as he noticed raised batons cutting a path for the chief of police's massive Bolero. The car kissed the stage and the fat, ponderous figure of Chief Rajkumar struggled out. He clambered directly up on to the stage, puffing, the steps only a few feet to his left. The chief never did have much of an eye for detail, Hariharan thought.

Rajkumar bestowed the thinnest of smiles on the mayor. He nodded to a flunkey, who immediately began lengthening the microphone stem that had been lowered to the level of the Swami's pallet. Sankara had been reading Gandhian aphorisms to his devotees in the days before his strength gave out. The press pushed forward from their demarcated area. Notepads, cameras and microphones bristled.

But this was Hariharan's show. He seized the microphone and regarded the crowds for a moment, then his eyes caressed the journalists.

'You've gathered to hear the words of the Mahatma. Yet the great man is still weak from his hunger strike.' He laid on them his most winning smile. A smile worth two elections and counting. 'Disappointing as it must be, you'll have to make do with me.'

A few laughs, at least.

'Now, some of you here today won't be satisfied by the outcome of this great sacrifice your Mahan has made. What? A promise to hold more discussions? More talk about this rise in vigilantism? *Arre baba*, have we not talked enough? you will say. What about action? We need action.

'I understand your anger, believe me I do. Persecution of minorities. Cow vigilantism. But we must address the root cause of these issues. Not just match violence for violence, until even our commendable Bengaluru police force –' here he smiled pointedly at Rajkumar '– will not be effective.

'We are a democracy and so we must uphold the rule of law. Your Neta embodies the conscience of our great nation. With all his heart, he welcomes discussion, debate. So this is why I –' and he put a hand to his heart '– have now arranged this cross-party group. And we will welcome input from all the enforcement agencies: state police, IAS and IPS.'

He looked again for a moment at Rajkumar, briefly down at the old Mahan still prostrate on his bed. Then he continued. 'But I promise more! I promise, here today, that I will go further still. I will bring in a new law . . .' He paused a moment, hearing the hush. 'A new law exclusively to deal with this menace.'

A reporter raised his hand.

Hariharan shook his head and continued: 'Come! All together, let us hail today as a victorious day for peace. All communities must stand united in our great secular nation. Jai Hind.'

The people applauded, some more enthusiastically than others. Hariharan did not mind. His victory was won. Time would dissolve this pinch-point. Indeed it already had, with a dribbled sip of orange juice.

He made his way off the stage, glancing at his watch, ignoring the press.

'Mr Mayor, a word.' Rajkumar, his voice full of bogus respect. With a rictus smile at the press, he turned to Hariharan. 'I do not appreciate your interfering in things that do not concern you.'

'Me?' said Hariharan. 'The Swami asked me to hand him the orange juice. I didn't know he'd invited you as well. Perhaps you can hand him his oatmeal. I hear that is his preferred food for breaking a fast.'

'I'm talking about Scotland Yard getting involved in our domestic homicide.'

'Good grief,' said Hariharan, 'that had nothing to do with me. News of your incompetence has reached the sanctified corridors of the central government, I'm afraid. The minister for the interior made the decision.'

Rajkumar could only splutter. He was so easy to wind up.

'Listen,' said Hariharan, injecting a little camaraderie into his voice. 'My advice is, take all the help you can get. Things

Marino Library

Items that you have checked out

Title: Cold sun
ID: DCPL3000036538
Due: 29/09/2022

Total items: 1
Account balance: €0.00
Checked out: 1
Overdue: 0
Hold requests. 0
Ready for collection: 0
08/09/2022

Thank you for visiting us today

are getting out of control on every front. International terrorism at the Red Fort, religious violence in Shivaji Nagar and Cooke Town. On the twentieth of next month you've Ganesh Chathurthi and Bakr-Id clashing. Next week, there's the anti-MNC march on ENOL Chemicals and traffic blockage at the Pepsi-Cola building on Cubbon Road. Plus, Twitter storms are increasing among the grassroots socialists. Protests brewing about the gang rape of that university lecturer. Tamilians facing drought again, organising a sit-in at the Vidhana Soudha. Oh man, how do you keep up with it all? And now, these Maharanis getting murdered in their own beds.'

Rajkumar's face grew visibly pinched. Extraordinary sight on a fat man. 'What can I do?' he said. 'The bloody CBI has taken all available resources and personnel to work the terrorism cases.'

'Exactly. So don't turn away any help you get.'

'Excuse me, sir, a word,' said a reporter, who'd had the cheek to climb on to the stage. The police constables were sleeping on their feet.

'I said, no questions.'

'For Chief Rajkumar,' said the wild-haired woman in shapeless Western clothes, clutching a notepad. 'About the recent spate of murders.'

'Then I'll leave you to him, Miss . . . ?'

'Kadambri, from *The Indian*.'

'Ah, a serious newspaper. Well, I have to go. Do not let the police chief off the hook till he answers your every question.'

He turned his back on Rajkumar and signalled his driver to fetch the car.

Chapter Four

Manu listened outside the kitchen for a minute before going in. His wife was instructing the maid about the correct preparation of okra. She wore a parrot-green sari, just this side of tasteful, and her hair, freshly washed, hung long and damp, the ends tied together in a knot. She had the kind of face that was beautiful in the classical South Indian way. Rounded cheeks, big fish eyes, thick lashes and eyebrows, plump lips. Healthy, vigorous, like a wriggling baby mammal. She noticed him and flashed a bright smile. 'Coffee?'

'Just water.'

His wife and the maid both scrambled for a glass. The maid found one first. The wife plucked it from her hands, filled it from the water purifier.

'I am showering and going out. Back at nine.'

His wife nodded, but her smile stiffened a touch.

Whistling a tune from last evening's *Movie Top Ten*, he showered himself anew. Drying off, he inspected his upper lip in the mirror. Took a small, sharp pair of scissors to trim his moustache. A millimetre here, a millimetre there.

In the bedroom, he chose a suit with care. Dark, of course. And a nice, cream shirt. No tie. He opened the corner wardrobe and picked up a shoebox from the bottom shelf, placed it on the bed. Then he opened the sock drawer. Two pairs of black socks.

His feet, thankfully, weren't the type to sweat when hot and constricted. He sat on a small chair and slipped on both pairs and then the shoes. Laced them up, tight.

He mulled over the aesthetics of the tableau he would shortly prepare. Perhaps it was time to add a little extra detail. Immediately, he knew what to do. Excited, he felt his appetite begin, the juices flow. He'd be hungry when he got back.

Outside, the driver came up. 'Where to, sir?'

'The boy will drive me.' The apology was implicit in his tone, for, after all, each man had his job, his caste, and it was as improper for his son to take the place of the driver as it was for the driver to take the place of the housemaid. Nevertheless, the change was necessary. 'You can go home.'

'OK, sir.'

He went to find the boy. He was cleaning the Scorpio's windscreen.

'All ready?'

'Yes, Papa.'

'Instrument?'

'In the boot, Papa.'

'Bag?'

'All packed.'

Manu stopped his desire to check things for himself. The boy could be trusted to get everything right. It was important for him, here at the cusp between boyhood and manhood, to be shown faith, to develop his confidence.

'Let's go.'

The boy nodded, not meeting his eyes, and threw the cleaning rag into the bucket. He slid into the driver's seat, switched on the ignition. A clanging racket burst out of the car stereo. The boy turned it off.

Manu slipped in beside him and observed the boy as he

expertly, and at great speed, reversed the Scorpio out through the driveway. Iron Maiden T-shirt, jeans, floppy hair, sneakers. The uniform of urban youth.

'Drive carefully,' Manu couldn't resist saying.

The traffic was mellow for Bengaluru, and they were in Ulsoor within minutes. Turning into a quiet, tree-lined street, they arrived at the Shangri-la apartments. The boy beeped. The gates did not open.

'The watchman's not here.'

The boy hopped out and pulled the gates apart. They slid open on their tracks. Driving in, they parked next to the elevator. The boy opened the boot while Manu pressed the button for the lift.

Waiting for the boy to fetch the things, he looked down and was impressed by the perfect crease on both his trouser legs. The maid was a good find on his wife's part.

The boy put down his backpack and the briefcase. 'I'll wait in the car, Papa.'

'Come with me.'

The boy raised surprised eyes to meet his. Manu could count on one hand the number of times the boy had met his eyes in the past two years. Manu was sure he wasn't imagining the spark of interest there, almost a flicker of excitement underneath the plaque of unreason in the irises.

They went up in silence, each intent on his own meditations.

Manu pressed the bell. The door opened after a minute.

'Sarita.'

There stood the woman, her beauty unmarred by a Lisa Simpson t-shirt and jogging bottoms. She smiled. 'It's a great pleasure to meet you. Though I must say I was surprised to hear you wanted to meet me, and so secretly.'

'I'm so very glad you *could* meet me.' Manu spoke with

sincerity, even a little fervour. 'A matter of the utmost importance, to me, and certainly to you.'

She was looking at the boy.

'He is mine. He'll be joining us.'

'Oh.' She seemed unsure what to think. 'You must be fourteen, sixteen? Still in school?'

The boy put the backpack by the door, shut it and slid the bolt.

Manu walked over to the sofa, perched on its arm.

The woman tried not to appear flustered, her eyes still on the boy. 'Can I get you a drink?' Like most people who failed to derive a response from the boy, she injected an extra note of determined sweetness into her voice.

The boy opened the backpack and brought out a folded tarpaulin. He went to the middle of the room and shook it open on the floor.

Manu pushed off from the sofa. 'Would you mind stepping over the tarp, little one?' He touched her elbow to guide her on to the tarp's blue expanse.

'OK.' She stared at the boy, as if trying to read his expressionless face. 'What's this, a trick?'

The boy hefted the air cylinder, placed it upright.

The woman watched with a puzzled smile as he depressed the pump a couple of times to check the suction. The boy then uncoiled the hose and gave Manu the steel-tipped nozzle.

'Stand very still, dear.' He deepened his voice, a mischievous smile under his trim moustache.

'Where's the camera?' she said, smiling back. 'Let me guess. *Celebrity Wind Up*? Or is it *Oh What A Hoot Shoot*?'

Manu held the nozzle to Sarita Mohan's forehead with his left hand. He used his right to depress the lever. There was a clack as the chain tightened and arrested the flight of the musket ball.

A sigh from the woman as she slumped against the edge of tarp the boy held up. He enveloped her, laid her on the floor.

'Perfect.' Manu smiled at the boy, although he wasn't looking his way. Already the boy was his successor in more than one way. His grandfather would be proud. He glanced at his watch. 'Tick tock. Let's press on.'

Chapter Five

A bald, moustachioed official in a blue shirt ran a long-nailed index finger along Patel's letter of invitation from the Bengaluru City Police Homicide Division. He tapped the maroon cover of Patel's passport and listened, as if the tone of polyurethane against human fingernail imparted to him age-old wisdom. It seemed an eternity, in fact, before he nodded at Patel.

'You have gun.'

'Sorry?' Patel patted his pockets guiltily, to see if the instrument of the man's clairvoyance had indeed appeared upon his person.

'You police officer from England. You not carry a gun?'

'I don't.'

'Like Indian police, you too carry lathi to catch criminal?' A mocking smile appeared upon the man's lips.

'I guess so.'

He stamped the passport with a sudden, hard movement, almost akin to assault, and pushed it back towards Patel.

'Thanks.' He knew his sarcastic tone was wasted on the Indian's ears.

Patel headed towards baggage reclaim. He wrestled his suitcase off a pile of luggage tumbling along a very short carousel and wheeled it towards the terminal exit.

As he walked he tried to remember the last and only time

he'd arrived in India before. He couldn't recall any of it. Had the air been similar, with a distinct weight and shape to it? A press of people against the security cordons, and with them, the pungency and mustiness of the tropics? Beyond, light from a cloudless sky poured through glass walls. Last time, he'd been twenty-three, in a cricket bubble. Last time was another lifetime.

He eyed the placards and lighted upon a beautiful woman gazing intently at the outpouring of passengers. She wore a green salwar kameez with a voluminous scarf that could not hide her erect bearing. Her hair was parted in the middle and loosely tied back. Her thickly lashed brown eyes rapidly scanned the faces that danced across her field of vision. Searching for her husband or boyfriend.

Peeling his eyes away, he noticed the card held by the man beside her. Spidery words spelled out, 'Officer Patil' and below, in tiny print, 'Scotland Yard'. The man wore a light grey button-up coat with a Chinese collar, and earmuffs in green camouflage print.

He met Patel's eyes, and turned sideways in a panicked manner towards the woman in green. The woman twitched a corner of her lips at Patel and extended a hand.

'You're not a moment too early, Mr Patel. I am Assistant Commissioner Chandra Subramanium.'

'You're the SIO?' Slightly flabbergasted that the vision of faraway beauty was, in fact, this flesh-and-blood policewoman with a no-nonsense air.

'Indeed.'

'What has happened?' He shook her proffered hand; a warm, small animal, rather brisk.

Ignoring his question, she turned to the man in the earmuffs. 'Ready, Ranga?'

Ranga took Patel's suitcase and marched off.

She turned to Patel. 'Let us talk in the car.'

Patel followed Chandra, breathing the dusty, warm air, marvelling at her nimbleness in three-inch heels. Clear, sharp sounds of busy people all around. Cacophony of car and rickshaw horns. Rapid mixture of English and native tongues.

Amid the jumble of vehicles and people, he stepped into the back of a four-by-four. It felt like entering a fridge. Luggage in the boot, Ranga and Chandra got into the front of the car. Patel, in his lonesome majesty, sprawled in the back seat, shivering in his T-shirt. It would not be polite, he figured, to ask them to switch the AC off. When the pilot had announced on landing, 'A beautiful, blue-sky day, twenty-four degrees,' Patel had taken off his jumper and packed it away.

As the car charged to the exit, a man holding a sheaf of yellow tickets leapt dangerously from the kerb and yelled something at Chandra. Patel held his breath, but Ranga showed no signs of stopping. Chandra's window went down a crack and she barked what sounded like expletives interspersed with the word 'police'.

Patel turned to see the angry shaking sheaf in the man's hand morph into a respectful wave goodbye.

'Wondering what that was all about, Mr Patel?'

He turned forwards. 'Not at all, Ms Chandra.'

One eye fixed on him from the rear-view mirror. She put a hand out and adjusted the mirror. Both eyes and the bridge of her nose came into view. Patel decided not to wonder about their road safety while the assistant commissioner repurposed the mirror as a window of communication. No doubt if the driver, Ranga, had need of it, he'd let it be known.

They sped towards a set of traffic lights that turned green just as Ranga crossed the stop line. He veered a sharp right, neither looking in the mirrors nor checking his blind spot. The car felt as if it might roll over.

'So, Mr Patel.' Chandra struck a tone that suggested she were in her sitting room, regaling a guest with small talk. 'I trust your journey was comfortable?'

'Fine. Fine.'

'Not too much turbulence?'

Patel groped for a seatbelt, and didn't find one. 'Are we going to the hotel first? I'd really like—'

'Unfortunately, Mr Patel,' interrupted Chandra, not smiling now, 'there has been a development.'

'What is it?'

'The fiend struck again while you were in the sky somewhere over Kandahar. A body has been found.'

'Is it . . . ?'

'I thought this is an excellent opportunity for you to look at the scene while it is still fresh.'

'Ah, well . . . '

'I've ordered that no one should touch anything till you get a good look.'

Patel swallowed, nodded. Ranga gave the impression of gliding through the traffic by not using the brakes at all. He simply pressed down the horn, and the vehicles around him scrambled. No need for a siren and flashing lights.

Patel's stomach panged. 'Could we please stop at a pharmacy, Ms Chandra?'

'Why is that, Mr Patel?'

'I need something.'

'Tell Ranga. He can get it for you.'

'No, thank you. I'll get it myself. If you can just stop for a minute. Is there one on the way?'

'Of course.'

Chandra spoke to Ranga. Ranga's head shook from side to side. Shortly, the car screeched to a halt.

Patel stepped out into the balmy air. He strode up to a little kiosk with a sign reading *Lord Murugan Chemist*. To his consternation, Chandra came with him.

'Bottle of Eno, please. A big one if possible.'

The man behind the kiosk counter frowned, concentrating on a point Patel felt to be the tip of his nose, and tilted his head first one way, then the other.

Patel waited.

Chandra said, 'Bottle of Eno.'

The man turned and disappeared behind some shelving at the back, and reappeared with a paper bag.

Patel looked into the bag. Inside was his salve for indigestion. Chandra handed the fellow some notes from her handbag.

'Thanks,' said Patel, as they returned to the car. 'Was he taking the piss?'

'The chemist? Making fun of you?'

'Mmm hmm.'

'Why do you think that?'

'I asked him for Eno. He nodded yes. Didn't get me any. You used the same words, same English. Then he fetched some.'

Ranga shifted in his seat, glanced back at Patel. Chandra's eyes reflected mirth.

'He nodded to indicate his lack of understanding, Mr Patel. It wasn't a yes. And I spoke in English because my Kannada is poor. I am a Tamilian who grew up in Kerala, and English is my lingua franca. You do not seem to realise how difficult your accent is to follow. You make no allowances.'

'I *am* English. I do not have an accent.'

Chandra's laugh was short and sharp as a striking bell. 'You have what is called the English accent, and it is most difficult to follow.'

'*Quite* difficult,' muttered Patel.

After a minute, she said, 'We will be at the crime scene shortly.'

'OK. Any background on the victim?'

'Sarita Mohan. Thirty-four years old. Businesswoman. Well known in certain circles. Featured in the *Economic Times*. Last year's Rising Star in *Entrepreneur* magazine. Last month she flew to Malaysia to collect a Foreign Business Leader Award. Shook hands with their prime minister. CEO of Mohan Autos, Mohan Petrochemicals and Mohan Finance. Single, lived alone. As far as we know, she last spoke to the building watchman yesterday at eight, when she asked him to run an errand. He was back by ten and stayed on duty till six in the morning. She was found by the grocer's boy who went to deliver milk, just after seven a.m. He called the police and ran away before they arrived. He's now missing, didn't go back to work. The maid's also missing, according to neighbours. She usually turned up at six a.m., had her own key.'

Patel could see nothing suspicious in a servant running away when the mistress was found murdered in bed. Probably the sensible thing to do in a country where the law invariably worked for the haves rather than the have-nots.

'Are there many young single women CEOs of business conglomerates in India?'

'Modern shining India, Mr Patel. There are more of them than you'd think, but fewer than there should be.'

They drove on tree-lined residential streets, passed weathered, well-kept apartment blocks and houses with iron gates manned by smartly uniformed men.

'This is a wealthy area?'

'The old money lives here, although a lot of them have begun to move further out.'

He thought of south Leicester, the middle classes moving out through Oadby and beyond over the years.

'I suppose,' said Chandra, 'this is a bit like Chelsea or Parsons Green.'

'You've been to the UK, Ms Chandra?'

'I spent a year in Cardiff.'

'What did you do there?'

'A masters in criminology.'

'Did you study the nature of Welsh crime?'

'I wrote a thesis on the nature of the Indian criminal mind.'

'And what was your argument?'

'The Indian criminal mind is no different from the British criminal mind. But to detect the criminal, a deep understanding of the culture is necessary.'

'Can a British detective catch an Indian criminal?'

'My thesis says it's improbable. Although it is within the realms of the possible. Then again, anything is possible. Even pigs can fly.'

She widened her impossible eyes. Patel felt his stomach tighten. It was terrifying and arousing at the same time. Her eyes, disembodied in the mirror, like some female deity's, seemed to be looking at all of him at the same time. The state of his teeth, the hair on his chest, his semi-flaccid penis. He felt light headed. As his mouth hovered between a smile and a grimace, Chandra moved hers.

'We have arrived.'

They stopped behind a couple of police jeeps and an ambulance, its lights silently flashing. Patel stepped out, freed from the car's merciless air conditioning. A number of male cops in khaki uniforms loitered by a pair of scrolled iron gates. The gates were slightly open – not enough to let a man through, and not close enough together to be shut. Chandra pointed to the gates and two policemen pulled them wider. They walked in and through the parked cars, past aimlessly meandering policemen, all the while watched with interest by neighbours and their servants, and a few, but not many, passers-by. This was a wealthy, exclusive area, after all.

His stomach protesting, Patel followed Chandra into the building, clutching the paper bag with the Eno. They stepped into an old-fashioned squeaky lift. A female voice boomed, 'Please shut the door, please shut the door.' A copper clanged the metal grille in place three times before the voice rested and the lift consented to take them up.

The hubbub reached them even before the lift opened on the fifth floor. At the end of a short corridor, a wide, painted door with a gleaming brass knocker stood ajar. He could see, inside, a bazaar of uniformed and plain-clothed men and women.

Patel put a hand on Chandra's arm as she made to leave the lift.

'Chandra,' he said, 'so many in there without protective gear, covers over their shoes, contaminating the crime scene.'

'Oh, don't worry. The forensics team has already been through there, much use that will be.'

'Why wouldn't it be useful?'

'We don't have access to the DNA lab.'

'Why not?'

'They are busy with more important matters.'

'Like what?'

'Jihadist terrorism. The Lakshar-e-Taiba has announced retaliation for the three Muslims lynched last week.'

'Good grief.'

'Indeed. Now let us go in and solve this case.'

She marched into the flat and announced, 'He's here.' The noise dipped. Several dark heads, similar to his own, turned to scrutinise Patel. Some looked beyond Patel, all expressive eagerness, and scanned the doorway.

Chandra said to him under her breath, 'The chief and I

learned your name only last night. The others only know it's a Scotland Yard officer.'

'Which is what I am.'

Chandra began to explain, but was cut off by a sing-song voice.

'Surely you are Indian, Mr Paa-til? From Gujarat?' A moustachioed officer, his epaulettes and chest bearing high-ranking insignia, ambled forth from a cloister of uniforms. He grasped Patel's hand with both of his.

'No, sir, I'm British. My parents were from Uganda.'

'Uganda? That is an African country, is it not?'

'Yes, sir.'

The officer looked him over, as if for signs of black. 'Ah,' he said.

'I was born in Leicester.'

The man looked unconvinced. 'The square? Like Trafalgar Square?'

Patel quelled the urge to produce his passport to prove his claim. He said, 'Leicester is a city in the East Midlands region.'

'Mr Paa-til.' The man's mouth turned down as if all this explaining was distasteful to him. 'We've been waiting for you.' His head slightly turned to Chandra, waited, lips pursed.

'This is Mr Rajkumar, our chief.'

'Let us waste no time in introductions, Mr Paa-til.' Rajkumar's vast belly undermined his attitude of briskness. 'Come and study the scene. Give us your expert thoughts.'

He pointed towards a closed door, plain and brown. Behind it, the dead woman waited. No matter how young she'd once been, or how pretty, Patel knew that once he opened that door, he'd be engulfed by the stench of violence, the fug of death. His stomach couldn't handle it just yet.

He took a breath. 'I'd like some protective gear. So I don't contaminate the scene.'

Astonished faces all around. Whispering and murmuring. A smile upon Chandra's lips as she ordered a flunkey to fetch his requirements.

While they waited, a constable approached Chandra. 'Ma'am, we found a phone under the bed. Forensics have bagged and labelled it. Charge is off.' He held up a clear-plastic-sheathed old Nokia. Patel remembered the black brick from the mid-1990s.

'Find a charger for it,' said Chandra. 'After fingerprinting, charge it, switch it on and note down what's on it.'

'Presumably it's not Sarita's phone.'

'Hers is an iPhone Seven. Someone's going through it now.'

'Who owns an old Nokia nowadays?'

'Museum piece. It's going to be a bugger finding a charger for it.'

The overalls arrived. Watched by all, Patel stood in the open-plan kitchen and donned the gear. Plastic overalls, gloves, hat, shoe covers. He placed the Eno on the counter, opened a cupboard and got out a cup.

When he ran the tap, he heard Rajkumar's voice from across the room. 'Tap water? You do not drink tap water in India, Mr Paa-til.' The chief's eyes alighted on a constable from the gathered minions. 'You! Get a bottle of Bisleri.'

Rajkumar watched, wistful and paternal, as Patel stirred the Eno, gulped it down, burped several times.

They waited to send him off, like relatives gathered to send off a favourite nephew on his first overseas trip.

'Now then.' Patel turned to Chandra with a chirpiness he did not feel. 'Let's get to work.'

She grinned from her own cocoon of plastic. The door to the bedroom was opened. He and Chandra entered. She closed the door behind them.

Patel took a shaky breath. There was a body on the bed. That much was obvious. He'd leave looking at it to last.

Thick, soupy light poured through gauze blinds on the windows. The ceiling light was on, the candescence golden rather than white, housed within an expensive brass pendant. Ms Mohan obviously had been a woman of taste. He looked at the window again. Curtains – thin, a kind of black silk, gathered at the sides. The bed – superking, some kind of satin cover, black, again. Her sari, the material of it, the colour, red, sucked at his gaze. He would look at it soon enough.

He wanted to get a sense of this person, this victim, without being tainted by the sight of her helpless, lifeless body, before considerations such as her looks, height and body size kicked in to colour his view of the matter. Sarah, he thought, would approve.

The wardrobe – half open. Slipping on the gloves, he put a finger on the lip of the door, far from the handle, and opened it fully. Row upon row of clothes, neatly hanging. Churidars, salwars. Nothing like the women of his family wore. These were delicate, beautifully designed, not garish, not a frill in sight. All the colours muted, the contrasts subtle. Chandra moved to stand beside him, looking at what he was seeing. Chandra's clothing, a churidar of orange and green abstraction, though perfectly adequate, was inferior in both taste and price to the dead woman's clothes. Chandra's clothes suited her profession, and didn't suggest any curves underneath. Feminine curves, Patel knew, would undermine her authority as an officer.

He placed a hand under a drawer and drew it towards him. Beautiful, well-made wisps of underwear. Did the scent come from the washing liquid, or had she used some special clothes perfume? He slid a hand among the silky nothings, feeling for a pouch of lavender or patchouli.

'You haven't looked at the body yet.' Chandra stood a bit too close to him, her chin nearly touching his shoulder.

He didn't respond.

He shut the drawer and opened the one below. Bras – luscious, expensive, silky, the cup size smaller than Sarah's.

Chandra shifted, cleared her throat, making a point of withholding comment.

He shut the wardrobe. The shoes would be in the hallway, by the front door. He doubted they would tell him anything different. The dead woman had expensive, obviously well-bred tastes, all fitting with the neighbourhood, and her station in life.

There was a dressing table next to the wardrobe. He wanted to look at her jewellery, her make-up. The table had a mirror facing the bed. That wasn't how he wanted to look at her body.

Time to face her.

Sarita Mohan lay neatly in the middle of the bed. Legs and toes together, arms by her side. She faced the ceiling as she floated on the black satin sea. He started with the feet. Unshod, nails painted a metallic grey, heels well-pedicured into softness. No dirt on those heels. A slim band of silver encircled the fourth toe on her right foot. His eyes moved up.

The red sari she wore in her death was traditional, the silk very different from the silk of the curtains, the colours from a different milieu than those of her clothes. It was a rose red shot through with gold thread, with a blue paisley motif border. Different from the saris his relatives usually wore.

'I'm assuming this sari is of the South Indian variety?'

'Kanchipuram silk, traditional wedding wear made in a southern district in Tamil Nadu.'

The red sari was altogether different to the rest of her wardrobe. In fact, she had only two saris in the wardrobe, one black with a deep rust-red border, the other a dark green with very muted black jari work. Both probably designer.

The gold thread, he knew – through knowledge gleaned from

reminiscing grandmothers – was actually silver plated in gold, woven through the silk. The silk itself was spun out of strands harvested from dead silkworm cocoons. Weren't the cocoons boiled with the pupae still inside them? He lifted some material next to her foot. Heaviness, he knew, indicated more silver shot through the sari. This was a light sari, more silk than silver. It was the kind of sari a bride from a poor family would wear.

No matter how physically far removed his upbringing had been from the subcontinent, knowledge of the subcontinent's cultures had nevertheless seeped into him. He knew them through the food and his family, through the relentless stream of television programmes always being watched at his parents' house, which also housed grandmothers and grandfathers who had carried with them the subcontinental way of life – thermals under saris, socks in sandals, bhajis, lentils and rice at every meal. Without changing a thing about themselves, they had managed to accommodate the cold, wet country outside into their lives. His presence here was incongruous. A native at heart, housed in a foreigner's skin. Except it was even the same skin.

She could easily be one of his cousins, he thought, and the horror of a life taken violently, before its time, seized him, not for the first time. He forced himself to look again at the dead woman, search for clues, without letting her humanity cloud his judgement.

The sari's pleats at the waist were evenly spaced, tied like a glamorous airhostess from those Bollywood films he'd watched as a child.

'Tell me about the sari.'

'Same as all the others. The killer, presumably, has some fixation with this old-fashioned sari. You've read the files. He kills them, drapes a sari around the corpse.'

'And the tailoring?'

'This is India.' Chandra shrugged. 'Hundreds of tailors in every area of the city, stitching blouses day in and day out. The sari could have been bought ready-made. A thousand sari shops. Designs like this are ubiquitous.'

'Still, he had to buy them somewhere, get the blouses tailored to fit. He had to know how to measure their ... you know ... chest size. And how did he know the measurements? By sight, or did he know them in a professional capacity? He could have done the tailoring himself. That's a real avenue for exploration.'

'The women all had different tailors from different areas. We checked them all out. No connections. Two of the tailors are women. All with solid alibi. Indians are never alone. We are already looking at the possibility the killer is a professional tailor.'

'And how are you checking this out?'

'We have a dozen men doing the rounds of tailors in the city, area by area.'

'Are they carrying photos?'

'Of the women?'

'No, the clothes. Visual aid jogs the memory better than just verbal descriptions.'

'Better still, each of them carries a cut-away sample of the saris. Only way to make a perfect match. Tailors never throw away surplus material.'

Patel nodded. Sarita's hands lay by her sides in complete repose, belying the manner of her death. No rings on her fingers. Her chest, under those pleats gathered on her right shoulder, looked nearly flat. Unusually for an Indian woman, no tasteful little gold chain, no pendant on her chest. Her head rested on the centre of the pillow, which had been pulled to the middle of the bed. Her face was drained of blood, grey-pallored, her eyes closed. Precisely in the middle of her forehead was a neat hole. Blood had run in two streaks from it and into her dark hair. Around her head, the black satin of the pillow cover and bed were stiff with blood. Something about the positioning of the bullet hole tugged at him.

'Any news on the murder weapon?'

'Not a clue. Ballistics cannot work it out.'

He turned to the vanity. No jewellery box. Just a vast array of make-up. He stared at them. If the pots and brushes of the dead woman's make-up held any secrets, they didn't yield them to him. He conjured up an image of her seated on the stool, checking her make-up, anxious to appear attractive, and his heart constricted.

There was a knock on the door and a voice: 'Madam?'

Patel picked up a tiny pot of smoky green mascara. 'MAC Green Goddess', it said on the side of the lid. He clicked it open and took his glove off, swiped a forefinger around the powdery paste and studied the silvery specks that had revealed themselves in the smoky green smeared on his skin.

Chandra, back at his shoulder, said, 'We have the grocer's boy from the corner shop in custody.'

'And why is that?' Patel rubbed his thumb over the silver green on his forefinger.

'He found the body and rang the police, then went back home to pack a bag.' Chandra picked up the MAC pot and put it down.

Patel shut the door of the make-up compartment. He wiped his fingers together and stood up. 'Let's go see what he has to say.'

'Nothing jump out at you?' Chandra's tone seemed carefully neutral. He felt a pang of pressure.

'I'm mulling over a couple of things,' he said.

At the door he swept a last glance around the room. There was something pristine about the whole set up. Nothing flash about Sarita as a person, either. She didn't even wear jewellery—

He said, 'Toe ring.'

'Toe ring?'

'Isn't it usually married women who wear toe rings?

'They come in and out of fashion among college girls. I wore my mother's when I was a teenager, but it became uncool by the time—'

'Wait. Sarita doesn't own or wear any other jewellery.'

'So?'

'The toe ring is too plain, too worn. Nothing else is that – what's the word? – rustic, except . . . '

'The sari?'

'You see?'

'OK.' Chandra didn't seem 100 per cent convinced. 'I'll have the toe ring checked out.'

She gave him an assessing look. He wondered what she was thinking. As though to confound him further, she said, 'Hmmm,' without elaborating.

Exasperated, he said, 'Let's go see the grocer's boy, then.'

Chapter Six

Five pot-bellied, scratching constables sat around Ulsoor Police Station's veranda, two gossiping, one on the phone, one drinking tea, one staring into the distance. They started, then flailed helplessly in the sudden presence of the assistant commissioner. Chandra gave them the ticking off they patently expected from her, then Patel followed her inside.

He blinked; his eyes adjusted to the gloom. A large room with twenty or so desks, two doors leading off to even gloomier interiors. The sound of sobbing came echoing out of the recesses. Everything, the desks of the constables and sub-inspectors, the walls with the Wanted posters, the shelves with the files and folders, the FIR cabinet, the very air itself, reeked of bureaucratic dust. Patel sneezed.

They entered the station inspector's room to wait for him. Patel walked over to the noticeboard, studied the Wanted posters. Mugshots of repeat offenders, their offences – rapes, burglaries, knifings – not dissimilar to those committed by his London crims. The difference: the jet-black hair and bushy moustaches lent the Indians an air of cartoonish menace.

The station inspector came bounding into the room and apologised for keeping them waiting. Then, casting squirrel-like glances at Patel, he led them at some speed through a corridor. They passed police lockups populated by lowlifes and prostitutes. Habitués, he supposed. They huddled or lounged, chatting or silent. Many stared at him as he passed. Chemical and metal smells: the ammonia in urine saturating the bricks, the metallic sourness of human sweat on iron bars. The stink of desperation, the musk of apathy. Bare bulbs glinted. Paan juice the colour of old blood stained the walls. Patel supposed the jailbirds waiting for whatever version of justice the Indian lords handed them had to chew on something to pass the time.

And finally, the inspector stopped, motioned to the sub-inspector, who took a key ring from a constable and opened the gate. They faced a wide wooden door with a glass viewing panel.

Chandra said to the inspector: 'We will take it from here. Please wait in your office.'

The inspector simpered and slunk away down the corridor.

'And you,' she told the constable, 'bring us some water and tea.'

The constable, a greying, moustachioed patriarch, hastened to her bidding, simpering also.

Patel thought he'd never witness such a thing – male subordinates utterly subdued by female authority – back at home. Not like this. Without resentment, without doubt.

'How do we handle this?' he asked her.

'I translate. We ask a question each, taking turns.'

'Has he got a lawyer with him?'

'Are you joking?'

'Is he aware of the option at least?'

'Why give him an excuse to delay the inevitable?' Chandra's tone was waspish.

'Dare I ask if there is a recording device in there?'

'You can ask.'

Patel expelled frustration. 'This is all very unorthodox.'

'Look, we just need some quick answers. Eliminate this fellow as a suspect.'

Patel hesitated, then nodded. He pushed the panel on the door and peered in. White light blazed at him. Unable to see anything through the glass, he pushed the door open.

The grocer's boy sat on a metal folding chair, a plastic table in front of him. He didn't twitch at their approach, or turn his head. He sat staring at his knees. There were two more metal chairs on the other side of the table, and to these Patel and Chandra repaired.

The boy looked up at last. His round saucer eyes swivelled from Patel to Chandra, from Chandra to Patel, as if unsure which one of them he ought to be focusing on. He looked about sixteen.

Chandra asked the first question. 'Name?'

'Ravi.'

Perhaps fifteen, thought Patel. 'How old?' he asked.

He waited for Chandra to translate, but the boy answered, 'Fourteen.'

Patel got up. 'Outside,' he said to Chandra and marched out.

In the hallway, he leaned on the shut door and bit down on his anger as he spoke. 'We cannot do this. He's a minor. There needs to be some protocol about that, even if it's different from what I'm used to. Can't put a boy in an adult cell. Can't use adult interrogation methods with a minor.'

Chandra didn't bat an eyelid. 'Don't act like a fucking social worker, Patel. This is the fourth murder. We are totally clueless. There will be a media circus when we hold a press conference about this one. We need leads, fast.'

Patel couldn't argue the logic of that point. He had his own protocols to follow, but he was out of his jurisdiction, technically. No skin off his back. Still.

'Is there an interview protocol I should have been shown?'

'No.'

'Do you have a complaints procedure?'

'No.'

'An ethics committee?'

'No.'

'Standards authorities or adjudicators who investigate police procedures and protocols?'

'Ha ha.'

Patel stared at her. She stared back.

'I wish to register my objections.' He leaned in. She didn't lean back.

'Who are registering your objections with? Your boss or mine?'

'Just with you,' he said, giving her the full force of his moral outrage. Then he said, 'Let's proceed, but handle him gently.'

They went back inside and settled back down in the chairs.

Patel began. 'You speak English?'

'Aaa yes, sir.'

'OK,' said Chandra, 'tell us what happened this morning.'

The boy shuddered as he began: 'I always take milk packet, super-skim, to madam in the morning. Normally, I ring bell, the maid, Sarala, open door and take milk. I think, Sarala, she missing too much of the work. Lazy lady. Today I ring, no answer. That never happen. If no Sarala then madam come to open. Then I see the door is open. Why? I thinking. I push it and something not right, I thinking.'

Here the saucer eyes screwed up to points. The boy shook his head. 'Sarita madam, always in Western clothes only, now wearing sari and tika, lying on bed.'

'Tika?'

His expressive Indian face clouded and he looked sideways, down on the floor. 'I know she is dead. I no touch anything, sir.' He flashed a look up at Patel, then quickly lowered his gaze back to the floor.

'Then what did you do?'

'I not touch nothing. I go to the hall and call the police from the landline. My cell, it not get signal from madam house.'

Chandra threw Patel a sharp look. He ignored her, kept his eyes on the boy.

'OK, why did you go home after calling the police?'

'I not feel so good, sir.'

'And why were you packing a bag?' asked Chandra.

'I want to go to my village, see my mother.'

There was a knock on the door and the constable came in with a tray. Before the boy's wary eyes, he placed down a plastic cup of tea and a rectangular packet of biscuits. Patel noted they were called 'Britannia Milk Bikkies'. The song 'Rule Britannia' slipped into his head.

They all took a biscuit. The plastic cup holding the tea was so thin that the boy had to hold it by the rim. His hand shook but he didn't spill it. *Rule Britannia, Britannia rules the waves . . .* Something about the boy was like a dog. Was it his expression, his general demeanour of one born to servitude?

'Let us start from the beginning again,' said Chandra. 'Can you tell us exactly what happened this morning? Take your time.'

The boy swiped the crumbs off his mouth, drank up his tea and some water, and began once more. Again, when he came to the part about finding Sarita Mohan's body wrapped uncharacteristically in a sari, his eyes slipped sideways. He stared at the floor while he spoke of his realisation that she was dead and described his call to the police. He wouldn't raise his eyes to meet Patel's.

When he finished, Chandra sent him for a toilet break with the constable stationed outside the door. A slow thumping began in Patel's skull. He recognised it as jet lag. Seven a.m. back home. He needed food, drink, and a pee. He ate another biscuit. Sweet and crunchy, made for children. It felt good. He ate another.

Chandra, who had been outside talking to the sub-inspector, came back in. 'He has told the exact same story to these fellows, too.'

'He's lying about something.'

'What shall we do?'

'Make him repeat till the thread begins to unravel? Standard op.'

'I have a better method, a faster one.'

'Oh yes?'

'You don't need to know the details. You cool your heels in the inspector's office. I'll send word when we hit the truth.'

'For God's sake, Chandra, he's fourteen years old. He's not a serial killer.'

'When I was doing police training in the Bihari wild west, I was routinely arresting rapists younger than this boy.'

'This isn't the wild west though, is it? Most fourteen-year-olds spend all day squeezing their pimples and wanking.'

'Maybe they do in your neck of the woods.'

They glared at each other for a long moment.

'Granted it's unlikely he's the killer,' said Chandra, 'although he's definitely hiding something. A couple of knocks—'

'No. I can't allow it.'

Chandra raised her eyebrows. 'From what I gathered from my stay in your country, our methods don't differ that much.'

'This isn't Guantanamo Bay. He's just a kid. My instinct tells me to take a different approach.'

'Ah.' She smiled. 'The famous Patel instinct.'

Patel felt faint. He needed proper food. Then a great big glug of Eno. Then a shower. He'd kill for a swim. He took a deep breath. His stomach pinched.

'Let me have a try.'

Chandra thought for a moment. 'OK. But if your try fails . . .'

The boy was brought back. Although he was only fourteen years old, he appeared older to Patel, who was used to molly-coddled British kids. This kid worked for a living. He was no feral youth, rapist or murderer. Nonetheless, he was hiding something.

'Son,' he said to the boy. Instinct made him deepen his voice, adopt a paternal tone. 'I know you are a good boy. You work hard for a living, and you respected Ms Mohan. I bet your employer values you, and wants you to go back to his shop as soon as we let you go. It is very clear to me you are innocent.' He looked the boy in the eye. 'But you are hiding something.'

The boy nodded in that perplexing Indian way. A head waggle. Some of Patel's relatives did that. It could mean either a yes and a no, sometimes both. You asked a simple question. It depends, they answered after a bout of nodding. Some Hindu thing. Truth itself depended on the perspective. Material facts were but maya, illusion. How could a British mind cope?

Patel frowned, tried unclenching his teeth. He couldn't tell if the boy was following his English. He was making himself sound like an East Midlands Gujarati. Well, his father. Sing-songy Indian. None of your clipped vowels.

Patel could see the boy's Adam's apple on his skinny throat go up and down.

'Look here, son.' Patel leaned forward. 'I know you are not telling us everything. Don't be afraid. Just tell us. It might be important. Help us catch the killer.'

Chandra was very quiet beside him. He waited.

The boy began panting. His fright-filled eyes strayed to Chandra, came back to Patel.

'Sir. Sarita madam. I seeing her for four years. She always in jeans, small top, foreign dress. High heels. Today, on the bed, she looking pure and holy. I make like this.' He put his palms together. His breathing eased.

Patel shifted in his seat as something in his intestines twanged.

'Beautiful, sir. Lakshmi, you know her. Goddess. I was going to phone the police. I take out my cell. My eyes full crying, wet on the phone. I wipe my phone with my shirt. I looking at madam. I see her this bit of sari.' He gestured toward his armpit, lifting the arm and shoulder. 'It had ...' He said a word in the vernacular, looking at Chandra.

'Slipped,' she said.

Ravi nodded. 'I thinking, all these policemen will come and see her. Her marappu has si-lipped. I not thinking. I put my phone in my shirt pocket. Usually I put phone in back pocket. I carefully, without touching madam, pull the sari to make her ... more, you know?'

He looked at Chandra again.

'Modest?'

'Modest,' repeated the boy, and turned bashfully back to Patel. 'And when I pull the sari to correct position, I turn and the phone – it si-lip to ground and go under the bed.'

'Which is why you went home and packed a bag?'

'I get fright, sir. I not want to go under the bed to get my phone. Under madam, you know?'

'Because she was dead?'

'Yes.' He forgot himself and looked too long at Chandra, blushed and turned to Patel. 'I not want the ghost to climb on my shoulders. I go backwards to the hall. The police, I am thinking, will see my phone and thinking all kinds of wrong things. I am not knowing what to do.'

That's it, thought Patel. Useless information. He opened

the second packet of Britannia Milk Bikkies and offered some to the boy.

Chandra called the constable and sub-inspector in.

'Take a statement and let him go,' she said to them.

Patel took the packet of biscuits and stood up. 'Oh, and get hold of the forensics team for the Sarita Mohan case. They'll be holding an old Nokia, black brick. Have someone take it to the grocer's and give it back to this boy.'

The bewildered policemen nodded slowly. Patel had slipped back to mockney from his East Midlands Gujarati accent. He looked to Chandra like the boy had.

She grinned, said to the policemen, 'Call up the Sarita Mohan forensics team. They will have a black, heavy Nokia phone. Tell them, take it back to the boy at the grocer shop.' She spoke in English, using more or less the same words.

'Yes, ma'am,' they chorused, and vigorously nodded to Patel their deep understanding.

Chapter Seven

'Lunch?' he asked Chandra. It would be an opportunity to establish some ground rules, clarify his role here, determine a plan of action.

She parked brazenly on a double yellow. 'Just a quick lunch.'

Patel hadn't expected the process of lunching to be quite so quick. They were at a steel and plastic establishment run by dhoti-clad middle-aged men. Patel found a couple of stools together on the pavement while Chandra queued in front of a dizzying array of hot foodstuffs. He perched, waiting, beside a man who was eating and gesturing and talking loudly to his meek companion who didn't seem to be listening. Chandra hadn't asked him what he wanted. He looked at the chalkboard menu. The letters were English but it might as well have been another script. She brought over two plates.

On his plate was a soggy affair of rice, lentils and mysterious spices that smelled quite a bit different from anything he knew.

'Bisi bele bath. A Kannadiga staple.'

Patel plunged his spoon in. 'I suppose you need hot food in a hot country.'

'I suppose.' Chandra tucked into her dahi vada.

A hiccup vaulted painfully out of his throat.

'Nice?' She indicated his dish.

'It's very nice.' Tongue coated with seventeen kinds of spices and ghee, he winced. His mouth felt full of red biting ants. He gazed longingly at Chandra's plate, with its puffed-up white vadas covered in a yoghurt sauce until, as her spoon cut in, he spotted pieces of green chillies.

'I was hoping,' he said as quietly as possible, given the surroundings, 'to have a run through of our options, construct a plan of action, if we could.'

The man who'd been digging his elbow into Patel's armpit swung his head in astonishment and stared.

'Sure,' said Chandra. 'Shoot.'

'It's a bit noisy here.'

'We'll go next door for a coffee,' said Chandra, pointing sideways over Patel's head with her spoon and then using it to scrape up the final bits of dahi vada into her elegant mouth, chillies and all. You haven't touched your bisi.'

He put his spoon down. 'I'll just have a lassi.'

Chandra shook her head. 'You can't mix lassi and coffee. Bad for the stomach.'

'OK. Just the coffee then.'

They sat in the coffee shop under a slow revolving fan suspended from a high ceiling. Patel, following Chandra's example, drank his coffee quickly, scaldingly, unwincingly. Chandra finished her conversation on the phone.

'Sarita's parents?' he asked.

She shook her head. 'They managed to get to the hospital and ID the body, but had to be whisked off to a different department and sedated.'

'Both of them?'

'Yes.'

'Seriously? What about helping us?'

'Wealthy people are more sensitive to loss than poorer people, it would seem.'

'Can't you make them? Just a couple of hours – we could use some information.'

Chandra shrugged. 'Big gun lawyers. We won't be able to talk to them till tomorrow at least.'

'Friends? Lovers?'

'Working on that. We have people calling everyone on her contacts list. Her secretary has furnished us with a list of professional contacts. ACP Kumar is looking into the business-rival angle, although it's unlikely someone's done a copycat to cover up other motives.'

'What else?'

'I've got uniforms knocking on neighbours' doors. Some curtain twitcher could've noticed a stranger. We already have an open telephone line for information about the previous murders. Manned twenty-four hours. This one will be added to the advertisement on all the news stations and dailies. We have, believe it or not, a hundred staff sifting through the nonsense we're getting.'

'Blimey.'

'Which leads us to the question. What is your role in this investigation?'

'What role do you want me to take on?'

'Shall I bill you deputy SIO? Be my sidekick?'

Patel made an expression which he reckoned was somewhere between a smile and a grimace. A very English thing. 'I've been given clear instructions. Officially, I'm aiding your force strictly in the capacity of consultant. But that is a broad remit.'

Patel knew Skinner, if nothing else, was right on the money with the designation. Pecking order was important. He would be in a much better position to deal with the Indians as consultant officer rather than Chandra's deputy.

'Frankly, I have enough deputies, constables and sub-inspectors running various strings of the investigation. I like this. Having my own consultant from London. You can stick around with me, and provide consultation.'

A fat lot of good his consultation had done so far. Patel felt the pang of slipping time, his pulse rate rising as he thought of the killer at large, stalking his next victim. Effortfully, he struck a jovial tone. 'You mean we can be partners, like those American buddy cop movies?'

In a voice dry as dust, Chandra said, 'Yeah, I'm Will Smith, you're that funny guy.'

While he thought of how to counter that, her phone rang.

A waiter came to hover by their table while she took the call, leaning this way and that to see if the coffee cups were empty yet. Chandra spoke in Kannada while Patel practised a 'hard stare' on the young man who wouldn't meet his eyes.

Chandra clicked off her phone, drew her whole focus on to the waiter. She curved her mouth into a snarl and barked something Patel couldn't follow. The man scooted back to the kitchen.

'New boy.'

Again, it struck Patel that Chandra's ferocity was something like that of a goddess – an angry one from the old, rural religion. Kali in a roadside shrine, the hair tangled and matted, tongue bloody. Or Durga riding a tiger.

As if she twigged what he was thinking, Chandra said: 'To be successful in a man's world, Mr Patel, a woman should constantly be on the offensive. Never give an inch, never spare a smile.'

Patel looked at Chandra's face. A smile, in fact, hovered over her lips. Her chin and nose tilted up, she cocked her head slightly, studying his face in turn, seemingly amused.

'I've seen that match, you know,' she said. 'The one where you hurt your wrist. I don't watch all that much cricket. But I was visiting my dad from university, and sat down with him. They made light of your injury. I guess no one knew it was serious. I expected you'd be back before long, and everyone else did, too. Never thought I'd meet you in a professional capacity, ten years later. Buy you lunch and tea and coffee, examine corpses with you.'

'Stop.' Lunch and coffee and corpses in the same sentence.

Chandra indicated her watch. 'Got to go. Sarita Mohan's autopsy's starting as we speak.'

Chapter Eight

The usual feeling of revulsion and a sense of his own mortality engulfed Patel as he descended towards the autopsy department. Usual for him, nowadays. He'd thought the queasiness would go in time but, if anything, it had intensified. The more corpses he chalked up in his career, the less his stomach liked it. He was reminded of a nun in a hospital drama, whose allergic reaction to copper worsened with repeated daily exposure till she began seeing Jesus.

The elevator had seen too many dead bodies. Liberal sprayings of disinfectant did nothing to disperse the death reek; its smirking, cold morbidity shone through the metal surfaces. Or was he now seeing things, too?

Sarita Mohan's autopsy was scheduled to begin at three, expedited not so much in order to provide fresh clues as to the identity of the killer, but so her powerful Hindu family could cremate her the following day, as per ritual.

'Through here.' Chandra led him into a very cold passageway stinking of formaldehyde.

A police officer waited in front of another set of doors. Nostrils flared like fish gills, he said, 'It's started.'

'Aren't you coming?' Chandra asked the man as she pushed open the door.

'Oh, no no,' he said, blanching like a root vegetable and turning away.

Patel envied the man his strength to show himself as weak. Already the second coffee he'd drunk, twenty minutes ago now, painfully rose up his gorge in anticipation of rebirth. As he followed Chandra in, he saw a table with a latticework screen in front of it. Through the scrolls, the pathologist, masked and hatted, bent over with a scalpel and pincers. A nurse in a blue sari, masked also, held a tray. The smell was unbearable. Chemicals combined with the onset of putrefaction.

A groan escaped his clenched teeth.

The doctor jerked up her head. She pulled down her mask with a blood-stained finger. 'You're late. I've already begun.'

Chandra went around the screen. Patel had no choice but to follow. On the slab, cranked up waist high, lay Sarita Mohan, split from shoulder to shoulder, chest to navel, vital organs exposed for study. As Patel watched, the pathologist measured the hole in her skull. Choosing a scalpel and a prong, she pierced and lifted a flap of skin, cut a slice and put it on a clean tray offered by the nurse.

Patel felt his vision growing black around the edges. Perhaps the chunky nurse would be able to stop him from pitching forwards on to Sarita Mohan's corpse.

'Dr Prakash,' said Chandra, 'anything different about this one?'

'Exactly the same as the others.' Dr Prakash spoke while prodding with a gloved finger the skinless flesh around the skull-hole. 'The bullet, or something like a bullet, has entered the forehead with great force so as to break through the skull plate. It has lodged briefly in the brain, cutting off vital nerves, destroying cerebrum tissue, causing massive haemorrhage and internal bleeding and almost instantaneous death.'

'And still no trace of the bullet?'

'It is puzzling. There is no exit wound, and there is no sign of a bullet. I just can't understand it. I'll be very interested to know –' she looked at Patel '– what kind of weapon would do this.'

'Oh, he isn't from ballistics, Dr Prakash. He's all the way from Scotland Yard, here to help us catch the bastard.'

Dr Prakash's eyebrows went up. 'Ah,' she said. 'You look familiar. Which part? I lived in the UK for a little while.'

'Patel was a famous cricketer some years ago. A long time ago.'

'Oh yes?' said the pathologist, and hummed over her tray of instruments, patently not a cricket fan. 'Fascinating case, isn't it, Mr Patel?' Dr Prakash bent over Sarita Mohan's forehead again. 'There is some kind of poetic elegance to the murders, is there not?'

'Well.' It was all Patel could manage.

The pathologist looked at him with fervour in her eyes. 'I studied English literature at York University, till I felt the pull of my true calling and came back to India to practise medicine.'

She put down the scalpel and extended her gloved hand, stained with blood and brain matter, right under Patel's nose.

Patel staggered back.

'Oh, sorry. Where are my manners?' She took her glove off and then grasped his unwilling hand. 'Priti Prakash.'

'This is Sergeant Vijay Patel,' said Chandra, affecting an incongruously pleasant formality. 'Ex-cricketer. Now a whizz-kid from Scotland Yard.'

Somewhere in his dull brain, Patel lodged a protest against Chandra's patronising tone. In spite of her rank, she was clearly younger than him, and ought not to be calling him a kid.

Dr Prakash was studying him. 'Although, you might say,' she drawled thoughtfully, 'one man's poetic elegance is another man's unspeakable perversion.'

Patel nodded with a puckering of his brows that he hoped indicated ironic detachment.

'You should come home for dinner. The two of you ... ' She turned to Chandra. 'Appa would love to see you. Come. I'll have them make Mysore pak. A Kannadiga delicacy, Mr Patel. You'll love it.'

'Mmmm,' said Chandra. She eyed the macabre tableau raised up like a Francis Bacon centrepiece, then met Patel's eyes. 'Sounds delicious.'

Outside, in the hospital courtyard, he checked his phone. A missed call from Sarah. And a text. 'Let me know if you can make it to dinner with Marty and Nina on the twentieth.'

His ordinary life, friendships and social outings with Sarah, seemed ridiculous at the moment, as if it was a life he'd watched on a telly soap, rather than lived. He felt not the least urge to respond, even just a yes or a no. He felt averse to everything – to corpses, to spicy food, to his domestic life, to aspects of his job, to his own skin and hair.

Chandra was browsing at a snack stall. People mingled and laughed, ate with gusto. He remembered how in his family weddings were sombre affairs and funerals a lot livelier. It seemed that wasn't a trait peculiar to his family. Relatives of the hospitalised wore religious marks and flowers in their hair, a conflagration of festive colours. Everywhere, he heard tones of relish as medical details were discussed loudly and proudly. He caught many English medical terms peppering the native tongues. There wasn't the brooding tension that suffused the air at British hospitals, where everyone whispered or stared at their feet in waiting rooms.

Chandra came to him bearing tall glasses of watermelon juice which they took to a little table. As she took a call, he forwarded ballistics reports on the previous murders to Scotland Yard, then picked up a newspaper someone had left on the next seat. The *Times of India* from two days ago. A raid on an abattoir. Scanning the article, he was surprised to learn that it was the police who had raided the perfectly legal business, following complaints about the treatment of the cows. There was an overly dramatic picture with the article. A man in a turban, a Rajput-like figure, held a double-barrelled shotgun to a cow's head. A tasteless photo.

Before he could read further, Chandra interrupted. 'Right, I know my plans for this evening.'

'A lead?'

'Not in the case of Sarita Mohan, not yet,' said Chandra.

'Then?'

'Someone I'd like to revisit. The first victim – the model Laxmi – her agent, Rahul.'

'Why do you want to visit him now?'

'Just got a call about his alibi. Doesn't pan out. Plus, there is something about him that pisses me off.'

'I suppose that's two good reasons.'

'On that topic, there is someone you shouldn't be pissing off.'

'It's a long list.'

'Rajkumar wants to see you. He wants to brief you officially, he said, whatever that means. As your immediate superior, I think it is my job to brief you on the relevant facts. But,' she shrugged, 'men will be men.'

'You mean boys will be boys?'

'Men here, like men everywhere, have their ways.'

'Rajkumar,' said Patel, cautiously airing his thought, 'certainly has a way about him.'

Chandra laughed. 'You haven't a clue. Let's go.'

Chapter Nine

Chief Rajkumar was holding the flesh between his nostrils in a pinch and jiggling it when Patel entered his room. On the desk in front of him were three telephones, one red, two black, and two mobile phones, lined up straight. Nothing else. Not a paper or a file.

Rajkumar continued to jiggle his nostrils even after Patel folded himself into a chair opposite.

Patel waited, recognising Rajkumar's wish to appear to be doing some serious thinking. An uneasy feeling bloomed in his chest. Was it heartburn from the coffee or was it, in fact, an instinct as to the designs of the chief inspector on one Scotland Yard detective? Patel couldn't tell.

Rajkumar finally allowed Patel the generosity of his attention. His gaze hovered around Patel's left ear, travelled to the face, met Patel's eyes.

'Afternoon, Mr Rajkumar. You wanted to see me?'

Instead of replying, Rajkumar let his attention drift past his right ear. He frowned at the door.

'Yes?' There was a rustle of clothing and throat clearing behind Patel. He turned to see a uniformed minion fidgeting.

'I am not to be disturbed,' said Rajkumar. 'I am meeting Mr Patel of Scotland Yard and showing him hospitality. Whatever it is, wait.'

He beamed at Patel. 'Have you had good lunch, Mr Patel? Shall I get you tea, coffee, samosas?'

'Water will be fine.'

'Tell Sarala to bring water. Bisleri.'

'Yes, sir.' A kind of reluctant whine from the deputy as he shuffled around to go.

'Remember, do not disturb unless it is very urgent.'

'Sir.'

'Is it urgent?'

'Sir.' The deputy shuffled slowly around again, his very flesh reluctant to respond quickly, such was his subservience to Rajkumar.

'Report needs signing, sir.'

'Bring it over.'

The deputy brought a thick sheaf of papers to the desk and stood stiffly by Rajkumar's side.

Rajkumar tapped the papers together, lay the pile on the table. He chose a pen from his front shirt pocket, one from four. He took precisely two seconds to run his eye on each page of the report. When he had finished, he tapped them together again, then began initialling each page. He squinted. Patel noticed the reading glasses still in his shirt pocket, gold rims glinting.

'Procedure, Mr Patel.' With an emphatic shake of his pen, Rajkumar signed his name, tapped the pages together one final time, and asked the deputy, 'What does it say?'

'Report inconclusive, sir. The expert cannot say what type of gun this is. Or even if it is a gun. No trace of lead.'

Rajkumar shook his head at Patel.

Patel said, 'I've sent a copy to London.'

'Have you?' Rajkumar seemed surprised that Patel could possibly have anything other than platitudes to contribute on the matter.

'Well, that is why I'm here,' said Patel. 'To help,' he added.

Rajkumar smiled, showing most of his teeth. 'Yes, of course, Mr Patel. We are privileged to receive Scotland Yard's assistance. And particularly *your* assistance.' He lifted his elbows off the table.

The deputy picked up the report and left.

Rajkumar pressed the fingers of both his hands against each other in a steeple, in front of his chest. Briefly, he rested his chin upon them and smiled, then held them both out, palms facing up, fingers tipped down towards Patel.

'Here we have Mr Patel, a celebrity no less. Coming to the aid of the hapless Indian police?'

Patel winced. 'I'm not a celebrity, Mr Rajkumar. That was ten years ago. No one remembers me any more.'

'No, no, not cricket. The famous catcher of the Dales Ripper, Mr Patel, are you not?'

'My picture graced the papers only briefly.'

In none of them was he even looking at the camera. Long-lens shots. For three days, the papers pursued him. He had refused all interviews. Then they dropped him to go after the next big story. It wasn't as though he was shy of the limelight. Just that he couldn't bring himself to take credit for what he considered a fluke.

'Famous, Mr Patel. I even read about it in the *Bengaluru Times*. "Patel Clean Bowls Serial Murderer."'

It hadn't been certainty that led him on over the Yorkshire Dales. Not a patient piecing together of a puzzle with the final piece dangling in front of his nose. He had just been knocking on every door in the village. It was his boss, in fact, who had suggested it, for a lack of leads had stymied them. His partner, John, had taken French leave to shag his mistress. Unfortunate timing. Suspended for a month.

Rajkumar smirked. 'You are too coy, Mr Patel. What a mass of talent you are. Brilliant cricketer with unfortunate injury first of all, then brilliant detective. A keen nose for hunting criminals, or else Scotland Yard would not have sent you to our rescue. Minister Goldblum would not have pressed upon our central government to accept the help.'

Patel swallowed the bitterness that any mention of cricket produced in him.

'I am here to provide any—'

'Do you know,' interrupted Rajkumar, 'how I learned of our good fortune, Mr Patel?'

'Fortune?'

'Your assistance, of course. I had a phone call the day before yesterday at six p.m. informing me to expect your arrival in the morning. Mr Patel, you were already en route by the time they thought of informing me.'

'As a matter of fact, I myself—'

'Curious, Mr Patel. For decades now, since Independence, in fact, we had no need of Scotland Yard assistance to solve our own domestic matters, for of course as you are well aware, Alex Goldblum's ex-wife was an Indian national residing in India. But now we cannot, apparently, do without your assistance. Do you know why, Mr Patel?'

Patel waited.

'It is a high-profile case, that is why.' Rajkumar leaned forward, pointed a finger at Patel. 'Only a famous cricketer turned famous Ripper catcher from Scotland Yard would do, Mr Patel, to catch our notorious Indian criminal. The Bengaluru police force with its hundred and seventy detectives isn't enough. It isn't equipped with such prowess, such brains as you, Mr Patel.'

'Our intention is to help, not interfere—'

'I spoke to your superior, Mr Patel.'

'Rima?'

'Superintendent Skinner. He very kindly rang me up while your flight was in the air, and he called you a take-charge type.'

As Patel was still taking in the meaning of what Rajkumar said, his phone buzzed. He ignored it.

'Your phone, Mr Patel.'

'Oh.'

In India, after all, a summons from your phone was a summons from a god. Rajkumar waited for Patel to check his phone, so he did. A text from Sarah.

'Who is it from?'

Patel felt this conversation was becoming ever more surreal. 'Oh it's nothing. Not work.'

'Family?'

'My fiancée, Sarah.'

'Oh yes? You are engaged to be married?' A ghastly smile from Rajkumar, either a leer, or an effort to be friendly, which, given the circumstances, was bizarre.

'Yes,' Patel said, unwilling to add more.

Unrelenting, Rajkumar said, 'Is your wife-to-be police as well?'

He imagined Sarah in a uniform. A sub-Chandra figure. 'Quite the opposite, in fact. She is an artist, a sculptor.'

'Oh yes. South India, of course, as you know, is famous for its sculpture. I must look it up. I like collecting sculpture and whatnot.' Descending into another realm of surreality, it seemed to Patel, Rajkumar flourished a pen and said, 'Your fiancée has a website, Facebook, Twitter handle?'

'Ah. I have no idea. Yes, a website. Just look up her name. Sarah Saunders. Google it.'

'Spelling?'

'S-A-R-A-H. And surname S-A-U-N-D-E-R-S.'

Rajkumar wrote it down. Then he pursed his lips. His expression changed once more, hardened. Without warning, he snorted like a bull. 'We will catch this fool murderer. Sooner or later. You are here, are you not, with your famous instinct, to take the credit when that happens?'

Patel drew a breath. Straight bat time. 'Mr Rajkumar, I'm here to assist.'

'You are?'

'Not interfere.'

'No?'

'And certainly not to take credit.'

Rajkumar opened his mouth, but Patel held up a hand.

'Believe me – Skinner, my boss, wants me to stay under the radar.'

'He does?'

'Yes. Please. I am very sure you don't need any assistance. It's politicians muddying waters.'

'Yes. Politicians. The mayor probably interfered too. That phony fellow.'

This surprised Patel. 'Sadiq Khan?'

'No, no, the Bengaluru mayor. Mr Hariharan. He is always interfering in police business.'

'I am your humble servant.' Patel dipped his head a tad theatrically. 'I'll be in the background, hidden away, helping out.'

'Do you know my son is into cricket, Mr Patel?'

What now? 'Erm, how charming.'

And just like that, Rajkumar's demeanour changed. 'You must come to the house, have dinner prepared by my wife, sign a cricket ball for my son.'

'Ah.'

'When all this is over.'

'Of course.' Patel forced a grin, thinking how the glamour,

the glory, the stardust still stuck to him from having shone so brightly, so briefly.

'Yes,' said Rajkumar, glowing himself, like an oiled bronze pot.

'Yes?'

'Yes,' repeated Rajkumar. 'Let us rise above, Mr Patel, or in fact, in your case, stay under, and we will do our jobs.'

'Absolutely, Mr Rajkumar.'

'I am starting to like you, Mr Patel.'

Good God. 'Thank you, Mr Rajkumar.' Patel rose from his seat.

Rajkumar lumbered up, shook Patel's hand. 'Watch out for reporters. They lurk everywhere and they will misquote everything you say.'

'I won't talk to anyone.'

'See you tomorrow, same time, for the next briefing.'

'Look forward to it.'

So it was going to be a regular tête-à-tête.

Rajkumar slapped Patel's shoulder twice in a gesture of camaraderie before shutting the door firmly on him.

As he made his way from the empty floor, it occurred to Patel that he'd never known an Indian to shut the door on a visitor. Queer fish, was Rajkumar.

Chapter Ten

The machinations of police politics roiling within his head, Patel slowly made his way out of the building. Chandra was supposed to meet him outside at six. He checked his watch. Half past five. His 'briefing' with Chief Rajkumar had only taken twenty minutes.

The sun was low in the sky, smothered in clouds. A nip in the air made him feel at home, and not in a good way. The street lights hadn't come on yet. The only glow of warm light came from a little kiosk on the pavement to the right of the building. The steam hiss and the clatter of metal tea pans lured him there. Hanging from strings were local weeklies, starlets on the covers. The *Bengaluru Times* had a blow-up of a Bollywood muscleman next to the lead about a new terror attack in Kashmir. Tea bubbled in an ancient contraption. Steam spouted up at the reading material. Three people stood sipping chai from half-glasses. Without asking Patel, the dark, shrunken man behind the stall held out a cigarette and a chai half-glass.

Just what he needed, in fact. Perfect communication without the barrier of language. He passed the man a note, was given some change. Lit his cigarette from a lighter, hanging, like the magazines, from a string.

He noticed two of the fellow customers were looking at him. Both wore harem pants, homespun kurtas, knitted shoulder bags. Both had long hair. Both held cigarettes. One a man, the other a woman.

The woman, her wavy halo of hair billowing in the breeze, put down her empty glass on a jar of boiled sweets, passed her cigarette to her left hand, and extended the right towards him.

'Good evening, Mr Patel.'

Patel looked from her to the man in his black-rimmed John Lennon glasses and lanky length of hair. A hippy, out of place and out of time. He knew them to be from the very privileged class of Indians who wore Bata sandals and spoke perfect, unaccented Tamil or Kannada to the maids, the stallholders, the auto drivers, and perfect, lilting English to Englishmen. They were the progeny of the movers and shakers of establishment. Children of ruthless businessmen, into Bob Dylan and socialist politics. He'd met one or two of their type at university, those that slipped the Oxbridge net.

'Good evening.' He shook the proffered hand. The man scribbled something in a notebook.

'How are you finding India, Mr Patel? And the Bengaluru police?'

'Charming, both,' he said. 'Are you from ...' He indicated the *Times* hanging from the thread.

The woman widened her eyes and smiled. 'Not from that gossip rag, Mr Patel,' she said. 'We work for the only paper that still prints news. *The Indian.*'

'I shouldn't be talking to you,' he said, throwing down his cigarette and stubbing it out. It had burned rather quickly to the filter.

She bent to stub her cigarette on the ground, straightened, tapped out a couple more from a packet. 'Goldflake?'

He took one. She took another and placed it between her lips. He caught the dangling lighter and held a flame for her, then lit his own. He berated himself for his weakness. His second cigarette in five minutes. His second, in fact, in two years. He dragged on it. Pleasure blossomed within like cancer cells.

The male reporter was still scribbling in his notebook, cigarette untasted between his lips, an inch of thick ash drooping from it.

The woman introduced herself as Kadambri, dragged on her cigarette and blew her smoke away from Patel. 'Can you tell us anything about the progress that's been made?'

'I am sorry. Anything for the press will be communicated to you by the police's media spokesperson.'

'There is no such person, Mr Patel.'

'Then I refer you to the office of Chief Rajkumar.'

'No one will talk to us, Mr Patel. We could help you, you know. Print details of what to look for in a potential killer. His habits, physical characteristics. We can warn all the women of the city.'

'I would advise against scaremongering.' Patel threw the cigarette down on the ground, stepped on it. 'I am sorry, I cannot talk to you. And if you come across any confidential information, don't print it. It would seriously jeopardise the investigation.'

'Oh come on, Mr Patel. From where are we going to get any information?'

He gave a small smile. 'You're wasting your time with me. I have to get on with the investigation. My colleague will be here any second now.'

'Where are you going?'

'Not home to a TV dinner and bed, I can assure you.'

'Are you going to interview a suspect?'

'Perhaps.'

Chandra had said something about the model's agent.

They were quiet for a minute. Kadambri stood observing,

or rather, absorbing, his every move. He ran fingers through his hair, flicked a glance at his watch, looked down the road for Chandra's green car. Kadambri's eyes moved with his every gesture, with the same mid-range focus of a snake's eyes that take in every gesture of a snake charmer.

'Why these women, Mr Patel?'

'No idea.'

'How does he pick them? Assuming he doesn't know them already?'

'Beats me.'

'Do you not know anything?'

'We have some theories,' said Patel, more in hope than knowledge. 'What do you think?'

'Me?'

'Yes. You are a young woman, strong, independent, professional, just like ... How do you think these women happened to be chosen?'

'Gosh, I can't imagine,' she said, looking nervous. 'He could be anyone I know, or don't know.' She glanced at her colleague. 'Him.' She glanced at the tea stallholder, who was listening intently. 'Could be him, could be you, for all I know.'

A feeble laugh emerged from them all. What she said was too close to the bone. Patel thought it must now be apparent to her that the police knew fuck all about the killer, and that fuck all progress had been made so far. He hoped she didn't print anything like that in her paper, alluding to him as the source.

'How does it compare, Mr Patel?'

'How does what compare?'

'You know.' Kadambri shrugged. 'Everything.' She waved her arms about. 'How things are in Europe and how they are here?'

'Europe?'

'Yeah?'

'Is a different kettle of fish.' He watched her frown as she deciphered his little idiom. 'Britain ... well, things are more straightforward there, I suppose.' Kadambri waited for him to continue. The nature of the discussion, he was aware, was metaphysical. 'My grandmother had a way of putting it. When you tell someone, "touch your nose", the Englishman will grab his nose like this.' He brought his hand to the front of his face. 'And the Indian, he will go around the back of his head to reach the front of his face.' And he did just that.

The tea stall owner, the male reporter, a couple of casual tea drinkers and Kadambri, all burst out laughing. Patel basked in the appreciative laughter. He wasn't exactly known as a wit back home.

Then, as if the darkness of the situation impinged on their consciousness, everyone fell silent all at once. Patel's cheeks felt the strain of his smile.

'Entertaining the natives, I see.'

He hadn't heard Chandra arrive. He turned, the smile fading from his lips, to see her assessing Kadambri. He turned again to introduce Kadambri, only to see her backing off, her man in tow. 'Good luck, Mr Patel,' she called as she jumped on the pillion of a motor-scooter.

Chandra raised her eyebrows at Kadambri's retreating back, and kept them raised as she said, 'Was that wise, talking to journalists?'

'Nah, just sharing a fag and a natter,' he said, purposefully striking a dismissive tone, relishing the uncertainty in Chandra's eyes.

Chapter Eleven

A woman in a giant toothpaste carton welcomed them to the party. Her face, arms and legs stuck out from holes cut into the cardboard. Her arms and legs were hairless, long and silky. Her face was painted over so thick it resembled a mask, with gold eyeshadow, gold lipstick and fake gold lashes. The cardboard tube bore, in dazzling gold lettering, the legend 'Colgate'.

'Welcome,' she said, with a smile one usually associated with an American politician. Patel wondered if the health of her teeth was an 'Essential' or a 'Desirable' in the job application.

'Oh good, we're early,' said Chandra, jangling her keys at a valet. She had made an effort for the party. She wore jeans and a sleeveless top, its back charmingly creased, huge hoop earrings that looked as if they were made of coconut shells, a bit of mascara and a dauntingly red lipstick.

A valet, with an obvious look of distaste, took Chandra's keys and drove her battered Maruti 800 away. Behind them a queue of highly polished Mercedes and BMWs was forming.

After directing them to the welcome drinks desk, the toothpaste woman turned towards some new arrivals with a strenuous spin on her high heels, her face shining like a benevolent moon from the hole in the tube.

'Sarah would say something apt.'

'About that woman dressed as toothpaste?'

'Yeah.'

'To be rinsed and spat out?'

'Something like that.'

'Who's Sarah?'

'My fiancée.' Patel looked away, as if it were some terrible guilt he was admitting to.

'Oh good,' said Chandra, pulling ahead of him through the doors. 'And I thought you were alone and unloved.'

Patel kept up with her stride. 'Why'd you think that?'

'It is an aura you project.'

'Do I look like I need someone to love me?'

Ignoring him, Chandra flagged an elderly waiter. She chose a cocktail from the tray he bore, then spoke to him in a low voice.

Guests were piling in. Tinkling laughter from astonishing beings – tall, ethereal and skimpily clad even by Paris couture standards. The most beautiful women he'd ever seen gathered in one place, and, erupting among them like boils, middle-aged men in suits.

Chandra turned to Patel. 'Rahul is here, but the waiter can't see him at the moment. I'll google a photo so we can both look out for him.' She brought up her phone and typed into it while juggling with her cocktail.

'This will be a while,' she said. 'Third World broadband. Want a drink?'

'No thanks.'

'It's free.'

'Tell me, what kind of party is this?'

'Oh, a peculiar one,' she said. 'Very common in Asia and the Far East. Once or twice a year, the company gives a treat for its hardworking managers and senior staff. Dinner in a five-star hotel. Fashion show. Disco.'

'Fashion show?'

'An excuse to parade semi-nude apsaras on stage so the men feel refreshed from their year-long corporate battles,' she said. 'And then they mingle. Free cocktails for all. Even us.'

'I don't see a stage.' Patel scanned the room. 'And it looks like buffet dinner.'

Patel made to go over. He was starving. He'd still not eaten a full meal since he arrived.

Chandra said: 'We need to find Rahul. If there's no stage, there might not be a fashion show, and he might not stay long.'

'Why's that?'

'He manages fashion shows, that's why. He's not just an agent.'

'Ah.'

'Drat,' she said, looking at her phone. 'Internet's slow even by our standards.'

'Let's ask around,' said Patel. 'Some of these models would know where he is.'

'I don't want word getting to him that we're looking for him. He might vamoose.'

Patel cast around for what he thought might look like a model agent slash choreographer of fashion shows. Definitely not a suit. Someone camp, dressed differently from the corporate types.

Then he saw a shimmer in the bar area. A beautiful woman, alone. 'I think I'll have that drink, after all,' he said to Chandra.

The young model perched at the bar, dressed in something white and diaphanous. She slouched, a manicured hand supporting her chin, an air of desolation around her chiffon cloud as she watched the bartender mixing a drink.

'Hello there.' Patel perched on a stool beside her. 'This is Chandra, I am Vijay.'

She shook her head in private mirth and the plumes of pink in her hair shook. 'Hello Vee-jay.'

'What's your name?'

'Gomti.'

'Any idea where to find Rahul?'

'He's around, somewhere,' she said. 'Telling someone how much he misses his wife, no doubt.' She giggled. Sniffed. Giggled some more. Then she abruptly stopped giggling, and a sly smile hung upon her lips as she appraised him.

'Do you know his wife?' said Patel.

She shrugged.

'We're wasting time,' said Chandra. 'I saw some people go upstairs.'

'Oh, he could be upstairs,' said Gomti. 'Just knock before entering the rooms.' She tried to suppress laughter.

'Bedrooms,' said Chandra.

'Mmm hmm. You look like a policeman,' she said to Patel, a flicker of interest coming into her eyes. Then she glanced at Chandra. 'You aren't a model.'

'She's my boss,' said Patel.

Chandra was staring at the stairs. Patel saw that there were, indeed, guests winding their way up, and waiters carrying down empty trays.

'I am going to check these rooms,' said Chandra. 'Want to come?'

'I shall talk to this young lady,' said Patel, 'while you go and check.'

Chandra disappeared up the stairs.

He turned to see the model studying him.

'Gomti, did you know Laxmi?'

'We were best friends.'

'Really? The police talk to you?'

'Yes.'

'What did you tell them?'

'Nothing useful. I cannot imagine who could kill her. She was so sweet, innocent really. But the police weren't interested in her character. Just my alibi and gossip about old boyfriends.'

'Did anything strike you as odd the last time you saw Laxmi?'

'I wasn't here. I last saw her over a month before she ... I was in Goa all week for a magazine shoot. Elle cosmetics.'

'Tell me about the last time you saw her.'

'Well, you know, it was at a party. There's some party every night. We had a laugh about something. Sometimes tears, sometimes laughs.'

'What about?'

Gomti considered. 'She'd gone to a meeting with a new client earlier. She had a low-cut top on and he couldn't take his eyes off her cleavage. So much that he went to put his glass on the table while staring at her boobs ... ' She dissolved into laughter, sputtered, struggling to control herself. 'Completely missed. The glass shattered everywhere. We laughed so hard.'

'Does this happen a lot? Men reacting this way?'

'What do you think?' The laughter was wiped off her face and she was suddenly grim.

'Do you think this man could be an obsessive pervert?'

'No more than anyone else. Laxmi seems to attract pervs. I am always telling her not to meet clients by herself. Going where they ask her to.' She paused, pursed her lips. 'Asked her to.'

'How do you meet clients, Gomti?'

'Oh, I always decide where to meet clients. Usually I make them come to the coffee shop near the Goethe Institute. Always in the daytime. Never at night. Laxmi – she wasn't careful. Too trusting.'

'Oh?'

Gomti touched the tears of laughter from earlier. Patel

plucked out a tissue from a box at the bar. She folded it up to her eye to shore up the mascara. Patel spied a silver tray behind the bar and held it up for her.

Gomti smiled a little. 'You know, when she started, she used to say yes to lingerie ads.'

'Is that a bad thing?'

'Yeah,' said Gomti. 'It's not like I'm a prude. Look at me. This costume is worse than a negligée. But it's what you say. Everyone knows you always say "No" to lingerie ads when someone asks you. When you start off. Saying yes straight away ...' – she shook her head – 'why, yes to lingerie ads means yes to blue films. Yes to be pimped off. These model agents, most of them are nothing better than pimps.'

'Maybe the agent pressured her?'

'Pressured?'

'You know, to be nice to someone, someone influential, rich. Can anyone pressure you like that? Rahul, for example?'

'Oh sure,' said Gomti. 'But it's nothing I can't handle. There is constant pressure, as you say, to drink, to do drugs, to have sex. Constant pressure.' She laughed, the drink went down the wrong way and she spluttered.

Patel handed her another tissue from the bar. Gomti took a moment to catch her breath. 'I've got this great story,' she continued. 'Once I was driven round and round Senatoff Road by a mafia guy. He said –' she laughed again '– he really wanted a friend he could have conversations with.'

Patel felt his blood go cold, but Gomti was laughing like it was a silly joke.

Chandra appeared.

'Found him,' she said, a tense nerve throbbing on her cheek. 'Let's go.'

'Thanks.' He touched Gomti's shoulder. 'Stay safe.'

Gomti winked at him and blew him a kiss. 'If you need to know anything else, call.' She dangled a limp wrist about her perfect conch of an ear.

Patel and Chandra walked up the stairs.

'Send someone around to get details of a mafia guy from Gomti,' he said, 'after we've dealt with Rahul.'

'Mafia guy? You'd think he had enough job satisfaction that he didn't have to moonlight as a serial murderer, too.'

'You never know.'

'OK,' said Chandra, 'but after we see what Rahul has to say. I have a good feeling about this.'

'How did you find him?'

'I had to ask the waiters. They've been warned not to talk. The rooms are also part of the deal, it seems. For drugs, secret meetings, entertainment of a private nature.'

'Whaddya know?' Patel shook his head. 'Gomti made models sound like purity and innocence.'

'Oh it's not all of them, I'm sure,' said Chandra. 'They probably hired hookers as well as the models.'

'Seriously?'

'The models, they all come from good families, with college degrees. They will go on to marry investment bankers, become film stars. They are for looking at, not touching.'

'And the hookers?'

'Why, they are just shit. They get trodden with the foot and the foot gets washed.'

'So, Gomti was right. Laxmi wasn't in the hotel room to provide a service.'

Chandra looked at him like he was an idiot. 'If the price is right, anybody can be had.'

A waiter came padding across the carpet runner, barefoot. 'This way, madam,' he whispered. He took them outside a room down the corridor and handed Chandra a key card, before padding back the way he'd come.

Chandra took a breath. In. Out. 'Now,' she said.

Patel put his shoulder to the door. Chandra swiped the key card.

They burst into the room.

On a vast bed, upon black silk sheets, the same colour and shimmer as Sarita Mohan's bedding, lounged a very big, dark man, with thick, matted hair lapping at his shoulders.

Although his eyelids fluttered open to see them, he seemed unable to process their presence.

Fried off his skull, thought Patel. Traces of a white powder on the glossy black side table. On the carpet, an empty bottle of Johnny Black on its side.

'Wha ...' said the man, half raising himself up. 'Put it over there,' he slurred.

'Mr Rahul,' said Chandra. 'We are the police. I'm here about Laxmi's murder. Your alibi didn't check out.'

'Police?' He spluttered. 'Laxmi? But I was at the cinema. *Godzilla.*'

'Yes, I know.' Chandra brought out her phone and swiped at the screen a couple of times. 'You said it was the eight o'clock show. And your friend Sanjay said he was with you. Then you said the 3D screen gave you a headache so instead of going to a party at the Sheraton, you got Sanjay to drop you at home at eleven p.m. and he went to the party alone.'

'Ye-ah,' stammered Rahul. He staggered upright, felt under the pillow, brought out a pack of cigarettes, fumbled for a match.

'Hang on,' Patel whispered to Chandra. 'How did you find that his alibi is false?'

'I checked the movie listings,' she whispered back. 'There was only a 2D show on at eight. The 3D show was at six-forty-five.'

Patel raised his eyebrows to show he was impressed.

'And to put this in context, Mr Patel –' Chandra raised her voice '– Rahul had a row with Laxmi at seven p.m. She wouldn't do a private show. What exactly is the nature of a private show, Rahul?'

'Oh, you know, just that some important clients want privacy. I just said, it's well paid, just a bit of flirting, harmless stuff, yaar.'

'Just flirting?'

'And bit of stripping.'

'Of clothes?'

Rahul put his hands out. 'No compulsion. Strictly voluntary. Big tips. I only take forty per cent.'

'Where were you that night, Rahul?' said Patel.

'At the show. We were late.'

Chandra shook her head. 'There is a record of you saying you were going to the eight o'clock show.'

'I'm getting a splitting headache. What will make you go away?' He reached for his wallet on the bedside table. He started peeling off 2,000-rupee notes from a bundle.

Chandra sat down at the foot of the bed and pinched one of Rahul's big toes through the cover. 'This is a murder investigation, Rahul. We aren't traffic cops at the end of the month.'

Rahul stopped. He seemed completely sober now. He shoved the cash back into the wallet, put the wallet back on the table. Patel could see the cogs in his head turning.

'That must be why I got the headache. I was wearing 3D glasses for a 2D film. That's right.'

Chandra continued to grip the big toe. 'You're pissing me off, Rahul. This is a very serious mater. You'll now have to come up with alibis for the duration of all four murders. You are officially a suspect.'

Rahul drew his feet and sat up, his lips set in a thin line. 'You are harassing me,' he said. 'I have connections. I know politicians, IPS officers. Minister Baburam's brother is my old college buddy.'

'If you haven't got anything to worry about, why do you need the protection of all these people? *Dal meh kuch kala hai*. Do you know the expression, Mr Patel?'

'Something fishy?'

'Yes,' said Chandra, 'except vegetarians in India don't eat fish. Care to translate, Rahul? No? Let me see – how do you say it?' She leaned slightly towards Rahul. 'Something black in the lentils.'

'You're harassing me,' said Rahul, 'when I'm dejected, absolutely dejected, at what happened to Laxmi. You're ruining my mental health. I'm going to sue you. I know lawyers. Some of my closest friends.'

'If you tell us where you were, Rahul, we can leave you alone to your solo entertainment.'

'I told you.'

Patel looked at a pile of crumpled tissues on the floor, sniffed the cloying rank air. He said, 'Where's your lover, by the way? Did you hurt her? Is that why she left?'

'No, no,' said Rahul. 'No lover.'

Chandra said: 'I can smell the sex on you, Rahul. If you don't co-operate, we will forcibly take a sample for DNA testing.' She turned towards Patel and winked.

'No, no sample. I need a lawyer. Give me my phone.' Rahul started feeling around for his phone.

Chandra said: 'You know the American expression, Rahul? If you want to play hardball . . .'

She shrugged at Patel. He got the drift. Rahul didn't.

She made two movements. With one, she was on all fours on the bed, bending over Rahul. With the second, she had her knee on his thigh, pressing down on the groin.

'Ugh,' said Rahul, surprised, then 'ugh,' again, in pain.

He brought his arms up to fend her off. She caught both his hands and pushed them over his head on to the pillow. Holding his wrists with one hand, she stuck two bent fingers up his nostrils and pushed till he screamed.

Patel found himself bearing witness to a geezer getting the harsh treatment from a woman in a salwar kameez.

Chandra's sing-song South Indian accent sounding all too incongruous, she said, 'I'll do this all night long till you tell me where you were when Laxmi was murdered.'

Rahul screamed.

Patel decided against examining his conscience in this instance.

She briefly let go. Rahul howled. The blood seeped from his nose. Chandra took her fingers to his nostrils again. He cried, 'I'll tell you, I'll tell you.'

She let go of his nose. 'Oh, do tell.'

'My leg . . . ' He squirmed.

'Na-ah,' she said. 'Spit it out quickly and I'll get off.'

It was then that they heard the toilet flush.

Very slowly, as though moving underwater, Chandra lifted her knee from Rahul's groin and slid off the bed. Patel himself, feeling heavy as though he were dragging wellington boots from a muddy pond, pushed off the wall. Rahul too, sat up in slow motion, as though forgetting the pain in his nose and groin. The three of them, painted figures in a Renaissance tableau, turned and stopped, watched the en suite door open.

A man – a skinny, well-dressed fellow – emerged, his pupils dilated all the way to Amsterdam. As if nothing at all had happened, as if he were just chancing upon some acquaintances, he said, 'Hi guys.'

He went to the door, put on his artfully weathered

brown brogues and stepped out, letting the door close softly behind him.

'That's Sanjay?' said Chandra.

Rahul nodded.

'You were with him that evening and night?'

Rahul nodded, looking away.

'Doing drugs and having sex?' Patel added.

He nodded again, not meeting his eyes.

'You know homosexuality isn't illegal any more in this country?'

Rahul did not answer. He was staring at the picture of a sunset hung above an occasional table.

'But drugs are,' said Chandra.

Ah, thought Patel to himself. Chicken shit. They were back to knowing nothing.

Rahul began weeping again. 'Don't tell anyone,' he sobbed. 'We're both married.'

'Ah, Jesus,' said Patel. 'Let's go.' Hours wasted. Hours in which the killer was edging closer to his next victim.

They left Rahul clutching a blanket to his bleeding nose.

Chapter Twelve

Chandra's little car puttered to a stop in the driveway of Hotel Top End. As Patel came around, Chandra's window lowered. Already she'd turned the volume of the stereo up. A high, effeminate voice shrieked in a mixture of English and Kannada. The music thumped.

He would be glad, he thought, of a few hours of quiet in the dark.

'I'll pick you up tomorrow morning,' said Chandra. All traces of make-up had disappeared from her face. A musky, sweaty smell rose from her. 'Wait, let me find my card.' Her jewellery clattering, she rummaged in the footwell.

He wondered what she was going home to. Would she creep in quietly, slip beside a sleeping someone? Or would she have to endure the waiting mother and father, who, while she was busting Rahul's chops, infested the dining table under the tube lights, fretting at the clock. Boiled rice, dal and two vegetables languishing on the table, going cold. Pickle in a jar. Yoghurt in the fridge. The mother rushing to heat the plate of food, the father pouring the water, Chandra sighing, fending off questions and exhaustion in order to make a show of eating.

She fished up a card. 'Toodle-oo,' she said. 'Be ready at seven-thirty.'

'Right,' he said. 'Have a good night, Chandra.'

'And you, Vee-jay,' she said, drawing his name out on her tongue, letting it linger before it left her lips. He found himself quite unexpectedly hoping it was the rice and lentils that awaited Chandra, and not a lover in bed.

He watched her little car turn and shoot down the road. Leaden feet, aching head, dog-tired bones, a bundle of disconnections in a country of disconnections, Patel dragged himself up to the reception desk. A woman, fresh as jasmine, punched in his details, took his passport for scanning and handed him the key card with the minimum of chitchat. She barely looked at his face. He could have been handing over anybody's passport.

The hotel was clinically white, surfaces gleaming, newspapers piled in artful fans on every table. A travelling businessman's dream stay.

The elevator bank was half hidden by an enormous wooden Ganesh and a bushy money plant. He got into a lift and summoned his floor. There were buttons for nine floors. A tenth button had a little handwritten sticker tacked on, which said 'rooftop pool'. No one had mentioned a pool to him. Gym, yes, massages, yes, beauty treatments, yes, but not pool.

The elevator pinged and let him out. In the room, his luggage waited by the wardrobe. The bed seemed adequate. The bathroom shone to European standards. The AC blasted cold air. Were the Indians trying to make preserves and pickles out of the travelling foreigners? First scorch them with the tropical sun, then freeze them with industrial-strength air conditioning. Except, it was chilly here in hilly Bengaluru; the sun couldn't quite scorch away the winter cold.

He turned off the AC. In the sudden silence that filled his brain, there resounded an echo of a scream.

He unshod his feet and left the shoes by the door. Padded to the bathroom, ran the tap, washed his face. The water ran down in grey rivulets, the filth of Bengaluru on his skin. He needed a shower. But it was all he could do to stagger to the bed and collapse on top of the covers. He shut his eyes and immediately, from the wings of his eyelids, the events of the day flounced onstage. He couldn't rest yet. He had to wind down. Empty his mind. Banish the swirling thoughts.

Flying down in the aeroplane. Chandra. Crisp, sexy, scary Chandra. The crazy traffic. The dead woman, clothed, then unclothed, shot, then cut open, a pair of tweezers removing a flap of skin. The nostrils of Chief Rajkumar, pinched, then jiggling, his unnerving bureaucratic stare making Patel jerk even now in a panic. Chandra again. Parading a variety of foodstuffs designed to traumatise his stomach. Rajkumar again. Giving him a deep pain in the gut the Eno couldn't reach. Eno, sparkling cold comfort. Sarah, his cold comfort.

He needed to check his phone. Drink Eno. Check his phone.

He sat up, rummaged in his pockets. Had he avoided looking at it all day on purpose? The Indians were always shouting into their phones. They shouted to hear each other above the noise. Their shouting created noise. Jostling, beeping, remarking, interjecting constantly.

'Empty your mind,' he said to the empty, low-lit room. The visions of dead women crowded in.

He shoved off the bed, prised his swimming shorts and goggles from the suitcase and fetched a towel from the bathroom. Pressing the button for the elevator, it occurred to him that the pool might be shut.

He got in the lift and went up. Was the hotel empty? Slightly eerie to not have encountered a soul so far, other than the receptionist. He could as easily be in some remote Welsh hotel in the winter as a metropolitan five-star hotel in the middle of the tourist season.

The elevator pinged open. A sign for the pool led him along a corridor. He passed rooms without numbers, and came to a lower landing that opened into a reception area for the spa. It was closed, the lights set low. He hesitated, then went past reception and into a short corridor. Massage rooms. Beauty therapy area. Men's changing. Women's changing. At the end, the doors were shut. A terminal blinked. He kissed it with his key card. Amazingly, the doors opened.

A great big, sturdy-looking canopy hovered over the rooftop to deflect the daytime sun. A blue shimmering expanse against the dark. At least twenty-five metres. Not another soul. No overhead lights. But the city's lights cast a radioactive glow over everything. In this half-light, he flung his towel on a deck chair, climbed over a rope (why was there a rope around the pool?) and peered in from the edge.

No water.

Instead, a giant crack split the floor of the pool.

The blue reflecting the starlight and the electric lights of the city was merely the painted pool floor. He imagined the floor cleaving under his feet. The tenth floor of a building. What kind of hotel, he'd asked his office manager, imagining an Art Deco haveli from the glory days of the Raj. Brand new, she'd said to him, handing him the paperwork for the hotel booking with a sparkle of accomplishment, as if newness was an indicator of quality.

The crack had foot-wide serrations in some places, and zig-zagged diagonally from one end to the other. He wished Sarah could see this. She would find it uncanny. Six years ago, she'd taken him to the Tate Modern's Turbine Hall to show him another giant crack on the floor.

'Piss off,' he'd said to her. 'This is just a great big fucking crack. This isn't art.'

He'd been angry with her then. A constant throbbing vein

under the skin of his temple. He couldn't now say why. The crack routing through the whole expanse of the Turbine Hall. Adults and children peering into it, someone dropping a chocolate wrapper, another caressing its edges. Some Mexican sculptress, or was it sculp*tor*, like ac*tor*? Did he make fun of that, too?

Sarah, with biting patience, explained how the crack was a challenge to the principles of architecture. They were in a cafe, people jostling her near their table, was that it? No, they were queuing up for lunch. The tone of her voice, its suppressed hiss, rage for rage, making people glance at them and look away. 'It is really important to me that you understand what I do, what I believe in.'

He had nearly snorted, but good sense prevailed and he pressed his lips together and nodded soberly instead. She'd already begun dabbling in what was to become her all-consuming oeuvre, her life's major work until now. Nude sculptures of orgasmic or orgasming women. In low moments, he referred to them as women jerking each other off.

And now, standing here, looking at the crack at the bottom of the rooftop swimming pool, he wondered how Sarah would make sense of this. He conjured up the little crease on her forehead, green eyes darkening into smoky emeralds as they intently focused on every serration of the crack. A challenge to architecture, no kidding.

A little GIF popped into his head, the type that ran on a loop over and over on someone's Facebook page. A muscular brown hand entwined in Sarah's auburn hair, smashing her skull against a serrated edge of the crack, in an endless loop.

He shuddered, suppressed a scream. 'Fuck,' he said to the night sky.

Patel stumbled and bumbled back to his room. His phone lay on the occasional table outside the bathroom. Two calls from Sarah, one from Rima, a voicemail, an email from Ballistics. He opened the email. Acknowledgement that they had received his request; they'd prioritise it over everything else, in light of the urgency, although they were short of staff, yadda yadda ... a prelim report would take a day or two.

Even as he looked at it, willing himself to call his fiancée, the phone rang. He felt a stone drop into the well of his stomach, churning up the acid pool once more.

'Sarah.'

'Hey,' she said. In that one word he could hear both dismay and relief. Was this a precursor to marriage? A lifelong meta-physical grinding against each other?

'Sorry I missed your earlier calls,' he said.

'That's all right,' she said. He could tell she was casting about for something to say that was somewhere between serious and frivolous. What did one say to one's fiancé on a long-distance phone call? Words that were casual, yet intimate.

'We need to talk,' she said.

'Now?'

'Were you in bed?'

'No. I mean ... won't it be better to talk in person?' His heart thumped. Was this it? The Conversation?

Her laugh sounded like an alarm bell. 'It's nothing serious. I just meant ... I didn't mean we needed to talk so *seriously*. You know ...' She seemed nervous. 'Just to keep in touch with each other ... you know what I mean?'

'Of course.' He was relieved. This wasn't the time or the place to talk seriously, although he knew they would have to one day, soon.

After a few more minutes of chitchat, about this and that of their day, but without the details on his part, tiptoeing around the important, relevant subject of themselves, filial duty to each other done, they hung up.

There was a new voicemail. Rima checking in, more or less in a semi-official capacity. He sent her a text. 'Skype meeting tomorrow?' Immediately the phone pinged. Rima. 'Yes, 9, UK time.'

He left the phone on the side table and stretched, naked, on the bed. He sat up again. His teeth ached. He'd held his jaw clenched all day. Pulling on a pair of shorts, he drew the bulky Billingham bag out from the closet. He drew out the files on the first three murders and put them on the little desk. To make space, he unplugged the kettle and set it on the floor by the dustbin. He opened the minifridge and plucked out a little can of Kingfisher premium lager. Popped it open. The clarifying sting of formaldehyde hit his welcoming throat. Sod the ulcers, he thought. He'd stock up on Eno tomorrow.

He opened the first file. 'Victim: Varalakshmi. P. Known professionally as Laxmi. Age 25. 5 ft 8, 54 kg. Medium-fair complexion. Identifying marks on birth certificate: none. Wheatish.' A detail about skin complexion. What would a white woman rate, he wondered. Rice-ish? A black woman, then? Rye-ish? Was the killer, in fact, picking and choosing victims based on their complexion? He went through more banal details, yawned.

They had taught him at university that a fast browsing technique was best to snag on any catchy detail. Skim read to draw in the essence of a text. The bits relevant to your topic will shine up like gems.

He sorted the papers right to left: PM report, FIR, newspaper articles, photos from fashion shoots, photos from the murder scene, some poor-quality printouts of selfies from her Facebook profile. He reread the FIR report, slowly – a sparse, dry account of the discovery of the murder. Hotel maid discovers a body in a luxury suite at 'The Park'. He read again the post-mortem report. 'Time of death: between nine p.m. and eleven p.m.

Stomach contents: partially digested pasta and vegetables; coffee. No sign of sexual activity, forced or voluntary. No sign of struggle. Fingernails clean, except for traces of foundation and lipstick. Fresh, unchipped green nails with two coats of lacquer strengthener.' Someone had written in the margin, *She having manicure that afternoon only*. He skipped to the description of the fatal wound. A hole in the middle of the forehead, one centimetre wide. Lacerations on epidermis indicated puncture with a hard, round object, size of an old-fashioned musket ball.

He put the report down and had a toilet break.

Back at the desk, he browsed through the incident report for the list of physical material in the room: clothes, coffee cups, shoes, cigarette butts. No shell casings. He looked at the photos. A dark stain on the forehead of a beautiful face. The living, breathing woman from the selfies and fashion shoots now a thin, long, inert body draped in a sari, its red colour merging into the red of the bedspread. A dark halo around the head where the blood had seeped and mushroomed.

There were close-ups. Patel examined the wound. His bile rose up in his gullet, and he poured down Kingfisher beer to scorch it. It was like no gunshot wound he'd ever seen. The hole, in every case, was neat and round, except for a slight serration at the bottom, visible only when the wound was cleaned of dried blood. He looked through the PM reports, found no mention of this peculiarity.

He reached again for the beer. Empty. He crumpled the can, threw it to the bin. The can caught the lip of the bin and, with a clattering of metal that pierced through his headache, fell on the floor, the last dregs of beer spilling from it. Sighing, Patel bent to pick up the can. That's when the tail of the *voila!* bird flicked in a corner of his brain. He recalled the murder weapon from a Hollywood film. Dropping the can into the bin, he fired up his laptop and opened his emails. Pressing REPLY to the email from ballistics, he typed, 'Could it be a cattle gun, like in *No Country for Old Men?*'

He looked again at the wound, but his eyes of their own volition slipped away to the dead woman's shoulder. He frowned. There was something different about the blouse. He opened the other two files and found similar shots – mid-shots, head-and-shoulder shots – of the victims. The blouses on Sabah and Anu were well fitting, and of a different shade of red. The one on Laxmi was loose, and everything about it was different. The thread was pink, not red like the others. The fabric was a richer, deeper red, with purple undertones, the colour of old-fashioned roses.

He wrote down in his notebook, *Chk abt Laxmi blouse diff frm others.* Putting that nugget aside for the moment, he read the newspaper reports about the model. A lot of fashion news. Bombay Fashion Week, one or two shots from Paris and Milan, rumours of an upcoming Bollywood debut, posthumously discounted as no more than a rumour. And what's this? A separate bundle of what looked like newspaper articles dated six months ago, pinned together. Scrawled in the top left corner of the first one: 'sex tapes'.

He rapidly went through the titles: 8 June 2018: WE'RE WITH LAXMI. NEWSPAPERS GUILD RELEASES STATEMENT SELF-IMPOSING BAN ON PRIVATE INFORMATION AND PAPARAZZI FODDER; 7 June 2018: EXCLUSIVE! LAXMI OPENS HEART ON TV AND IN PRINT!; 6 June 2018: DEFEND LAXMI TWITTER CAMPAIGN GAINS 60,000 LIKES. HERE'S A SELECTION OF TWEETS FROM THE PUBLIC SUPPORTING LAXMI AGAINST IMMORALITY CLAIMS BY BJP ACTIVISTS; 5 June 2018: ICLOUD NOT A SECURE PLACE FOR YOUR PRIVATE INFORMATION. NO SURPRISE THERE! *Sidebar:* HISTORY OF LEAKS FROM ICLOUD; 4 June 2018: OPINION PIECE.

WHY DOES SEX SHOCK A NATION OF A BILLION?; 4 June 2018: TOP WRITERS AND ACTORS SUPPORT LAXMI AND CONDEMN SOCIAL MEDIA TROLLS; 3 June 2018: WRITER KALKI DEFENDS LAXMI. LAXMI'S VIDEOS PRIVATE AND NOT FOR PUBLIC; 2 June 2018: LAXMI SAYS 'NO COMMENT' TO ALLEGATIONS OF IMMORALITY; 1 June 2018: SEX VIDEOS OF TOP MODEL LAXMI LEAKED ON THE INTERNET.

Sex tapes, he wrote in his notebook. *Storm in a teacup 6 mts ago, or did it bring her to the attn of killer?*

He tapped the back of the pen on the desk. Could it be connected? Would it be a motive? The immorality angle? How does it fit with the fetish with the sari? Do the women all resemble someone in the killer's life?

He looked at the TV. There would be BBC World and CNN for news. He looked at the bed, the slight depression where he had lain earlier, oh so briefly. He could get some much-needed rest, wake up fresh in the morning buzzing with ideas. Or he could do what he must. He dragged his laptop over, opened a search engine and typed.

'Laxmi sex video.'

After several misleading YouTube videos that came up with 'content removed', he found the goods on a link from someone's sleazy blog, in among 'genuine honeymoon' videos.

The screen within the screen switched on. A hand moved away from the viewfinder. View of a bed. It was hard to see the colours of the sheets. Just a pattern in the design was visible. The lights were low, there to set the mood rather than the set-up for filming. A man and woman approached each other, met in front of the bed. They kissed for a long time. At a pace quite slow by Hollywood standards, they moved from first to second base. They were standing at an angle to the camera. Her body wasn't in view, just part of her arms and his hand at her breast. He cupped her breast. She fondled his arse. Through his boxer shorts, his bum looked firm, muscly. His legs were long, beautiful.

The man's name was Rocky. Patel had read in the file that he was a model too, and they had been an item for eight years. Laxmi's murder had so devastated Rocky that there'd been a suicide attempt. His family and friends now didn't leave him alone. In the film, his arse moved closer and rotated against her waist. Rocky had an iron-clad alibi. On the night of Laxmi's death, he was shooting an episode for *The Big Next Model Hunt*, an MTV India production, on Anjuna Beach, Goa.

The couple finally undressed. He almost expected them to have folded the clothes first and put them away in the cupboard. But they just left them in a neat pile on a chair, the edge of it just visible in the shot.

Patel yawned. He was watching sex between people who had been together so long that their passion had funnelled down into mere habit. He wondered if the videoing of it was meant to rekindle their mojo. Something suggested by *Cosmopolitan*. Five ways to put the *bonk* back in bonking. It seemed they were enacting a lovemaking pretty much like it was every time between them. A sweet and sad ritual. Sad because anyone could see this video. And because now she was dead.

He thought of Sarah and himself. They too did the same thing every time nowadays, often on a Tuesday night, or a Thursday, after showering and brushing their teeth. If one of them forgot, the other grimaced, prompting a reprieve from the proceedings for a brief tussle with brush and paste, the desire ebbing every second, the toothpaste like disinfectant poured on the intimacy of the kisses.

On the screen, Rocky had his perfect ass to the camera while he bent over Laxmi, her svelte legs, with surprisingly thick ankles, around his neck. Patel didn't think he was going to find

out much from watching this domestic sex video to its conclusion. His hand hovered over the close button, but just to be on
the safe side, he skipped through the tediously long humping to
the end, where the couple, sated, lay side by side, stroking each
other's faces. He hadn't missed anything useful. He closed the
screen, shut down his laptop. He couldn't see what could link
the sex video to Laxmi's murder.

He browsed through the other files, and then, fighting fatigue,
made some notes.

Wht connects the 4 wmn?
mid 20s to late 30s.
all upperclass, powerful, well known
but very different circles.
1. fashion model
2. writer & activist
3. British politician's ex-wife, Indian tennis star's fiancée
4. businesswoman

He looked again at their photos, mostly from the press and
gossip columns. So, he thought. So . . . all were attractive women
of childbearing age. He rated them based on attractiveness from
one to ten. From first to latest victim, they were 10, 6, 7 and
6.5. But if were one to have traditional Indian tastes, and Indians
liked curvy figures and thick hair, it would be 6, 8, 9 and 6.5.

And this was based on looks, not their personalities, social
agreeability. In real life, their attractiveness would depend on
their actions, too. But he only knew them in death, and from
media reports, not life.

It felt obnoxious to be rating dead women on their attractiveness, like a teenager picking his zits while dreaming some
housewife would put an end to his state of virginity.

He rubbed his aching eyes.

Still, he looked at the numbers again and they were all above six out of ten, whether one's tastes were Indian or not. He wrote down: *All 4 attractive.*

Then a sudden image came to him, of chubby Kajol dancing in a Kollywood film. She wore a short black dress, pumped her thunder thighs to an A. R. Rehman song. Sarah had said something memorable about it.

Scrunching his eyes, he dug deep into his addled, exhausted brain and drew out the whole memory for examination. They had been visiting his parents in Leicester. As usual, the TV was on a Sony or a Zee channel. It was the day before Diwali. His nodding granny perched on the sofa. Sarah sat with her companionably while Patel's mother fed him laddoos in the kitchen, straight from the stove. After he'd eaten three, his mother piled a plate for Sarah. When he took them out to her, Sarah was sitting with eyes glued on the mesmerising, carnivalesque song-and-dance routine. She said, 'Isn't that a bit risqué for India?'

'Hardly,' he said. 'She's dressed modestly by Indian movie standards.'

'Kajol,' interjected Naani, who was by then at least two cards short of a full deck. 'Famous. Very famous. Daughter of Zeenat Aman.'

'Not Zeenat Aman,' he said.

'How would you know?' said Sarah to him.

She meant how did he know what was and wasn't risqué in India. But he did know. He'd known plenty of real Indians at the university, and he'd watched endless movies and followed the news. And of course, there was cricket. Indians infiltrated anything to do with cricket in the UK. He'd seen the posh Indian girls given access to the cricket players. Golden skin, little dresses and long curtains of hair. He knew there were pious, god-fearing Mother India types. He told her that. Told her, 'They can go both extremes in film and in real life.'

Sarah looked unconvinced.

He said, 'All over India, in cities especially, there are lots of Westernised women. More than you'd think.'

But Sarah wouldn't be persuaded. She politely ate half a laddoo and gave his mother faint praise, generous by her standards, but the kind that left his mother cooking up a storm to compensate for the rest of their stay, only irritating Sarah further.

Patel finally allowed himself an ironic smile. He'd figured out something that connected all four women. One word to describe them all. *Westernised*. He wrote it down and underlined it.

Part Two

Chapter Thirteen

Eyes closed, Manu envisioned the perfect man emerging pure and glorious from a great fire. Fiery orange tongues devoured gristle and filth that crackled and hissed. Blackened bits of char flew out in a fan behind him. Untouched, unmoved, face smooth and unlined, the perfect man, Manu-purush, opened his calm, purposeful eyes and gazed upon the new world.

Manu opened his eyes, studied the screen in front of him. His fingers tapped out the words on the keyboard.

'There will blaze a Great Fire to consume impurities of womanhood that taint Man, and He will emerge pure in head and body, tall and strong, to own the world. He will right all wrongs for ever.'

He thought for a moment, then typed 'The Fire That Burns Pure' in the box marked TITLE and clicked the PUBLISH button. After a few minutes checking his emails, he opened his blog and noticed someone had already read his post and commented on it. ShivaShiva wrote, 'Great Stuff.' ShivaShiva lived online. He was a fan of Manu. Manu had six or seven devotees. Not nearly enough, but very soon, when his work was known ...

He checked the bean counter on the Amazon page for his book, an earlier effort than the blog at disseminating his ideas, and found no change in the sale figures. The entire sales figure for *The Teachings of Manu* by Valarmiki still stood at a mere three copies. Manu shrugged. Such was the nature of his work, it had to be kept secret. No one knew about it, and no one read it, even though it was available for all, to learn from and be transformed. A shame he couldn't publish in his own name. Tempting as it was to gain credit for his work, to proclaim his faith, so to speak, it wouldn't do. It just wouldn't do.

He tapped his fingers on the desk, dissatisfied. But onwards and upwards, he told himself. There was work to do. He stood up from the desk and went to the wardrobe. He shook out a sari and blouse, went to find his wife.

Manu pierced the layers of silk with the safety pin and secured the sari to the blouse. Not a wrinkle. He was pleased. It had taken him a lot of practice to get it just so.

He looked over his prone wife at the boy, who was setting the pleats of the sari in the shape of a fan.

'Nice job.'

The boy grimaced. He did not enjoy familial interactions. Typical teenager. Manu felt fondness and frustration jostle within his breast as he contemplated the boy.

'Now's the tricky bit,' he said. 'Ready? On my count.' He held his wife under the shoulders. The boy grabbed her by the knees. 'Three ... two ... one ... lift.'

In one smooth motion, they lifted her on to the couch.

All the pleats were still in place, and every strand of hair. Manu was satisfied. He nodded approval at the boy, who refused to meet his eyes, refused to take pride in enacting this sacred ritual.

Irritably, Manu grabbed the little bottle of ammonia, wafted it under his wife's nose. 'Amba, Amba, wake up.'

She woke up, eyes wide like a startled herbivore, and looked

down at her clothes. She took a hand to her hair, which he and
the boy had combed and braided earlier.

'Oh,' she said. 'I was in the kitchen . . .'

'Now you are here. And gloriously transformed. Want to look
in the mirror?'

Amba shook her head jerkily. 'What time is it? I need to
make dinner.'

'Your clothes are over there. Change before you go.'

She nodded meekly and went over to the chair by the side of
the painting.

Manu settled on the couch.

'Come here, boy.'

The boy came to him, knelt beside him on the floor.

Manu drew the boy's head down on his lap, and there it lay,
warm and nestling. He tapped the boy's cheek as he watched
his wife change her clothes. Things were going well. So well,
in fact, that his heart quickened, desiring more. The desire to
find another one of those shameless, strutting cunts, ripe for
transformation.

He saw the woman the next morning as he walked up the steps
of the Secretariat. Noticed the back of her head, the mass of
black curling hair, medusa-like, corrupting the very air around
her. She wore a tunic like a shapeless gunny sack, which was at
least modest by current standards, although the sun in front of
her, as she raised her arm to drop cigarette ash on the pavement,
permitted the silhouette of her curving waist to show through,
and the darker outline of her underwear.

He smoothed his frown of disapproval before he approached
her. But it was too soon. This wasn't the way he found them.
He had a meeting in five minutes, plus there was something
familiar about her shape, and her hair. He stilled his heart,

swallowed his desire, sucked in his breath, too, in case she felt it on her neck. Thus he retreated swiftly from her, and walked into the building.

But it was meant to be. Two hours later, his head full of policing needs for the new Timmipur four-land flyover, on the way to another mundane, irksome meeting he beheld the medusa-woman arguing with a secretary.

Chapter Fourteen

His eyelids fluttered open to six-forty-five a.m. on the phone face, but Patel tried to cling on to his dream about breakfast. The fact of staying in a hotel had stirred in his British breast the anticipation of a full English. Crisp bacon and sizzling sausages, a cavalcade of toast and the wobbling yolks of eggs.

He came awake, slumped at the desk, neck in a cramp, head flopped on top of the files he'd been reading in the early hours. He'd fallen asleep in the middle of writing something in his notebook. A blotty smudge to prove it, the pen still in his hand, staining his forefinger. He spent a few seconds trying to decipher what he'd been writing, and gave it up as a bad job. He headed downstairs to the restaurant.

Plate in hand, Patel grimaced in front of the breakfast buffet. Cold toast set up in a rack, a row of cardboard squares, next to limp, over-fried eggs and burnt chicken sausages that smelled like yesterday's dog's dinner.

Chandra bustled into the dining hall with a bunch of newspapers.

'You're early,' he croaked.

She gave him a puzzled look, failing to understand his point, then magnanimously shrugged off his inanity.

She took a look at the English breakfast options and declared:

'That's disgusting. Go to the other counter. There is a chef making fresh dosas on demand.'

Patel opened his mouth to protest, but Chandra cut him off: 'Find a table. I'll get us both some food.'

He looked at the toast, eggs and sausages once more, lifted a limp, reluctant hand towards the ladle delving into soggy mushrooms the colour of despair, and simply could not bring himself to do it. He went to find a table.

'This isn't bad,' he said a little later, tearing and folding a piece of dosa, dipping it into sambar and smearing it with coconut chutney. If he alternated each mouthful with a spoon of yoghurt, he might just survive the fire in his mouth.

'Have you seen the papers yet?' said Chandra, swiftly demolishing her own dosa with a knife and fork.

'No,' he said. 'Has the murder made it to the front page?'

'In all the papers. But guess what else is on the front page of the biggest circulating paper in four states?'

'What?'

He couldn't imagine what. Another bunch of refugees drowning? Leonard Cohen winning the Nobel Prize? Another clue in the missing Maddie saga? But of course, he was thinking of the UK papers.

'Are you going to tell me?'

Chandra, like a game-show host delaying the result in order to inflate the suspense, cut a big piece of dosa, dropped some chutney on to it, rolled it with her knife and fork, speared it into her mouth, chewed twice, swallowed, took a sip of water and, only then, leaned forward to stage-whisper, 'It's you.'

'Me?'

'You are the front page news.'

'Get off.'

She produced the paper. It was *The Indian*. The bold banner headline said GENTLEMAN STRIKES FOUR. A few paragraphs on the latest victim. Then there was the large insert, coloured, boxed and with Kadambri's byline with her Twitter handle, @kadswrites. In a spidery font designed to haunt him, *Scotland Yard Sends Spinner to Clean Bowl Serial Killer.* Even had a photo of Patel bowling.

His appetite left him. He pushed the plate away and scanned the article.

The Indian government has sought and obtained help from the best in the world at detection, a police force at the very forefront of modern detection. DI Vijay Patel of Scotland Yard flew in yesterday from London, and was brought straight to the Ulsoor crime scene, where the latest victim, Ms Sarita Mohan, was found early this morning. He has offered his insights to the Bengaluru Homicide Department. In an exclusive to this paper, he warned against encouraging the killer by publishing speculative information about his preferences in victims, or indeed, any details about the investigation, which would only encourage copycats and the unhinged looking for publicity. This reporter was struck by the impression that Mr Patel, thorough professional and a gentleman to boot, could inject some much-needed zest into our City Homicide Department, show our coppers how to do things in style. Perhaps there was a reason, after all, for his promising cricket career to end abruptly. For otherwise, he wouldn't now be on hand to catch this psychotic killer preying on the good women of Bengaluru. Yes, our cops need help to catch this monster, and they have help from the best. Good Luck, DI Patel!

He groaned.

Chandra smirked. 'You're not a DI. They need fact checkers at that paper.'

'She really has made a mountain out of a molehill.'

'She sounds very impressed with you,' said Chandra, archly. 'You gave her an "exclusive".' She made quotation marks with her fore and middle fingers.

'Look, I just lit her cigarette, that's all.'

'Tell that to Rajkumar.'

Patel groaned again.

'Oh lighten up. Today's headlines, tomorrow's old news.'

'I suppose.'

'Nice picture, too. Youthful look.'

'To change the subject,' he said, 'what's with the "Gentleman Strikes Four"?'

'Oh it's a sick joke. He treats the victims so nicely. No sexual assault, just pretties them up, makes them look like ladies, in fact. What a gentleman. Some Hindutva asshole started it on Twitter. It caught on.'

'Sick,' said Patel.

'Kadambri calls you a gentleman.'

'Takes one to catch one,' said Patel, lightly. But it irked him. Was the sub-editor of the paper snoozing?

'Are you going to finish that?'

'What? No.'

Chandra pulled his plate towards her and set to finishing his dosa.

'Oh well,' he said. 'I'll have to avoid Rajkumar.'

'You have a five p.m. briefing with him.'

'He told you?'

'It's my job to make sure you get to it.'

'All I need is a fucking babysitter,' he mumbled.

Chandra frowned, chewed silently, swallowed the last bit of dosa. 'Ask me why I'm here half an hour early.'

'Why are you early?'

'Fact of the matter is, Patel, there's been a development.'

'Do tell.'

'An anonymous call from Bannerguda dam thereabouts.'

'That's where the second victim was found.'

'Yes. Last night, a man called. He has some information about the victim and will only speak in person. We are meeting him at the village at nine. I've been hoping for some information about Anuradha's driver, Bupathy, who took her there and waited for several hours. He has no alibi for three of the murders. But I can't get anything else on him.'

Patel's fatigue drained away as blood pumped into his brain. 'Anuradha was the second victim? When did you arrest the driver?'

'After Sabah Khan's murder. The third. He didn't have an alibi.'

'He didn't have an alibi for the first – Laxmi's – either?'

'Nope.'

'Why didn't you arrest him straight after Anuradha's murder as a suspect?'

'He went home and called the police after Anuradha didn't come back from the dam. I thought he can't be that stupid. The one thing we know about Gentleman is that he isn't stupid.'

'This Anuradha,' he said. 'Hers is the only murder outside the city. Forty kilometres away, isn't it?'

'Yes. The dam's out in the sticks.'

'Sticks! You pick that up in Cardiff?'

Chandra smiled. 'Yes.'

'What about the obvious development?'

'What's that?'

'Bupathy was in custody, wasn't he, when Sarita Mohan got murdered?'

'We have no leads at all on Sarita Mohan so far. Her maid is still missing. I have people sifting through everything, talking to everyone she knew. This is the best lead we have.'

'I've never seen a dam,' he said, 'outside of films such as *Chinatown* and *Force 10 from Navarone*.'

Chandra sipped her coffee. 'You want to see it? There's nothing there.'

'I'm curious about where Bupathy waited. Why she would go so far alone, and in the night, and how come he didn't see anyone or anything? Someone should have. It's India, after all. You are never completely alone anywhere.'

'Ah, but Mr Patel, India is also where no one notices anything, even if it is under their nose.'

Patel gave Chandra's nose a speculative look. 'All the same, I'd like to see the place, and ask some questions about where the driver waited.'

'If we leave now, we can look at the dam, meet the anonymous caller, and be back at midday to talk to Bupathy.'

Patel sipped the last of his tea. Milky and over-stewed, he knew it would sit in his stomach and churn things up. His fingers itched to light a cigarette. He knew there'd be a little kiosk outside the hotel. There was one outside every big building, at every street corner. He'd ask Chandra to stop at one so he could buy a packet. He'd share with her his thoughts from last night. Show her he had some use. He needed to smoke. When they caught the killer, he could quit again.

'Let's go,' he said.

Chapter Fifteen

Chandra drove with both windows down. The breeze puffed her dupatta against her cheek like an amorous, persistent blowfish till she snapped it off and thrust it out of sight. The city was far behind them. Tired trees swayed and so did thin dark men on rusty bicycles, some in gleaming polyester shirts, some holding mobile phones to their ears, all oblivious to thundering lorries that missed them by a whisker. Little dusty shops next to little dusty bus stops, the waiting buses pumping out diesel fumes; the souls onboard, all eyes and ears, little dark devils from a lithograph, looking at Chandra's little car as they would an alien spaceship, though one that, if unfathomable, was nevertheless a familiar sight. Clumps of houses stood amid agricultural land. The red earth bore bare winter crops.

They came to a dirt road that ended in a grassy knoll. Beyond, a clump of rocks, and beyond those rocks, the wall of the dam loomed into view. Chandra turned off the engine. The morning chill was evaporating. A watery sun in the sky.

'It's like the English summer,' said Patel.

Walls of the dam stretched high and wide, curved at an angle. They followed the curve of the wall to a roar of rushing water. The sluice gates were open. A man dressed in jeans and a purple T-shirt stood on the rampart at the edge of the water-fall. Even above the noise of the water, Patel could hear him.

He was bleating. Patel wondered if he was the local loony. He was about to ask Chandra when he saw a goat emerge from a culvert. It clambered up the steep embankment towards its bleating master.

Chandra picked a path along the rocks, led Patel down where the embankment sloped into the riverbed. They walked a few hundred yards to a wide, flat area where a swathe of silt was being deposited, along a curve where the river meandered. She stopped, hesitating, searching. Patel was intensely aware of the dam looming over them. He thought of Hans of Holland, finger in the dam.

'There.' Chandra pointed.

A stick on the ground, and attached to it a piece of raggedy yellow tape. Patel bent to examine it. Five centimetres long, with an uneven serrated edge. It looked like small sharp teeth had chewed it.

Chandra looked over to the rocks on the bluff in front of the car. 'Bloody goats.'

'Goats ate the plastic tape?'

'Must have. The villagers know to keep away.'

Sure enough, hoof marks dotted the basin and then disappeared into harder ground. Where the body had lain, there were no markings, nothing at all, just the smooth expanse of continually deposited silt, and the stick with the bit of yellow tape on it.

If Sherlock Holmes were here, mused Patel, even a month after the murder, he would have had his nose in the fresh silt and come up with half a dozen clues. But who in the real world actually picked up clues from a stone-cold murder scene? He hitched up his trousers and squatted where the hoof marks disappeared. The ground was dry, grass sprouted like teasing hair on a bald head. Caught in the grass, all kinds of garbage – faded biscuit wrappers, grubby plastic bags, broken bits of tat.

Even as he poked around, people were emerging. Villagers, goatherds in formal shirts and trousers that were washed over and over and stained by rough living, men of leisure in lungis, a couple of women in nighties carrying their washing. All stopped to watch the two city folk poking around at the scene of a murder already a month old and half forgotten.

Echoing Patel's thoughts, Chandra said, 'It is only in detective novels that culprits are dropping buttons and whatnot, bits of clothing have laundry marks, or people leave behind a rare snake-skin wallet that is only available from three boutique shops. You pick something up and it leads straight to the murderer via a couple of twists. In real life, people carry crap that is all made in China. The only good lead is personal information.'

'Information from someone who knows what happened?'

'Yes. That is what I am hoping for at the village. Granted we must gather material evidence. We have a pile of stuff from every murder scene – we don't know if any of it is relevant to the case or not. When we do get a clear lead, which could be a matter of a fluke, at least we can then use the stuff we have to help build a scenario or to corroborate evidence.'

Patel picked up the biscuit wrapper. 'When we find out, for example, it is the son of the Britannia biscuit tycoon, we present this in court as corroborative evidence.'

'Funny, Mr Patel,' said Chandra, but she did not laugh. 'This is the stuff that has gathered since the murder. Every single object found at the crime scene has already been bagged, dusted for prints, its antecedents tracked.'

'How many?'

'A hundred and fifty three. Off the top of my head I recall a hair-oil bottle, Parachute brand, empty, missing its cap; a mobile phone case cover, black, cracked; a Juicy Fruit chewing-gum wrapper; a rusted Wilkinson Sword razor blade.' She shook her head in exasperation. 'The foot patrol unit has been to every hut and hovel in the surrounding villages, and the locals shown the list of items together with photos.'

'You think something will come out of it?'

'Nothing so far. But you never know. We have collated all the information we can. All indexed and cross indexed, alphabetised, colour-coded.'

'Wow.' As useful, he thought, as polishing crap.

Chandra smiled. 'You remember the Yorkshire Ripper case, Mr Patel?'

'From the seventies? Before my time.'

'The study of that case was my special project while at Cardiff. They took the Ripper in for questioning nine times. They didn't collate the information. Files were sitting all over the place. A friend of Peter Sutcliff wrote to the police to convey his suspicions. They took down his message. Nothing happened. Then he visited the police station. His messages were sitting in the filing tray for over a year while Sutcliff murdered three more women. For want of a shoe, the kingdom was lost. So as soon as I was brought in on this case I demanded the three best secretaries in the HQ, including Rajkumar's personal assistant, to organise all the information.'

'I am impressed.'

'Don't be,' said Chandra, her voice hitting a harsh note. 'We haven't got anyone with the raw talent to sniff out the killer.'

'Is there such a thing?'

'Sure.' Chandra narrowed her eyes. 'You.'

'I'm not so sure about that. We all have to plod through the boring stuff. Talk to everyone, chase up every lead, and ninety-nine out of a hundred come to nothing. Sometimes the right clue is under your nose. But if you don't know what you're looking for . . .' He shrugged, thinking of the old man who turned out to be the Dales Ripper. Sometimes you sure get lucky, he thought. But he said: 'Every shadow and stone is relevant. You're doing the right thing.'

Chandra brightened. 'And that is why we are here, one month after we could have found anything useful in this terrain, sniffing at the grass and goat pellets.'

Patel shook his head. He could tell Chandra was teasing him. 'I need to know the landscape so I can imagine the actions of everyone involved. I cannot fathom how Anuradha was persuaded to come such a long way. Surely the killer isn't some goatherd living in one of the village hamlets. He's got to come from Bengaluru itself, or some affluent surrounding suburb.'

'Whitefield or Koramangala.'

'So he must have driven. And what do you see here, Chandra?'

'The dam?'

'No. The road. The one dirt road – the only one to and from the dam. Someone was bound to have noticed a stranger. Was her car parked here?'

'No. Anuradha had Bupathy stop at the village and came on foot with a torch.'

'OK. Then we better go meet our man.'

Making the tight U-turn with unnecessary speed, Patel wincing in anticipation of the crunch of rock against fender and thankfully disappointed, they blatted back down the dirt road.

Chandra slowed at a clump of brick houses and a shop. She turned off the road, parked under a tree. Cut branches of bananas hung outside the shop. Shrivelled-up vegetables and fruit sat in a couple of baskets. On the stoop, two men sat smoking cigarettes, watching the road, one in a white shirt and dhoti, the other in trousers and a singlet, sporting camouflage earmuffs.

Shuffling noises from behind the tree trunk. Watching with

red, baleful, eyes, a good-for-nothing fellow, the type who seems to plague Indian street corners. He leant against the tree, wearing just a lungi, smoking a beedi. Hair the colour of dry rust skimmed his shoulders. He stared at the car and spat in the dust. A pye-dog came from the doorway of a brick house to sniff at his spit, then cocked its ear as Patel opened his door to step out. Wagging its tail, the dog nipped over to greet him. The men on the stoop paused their chatter to review the newcomers.

The man in the lungi pushed off the tree and came to gawp at Patel. His teeth needed serious attention. Brown stains and rot. So this was the village loony, he thought.

'Police,' said Chandra. She asked him a question.

The man in the lungi ignored her and said something to Patel.

Patel said, 'You talk to her.'

He deigned to look at Chandra, his hand seemingly unable to stop itself from cupping his private parts as he gave her his attention.

'Bloody oik,' muttered Patel as Chandra repeated her question, ignoring his hand.

The man replied with what seemed to Patel an arrogant tone. She spoke again. He answered.

Chandra said to Patel, 'This man claims Bupathy parked his car right here where we've parked. Then he waited at the toddy shop for several hours. Surprisingly, he didn't drink toddy, only drank water from a bottle and ate fish fry.'

'Toddy shop open that late?'

'Open twenty-four hours,' the man said to Patel.

The better-dressed man from the stoop came out to see what was going on.

'Hello there,' he said with a big wide smile, like a pastor from the American deep south. 'I am Ravindran, the headman of this village. You are police from Bengaluru? I thought the investigations around this area have drawn to a conclusion and there is nothing more to discover.'

Underneath the headman's moustache, his smile was too wide. Was there anything going on in the village he was keen to keep under wraps? Or was he just raising a mild objection to the lives of his villagers being disrupted by the police enquiry? The man wearing earmuffs suddenly threw down his cigarette, came up to the headman, whispered rapidly and gutturally. The headman's demeanour changed. He turned effusively towards Patel.

'You are Mr Patel from Scotland Yard! What a pleasure to meet you, sir. We've been reading about you just this morning. Anything you need, we're here to help.'

Earmuffs had run back and now reappeared with two bottles of cola, complete with straws.

'Our local Bindu-cola,' the headman said. 'Very famous. Please to have.'

By now, a small crowd had gathered. The villagers waited, whispering. The men in long-sleeved shirts of varying hues and the women in saris or nighties. A few young children stared.

Chandra spoke to them. One or two hesitantly answered. Patel felt the frustration of being the outsider, unable to speak the language, until Chandra said to him: 'I don't think they understand my Kannada. I'll try Tamil.'

When she spoke again, Patel saw a couple of faces frown. He remembered they were at the border. The dam divided Karnataka and Tamil Nadu more than physically. He recalled reading there was a water dispute between the states.

But it was too late to stop Chandra. She spoke for a minute and waited.

No one answered.

The headman spoke in earnest. There were monosyllabic

replies. A woman left the crowd and entered her home a few metres away. Others turned to leave.

Chandra said, 'None of them seen to know anything about strangers on the night of the murder. All we have is this man saying Bupathy waited at the toddy shop. No other cars. No other men.'

'That can't be it? Someone must have seen something.'

'In India, Mr Patel, either everyone sees everything or no one sees anything.'

'Who do you think phoned?' said Patel under his breath, 'the headman or the loony?'

Chandra shrugged.

The headman put a hand on Patel's shoulder, angled him away from Chandra. 'The thing is, Mr Patel,' he said, as if he were doing a *between us men*, ignoring Chandra's presence, impossible as she was to ignore, 'the dam used to attract all kinds of couples from Bengaluru in the night-time. They would drive and park there for privacy. The villagers did not like such immoral activities. So we gave warnings to some of them. Nowadays we don't get many in the late evening time. If they come, it is in the midnight when we are all sleeping. So it is possible there are one or two, even three or four cars in a week at midnight passing on the way to the dam which someone could have seen and ignored.'

Patel nodded, thanked the man and waited till he went back to the stoop. He turned to Chandra and said quietly: 'You'd think otherwise, wouldn't you? If they're so het up about immoral couples, they would be waiting and watching to go warn them or take some village thugs to rough them up.'

'That would be more logical.'

Patel watched the headman's eyes shifting this way and that. People had wandered off. Now only Lungi, Headman and Earmuffs remained. The pye-dog still waited for a titbit from Patel.

Chandra said, 'I think this man –' she indicated Lungi, '– is the only one forthcoming.'

Lungi, Patel noticed, was scratching his balls quite intently. Patel's mouth soured in distaste. 'Are you sure?'

'Oh yes. Let's take him along to the toddy shop and buy him a litre.'

'You mean a pint?'

'A litre, Mr Patel, is nearly double of a pint.'

'Madness,' he said.

'Have you ever had a yard of ale in one of your pubs?'

'No.'

'Gosh, you haven't lived,' said Chandra, and turned to instruct Lungi.

His face lit up. He beckoned them to follow him. The headman frowned after them.

Lungi led them around the shop corner, down a road that ran between small brick houses in a variety of shapes and hues. They came to a clearing near a clump of coconut trees. From here they had to look up to see the brick houses. Further, beyond a foul-smelling ditch, were mud hovels and huts where presumably the farm labourers and household help lived.

The toddy shop was a thatched, temporary construction. A tiny reception area with a table led into a room with rudimentary seating of school benches, some broken.

They sat and waited. The dog had come in with them. Lungi and the dog sat at the other end of the room, which was just as well, Patel thought. He didn't want Lungi too close to them. While they waited for the owner to appear, Chandra entertained him with a story about 'Mahila sangas' in Maharashtra who had recently organised female goondas to rough up toddy sellers and wreck toddy shops.

'They like to pour the toddy into the drains,' she said. 'Last week there was a video taken on someone's mobile, as the Mahila sanga in North Tillipet poured close to twenty thousand litres of toddy into the local buffalo pool.'

The buffaloes must have a had a good wallow, thought Patel. When the owner of the toddy shop appeared, the first thing Chandra did was to order a mug each of toddy for all of them, plus plates of rava fish fry and chilli chicken.

When Patel gave her a look, she winked and said, 'Carrot before the stick, Mr Patel. Plus, it's lunchtime.'

'It's only nine o'clock.'

'Well an hour here or there,' she shrugged.

A man appeared at the doorway, spotted them and turned away.

'We are putting off customers,' said Patel.

'They will sit on the bench outside. Out of respect.'

Patel thought the no-good mid-morning toddy guzzlers could probably read the big invisible sticker on his forehead that said, 'Copper'. Some instincts, he thought, traversed culture and language barriers.

Lungi was intently picking his nose in the corner.

'Did you notice,' said Patel, 'the headman wasn't keen on us lingering?'

'He was very smiley.'

'Fake smile. I reckon the villagers were sullen and tight lipped because they don't want to co-operate. Why, do you think?'

'Could be any number of reasons,' said Chandra. 'Indian police sometimes have that effect on those they serve.' She spoke as if she weren't police herself.

The owner appeared with three plastic mugs of toddy and plates of food.

'All freshly made just now only, sir.' He too, ignored Chandra's presence. It was as though a modern city-bred woman was such a threat to their masculinity that they hoped ignoring her presence would make her disappear, thought Patel.

The chilli chicken looked greasy beyond reckoning. Patel didn't want to find out if the red in the fish fry was food colouring or chilli powder.

Chandra dug in. His stomach rumbled. Throwing caution to the wind, he ate.

'I've never had this before,' he said, wincing from the chilli treatment.

'Rava fry. Mangalorean speciality.'

The man returned with a small bowl full of fresh green chillies, and placed it under Patel's nose.

The pye-dog un-merged itself from where it had blended into a corner and approached Patel, in whom it had identified a potential benefactor. The shop owner, just then noticing the dog, began shooing it away. The dog slunk off, its tail cupping its anus, and squirmed under the school bench, trying to get under Patel's legs.

'Leave it,' Patel said to the owner.

Lungi cackled.

The owner looked affronted. 'But it's a dog.'

Chandra said, 'Leave it.'

The man said sullenly, 'If you say so, miss.'

'Sit down. We need to talk to you.'

He stood, nonplussed.

She said, 'You understand English?'

'Of course, miss,' said the man with a great grin of his brown, corrupted teeth, a match for Lungi's.

'We have some questions for you.'

He sat down.

'Did any police talk to you about the murder of Anuradha since last month?'

'Only for chitchat.'

'What do you mean?'

'Just when stopping for thirst purposes. When they doing the rounds with the list of items they finding on the riverbed. I myself has nothing on the list.'

'I have on good authority that Anuradha's driver spent several hours here waiting for her return. Seeing as you have all local customers, apart from the occasional policeman or police-woman, you would have noticed a stranger like him, spending so many hours and not even drinking toddy.'

'Of course, madam. He was very nice man. I even offered a glass for free and he refusing with smiles. Then he getting very worried. The time is getting late. He looking at his watch one minute, asking me the time the next minute. I tell him, what for you have watch if you can't read time? He looking at the road up and down, like this and this.'

'Wait – he sat here and kept going out to check the road?'

'Oh no, sir, he not sitting in here. Here was full of drunkards making stink with burping and belching eating. Excuse me, I not meaning people like yourselves. The good caste people of the village only. Normally only the scheduled castes sit outside, but he insist. He very tense.'

'Let's take a look outside,' said Patel.

The three men who had been slinking on the bench outside scattered to the winds. The dirt road passed the toddy shop, curving away from the brick houses and skirting the hovels of the low castes, then stretched north towards the distant, invisible lure of Bengaluru.

A clear quarter mile of the road was visible in each direction. 'What time was Anuradha's death estimated?' asked Patel.

'Between eleven p.m. and one a.m.'

'Till what time did the driver wait here?' he asked the owner, who had come out to study the dirt road with them.

'Till one at least. I remember him saying, "It's one o'clock. It's really too late." Not for me, brother, I told him. These drunkards will drink till dawn when their wives come to fetch them.'

Chandra said to Patel, 'That corroborates Bupathy's evidence that he was here till one a.m. before going to the dam. He didn't find anything there. It was too dark to see much. So he went home and alerted the police. By the time the police sent a constable to look, the sun had risen, and the goatherds had seen the body and were standing around gawping at it.'

She turned to the shop owner. 'Did he tell you where he was going when he left?'

'I said, "I am just going behind the hut for a number one." But when I come back, he is gone, and just leaving some cash on my table under a stone. Very irresponsible of him. Should have waited one more minute for me. A drunken lout – this fellow inside, in fact,' he said under his breath, 'was standing there making big eyes at the money when I coming back.' Raising his voice, he said, 'I keeping all money in very strong Godrej steel locker. Impossible for any chootiya to break into.'

'Language,' said Chandra.

'Sorry, madam.'

'Go about your business,' said Patel. 'We need to chat.'

'Sir?' the man was puzzled.

Chandra said, 'He said, go and do something else. We need to discuss.'

'Oh,' beamed the man. 'Discuss, discuss. I will go.'

He went.

Patel said, 'If Bupathy sat here after Anuradha left on foot, and waited from ten p.m. till nearly one, he was in a good position to see a car that could have gone past either on the way there or on the way back, or both.'

'I was surprised,' said the owner, who hadn't gone far, after all, and was polishing a bottle with a rag in the corner of the reception area, 'when I read in the *Kannada Malar* that he was arrested as a suspect. The man was so polite, so nice, he didn't even drink toddy, and he was a mala.'

'What's that?' asked Patel.

'Oh,' said Chandra. 'He was doing a day fast in order to do the pilgrimage to Sabarimala. They wear only black, no alcohol or sex or cigarettes, no bad habits. Only vegetarian food.'

'Although he ordered fish fry,' said Patel.

'That's true.' The owner nodded.

Patel said, 'Hmm, mala in a toddy shop.'

'To sum up,' said Chandra, 'if there was a vehicle going towards or away from the dam between ten p.m. and one a.m., there is a very good chance the driver saw it. We know there is a high probability he's innocent as both the toddy-shop owner and Lungi say he was here from ten till one.'

'Actually,' said Patel, 'only the owner said he was here till one. Not Lungi. All we know is he saw that the driver didn't drink toddy, just bottled water, and ordered fish fry. That could've been at ten p.m.'

'He stood over there eyeing the money the driver left after one a.m.'

'Let's ask him,' said Patel.

When they went back in, they found the pye-dog standing on the table, licking a plate clean. The tail wagged as the dog ate, one eye warily on them. Chandra shooed the dog out. Lungi sat in the corner, in the same posture they'd left him in. But all three toddy mugs were now in front of him, empty.

Lungi spoke to Chandra, hiccupped. His toddy-reddened eyes ranged blearily around the room. Chandra said to Patel, 'He thought we'd gone and didn't want the toddy to go waste.'

'I am quite happy to be going back to Bengaluru sober.'

Chandra said to Lungi in English, 'So on the night of Anuradha's murder, you were here from ten p.m. till at least one a.m.?'

'Me live here,' said Lungi. 'Owner my brother. He pawn my mother's dowry.'

'That's true,' said the owner, coming in, 'but not about our mother's jewellery. I got a small bank loan.'

'Explain,' said Patel.

'He is my younger brother, a good for nothing, useless fellow, and if I hadn't promised my dying mother to look after him, he wouldn't be drinking up all my profits.'

'Ah,' said Patel.

Chandra said, 'Looks like we haven't learned anything useful here, after all. Shall we head back?'

Lungi said, 'Check his phone.'

'Sorry?' said Patel.

'The driver. He make call, twice. I listen, I try. I not hearing anything. The driver speaking in very low voice, looking left and right to see if anyone listening. Then when I peep, he switch phone off.'

Patel and Chandra looked at each other. 'Bupathy rang the police after he got home,' he said.

'Precisely. And we checked the mobile phone he gave us. There were no calls made or received, all evening and night.'

'Right. Let's go talk to him.'

Chandra smiled at Lungi. 'You've provided very useful help to us today. Come outside. We need to reward you.'

Licking his lips, Lungi got up, adjusted his privates, staggered outside. The scowling owner, no doubt feeling slighted at Chandra's favourable treatment of his family's black sheep, came along too.

Outside, Chandra said to Lungi, 'Put your right hand out.'

Lungi extended his right hand.

She unhooked the short lathi that hung from her buckle.

'What . . .' began Lungi.

'What?' said Patel.

She brought the lathi down on Lungi's outstretched hand.

Lungi howled. He doubled over, clutching his hand.

Chandra said to Patel: 'Hopefully it will hurt long enough to instil some manners in him. There is a saying in Tamil.' She turned to Lungi. '*Nalla mattuku oru soodu.*'

'What does it mean?' asked Patel.

Chandra shrugged. 'Difficult to translate.'

'A single burn for a good cow,' said the toddy-shop owner, happily.

Curiouser and curiouser, thought Patel.

Chandra took out her wallet, peeled off a 500-rupee note and gave it to the owner of the toddy shop. 'Half for toddy, half for food. For your brother. You promised your mother to look after him. That involves feeding him, too, and not just toddy. Understand?'

The man nodded, open-mouthed.

Lungi finished howling and remained standing with a pained expression on his face, still clutching his hand.

Chandra ignored him and continued to the owner: 'I'll send a constable to take a written statement this afternoon. Make sure he is in good shape to give it.'

Chapter Sixteen

'You don't have an appointment,' the secretary said, flatly.

Kadambri made her voice sweet. 'He said I can drop by any time. I have a deadline to make.'

The secretary had her lips pursed and eyes focused on the computer screen. She wasn't going to be swayed.

Kadambri had barely begun to pester her when the chief of police appeared, surprising the secretary somewhat. Her pursed lips came open and her eyes widened at the sight of Rajkumar, who was rather out of puff and unable to speak, merely grunting.

'Mr Rajkumar, is the mayor expecting you?'

Rajkumar looked confused, as though he had been pre-occupied with important matters and had wandered in there by mistake.

Kadambri seized her opportunity. 'Any leads on the new case?'

'Eh?' said Rajkumar. 'What is she doing here?' he said to the secretary. 'Never mind. Is the mayor in?'

'He's at a meeting, sir, but if you like, I can ring him on his mobile?'

The secretary helpfully picked up the phone.

'Might have the phone switched off,' said Kadambri. 'If you tell me where he is, I can run up and fetch him?'

The secretary glared at Kadambri's insolence and began dialling.

'No, no,' said Rajkumar. 'Leave it. I'll get in touch myself.'

'What did you make of my article, sir?' said Kadambri.

'What article?'

'About your police prodigy. Mr Vijay Patel.'

That did the trick. Rajkumar found his puff and Kadambri scrambled to get his quotes down. But with supreme effort, Rajkumar brought his feelings about Scotland Yard involvement under control, and warned Kadambri 'not to spread untruths'.

He'd barely left when the mayor walked in, preoccupied with the papers in his hand. Kadambri jumped up to accost him before the secretary could get involved.

Hariharan recognised Kadambri as the journalist he'd spoken to at the Swami's fast-breaking ceremony.

To Kadambri's relief, he said to her, 'Perhaps I may have a few minutes, while I walk to my lunch meeting.'

She broke into a toothy smile. 'That would be wonderful, Mr Mayor. Mind if I record you? So much easier to transcribe ... I have a two p.m. deadline ... just a couple of questions ... '

'Let me get my briefcase. I won't be a second.'

He shut his office door and leaned against it, eyes closed for a moment. Meeting after mindless meeting with lumpen officials. Her breezy presence, the disruption to his working day, was a welcome balm. He pushed off, took possession of his briefcase and went out, threading a paternal expression on to his facial features.

They walked. She told him about the article she was writing. Asked him for updates on the cross-party committee to tackle cow vigilantes. His mind wandered; he found it difficult to hear what she said.

To her surprise, he said, 'Have you noticed how the house sparrows are disappearing?'

'They are?'

'Yes. So little and helpless, yet so bold, trusting, entering people's houses and pecking from human hands.'

'So why are they disappearing?'

Instead of answering, he said, 'Do you know the robin? The little English bird, red breast more orange than red, perches on a garden rake when the gardener pauses for a moment from his toils. Chirps in friendly inquiry. Then hopping back and forth inches from the sharp tines, grubbing, pecking at titbits, pulling worms out with weeds and grass roots.'

'Did you see this on the Discovery channel?'

He grinned with just his teeth. 'Just imagine if the sure-footed robin should ever misjudge a hop, the tine coming to contact with the soft flame underbelly of the bird the size of a child's palm?'

Another bloody poet, thought Kadambri. Something about her made the men she met wax lyrical. She said, 'Mr Mayor, I hear you are having a party at your house. Is this something to do with the situation?'

'Sorry, my mind has wandered. Ask that again?'

'You are inviting the great and the good of Bengaluru to your party tomorrow night, to put their minds at ease?'

'Oh yes, they all have daughters they worry about.'

'You should invite Mr Patel.'

'Who?'

'The Scotland Yard detective. He seems competent, despite the suggestions from Chief Rajkumar. I spoke to the Chief just minutes ago. He was in your office, looking for you. Said he had a meeting, but your secretary didn't think so. He must have a lot on his mind. Looked confused, then seemed to forget why he was there. He left, declining your secretary's offer to ring you. Anyway, Patel's presence at your party might lend your guests some reassurance.'

'Rajkumar considers this detective incompetent?'

'Let's say he expected Patel to toe the line, remain invisible, not to grab the headlines the day after he arrived on the scene.'

'That is your doing.'

She shrugged, a hint of a smile upon her lips.

'May I see the paper?'

She rummaged in her bag and brought out a folded newspaper. Hariharan stared at the picture. Long, unruly hair flopping over the forehead and away in the wind, coming into bowl, Vijay Patel at the zenith of his short, illustrious career in cricket. He studied the title of the article.

'I went through four newspapers at breakfast,' he said to Kadambri. 'Ran out of time before I got to yours.'

'I won't be insulted,' she laughed. 'What do you think?'

'He was a cricketer. Now he is . . . ?'

'With Scotland Yard. Here to help catch our own Ripper. Invite him to your party.'

'I'll think about it.'

'Say you will.' She spoke to him as though he were a favourite uncle.

'Very well. I will.'

'But he won't know anyone there.'

'Won't he?'

'He's met me.'

'Ah, I see. You'd like to be invited yourself.'

She gave him a guileless, charming smile, born from the confidence bred into her by a wealthy, loving family. A smile someone like him had to learn from scratch.

'I'll invite him. And you can come too, but without your notepad.'

'Of course.' She flashed another toothy smile. He smiled back this time.

'See you tomorrow then.'

Without further ado he turned on his heel and walked back, clutching the newspaper in his hand. His thumb rested on Patel's face framed by the windswept hair, features set in a grimace that was a second's preparation before releasing the leg break that won him the third in a hat-trick of wickets, and the title, 'man of the match'.

Chapter Seventeen

As the highway widened on its approach into Bengaluru, the traffic murmured and gurgled. But by the time they passed the overhead *Indian Telecoms Welcomes You to Bengaluru City* sign, the traffic had condensed into a churning sea of braying horns. Chandra drove one-handed while studying her phone and swiping icons.

'The autopsy report's just come in.'

'That's quick.'

'Let me read it to you.'

Patel grappled for something to hang on to as a rubbish lorry swung in front of the car, spewing torn plastic bags of filth. Chandra casually took her eyes off the phone to glance at the lorry, then accelerated towards its hellish maw while pressing the horn with the only hand that was on the steering wheel.

The rubbish lorry pulled away. Chandra's attention back on her phone, she began to read, 'Time of death ...'

Patel reached over and took her phone. 'Let *me* read it out. Please.'

Fighting motion sickness, he raced through the report and read out the highlights. 'Time of death between eight and ten p.m. Cause of death: significant intracranial haemorrhage and frontal cerebral injury, just like the others. No exit wound. No soot, no gunpowder stippling, no particles surround the wound. No remains of projectile recovered.' He looked up. 'The details are identical to the other PM reports.'

'No trace of metal in this one, either?'

'Nothing visible.'

'They would have sent samples for further testing.'

'So the new samples can join the old samples in the DNA queue?'

'I'm afraid so.'

Head swimming, Patel skimmed through a description of all the different organ systems. No surprises there. He came to the Items of Evidence. 'Fingernail clippings and scrapings, blood specimens, hair and tissue samples, sexual assault kit . . . ' Patel looked up from Chandra's phone and waited for the dizziness to pass. 'Nothing new.'

They were now stuck in a traffic jam. A truck had stalled in the middle of the junction. The driver and a small crowd stood around, arguing. Patel thought the situation was not dissimilar to the one he was in. He fought a feeling of frustration. The only lead they had was to do with Anuradha's month-old murder. And it was nothing more than a scratch in the dark, based on a theory concocted by a filthy, crotch-grabbing drunk from a village toddy shop. Really, they were flogging a dead horse. They needed to be investigating the latest murder, but they had zero leads. He looked at his watch. It was already twenty-seven hours since Sarita Mohan's body had been found. But then, time was a fluid concept in India.

The traffic intensified. Necks craned out from windows and over handlebars of scooters and bikes. Although the problem, in the shape of a twenty-foot articulated lorry, was clearly visible for half a mile, still everyone beeped continuously, as if through some Indian mode of transmigration their desires could be carried out; the shrill honking could physically move the truck from their path.

Then in the blink of an eye, as if that magic did occur, the truck was moved and they in turn were moving.

'Still nothing on the maid?'

'Twenty constables are combing through her slum and ancestral village,' said Chandra. She zipped around the inside of a meandering auto.

They crawled alongside a bustling marketplace selling bright plastic tat and more varieties and hues of fabric than Patel had thought possible. An assault of textures, patterns ... if there was a pattern that gave a hint of the killer's identity, he couldn't see it.

He could only declaim the obvious. 'Nothing remarkable in the autopsy. Same as the others.'

Chandra sighed. 'He's too darned clever.'

She negotiated a maze of a junction. 'One new thing, though.'

'What's that?'

'The fact that Sarita was murdered in her own home. No forced entry.'

'Do you check before opening your front door?'

'Yes. I have a spy glass and a chain.'

'Ah.'

'And my building has twenty-four-hour watchman service.'

'Still, there's no guarantee she only opened doors to men she knew.'

'I cannot shake the feeling that he must be known to all the women.'

'Why?'

'Purely because, well, like attracts like. A man in posh circles would have more access to posh women. It's logical.'

'Aren't you forgetting the daddy of them all? Jack the Ripper?'

'I did a paper on him as well at Cardiff. It's true that most experts agree he was an aristocrat. Yet he killed hookers, after soliciting them from the streets.'

'Which disproves your theory about class.'

'It's prostitutes who are classless. In the Ripper's case, remember it was the Victorian times. Women weren't so . . . accessible. Only prostitutes put out and were willing to be alone with a man. In pretty much every other class a woman would insist on a chaperone.'

'I find that hard to believe.'

'Well, OK, it might be a generalisation, but –' she raised a finger to emphasise her point '– prostitutes have, all through history, catered to every class of men. Even in this country, a prostitute is never asked her caste and doesn't ask it of her clients, either.'

'So, presidents and priests alike, desiring anonymity, could swing by in their car for a bit of action in the front seat or behind a tree.'

'Very graphic,' said Chandra, mock-widening her eyes. 'But in this case, the murdered women are from the elite, privileged class. No way a poor, lower-class man can have private access to them.'

'Except we know the grocer's boy went up every day to deliver milk.'

'Yes, to the maid.'

'The missing maid.'

'Yes.'

'That leads us back to square one.'

'We are here.'

'Here' was a police station, painted a jolly yellow.

Shivaji Nagar Precinct was bigger and busier than the Ulsoor Police Station. While they waited for a sub-inspector to escort them to the cells, Chandra studied the Wanted posters on the noticeboard. Patel studied her profile, while looking in the general direction of the posters. Her clear, unlined brow dipped on to a neat, straight nose with no tilt in it whatsoever, and under the generous mouth was a hard, stubborn chin. There were circles under her eyes, and he tried to remember if they were new.

The smiling sub-inspector Rakesh with his neat little teeth took them through the station innards, again like Ulsoor, displaying the wreckage of humanity in cages, although here the paan stains were fewer and the smell of piss less pungent.

Rakesh himself, without the aid of a constable, opened the door to the cell. He handed a phone to Chandra and left.

Patel's phone buzzed. He took it out to turn it off, then saw it was Rima.

He'd forgotten all about the nine a.m. Skype call.

'I'll join you in a minute,' said Patel. 'Got to take this.'

Chandra nodded, and he didn't like the set of her jaw as she strode into the cell.

'Hey Rima.'

'Hey lover boy.'

'*Inspector* Rima, sorry I couldn't call you at nine.'

'It's eight o'clock in the morning.'

'Oh. Right. Of course. Well.'

'Got company, have you?'

'No. Yes. Just about to interview a suspect. Sort of.'

The constable was watching him, slack-jawed, listening without the pleasure of comprehension. He didn't care if Patel knew.

'Listen, said Rima, 'Skinner's been going about looking pleased with himself.'

'Well, he would, wouldn't he?'

'That bad, huh?'

'Not quite, but it isn't a bed of roses, either.'

'I can help you on the sly.'

'Oh yeah?'

'I can do some digging for you, this end.'

'You could pester Ballistics for me . . . I sent them reports. The murder weapon is descended from Asgard or some such. Eludes human comprehension.'

'What about Goldblum?'

'What about him?'

'He smell fishy? Shall I dig up dirt on him?'

'I'm sure he's got plenty of dirt, but not relevant to the case. This is clearly a local psychopath.'

'Clear to you, or the police psychiatrist?'

'They don't have one looking at the case, I don't think.'

'Want me to rustle up a yardie shrink to look at it?'

'Would you?'

'Only for you.'

'I owe you.'

'I'll collect. Don't worry.' Then she told him in a few choice words how she'd collect, and Patel felt his face turn red. The constable was still watching.

'Right,' he said. 'Speak later, then. Bye.'

When Patel pushed open the door to the interrogation room, he heard Chandra's voice but couldn't follow the words.

He stepped in to see Chandra push someone. The man, who could only be Bupathy, stumbled and came to his knees against the bedhead. His black dhoti came loose and trailed on the floor. Chandra bent one knee and lowered the other on the floor like she was about to stretch her hip flexors. She brought one hand up and grabbed Bupathy's throat. His head went up against the metal railing. Clang. She removed her lathi from its belt with her other hand and thrust it against the rudraksha beads on Bupathy's windpipe.

'Come on, tell us the truth,' she said.

Patel took a step towards her, and stopped himself from intervening. He didn't know the nitty-gritty of Indian law, but Bupathy was a god-fearing mala. If it was the UK, the case would be shut down. Chandra would have to appear at a disciplinary hearing. But they were not in the UK. He shook his head; tried to clear the cobwebs in his brain. Five hours' time difference shouldn't cause such jet lag.

Chandra pressed on her lathi. Bupathy moaned. His rudraksha beads clacked against the metal. His black dhoti rode up as Chandra's thigh pressed against his.

It occurred to Patel that although god-men ruled the nation, god-men could also be kicked by policewomen. The rule of law held the dizzying complexities of India like a rope held a bundle of snakes. The profane ground into profound even as the policewoman's knee ground into the devotee's black-clad thigh. He could save himself the bother of the pilgrimage and declare Kali came to him through Chandra.

'Chandra,' Patel said. 'May I have a word?'

'Not now.' She pressed down.

Bupathy sobbed, a strange, strangulated sound, like painful hiccups.

Patel put his hand on her shoulder. 'Please stop.'

Chandra turned around, fury all over her face.

'Outside, Patel.'

They marched out to the corridor, leaving behind the quivering Saami clinging to the cot bars as if to life itself.

Chandra shut the door, leaned against it. 'You have no business—' she began.

'It *is* my business,' said Patel. 'I've been sent here to *make* this my business.'

'I was doing perfectly well on my own.'

'Your government approached Scotland Yard.'

'And you are our Great White Hope?' She raised her eyebrows.

'I might ...' started Patel, but what could he say to defend himself? How could he claim to be some genius come to crack the case for the Indians when he knew fuck all about it? He'd contributed nothing yet. More than that, he was a fraud, as Chandra's expression seemed to say, an Indian who wasn't an Indian telling her what to do, questioning her methods. But how could he not question them? Wearily, he said, 'What are you trying to achieve here?'

'I want information fast, before the next victim is stretched out on a cold slab.'

'How can you know he's telling the truth with your lathi crushing his Adam's apple?'

'They usually do.'

'He'd say anything to breathe.'

'Excuse me.' A sardonic voice. They turned to see a man in a suit flanked by a couple of police officers. 'I am sure you have matters of the greatest importance to discuss, but if you could move away from the door to do it, please?'

'And who are you?' said Chandra.

The man smiled. There was no humour in the smile. Skin the colour of refined wheat puckered over two and a half chins. He wore a black suit with a white shirt, black tie, pressed professionally by a dhobi. Papers in hand, folded lengthwise. Lawyer. Rich one.

'Barrister Ajay Mehra. Here are court orders to release Bupathy.' He handed Chandra the papers.

'We're still interviewing him. You'll have to wait half an hour.'

'If I do not see my client in the next sixty seconds, you will be answering a sessions court on Monday as to why my client was being questioned without his lawyer's presence, and why he was in jail for forty-eight hours without a shred of evidence for any wrongdoing.'

'I didn't know he had a lawyer.'

'You can tell that to the judge, miss.' He smiled patronisingly and raised his eyebrows to the officer next to him, who said, 'Sorry, madam, I am helpless in this matter.' The name on his lapel read 'Inspector Dandiraj.'

Chandra stepped aside. Dandiraj gestured to a constable who opened the door. The barrister wafted through, leaving a whiff of sulphur.

'So we have nothing to argue about,' said Patel.

Chandra looked dead level at him. 'We had *one, tiny* inkling of a lead. All I needed was two minutes. If not for your conscience, we might actually get somewhere.'

Patel shrugged. 'I'm a policeman. My job is to uphold the law.'

'What do you know of how the law works here?'

'You're sure teaching me.'

Chandra's phone rang. She looked at the number, turned slightly away from Patel and spoke.

'Mmm hmm, mmm hmm,' she said. 'We'll be there –' she looked at her watch '– in . . . ' she dragged the word, eyeing Patel, 'one hour.'

She shut the phone.

'What is it?'

'The maid's husband has been found.'

'Shall we go?'

'Yes, but first, I need to find out who this barrister fellow is.' She plucked the court orders from her back pocket. 'Come with me.'

In Inspector Dandiraj's office, she signed into his desktop, and scrolled with his cordless mouse.

She typed the barrister's name into Google. They

waited. Chandra jiggled the mouse. 'Bloody telephone modem,' she said.

With the hourglass siphoning sand in place of the cursor, she walked over to the shelf of files.

Browsing, she murmured: 'The HQ has broadband. Here, in the undesirable parts of the city . . .' She picked a file from the shelf, laid it on the desk, opened it.

Patel came closer to look, his arm brushing hers.

It was Bupathy's arrest file. He glanced over at the computer screen. The Google search came up with the barrister's contact details.

Chandra tapped a finger on Bupathy's bio. 'Bupathy lives in Cooke Town. Bentley Street. Ironic name, because the houses on it are modest. Old neighbourhood, old houses. Unlike in the UK, Mr Patel, here old usually means poor.'

'Thanks for that lesson in comparative studies.'

She pursed her lips at him. 'Let's see.' She glanced over at the desktop screen and clicked on a link. 'The lawyer, Mehra, on the other hand, has offices on Parliament Street, the most expensive real estate in the city. At his elbow, he has the American Embassy, at his ass the Secretariat.' She clicked on another weblink. 'And his humble home is in Jayanagar, Windsor Gardens, a gated residential for millionaires, with its own gym, and a swimming pool as big as the Bay of Bengal.' She clicked off the browser. 'He charges fifty thousand rupees a day. Five thousand an hour. No way can Bupathy afford him.'

'His rate's on the website?'

She shrugged. 'That's the ballpark, anyway. And the man is lead partner in his firm. He should have sent a minion for this kind of thing. It must be great urgency and pressure from his *real* client that's sent the man himself scarpering to the judge and turning up at a police station in Shivaji Nagar Precinct.'

'Curious,' said Patel. 'Let's look at his clients, then.'

'Confidential,' said Chandra, 'but easy enough to find out.'

She looked at Patel, with the same assessing look she'd given him earlier, as if playing out something about him in her mind.

'I have to make a call,' she said. 'Then we will go see the maid's husband.'

She punched numbers on her phone as she walked out. 'I'll put someone on to the barrister,' she threw over her shoulder, with the phone pressed against her ear.

Chapter Eighteen

A man sold vegetables from a handcart. A couple of women, pristine goddesses in bright yellow and blue starched-cotton saris, daubs of vermillion on their powdered foreheads, marigolds piled on their hair, chose brinjals and onions heaped in wide straw baskets. Melons and coconuts teetered at one end. The cart occupied a spot where the road abruptly narrowed and turned into an alleyway, changed in character, with loose stones, mud and potholes, just wide enough for a small car.

Presumably not wide enough for a steamroller or tar spreader, Patel noted as they squeezed past the cart and past the wary eyes of the vegetable seller and his customers. Nor any rubbish lorries. A huge mound of torn-up paper, discarded plastic and reeking food scraps, buzzing with flies, sat right in the middle of the alleyway. A manhole missing its round iron lid, probably stolen. An open culvert hugged the dirt road, its surface slick and oily, reflecting back the huts and hovels looming all higgledy-piggledy. Paths veered off in all directions, compact apartments built atop each other at crazy angles up and down the hilly terrain like wooden blocks stacked up by a toddler.

'It's here, somewhere,' said Chandra.

A little naked boy stood up from beside the drain where he was squatting. Leaving a conical pile of glistening brown shit on the ground, he skipped off.

'Glorious,' said Patel.

'Hey, you,' Chandra called to a man leaning against the door of a hut, smoking a beedi. He glowered over his moustache and yelled something across the rubbish pile.

Three men appeared, looking a little too well fed to be slum dwellers.

'Trouble,' Patel whispered.

Chandra's hand went to her lathi as she yelled out her question. One of the men burst into rapid-fire Kannada. Chandra spoke haltingly in her bad Kannada. The man looked furious. He spat. A glob of spit fell on the ground next to Patel.

'Paat-il,' he said.

Chandra looked at Patel, raised her eyebrows, said, 'He says you are having an affair with his wife.'

'His what?'

'His wife.'

'I don't understand–'

Before she could speak again, two of the men launched themselves on Patel. The first thug threw a punch. Patel instinctively turned his shoulder to block it. At the same time, he kicked out at the other thug. Scrabbled backwards, shoulder throbbing. Stole a glance at Chandra.

First man down, second grabbing at her left arm. She thrust the pointy end of her lathi into his midriff while reaching into her back pocket.

His own assailants moved and Patel found his feet treading air, his bottom crashing on to the ground. He swore, lunged up. The men jolted back as if he were a rearing snake. Shouts and screams of rage from the men attacking Chandra. Patel became aware he was shouting, too.

'Get back, you fuckers. Back away now.'

But it was Patel who was backing away from the men, and

them edging forwards. He reached a hand for the radio that wasn't there, to call for the backup that wouldn't come. I'm in India, India, a voice inside him shrieked.

The men sensed his hesitation. They leapt. He turned and ran, chest tight, aiming for the cart that was blocking the alleyway. The cart's owner and his customers had fled. He saw in his mind's eye the sickle half buried under a pile of melons. Someone grabbed at his ankles, tugged his shirt.

Scrambling madly, onions and tomatoes tumbling, Patel reached the melons. His fingers gripped the handle of the half-buried sickle, a well-deserved miracle. He spun about and lifted it like Thor his hammer.

The sickle changed dynamics. The thugs wilted. Stepping back, they looked at each other, seeming to find nothing mutu-ally reassuring. Patel roared at them, giving into emotion on a subcontinental scale. The men melted into one of the myriad paths winding away through the huts. Patel, disconcerted by this sudden and wholesome abandonment, was left holding the sickle up in the air, like a hero in one of those rural action flicks, the posters of which peppered the city's buildings.

Chandra. He turned to see. Her back to him. One of the thugs in front of her. A scream split the silence. Chandra stepped to the side and he saw her arm come down. The thug staggered away, howling, grabbing at his eyes. Chandra's hand pushed a small object into her back pocket.

Pepper spray, Patel realised. Those things worked. Then he noticed the other thug on the ground, unconscious, a red wound on his forehead. Chandra turned, saw his own attackers running up between the hovels.

She yelled to Patel, 'Go after them.'

Patel obeyed. Still wielding the sickle, he bulldozed past the hovels, upsetting women who squatted in the narrow paths shelling peas or peeling onions and garlic, gossiping. Through the dark huts and out again. Some men slept, some simply sat, doing nothing.

'Sorry, excuse me, sorry,' Patel threw left and right as he ran. A woman drew her feet back under the woven winnowing tray that held shallots and a penknife. Coconuts scattered right where they'd waited for the women to break them. He startled a woman nursing her baby. It set up a howl behind him.

Ahead, he saw a flash of blue lungi, a white-clad shoulder disappearing around a corner, black curly hair bobbing out of sight. He twisted and turned with the paths, the pounding of his heart setting off his eardrums to thrum, unable to hear above his breathing, wheezing.

Patel collided with the two men at a set of traffic lights that appeared out of the blue where the slum ended. A busy junction, three major roads. Blasts of tempestuous horns. Patel, through the dust, saw the reason for the men's hesitation. Traffic police. Just yards away, on the side of the road, two uniforms sat in a jeep, all their attention on Patel and his two goondas.

'Police,' yelled Patel. 'Grab these men.'

He leapt on the nearest thug. His fingers grasped, then slid, missed, then snagged in the cuff of the white shirt. At the same time he saw the other thug lurch on to the road. The jeep's door opened, a copper's boot slid on to the baked tar, his teeth exposed in an effort to kill the inertia of his khaki-clad bulk. He plunged into the traffic after the second thug. The horns set up a chorus. The policeman ploughed through cars and scooters towards the thug stuck between a tempo and a bus.

'Gotcha.'

A nonchalant aunty paddled past on her scooter, oblivious to the whole caboodle, intent only on edging forwards, all ready to launch herself ahead of other, more cumbersome four-wheel traffic.

Patel's attention snapped back to the man thrashing in his arms. He squeezed harder on the chest-lock. The man grunted, twisting. His bare knee came up against Patel's groin. Patel writhed away, but the thug pulled loose, brought an arm up and, suddenly, something glinted. Patel felt his vision explode.

Next thing he noted: the aunty still paddling, but the screen was tilted, the camera fallen on the floor. She paddled upside down past a slack-jawed auto-driver half out of his seat. 'What a lot of fuss.' She waggled her head at him. The screen blinked, the aunty replaced by Chandra's face, her mouth opening and closing but no sound coming out. He reached for the remote to switch the volume back on. Blacked out.

Chapter Nineteen

Patel held the stem of his broken spectacles and squinted at the blurry traffic. This, he thought, must be what they meant by the expression *at sea*. He rattled and shook along with the rattling, shaking, swerving autorickshaw, its driver unconcerned with the traffic around them or the traffic rules. The ride, like everything else in this trip to India, disrupted his being right to his core. His body shuddered and bounced as the auto bounded over potholes. His elbow throbbed. His ankle twanged. His ears rang.

The bandage on his head flashed at him in the little rear-view mirror. It made him unrecognisable to himself, and to ponder about who he really was. A mollycoddled Indian boy who became a serious cricketer, then unexpectedly and in all too discombobulating a manner, an ex-cricketer by the time he turned twenty-two. *Retired hurt* flashing on the scorecard on the screen as he walked away from the pavilion nursing his wrist, shrugging off the pain. Equanimous about the physio, the surgeons. Temporary, he'd thought, it's only temporary. Then the words *for ever* sinking in his brain, the hurt settling deep. *Retired hurt* for ever. A few times he had got dressed and picked up a bat, intending to go and break the surgeon's skull in, but he was not that kind of person. He had smiled and thanked him, actually *thanked* the surgeon when he informed Patel of the permanence of his injury due to the failure of the tendon operation. Thanked him. Smiled at him. So fucking polite. Such an English gent.

The auto swept around a corner. Patel's body slid on the Rexine, his ankle painfully jolting the auto's metal lip.

'Steady on,' he said to the oiled head of the driver, who looked at Patel in the mirror as though he were a strange, mad animal.

Looking again in the mirror he saw a wildness in his eyes he'd never seen before. Not once in his life had he gone off the rails, become, even for the briefest time, a strange, mad animal. After the injury, everyone complimented him on his sensible attempts to pull himself together. He took his mother's advice, enrolled on a criminology course. He'd been the odd, mildly famous mature student. No one on his course had been that into cricket. It wasn't a posh uni and the course was full of working-class white kids. He did not hang out with them. He was too old to binge drink, and while he liked a drink, he was much too sensible to get into altercations or fisticuffs. From time to time a cricket enthusiast circled him till the stars in his eyes faded and Patel lapsed into someone all too human and boring. Later, too, while his job as a police officer involved subduing trouble-makers, there was always back-up, procedure, certain standard phrases you used to address the drunk and disorderly or violent individuals. He attended training courses on gentle and effective physical methods of restraint and arrest, always, always with a partner beside him, all done to the ritual of reading rights.

The auto jolted him again. Pain shot up his bruised elbow.

But *this*. This unpredictable madness. Chandra dealt in this every day. Policing by the skin of her teeth. She selectively used or discarded the law according to her own idea of what was right or wrong, and how things worked. A sheriff of the lawless Wild West, those films he loved as a kid. Really, the 'West' he was from, law-abiding England, was just a myth the Indian rich believed in. However, the Indian wealthy were physically trapped in the East, where poverty and lawlessness, unsentimental fatalism and merry-go-round logic made the whole place a beast of eccentricity that toyed with their petty Western aspirations. He was in the lawless East. Mind-bending, eccentric East.

A blurry-eyed and seasick Patel was dropped off at his hotel foyer.

'Afternoon, sir,' said the receptionist, completely uninterested in the bandage on his head, the bruises on his face, his dirty, scuffed clothes, the tears at the elbow, the blood seeping, drying at his knee. She consulted a Post-it on her computer screen. 'There will be a car to pick you up at seven. Message from a Mister Chandran.'

'She didn't say what for?'

'No, sir.'

He looked at his phone. Battery dead. Once in his room, he plugged it in to charge, and waited. Chandra had taken the thugs into custody for questioning, leaving Patel unconscious with the two traffic policemen. They had dragged him into the jeep, driven him to hospital. He came around, was examined and exclaimed over by doctors and nurses, had tests conducted to see if his brain was still functioning, endured unnecessary fuss over his concussion. Two nurses applied a dramatic bandage when a plaster would have done. Finally, he'd been allowed to leave.

After several minutes, the phone made itself available for use. Voicemail from Chandra. 'We are going to a party. Be ready at seven.'

Another party. Patel's head hurt too much to think. He was without the will or the wherewithal to question his path through the Indian jungle. Chandra hacked a trail for him and he simply followed. At least he'd escaped his 'briefing' with Rajkumar.

Patel resisted the bed, and ran a bath. He checked the time.

Six-thirty. He slipped into the watery warmth and groaned out loud. He'd close his eyes for ten minutes, he decided, just to restore himself, to settle the heady, disjointed feeling from all the strain. Just ten. Then he would have twenty long minutes to insert his aching limbs into a suit, the wrinkle-proof faux linen he had rolled up and shoved in the corner of his suitcase. The best twenty quid he'd ever spent in Topman in January. He preferred that to the two Armanis he'd splashed out on during his heady, but brief cricketing rise. He lay in the bath, his mind emptying at last, and the strong Indian painkillers began kicking in.

His heart thumped in its cage, broke out through the cracked ribs and became a frog trying to leap out of the watery grave. The little webbed feet, stepping and springing upon lumps in the water, drowned unnameable creatures in the murk. Time was running out. The reeking liquid seeped into his lungs, each breath a struggle ...

Patel woke to the twin sounds of his phone ringing and a fist banging on the door. His head slumped forward, chin touching the water. A thumping in his temples too. The bath water was cold. Steam had condensed and trickled down his head from the tiles where his head had flopped back. He scrambled out of the bath, wincing and cursing, scooped up his phone. Sarah.

'Hello?'

Sarah spoke in a rush. He couldn't hear her words over the sound of the banging door.

'Hang on, hang on.' He checked the time. Seven-thirty-five. Hurriedly draping a towel over his midriff, Patel cracked the door open. Chandra.

'Hold on a sec,' he said into the phone.

'All right?' said Chandra. 'The cab-wallah tried to ring you from reception. But there was no response. They rang me. I couldn't think of where else you could be. But the state you were in, I thought you were probably fast asleep.'

'Give me two minutes.' He shut the door again.

'Yeah, Sarah?'

'Maybe I'll call later.' She sounded serious. There was something in the air.

'Oh wait,' he said, as Chandra banged on the door again, louder.

He opened the door again.

'I'll meet you at the mayor's party,' said Chandra. 'Your cabbie is waiting by the reception. He will recognise you from the papers.'

Patel shut the door once more. 'Hello?' he said, and received silence from the other end.

Sighing, Patel went back into the bathroom, removed the bandage from his head, and inspected the wound. Dried blood. Bit of swelling. He stuck a little plaster on it, and ruffled his hair over it. Good as new. It was while knotting his tie that he realised Chandra had been wearing a sari. He could not recall how high the waistline was, how much of her navel showed, whether her bellybutton peeked, if it was round or oval, whether her stomach curved in sexily or curved out sexily, if her pallu was gathered high on her shoulder exposing part of her blouse-clad breast, or whether it was modestly let down all the way, covering her like a blanket, with no hint of the untold treasures beneath.

Patel had to wait a full five minutes – fully suited, hair brushed and gelled, shoelaces tied – for his hard-on to subside, before he could walk down to reception.

And then only while he was on the stairs, the fog of desire (that lay upon the fog of painkiller-subdued pain) in his head cleared a little and he recalled Chandra's words. Papers, she'd said. The receptionist eyed him with a curious intensity as he approached the stack of complimentary newspapers by her elbow.

'Evening papers?' he said.

'Yes, sir. Vernacular only. One Tamil, two Kannada.'

Patel picked up three papers and laid them on the coffee table. With his back to the staring receptionist, he studied them. Amid all the swirling strangenesses that were the Tamil and Kannada alphabets, the only familiar thing was his own picture, lifted off the internet from God knows where – somebody's Facebook page, perhaps – three years younger, mid-blink, with a half-smile of drunkenness, lifting a glass of ale to someone at a retirement party in Manchester. A sigh escaped him. The other two papers had him in cricketing whites, coming in to bowl, feet flying, wind-sheared cheekbones and bug-eyes, concentrating, biting his lip. The picture from his Wikipedia page.

He put the papers back. He could guess the contents of the articles. Most probably a rehashing of Kadambri's *The Indian* story. Opinion, speculation and hope. The last unwarranted.

A skeletal little man approached. 'Sir, car ready,' he wobbled his head.

Chapter Twenty

They drove into some kind of hidden millionaire's enclave, right in the heart of the city. Not a speck of rubbish was visible on the well-lit roads canopied by leafy trees, the wide pavements empty of pye-dogs and loiterers. They rolled along short, broad streets, occasionally passing another luxury car, and turned into a private drive that cut through a wide lawn where the grass had been meticulously cultivated to nearly English standards. They stopped at the pillar-flanked front door of a sprawling house.

Patel creaked out of the car and for a moment watched other cars arriving with other guests. In the dark, spotlit with yellow gas lamps, precious stones twinkled among the guests' clothing. With the rattle of bangles and the swish of silk, Bengaluru's finest made their way to the house.

He too went in, found a table with refreshments. All liquid, tempting. In spite of the strong painkillers, his head thumped. It was either very dim in there, or his vision was blurry from the concussion. A waiter appeared and the words slipped out. 'Scotch and soda.' Then the drink was in his hand. He stared at it for a second. Two generous fingers of the good stuff with very little of the soda. What the hell. He took the drink outside, found a corner by some kind of outhouse, away from those chattering, and lit a fag.

'Hey there.' Kadambri stepped into the light from the side of building. She dragged on her cigarette, crinkled her eyes at Patel, smiled. 'You look a bit battered.'

'I'll say.'

'Didn't think he'd actually invite you.'

'Was it on your recommendation?'

'Yes.'

'I did wonder why I was here.'

'Your presence is meant to reassure the crème de la crème that their women are safe.'

She smiled at him through a wave of smoke. She wore thick, glittering lipstick and heavy kohl. The whole look was something out of a Rembrandt painting, reset in a modern, multicultural context. The mood, the brooding sexiness.

His eyelids drooped. A wave of something passed over him. Shouldn't have drunk the Scotch so quickly.

'Do you feel reassured?' He didn't quite manage to say reassure right.

'I confess not, Mr Patel. You look like you need a bit of help yourself.' She put her free hand on his shoulder, as if to steady him, and he had to stop himself from leaning on her.

'Thanks for the glowing write-up.'

'Slow news day.' She laughed. How different she was from Chandra. All easy and smooth and cool, and yet, with the same steel to her backbone. A quieter sort of strength. 'You know, what you said outside the police HQ really stuck with me.'

'My variations on "no comment"?'

She laughed again. 'About the killer being someone familiar. Like Jekyll and Hyde. It could be a powerful man with a public and a private face. Then the women don't have a chance, do they?'

Patel frowned. 'I didn't say that,' he said. 'You want to write up your speculations, then lend them authenticity by pretending I said them.'

Kadambri silently puffed away, as though he hadn't spoken, unconcerned by the origins of her dubious information. Patel thought of the stats of violence against women. Usually a man well known to them, in most cases their partner. But all these women barely knew each other, so how could they all know the killer intimately?

Patel found himself saying, 'I wish I had a theory. Any theory. But the fact is, I haven't a clue about the killer's identity. But don't print that.'

Kadambri smiled. 'So we're both flailing in the dark.' She stubbed out her cigarette. 'Let's go in. I need a drink.'

He glanced at the house, the movement of his head too quick. He briefly saw stars. The cars three-deep, dropping people off. The front of the house crammed with guests, knocking back the booze, talking loudly. He couldn't think of anything worse than being pecked at from all sides by tipsy people he didn't know, people who read the papers, watched cricket.

'I'm just going to stay here a few minutes, smoke a few fags.'

Disappointment on Kadambri's face. She'd probably wanted to show him off. 'OK,' she drawled. 'Come and find me. I'll introduce the mayor.'

Patel dragged on his cigarette and wondered where Chandra was, and what happened to the two thugs she'd taken into custody. The cars were backed up all the way down the drive. The guests were beginning to spill out of the house. One or two glanced his way. Soon somebody would come over to chinwag. He stepped into the darkness where Kadambri had been lurking. What was this? Servants quarters, some kind of annex? He looked around the corner of the little building, to a pool of white light from a bulb on the annex wall. Half-hidden by a thick tree trunk, a youth with cherub cheeks was polishing a vintage motorbike. A low-rider, the black gleam of the engine inscribed with the logo, Royal Enfield. Wide seat, red leather. Leather tassels hung from the handlebars and wing mirrors.

'Nice ride,' said Patel.

The youth grinned. He wore a T-shirt with the Lacoste crocodile on it, and tracksuit pants. In India, the poor youth dressed smartly and followed cricket, the rich youth wore tracksuits and trainers and followed football.

'You live here?' asked Patel.

'House is full of pigs,' he said, eyes on Patel's shoes. 'I'm staying away.'

Patel nodded. He could see the young man's point.

'You want to ride?' He held out the keys, not looking directly at Patel.

'I'd love to,' Patel said, gazing longingly at the Bullet, 'but I'm afraid people are expecting me at the party.' He suppressed a shudder. Rajkumar, no doubt seething about the press coverage. Chandra looking sexy and dangerous, waiting to toy with his sanity.

The youth held the keys out to him, either insisting or unable to understand Patel's *English* English.

Patel said, 'No thanks,' nodding at the same time Indian fashion.

The youth lowered his hand, expressionless, put the key in the slot. Patel threw down the cigarette stub. He was sorely tempted, but he stepped away from the tree to glance back at the house. Chandra stood at the entrance, talking to someone, but her eyes on him. She waved. The woman had hawk eyes.

'Better go,' he said.

The boy began pulling the cover on to the motorbike, his features inscrutable in the dark.

Patel crossed the lawn, but Chandra had wandered off. He went looking for her. Inside the house, people stood in threes and fours. Decorous female murmurs were punctuated by male laughter. A tinkling of music, Indian, classical with jazz notes, some kind of artful fusion. Canapé trays floated around the room. There was nothing official or stately about his surroundings. A tasteful simplicity in the décor masked the extent of wealth on display. Classical paintings of kings and queens, minstrels wielding tambourines or nymphs lounging modestly by forest streams. Traditional silver lamps. Floating towards him were cocktails in swirls of pink, yellow and green, adorned with sprigs of mint and slivers of limes. No doubt the exotic alcohols from the far west mixed with local aphrodisiacs or digestive aids.

Cocktail in one hand, canapé in another, he spied Rajkumar booming over the heads of half a dozen nodding, moustachioed courtiers. Patel backed into another room.

Cocktail in hand also, eyeing his canapé, Chandra came towards him. Her eyes shifted to his and she smiled. 'Hello there.'

Patel didn't know if it was her perfume swirling through his nasal passages or some kind of room freshener.

'Hello, Chandra.'

A shimmer on her eyelids. Green eyeshadow with flecks of gold in it. The same colour as Sarita Mohan's eyeshadow. But the flecks in hers were silver. Chandra wore a rosy shade of lipstick slightly smudged by the cocktail glass; its rim bore the imprint of her lower lip.

'Missed the five o'clock briefing with Rajkumar.'

'Yes, the papers have been phoning him all morning to ask about you. He's probably counting the ways he can punish you.'

'He's angry?'

'Yep.'

'At me?'

'Yep.'

'What did I ever do?'

'Breathe.' She looked sideways a moment, where a suited man loomed, but he was only turning to go into the other room. 'Listen, I have to tell you something.'

'Those men you picked up?'

'No no.' She put a hand on his chest, leaned towards him. 'It's something personal.'

Her smoky, green-fringed eyes blinked, close to his face.

A stranger's voice shattered the moment. 'Just the two people I wanted to see.'

Chandra's hand fell away. They turned together.

A warm smile lit a handsome face with a Clark Gable moustache – a well-groomed man, glowing with health, sparkling eyes, teeth, hair in a cultured, forties style, parted on the side.

'Hello, uncle,' said Chandra. 'Mr Patel, His Honour Mr Hariharan, the mayor of Bengaluru.'

Patel shook his hand. Soft and cool, with a touch of reassurance. The smile increased in wattage as he appraised Chandra. 'In a sari, at last. It suits you. How's your father, the old rascal?'

'The same,' said Chandra. 'He's taken up watching test cricket. Tries to coach the Indian team from the living room. Last weekend I was home and they were losing to Sri Lanka. He threatened to have them all arrested. Still thinks he's a policeman.'

'That scoundrel was always into cricket. We used to sneak off from college, climb the wall into the MCC and watch them at nets. Smoked grass, drank beer. Don't tell your mother.'

Chandra laughed. 'I certainly will.'

'He would love to meet Mr Patel. Are you taking him?'

For the first time since he'd met her, Chandra looked lost for words.

'We are in the middle of the investigation,' she said after a moment.

'Why, yes, of course.' The mayor gave the tiniest wink. 'Wouldn't do to mix work with pleasure, eh?'

Patel felt himself flush.

'I better go and see Rajkumar,' said Chandra. 'Need to update him on the afternoon's events.' She widened her eyes meaningfully at Patel. 'I'll try to keep him in the other room.'

They watched her disappear into the mix of people.

'Mr Patel,' said Mayor Hariharan. 'You are finding yourself suddenly the toast of the town. How must you feel?'

'Strange,' said Patel. He did not want to be the toast of the town. He had a job to do. Why did Chandra leave? What had happened to the thugs she'd arrested earlier? Where was the missing maid? The mayor was waiting for him to continue, so he added, 'Very.'

'But, of course, Mr Patel. Come, people are dying to meet you. All the important people of Bengaluru are here.'

Eyes that had peered at him curiously, even surreptitiously until then, widened with delight as the mayor introduced him. They went through one room after another. A hundred introductions swirled in the golden light, fluttered like moths before expiring in the cavern of his injured head. The faces and the names were all too unfamiliar. His head buzzed from the assault of so many introductions. His ability to respond appropriately faded by the minute till he could only dumbly nod as people told him about themselves, about those next to them and the others they hadn't brought to the party, all in a befuddling English: loopy, elliptical, convoluted, peppered with Americanisms and English archaisms he associated with colonial times.

The mayor's eyes often rested on Patel in the middle of fielding seven different conversations at once, trying to read him.

Patel began to get impatient. How could he small talk strangers at a party when a madman was out there killing women? Fair enough, his presence as a Scotland Yard representative was meant to reassure, but for heaven's sake.

Finally, Hariharan said, 'But you must have had enough of meeting new people, Mr Patel. Let us go somewhere quiet so you can have a moment to restore yourself.'

Not a bad idea, thought Patel. He needed a bit of restoration. He followed the mayor through a set of doors on the veranda. The evening had drawn in. No stars were visible in the polluted sky. They strolled across a lawn that had remained dry and prickly in spite of the signs of recent watering, and through some sliding doors to a kind of posh den. A sofa with its back to the doors faced a wall. The mayor shepherded Patel towards it.

'Scotch?'

Even as Patel nodded, a servant he hadn't noticed handed them glasses. They sat on the sofa, side by side, enveloped in an odd kind of cosiness. They sipped without speaking. The Scotch softened the edges and prickles of the day. Patel became aware that a painting faced them. Or rather, that they faced a painting. In fact, the very purpose of the sofa was to view the painting. He felt transported from southern India to the sophistication of Tate Britain, where such things were possible, or in fact, seemingly permissible. Experiencing a painting in silence seemed a curiously anachronistic activity in the bling chaos of modern India. The shrill and brittle quality he associated with the wealthy and powerful denizens of the Third World did not apply to the mayor. He was old school, a man of refinement.

The murk of painkillers and booze parted a little and the painting came into focus. A blue expanse. Forms shimmered darkly into view and disappeared before they could quite achieve three-dimensionality. Rounded organic forms lumped in the foreground, evoking ideas of bodies, limbs, languidness.

'Sarah would like this.' The thought slipped from his mouth.

'Is Sarah your wife?'

'Fiancée,' said Patel, trying to sound confident, as though stating a fact. The final syllable of the portentous word, the ée, had risen in pitch despite his attempt at control. A question, if only to himself. 'She's an artist. A sculptor.'

'I see. I myself cannot pretend to understand, or even appreciate art. Most of the stuff came with the house, my wife's family's. But this. This is one of the few things I acquired for myself. It really captures me, you know, Mr Patel. It is sophistication. The colour blue. All those dark shades of blue, the mesmeric forms. It is your colour, is it not? It is in your flag. When it comes to cricket, of course, we both wear blue. Although yours is a classier shade.'

Patel nodded, the Scotch sliding effortlessly down his throat.

'Do you not think it a dichotomy, Mr Patel, to be a man of some taste and also a politician? In a place like India, I mean.'

Patel smiled. 'Yes. I had a very different mental image of the typical Indian politician.'

'White dhoti, criminal record, no English?'

'Provincial, yes,' he said, diplomatically.

'But then, you would know all about a dichotomy, wouldn't you? A dazzlingly successful cricketer. Now a dazzlingly successful police officer.' The mayor beamed. 'Perhaps the only one in the world.'

'Hardly,' Patel said, demurring not so much to the contradiction in his chosen professions as to the adjectives dazzling and successful. 'I just muddle along, really.'

'But I have seen your bowling.'

'Cricket ended ten years ago. I'd barely begun ... to be a success. Now, all this. I am by no means Sherlock Holmes.'

The mayor laughed, but not unkindly.

'What do the evening papers say about me?' Patel asked, beginning to relax. 'Haven't had a chance to ask.'

Hariharan smiled. 'All good things.' He tipped his glass this way and that, as if studying the play of light through the remaining half finger of Scotch. Patel had drained his.

'So what do you make of the painting, Mr Patel?'

Patel squinted, studied the abstractions on the canvas, gathered his thoughts. After overcoming his resistance to engage with anything he considered highbrow, he found himself quite mesmerised by the artwork.

'Things taking shape,' he said, 'as though the forms are gaining definition, something momentous about to emerge from a kind of creative murk?'

The mayor smiled. 'You are a perceptive man, Mr Patel. It is in fact, exactly how I view it. The excitement makes my nerves sing, at the thought of being at such a threshold of monumental arrival.'

Steady on, thought Patel. The man was getting a bit carried away. He felt a bit edgy all of a sudden, as if they were sitting too close. But he hadn't noticed either of them shifting position on the sofa.

'Listen,' said the mayor. 'I wouldn't worry about Rajkumar. He's more bark than bite. He's just, you know ...' An almost Gallic shrug. 'He's feeling a bit snubbed that expert help is flying in over his head.'

'I know.' Patel sighed. 'I wish the papers didn't call me a knight in shining armour.'

'But you are!' Hariharan laid a paternal hand over his for a fleeting moment. Patel could sense his good judgement in all things, his sympathetic effort, his control over physical expressions of emotion. Elegant and masterful, like the painting they had been studying. The lightest touch of his fingers, fore and thumb, on the hairs of his wrist.

Patel sighed. 'The assistant commissioner is not a fan of being rescued, I think.'

'Two heads are better than one, Mr Patel. Chandra is fierce but even she needs a sounding board, even, dare I say it, a restraining hand. And Rajkumar needs to be kept on his toes. He can be a bit smug sometimes about the Bengaluru police's good track in criminal cases. But let's face it, even a Scotland Yard mosquito is better trained and better equipped to catch a criminal compared with the pot-bellied Indian constable.'

Patel laughed. At his first press conference in Oz, before his big debut, he had *hmm*ed and *errm*ed so much, so nervous was he, that an Aussie reporter had snapped, 'Er, mate, what are yer, a mosquito?' The yellow press had dubbed him 'Mosquito' for three days, till he took five wickets for seventeen runs, and became, in quintessentially Aussie terminology, 'Boomerang Patel'.

The male servant reappeared, and dipped his head towards the mayor's ear.

'One cannot catch one's breath, Mr Patel' Hariharan sighed after the servant left. 'Apparently, Minister Madhavan's looking for me. If I do not go and kowtow he will take it as a personal insult. And you better come with me. Don't want you poking around unearthing state secrets.' He laughed.

They made their way back to the party.

Booze had oiled the joints, loosened tongues. People were more languid and – if possible – noisier. Chairs had been dragged into groups. Waiters moved around with trays, plucking empty glasses from guests' hands, replacing them with full ones. Patel's

Scotch glass was whisked away and he now held another, darker drink. Rum? He couldn't recall what he'd asked for.

A tall, stooped man introduced himself and a short, sloping woman stood mutely by. The man began describing his job in detail to the top of Patel's head. How many men under him. How many over. His prospects for promotion. Patel found himself in a circle of people sagely nodding. His eyes wandered. They touched upon the yellow lights in hooded lamps and ceiling pendants, an elegant mishmash of European and Indian designs, alighted on those classical paintings again, blouse-less bathing women in flowing drapes, and the furniture. A fat woman spilled over an intricately carved chair. The soft furnishings bore prints of lotuses and elephants and all things Indian. Now he saw paisley everywhere, in furnishings, in many of the saris. Some kind of paisley revival. A chill in his heart. The dead women's saris were bordered in blue paisley.

The tall man asked a question. Patel's eyes alighted on Chandra at the entrance, talking to someone who looked suspiciously like Rajkumar in profile. The tall man waited. His wife nodded up encouragingly at Patel.

Chandra's eyes searched the faces. He willed her to see him. She did. She said a word and began moving his way. It was a long way, from where she was to where he was. People lapped like waves at her little boat. Patel realised he was holding his breath.

As he breathed again, Chandra's eyes shifted focus to half a centimetre behind his left ear. They widened. Who did she see? Patel turned. Behind him, a man in a well-cut suit was talking to a servant, or a driver. The second man abruptly looked down, turned and walked away. The suit continued talking to thin air for a few seconds, then stopped, jerked his head towards Patel, and just as abruptly as the second man, left the room. Patel followed. First one man, then the next rushed past a potted plant and through a door, leaving crushed toes and angry exclamations in their wake. Patel couldn't see what was behind that door.

Chandra was beside him.

'Was that . . .?' began Patel.

'Driver Bupathy. Shaved his beard, changed his clothes.' She raised her eyebrows.

The alcohol on Patel's brain dropped away. His head cleared. 'Who was the suit talking to him?'

'No idea. But he sure moves quick. Let's go.'

Patel mouthed 'Excuse me' repeatedly as he pushed and shoved his way through the guests. The doorway led to a service lobby, then an anteroom that opened into another living room with scattered guests. They were at the side of the house. Through the windows he saw a row of cars. One of them was backing out fast. He rushed out as it made a tight turn.

Chandra caught up with him.

'You can't go very fast in your sari,' he said.

'Bugger off,' she said.

The car screeched up to a pair of gates and blasted its horn.

'No watchman,' said Chandra.

'What make is it?' Patel squinted in the dark.

'Big white car. Probably a Lexus.'

'I'll text you the number when I see it.' Patel thanked providence for the extra moments. He looked around for a vehicle.

'We'll never catch him. My car's on the other side . . .'

'Too far.'

To his dismay, the gates were opening. A moped puttered in. The rider balanced an enormous shopping bag on his lap. Two more hung from the handles.

Patel ran to him. 'Stop. Police.'

The Lexus scraped against the gate as it squeezed through.

Chandra pulled the bags from the moped, dumped them on the ground. Booze and party snacks tumbled out.

'Sorry,' said Patel. 'Need bike to catch criminal.'

The man spoke rapidly.

'He says if you let the throttle go it will switch off,' said Chandra. 'Button start doesn't work. Kickstart only.'

'And much too slow,' said Patel, eyeing the two-stroke engine. 'There's got to be something better.'

'What about that one, sir?'

'Where?' said Patel. Then he saw it. Oh yes!

Under the tree, beneath a tarp, the Enfield.

'Do you know how to ride it?'

'I'll manage.'

He recalled the boy had left the key in the ignition before he whipped the cover on. But it wasn't there. Had it dropped to the floor? He was craning to look, when the moped man said, 'Key, sir?' He held out the key to Patel. The servant class, thought Patel. Keepers of the keys.

He hopped on, kicked. The Bullet boomed to life.

'Take the right into the city,' yelled Chandra as he cruised to the gate. 'I'll organise roadblocks.'

Patel burned rubber, thought about Indian legal alcohol limits.

He'd ridden a motorbike briefly, before witnessing a mangled mess of a biker being picked off the barrier at Blackwell tunnel. He lacked the guts to put his life on the line after that. Just as he lacked the guts to stop Sarah from thinking he'd seduced her, loved her, wanted her babies.

But now, the Enfield's thrum, a passionate heart under him. This was a last hurrah. He was in India. His fate was in the hands of kitsch, capricious gods.

He turned right at the end of the road. Within seconds, he spotted the car at the traffic lights. Just as he braked beside it, it screeched through the red lights. He followed, twisted blindly around bends, trying to keep up.

Ten years ago, on the morning of his wrist injury, the driver of the car that took him from his hotel to the MCC ground had said to him, 'Why you putting seatbelt? You expecting I crash? Ganesha won't let.' The little ivory Ganesh stuck with superglue on the dashboard, smothered in fresh marigolds, had indeed ensured they didn't crash, in spite of the driver steering like he was on a suicide mission. After safely delivering Patel to the dressing room, Ganesha had turned his attention away from Patel, left him to tear two tendons in his wrist.

The Lexus braked and turned abruptly into a side street. Patel zoomed past, braked, screeched around and followed, wheels sliding and straightening. He turned the bend to see the Lexus slam against the corner of a food cart. The cart holder shrieked as a biryani pan took flight. Patel ducked as a Petromax lantern whizzed past, missing his ear by an inch.

The Lexus raced, dodged and slunk behind trucks, trying Hollywood tricks to shake him off. He managed to hold on.

Who was in that car? He couldn't read the registration number. Too dark. Perhaps it was deliberately smudged over. The cheek of Bupathy to come to the party, where half the police force was present. Why would he do that?

A knot of vehicles. The Lexus was getting away. He tried to focus on the unpredictable Indian traffic, told his mind to disengage from road safety rules drilled into him since boyhood. But how could he?

Road block. The car slowed for lathi-waving policemen. Patel went down the gears. The Lexus screamed into the barriers, smoke in its wake. The cops scrambled from the crunched remains of the plastic barricades. Patel sped in pursuit.

He expected the coppers to jump into a jeep and come after

them, but no one did. Red light. Busy junction. The Lexus scraped past a bus and careened downhill several hundred yards ahead as he was forced to slow down. Tightly wound into a ball at his very core were the lessons of road safety, all the years from pre-school onwards. Now he simply had to abandon all of it, rip up half a lifetime's behaviour pattern.

He opened the throttle, punched the gears up. Through the red lights he sped, holding his breath, looking neither left nor right. A blast of horn. His left ear rang. Panic shut his eyes. Something slammed into his leg. A sharp rip on the flesh of his leg. He was spinning, but the bike's two wheels were still on the road. He heard a thump behind him as a vehicle hit an immovable object. He opened his eyes. The Lexus was in front of him.

A buzzing and a ringing near his groin. Still riding, he stretched out his left leg reached into his pocket and retrieved his phone.

'Chandra. I can't see the car reg.' One hand on the handlebar, he zipped around an auto and in between two cars.

'Never mind ... Bupathy's boss. P. Krishnamu ... Selvi Gangammai Street, Whitefield.'

'What street? Is Whitefield the area? House number?'

The line cut off. He slipped the phone into his shirt pocket. The Lexus pulled further ahead. A van swung in front of him.

He braked. Pressed the clutch by mistake. The bike jumped and stalled. Something slammed into his back.

An auto had slammed into his back tyre, but while already braking. By the time he'd managed to get back on the bike, the Lexus was gone. He followed road signs to Whitefield. Thankfully, it was a suburb with big, gated houses, not an inner-city warren. He stopped at a street sign beginning Selvi ... A khaki-clad watchman from a nearby house rattled his stick on the iron gates to announce his presence.

'Which house white Lexus car?' Patel asked him.

'Here no number,' said the man readily. 'House with parrots on gates.' He gave directions.

When Patel arrived at the bungalow, it was bathed in gloom and dark. His headlights picked out a row of metal parrots on the gates. He nodded to himself in grim satisfaction. Not a light was on. He checked his watch. Eleven-fifteen p.m.

The bungalow was wreathed in darkness. Wincing, Patel lifted his leg over the bike, pulled it on to its stand. No watchman emerged from the gloom to ask his business. The white Lexus slept. He touched its bonnet as he approached the front door. Still warm. He crossed the portico, watching for any movement through the windows. But it was pitch dark and the windows were heavily stencilled with iron bars. At the door, he paused, wondering whether to ring the bell. He looked at the door again. A heavy brass knocker in the centre, shaped like an elephant's head and trunk. He lifted the trunk and knocked. The query boomed through the air, resounding against the walls, the windows and the ground. Nothing stirred. He pushed the door. It sighed inwards.

Right, he said to himself and hobbled over the threshold. As his eyes were adjusting to the darkness, he heard the squeak of a chair. Fight or flight? He saw vague shapes: sofa, armchair, coffee table.

'You found me,' said a voice.

'Turn on the lights.'

A lamp clicked on, yellow and gloomy. The suited man from the party sat in the armchair, nervously poised.

Patel said, 'Did you hope I'd ring the bell and go away when no one answered?'

'Yes.'

'You shouldn't have left the door open.'

'I did?'

'Yep.'

'Maybe I really didn't want to hide.'

'Changed your mind?'

'You'd have come tomorrow morning, or evening, the next day. Where would I go?'

Patel's pulse quickened. He stepped over the threshold.

'Mehra is your lawyer.'

'Yes.'

'Bupathy your driver.'

'Mostly do my own driving.'

'Anyone else in the house?' Patel's eyes darted around the room. Doors led into unfathomable interiors, a stairway around a bend. Surely a place like this had servants.

'I sent everyone away ten minutes ago.'

'Who's everyone?

'Watchman and maid. Bupathy drove them away in the other car.'

'Where will they go?'

'I don't know. But they'll be back before morning. I'll tell them something. Give them money.'

'If you're still here,' said Patel.

He needed to call Chandra. He should have rung her before coming in. But he hadn't known he'd find the man sitting in his own living room. Now he was here, he had to hear the confession first.

'So what do you know about Anuradha's murder?'

'Are you close to catching the killer? Isn't that why you've been brought here?'

Patel wondered if he was playing games.

'How do you know Anuradha?'

'We were friends.'

'Why did you and Bupathy run from the party when you saw me?'

The man hesitated. Shit, he knows I know nothing, thought Patel. 'I had urgent business.'

'You're sitting in your own front room with the lights off. You sent away your servants.'

'Staff,' corrected the man. 'Seems you are just here fishing for information.'

'So tell me.'

'Do you even know my name?'

'P. Krishnamurthy.'

'You have nothing on me. Why would I volunteer information? I need my lawyer.'

Patel sat down. He couldn't bend his stiff knee. He leaned back on the cushion, stretched his leg along the sofa. 'We can arrest Bupathy, extract information from him.'

'Bupathy won't say anything. My lawyer will have him out in an hour.'

'We'll book him in at five p.m. on Saturday. By the time your lawyer comes knocking with a court order on Monday morning, Bupathy will be ready to sign anything we ask him to.' He winced, embarrassed to be adopting Chandra's methods, even in a lie, then took a punt. 'Or we drop hints to the press about your involvement, and watch your friendship with the mayor evaporate.'

A strange expression came into the man's eyes. He scrunched up his whole face like a handkerchief, bared his teeth. Then he threw his head back. The cords on his neck stood out. Under the chubbiness, there was a good amount of muscle. A sound like a door creaking came from the man's clenched jaws.

He's angry, thought Patel. He calculated the time it would take him to reach the lamp by the stairwell, knock off the shade and have to hand its nice thick stem to protect himself with. P. Krishnamurthy could be hiding a weapon under those clothes. Knife, torch, gun. Should he move now, or risk waiting? No, move. But before Patel got up, the man unclenched his fists, brought his head back down. To Patel's surprise, Krishnamurthy sobbed.

Between gusts of tears, he managed to sputter, 'Please ... who killed Anuradha ... the papers think ... if anyone can ... this monster, it's you.'

'Ah.' Patel's hope of solving the case that night evaporated. He settled back on the sofa, sighed. 'Start from the beginning,' he said. 'But first, have you got any painkillers?'

'No. Just whisky.'

A sobbing Krishnamurthy spilled out the old tale of forbidden love.

'You know, you could have pulled me aside at the party and told me your story,' said Patel, gingerly feeling his tender head, glancing at the empty whisky glass, deciding against another.

'Sorry, Mr Patel.' Krishnamurthy laughed embarrasedly. 'Bupathy panicked. And I panicked. Not expecting you and Ms Chandra at the party.'

The story over, Patel took his leave, only to find the bike wouldn't start. He shook it side to side, reckoned the tank to be empty.

Krishnamurthy rang Bupathy. 'He'll know what to do.'

Bupathy appeared in a little while from wherever he'd been sent to hide. After a minute of sheepish handwringing in his pursuer's presence, Bupathy rooted out a siphoning tube and while draining petrol from the Lexus into the Enfield's tank, he said: 'It's lucky for me it's you, sir, who came after us tonight. The Indian police wouldn't have believed us, or even if they did, they would have given me a hard time anyway, for revenge.'

'You mean for not telling the truth in the first place and saving them a lot of hassle?' said Patel, but Bupathy didn't seem to have an antenna for irony.

'Indian police not so nice. You are a very kind man, Mr Patel, sir.'

Patel shrugged, too battered to feel flattered. 'It's not kindness. It's logic. Your actions on the night Anuradha was murdered, especially the business with the phone, make you look suspicious of skulduggery, not murder.'

Bupathy tapped on his own skull, nodding, then pulled the tube from the Enfield and closed the tank. 'All done, sir.'

'Wait, Bupathy.' said Patel. 'Tell me about your wait in the toddy shop. You were looking down the road the whole time. Did you see a vehicle going towards the dam?'

'Oh, sir,' said Bupathy, 'I didn't see a single car going or coming. Just a couple of villagers stepped on to the road from their hovels or huts from the lower side, perhaps going to the grocery store by the big tamarind tree, and back they came clutching their bags full and heavy.'

'No one else?'

'No one else.'

'You sure?'

'I am sure.'

Patel kicked the pedal. The engine coughed and died.

'Oh, there was that cycle.'

'What cycle?'

'Just a dirty slum fellow on a cycle.'

'Going or coming?'

'That's the thing. He wasn't going towards the dam. He was coming from it.'

'Describe him,' said Patel, feeling his pulse quicken.

'Couldn't see clearly in the moonlight. He was the only one who didn't get off the road and go into the slum. Instead he sped onward towards the Bengaluru highway and disappeared from sight.'

'Did anything about him stand out?'

'Just a dirty slum fellow,' Bupathy repeated, as if the fellow had been beneath his notice, really. 'He was singing a rude film song, and he was young, although the song was old, an Ilayaraja hit from the eighties. He wore a lungi and a shirt.'

'The bicycle?'

'Old cycle. A Raleigh or a Philips.'

'Anything strike you as odd?'

'He had a big gunny sack on the pillion. I remember thinking that's a lot of groceries for the evening meal.'

A vein throbbed in Patel's temple. 'What time was this?'

'Oh about an hour after madam left. But I wasn't worried then. It was not even eleven o'clock.'

'Hang on,' said Patel. 'People don't buy groceries at eleven at night.'

'People work shifts in the leather factory half a mile from the dam along the river. They cook at odd times.' He shrugged.

'But there is no road beyond the dam.'

Bupathy gave him a look. 'Not for cars. But cycles can go on paths between fields, and across the riverbed.'

'And you're certain he didn't get off the road and enter the village?'

'Yes, sir.'

Patel kicked again. The Bullet roared into life.

'Oh, and Bupathy?'

'Yes, sir?'

'What happened to your fast?'

'After so many days in jail, sir, I thinking I want chicken biryani, rum and nice woman.'

'Fair enough.'

Patel winced at every jolt on the roads back to the hotel.

Chapter Twenty-One

It was gone one when the Enfield puttered to a stop outside Hotel Top End. Patel patted once on the fuel tank, and hobbled into reception.

En route, he'd rung Chandra and told her (shouting over the roar of the Bullet, Indian-style) to call off the arrest party – P. Krishnamurthy was innocent. Not an evening he'd chalk up as edifying. Perhaps in the hallowed sunlit years of his retirement he'd look back and smile at his foolishness.

The receptionist, bright hard jewels for eyeballs, said to him, 'What can I do for you, Mr Patel?'

'Room service still available?'

'Sorry, Mr Patel. Closes at ten.'

'I need some food. Please. Just anything. Some toast, plain rice, anything.

'Well, Mr Patel, they are making the night-shift staff something light. Would you like some of what we have? Nothing special.'

'Something light,' he repeated.

'Chicken curry and chapattis, Mr Patel. I'll ask them to send some up.'

'I'm very grateful,' said Patel, and meant it. All he'd had by way of sustenance since the morning at the toddy shop were a couple of canapés at the mayor's party, the Scotch, two cocktails and the whisky in Whitefield.

He entered his room, flicked the light switch on.

'You look a mess,' said Chandra. She was perched on his bed, still in her sari, a little dishevelled.

'Hello, Chandra.'

'You are limping.'

'It's nothing.'

Chandra raised an eyebrow. 'So what did you find out?'

'Excuse me,' he said, suddenly very aware that he reeked of rancid grease, petrol dribblings and drying blood. 'Let me get cleaned up while I talk.'

In the bathroom, he stripped off with the door ajar and summarised Krishnamurthy's story for Chandra.

'It's all the usual Bollywood stuff,' he said. 'P. Krishnamurthy is the owner of a chemical factory on the other side of the dam. She campaigned against his releasing untreated effluents into the river. Mortal enemies fell in love, started an affair. Though he's estranged from his own wife and family, he's still legally married, so they kept it a secret. He promised her he'd mend his polluting ways. She began campaigning about other issues.'

'So why was she at the dam that night?'

'From what Krishnamurthy has been able to piece together, from her comments to Bupathy on the drive, she was meeting someone with information about dodgy activities at the dam. Possibly Krishnamurthy's.'

'Ah, so she didn't improve him, after all.'

'Guess not.'

'So the killer knew about their affair, and lured her to the dam with some pretty sophisticated chat. My head's spinning.'

'And the only suspicious person near the dam was a bum on a bicycle.'

'This is getting woollier by the minute. I may give in to my aunt's wishes and go to her personal astrologer, after all.'

'What for?'

'He claims he can draw up the killer's natal chart.'

'That's not a bad idea, in the circumstances.' He was only half-joking.

Patel turned on the shower, stepped in, and let the hot water drum on his back, eyes closed.

Chandra's voice came alarmingly from the doorway. 'So why was driver Bupathy acting dodgy, different phone numbers and whatnot?'

'Bupathy runs a service for well-known, important people who want to keep their activities secret. He promises complete anonymity for ferrying them about town to secret rendezvous.'

'Ah, that's a niche service. I bet his car has blacked-out windows,' said Chandra. He heard her voice fade away and she left him in peace.

Patel felt the day's dust and disgust and disappointment slowly drain away. The hot steam fogged his brain into a soothing state of numbness. After several minutes, he turned the shower off, dried himself, draped the towel around his waist, kicked his dirty clothes into a corner and stepped out.

Chandra was peering through the little window. Its glass was frosted, barred with steel, locked and painted shut.

He said, 'In the daytime you can see the blank wall opposite.'

She turned. 'I was wrong about you.' She moved close and tilted her head.

'What were you wrong about?' he said, sounding croaky.

There was a knock on the door. 'Room service,' a voice called.

'Let's talk while I eat,' he said.

Two mouthfuls in, his tongue began to burn. He grabbed a beer from the fridge, that old English remedy. It was like pouring oil on fire. Nevertheless, he wolfed down the rest of the meal. It had always been a source of amusement to his university friends that an 'Indian' like him couldn't tolerate spice. 'But you eat it every day at home,' someone once exclaimed. He had to explain that, at home, Gujarati food was simple fare. Shunning meat, onion and even garlic, it tended to be more sweet than hot. The curries that came in varieties of hot, very hot and Mad Dog Hot were British-Punjabi bastards, probably unrecognisable to most Indians. Parts of south India, he now realised, were into British-bastard-hot.

A huge belch erupted out of him, much to his embarrassment. Chandra, checking her phone, didn't look up. He wiped the plate with the last piece of chapatti, ate it. Then he gathered up the detritus, took the tray outside, swung the door back and forth to air the room. Chandra leafed through the police reports. A sliver of waist at her back, and her long neck, exposed by the sari. Hair in a plait. Little hairs curled at her nape.

He finished fanning the room, shut the door, nipped into the bathroom for a quick rinse with mouthwash, wondered about the logistics of getting dressed. Should he take his clothes to the bathroom? Or brazenly and nonchalantly pull on his briefs under his towel, then discard the towel and put on a T-shirt and trousers? He didn't want to look like a prude by going into the bathroom to dress and at the same time he couldn't summon up enough suave to dress in front of her. Not very American buddy movie, he thought.

Chandra looked up from the file. 'I've been trying to tell you something since the party.'

'Oh yes? What were you wrong about?'

'I was angry that you showed up without us asking for help. And I have read about you and I have read between the lines of all the interviews you refused to give.'

'So?'

'Rajkumar and I agreed one hundred per cent to not co-operate with you.'

'Eh?'

Chandra's cheek twitched, as if she was trying not to smile. 'You've infuriated me since the moment I picked you up from the airport. With your superior resources, your superior morals. A white man in dark skin.'

'That's harsh.'

'Rajkumar asked me to keep a close eye on you. I would've gladly left you by yourself, see you fuck up royally all on your own. But hey, I had to obey orders.'

Patel needed to sit down. The whisky was wearing off. His leg throbbed. His head thumped.

'I wanted to ruffle your feathers a bit.'

'You did?' He sat at the edge of the bed, towel wet and chafing at his waist now. He kept his knees pressed together.

'So I got these goondas to ruffle you up at the slum. I was angry about your interference when I was questioning Bupathy. Sick of your sermonising.'

'Goondas. At the slum. You asked them to ruffle me up?'

'Just to straighten the creases. My thinking's this: here's an evil madman murdering innocent women. Time is a luxury. There is a difference between upholding the law and getting bogged down by legalities.'

He was still stuck on her last point. 'Did you just say you'd *arranged* for the goondas to beat me up?'

'Anyway, those idiots messed up. They attacked both of us instead of only you. And I appreciate you coming to my aid.'

'My pleasure.' He dripped sarcasm.

She came closer. 'And later, going off on the Enfield. Look at you. Taking such risks to your own life. Never mind it was a wild goose chase.'

He struggled with the main point. 'You hired thugs to beat me up?'

'Technically, free labour. They owed me a favour.'

And then she was crouching, hands on his cheeks. 'I was wrong about you.'

He wasn't sure what to think.

She leaned back, awkward. His towel! He sat up, clutching at his waist. Thank goodness, it was still in place.

Chandra was looking away, and down. Was she blushing?

'Hey,' he said. Surprisingly, he felt no rancour. Strangely he felt flattered that he'd affected her enough for her to hire thugs to thump him. He leaned forward.

She met his eyes again. For a long moment they stared, then they kissed.

Her hand tugged at the towel. He'd worried it would fall off in front of her, and now she was pulling it off. He grabbed her hand. 'Stop.'

'Take my clothes off,' she said, and the sari fell from her shoulder, revealing a very low-cut blouse. His mouth dry, he put his free hand on her shoulder, as if to steady himself.

Lust was a blind burrowing worm, spineless, earless, sightless, not knowing the head from the tail, searching into the soil. But he wasn't a worm and would not be consumed by lust. He ached in all kinds of places for reasons that momentarily eluded him and now a new ache began; he felt the biology trying to take over from the brain, felt the desire to ravish her take hold. Oh, to sink into the quicksand of oblivion . . . but there was a woman in peril . . . Chandra's blouse had little hooks.

He let his hand fall away, caught his breath, slowed things down in his head. Felt the tiniest easing. He was able to say, 'Should we?'

'Why not?' She pushed him down on the bed, lay her length upon him, groin against his through the flimsy layers of her sari. Then the swell of breast rose against his nose, her hands on the back of his head. He felt overpowered, then she slid down to kiss him again.

Like a rope thrown to a drowning man, his phone beeped.

Without ceremony she swung away from him, reached over to the bedside table and picked up his phone. Then, straddling him again, she held the phone with one hand, studying it. With the other, she fished for his balls in the river of her sari.

'Text message,' she said, now stroking his hard-on.

'Huhn.'

'Sarah. "All OK? Called a couple of times. Kiss." Oh, and another one from earlier.'

'Ah,' he said. Her thumb circled the head of his penis.

'Rima Seth. "Goldblum hiding something. Still digging." Two kisses.' Chandra smiled. 'Which one's the boss? Which one the fiancée?' Her hand now stilled, Chandra waited for a reply, her expression studious, still holding his phone with her free hand. All he could do was grunt idiotically.

Even as he fought to control himself, his phone shrilled in Chandra's hand. At the same time an A. R. Rahman ballad blasted from her handbag. He shut his eyes, and through almighty effort, brought himself under control.

His phone, still ringing, landed on his chest. He felt Chandra shift, leave the bed. When the throes of conscience and desire subsided, he looked at his phone. Number withheld. Chandra threw words scattergun into her phone.

'Hello?' He sounded, thankfully, like one who had been roused from sleep. He breathed relief it wasn't Sarah or Rima at the other end. Just an unintelligible Indian voice caught up in a panic.

Then the air went out of his lungs. The news seeped into his skull.

'Be there in ten minutes,' he said. He hung up and watched Chandra as the news sunk into her too.

All he could say was, 'Sorry, for . . .' He couldn't say what, so shook his head at having to apologise, for apologising was in his national character.

She nodded, distracted. He sprang from the bed and rolled into the bathroom. Chandra came in after a minute. Her sari was back on her shoulder.

'I'll go home, change,' she said. 'Meet you at HQ.'

He nodded, unable to meet her eyes. She left the room without meeting his.

Chapter Twenty-Two

The early hour notwithstanding, a gaggle of reporters and TV crew clogged the wide foyer of the police HQ. Head down, shoulders hunched, Patel swatted away questions as he ploughed into the building.

He was directed to the incident room, a long, wide space with a claustrophobically low ceiling, too many fluorescent lights and tiny windows. Chief Rajkumar presided, a fat crow at the front. Groups of policemen and women, some in plain clothes, huddled over desks. Someone stood poised with a marker pen next to a whiteboard. The smell of hair oil, reminiscent of his childhood, pervaded the air. Maps of the city were spread on some tables, locations marked. Laptops lay open with Google Maps and Google Earth switched on. Rajkumar relayed a series of instructions in a mixture of Kannada and English to nodding, note-taking officers.

Chandra, back in her no-nonsense salwar kameez, was involved in a briefing with some officers. She called out, 'Mr Rajkumar.' When he ambled over, she said: 'We need to draw up search perimeters. Nerumal here will divide the city into search zones and assign constables and volunteers to each. We will also issue bulletins through the press, asking Bengaluru residents to be vigilant.'

Rajkumar said: 'I'll pull men from other cases temporarily

to conduct the search. But what do we tell the press? There are even TV crews.'

He glared at Patel, as though he'd personally invited them.

'How did they know?' Patel asked Chandra.

'Her boyfriend.'

'Have we got his statement?'

Chandra raised her eyebrows at a deputy, who ran from the room. 'On its way.'

Chandra was called away by a subordinate with a logistics issue. Patel sank down into an empty chair at a table with a huge map of Bengaluru. He saw the vast suburb of Whitefield. His eye travelled west. He saw the markings for Koramangala, and the dense centre, ringed with Ulsoor, Shivaji Nagar and the beginnings of Jayanagar. In the centre, prominently italicised, were M.G. Road and Brigade Road, and within a mile, Parliament Road, featuring the offices of driver Bupathy's lawyer, then Senatoff Road and Eldams Road – where he had lunched – converging on the racecourse and the Gymkhana Club. He had read in the guide book that all the good pubs were in the Gymkhana area. He hadn't the slightest inclination for a drink, he realised, with some surprise.

The deputy who'd rushed out of the room came back waving breathlessly the boyfriend's statement. Patel skim-read the three-page yellow foolscap before starting over, reading everything carefully again.

Kadambri had come back from the party at eleven-thirty and told her boyfriend, Vincent Selvappa, that she had a lot of material for tomorrow's news story. Vincent was fixing them drinks when she got a call. She said, 'I have to nip out for a quick meeting. This could be important.' He was used to this. Kadambri was brave, ambitious and relentless in her pursuit of stories, and her job was her passion. She never switched her phone off, took every call. She would go out at all hours to chase up a lead. But she was not stupid. She usually took along a male photographer, or Vincent himself, to potentially dangerous situations. 'Want me to come with you?' he'd asked, regretting the two drinks he'd already had. She'd said: 'No no, it's quite safe. I'll be fine on my own.' It was obvious to Vincent that the source, whoever it was, wanted to remain secretive. He automatically, perhaps foolishly, assumed, given how relaxed Kadambri was, that she was meeting a woman. She had a special interest in female-orientated stories. Vincent was relieved she didn't want him to go with her. He wasn't a fan of chick talk. He went to bed around one, and was woken by a text message three hours later. 'Help me. I will be clothed in red.' It took him several minutes to understand. He tried her phone, it was disconnected. So he called the number on the police information poster stuck on Kadambri's pinboard.

Patel stared at the map on the desk, his mind racing. She'd been to the mayor's party. Was it someone there? Or was it an old acquaintance? He recalled her words at the tea shop. *Could be anyone. You, him, or him.* He went to find Chandra. She huddled in conference with Rajkumar at the other end of the room.

'Kadambri went straight home from the mayor's party,' Chandra was telling Rajkumar.

'How do we know this?'

'We found the cab-wallah.'

Patel said: 'I'll get a list of the guests at the party. We must search all their known premises.'

'Would stir things up,' said Chandra.

'So what?' said Patel.

'They'd be eager to co-operate or it will look suspicious,' said Rajkumar.

A constable rushed in and summoned Rajkumar to his office.

Chandra, alarm on her face, went with them, leaving Patel in the busy incident room.

Telephones shrilled. Policewomen and men answered. A mixture of languages assaulted his ears. A tea boy was collecting empties.

'Tea, sir?' he asked Patel.

'Please,' he said. He needed to ring the mayor, ask for his guest list. He looked around for a free secretary. 'Excuse me,' he said to a policewoman two desks along. She turned, hearing his voice, and he noticed the receiver pressed to one ear. She smiled at him. Patel smiled back. Her smile froze, then faded, her ear still on the receiver. Her eyes widened. She slammed down the phone just as the door burst open.

For all his bulk, Rajkumar gave the impression of flying over the desktops.

He said to Patel, 'Someone calling himself "Gentleman" has issued a message to the press, to six major newspapers. A personal message.'

'To whom?'

'To you.'

The stunned room gaped at Patel even as Patel gaped at Rajkumar.

'Sorry?' he said.

The woman turned towards him. 'Any second now. Fax is coming.'

An excruciating wait followed. In the strained air, Patel sat with his head down, his thoughts at a hundred miles an hour, catching snatches of English as the cops, Rajkumar and Chandra presiding, divided up search areas, assigned what to whom and determined how many searchers they could spare. Efforts were being made to track down Kadambri's whereabouts last night.

The policewoman waved a paper in the air. The fax. They all crowded around as Chandra read it out.

> *From within the depths of his eyes,*
> *One Manu looks out and recognises another*
> **Manu, Chapter XIV, *The Signs of Manu***

The arrival of Mr Patel of Scotland Yard is a sign – a sign of the righteousness of my work. Well done, Kadambri, in spite of your immoral ways and your smoke-clouded female brain, for recognising the 'Gentleman' in Mr Patel. He and I are cut from the same cloth. Now comes the time for ritual cleansing, preparing our bodies to receive our higher selves. Go and bathe in the purest Ganga, Patel, while I ritually cleanse this unworthy female to receive benediction. May she become elevated to receive the Goddess upon her. May she become worthy.

As the old song goes … *A woman is born to cry, a man stands tall as a sky.*

Every face in the room was turned towards him. Rajkumar broke the silence. 'Bloody hell, Patel, what have you done?'

'Me?' said Patel. 'It's the papers. I haven't said anything. They've made me up to be something I am not.'

'You're no gentleman,' Rajkumar snorted.

No one laughed.

'Wait a minute,' said Chandra. 'Looks like he intends to release her alive.'

'How do you gather that?' said Rajkumar.

Chandra quoted, 'Then she can become worthy?'

'It could mean anything,' said Rajkumar.

'But what has anything to do with me?' said Patel.

Rajkumar said, 'One thing we know you've done is sign the death warrant for that poor girl.'

'She's not a girl,' snapped Chandra. 'These are all women. Send the note to Dr Bindra.' She turned to Patel. 'He's our psychologist.'

Rajkumar shook his head. 'They found an unexploded device at the Meenakshi Temple in Nandavanam. Dr Bindra has been whisked away and is uncontactable.'

Chandra mouthed an expletive.

Rajkumar said: 'Mr Patel, please send a copy to your Scotland Yard experts. We need a psychological profile based on this note and all the case details, and after that we need to address this –' he floated his hand, searching for the appropriate expression '– this *bond* between the two of you, how we can use it.'

Bond between them. Patel wondered if he'd seen them at the party. Kadambri and him, chatting by the tree, smoking. Then Chandra and him, flirting, rushing out together. Suddenly afraid, he said to Chandra, 'You are not safe.' He wished he were saying it to her alone, rather than in a roomful of people. 'If he sees you – he probably already has – he will come after you. You're damned by association.'

'I wish he *would* come after Chandra,' said Rajkumar. 'That would be the best thing.'

'What do you think I am, Mr Patel?' said Chandra.

He couldn't understand why the room suddenly felt cold. Then he did. Chandra was as far from a pretty damsel as he was from a sodding knight . . . or gentleman. He'd seen her in action. A tough police officer, some kind of martial arts expert. And mentally, far tougher than Patel. In all probability, she'd break every bone in the killer's body before the asshole pervert could lay a finger on her. But he remembered what Goldblum had said about Sabah Khan. Her black belt in karate hadn't done her much good in the end.

Patel, sitting in his plastic chair, resisted the overwhelming urge to sink his head down into the desk. Put his arms over his head, beg mercy, beg leave. Go back to his quiet London life, resume his semi-anonymous, unremarkable existence, a life of dissolution and drink, give in to the inexorable pull of an unhappy marriage, all the while cursing the fate that stole his cricket career and stellar path, cursing his impotence in the face of the external influences in his life, which buffeted him high and low on the winds of chance like some grubby plastic bag, a plaything pawed at by cats like Sarah, Rima, Chandra, and now this murdering nutter.

'Right.' He made himself assume an efficient, neutral tone. 'I'll get this off to the Yard.

'Could you show me the photocopier?' he asked the friendly woman constable.

He faxed copies off to Rima, then rang her, well aware of the time in the UK.

She picked up on the second ring. Instead of a greeting, he heard a string of expletives. Eventually she stopped, fully awake, and he told her what had happened. She did not speak for several seconds, then said: 'I'll Skype you in one hour. I'll have Dr Brenner with me. He is our best offender profiler. I'll have him read the note and suggest how to proceed.'

Patel had forgotten how efficient his colleagues could be when needed. 'It's one in the morning.'

'You need your arse saving. And ours. Can you imagine the diplomatic nightmare this is going to cause?'

Patel muttered, 'See you online in an hour.'

'There is no internet,' said Chandra. She'd been standing by his elbow, listening.

'Excuse me?'

'Happens now and then. First world technology, Third World wiring.'

'Let's find a cafe with wifi,' said Patel.

'Coffee shops. There's a Barista and next to it, Coffee City or Palace or Universe, on M.G. Road.'

'Nothing closer?'

'We'll be there in ten minutes.'

The Barista was in the Wigan Building, a big department store. Chandra sprinted up the front steps. Forlorn unfurled umbrellas drooped over the outdoor tables set up in arena-esque concentric circles. She slowed down and stopped, visibly dismayed at the sight of the empty, unpeopled tables.

Not a fly or a crow, as the Indian expression went.

'Perhaps they haven't started outdoor service yet,' muttered Patel.

Chandra nodded, pointing at the order counter. They went closer. A notice read, *Open 9.00 till 7.00 Monday to Sunday.*

'Damn,' said Chandra. 'It's not even seven o'clock yet.'

Patel looked at his watch. 'Meeting in fifteen minutes.'

'Postpone it?'

'Every minute counts. We need to tailor a response.'

Chandra banged her fist on the noticeboard.

'The other cafe?'

'No,' she said. 'Only the chai-wallahs open so early.'

His eyes scanned the walkway across the road, the buildings behind it. 'Private houses? Businesses?'

'There are some houses behind the Life Insurance Corporation.'

'Let's knock on one.'

A sleepy memsahib opened the door to Chandra and Patel. Still in her nightie, she yawned, rubbed her eyes, then gawped when she realised it wasn't the maid or the milkman she'd expected.

'Police,' said Chandra briskly. She flapped open her ID through the gap in the door. 'We need to use your internet.'

At eight o'clock, the entire family, mother, father and three young children leaned over Patel and Chandra's shoulders. As Rima's face appeared on screen, seven-year-old Singh pushed himself between Patel and Chandra for a better view. Patel said to the smiling father Singh, 'Don't you have things to do, like getting ready for school?' He raised his eyebrows, gave a pointed look at each of the children.

'Ah, but of course,' boomed father Singh. He hustled his family out of the room.

'Hello, Rima,' said Patel.

She moved the laptop to include in the frame a slight man. 'Here's Dr Brenner, who's schlepped across town to be here.'

Dr Brenner gave a dry chuckle. 'The dead of night gives me a chance to gun my Audi down Gower Street.'

His tone turned serious. 'Now, I've not had long to study the letter from this Gentleman, as he calls himself—'

'The name coined by the media,' Chandra interrupted. 'He's simply chosen to accept it, as a kind of compliment.'

'Indeed.' Dr Brenner put his hand up, frowned. 'I'll do the interpreting, if you please, miss. Frankly, I need at least a day or two to look at everything before even beginning to draw up a psychological profile.'

'We don't have a day,' Chandra said brusquely. 'He's got a hostage.'

Patel said: 'Should I communicate with him through the media? Delay him, somehow?' Flashes of the horrors in the Yorkshire dungeon assailed him. 'What should I do?'

Dr Brenner pursed his lips and said sternly, 'It is really not a good idea to jump the gun and make assumptions based on a note and leap into action without a plan.' He glanced at a piece of paper in front of him. 'Barely a hundred words. I haven't had a chance to study each case, each scenario, all the details, which is what I'll need to do before beginning to draw the barest outline of his psychological make-up . . . '

Chandra said, 'Can you at least suggest something based on what he thinks about Patel? We faxed you the article Kadambri wrote about Patel with his note. That is all *he* knows about him. So. What does he think?'

Dr Brenner nodded for a few moments. 'Let me read all the material about Patel the killer's seen. It's all online, right? Let's reconvene in ten, twenty minutes.'

Rima picked up her laptop and came out into the hallway. 'I'm going to fix up some coffee,' she said, walking while carrying her laptop. It faced away from her. Patel had a view of the corridor that led to the staff rec room.

'Never seen it so empty,' he said.

'Everyone's out of town. Holidays. The criminals with cash are in South East Asia for some poontang.'

'What's poontang?' said Chandra.

'Pussy,' said Rima.

Rima was being provocative. She placed the laptop on a table, turned her back to them and made coffee.

Chandra engrossed herself in watching Rima make coffee as though it were a movie. A tap-tap off screen. Rima looked towards the door, which was out of view, and nodded. 'Be right there, John,' she said.

Chandra's arm brushed against Patel as she tried to catch a pen that had rolled away from her.

He heard the rattling of kids getting ready for school. The mum dashed into the kitchen on her tiptoes, and on tiptoes carried away a packet of bread, smiling apologetically as she disappeared into the bedroom to feed her children.

Rima and Dr Brenner were now back in her office. The psychologist wore a deep frown between his eyebrows, almost a furrow.

'Ms Chandra,' he said, 'I know you're lead investigator, and you outrank Mr Patel here. He is, I understand, over there in the capacity of a consultant.' His voice turned soft. 'I do not want to sound patronising, but please, will you be careful every moment, and perhaps you would consider, if you haven't already, asking your chief to assign you a bodyguard?'

'Why?'

'Because of your association with Mr Patel.'

Patel said, 'Chandra can take care of herself, doc, and hopefully me too.'

Dr Brenner frowned some more, and said, 'Regarding his views, I've read the newspaper article as carefully as I could in the ten minutes I had with it, and also the note. What's obvious is that this fellow loves the title "Gentleman". He feels that's exactly what he is – somewhat like, well, I suppose, The League of Extraordinary Gentlemen, who fight for the Empire, but that's me getting carried away.' Dr Brenner cleared his throat, took a sip of coffee. 'First of all, he's an Anglophile. He probably loves the colonial romantic version of British culture the Victorians sold to the Indians as something to aspire to.'

Chandra nodded. 'Here in the south, a lot of people, especially Tamils, prefer the old British rule to Hindi-speaking Delhi politicians.'

'But as you said –' Patel turned to Dr Brenner '– you haven't had time to reach definite conclusions.'

'Well I haven't had time and material to draw up his psychological profile and family background, but he's definitely an Anglophile, hence his attachment to you.'

'Because I'm British?'

'Well, here's the conundrum. I'd imagine an Anglophile would associate Britishness with a white-skinned person.' Brenner put his hands up. 'This is not my area of expertise. I'd like, in fact, to contact SOAS, see if someone there could shed light on this phenomenon. Anyway, even by Indian standards, Patel is rather, well, dark of skin. Moreover, Patel has a distinctive West Midlands accent, not quite the clipped tones an Anglophile, in the traditional sense, might idealise.'

'East Midlands,' muttered Patel. He was sure Dr Brenner didn't mean to be so personal, but he felt like a frog in a lab being dissected, his internal organs found wanting.

Dr Brenner shrugged, as if thinking, Potato, potahto.

Chandra laid a hand on his knee.

Patel said, 'OK, so I release a statement, from one gentleman to another, asking him to spare Kadambri.'

'Absolutely on no account must you make any kind of appeal. You cannot predict what a highly unstable person would do if he knows he can toy with you ... by toying with his prisoner. Anything you say might ... "encourage" him, the wrong way.'

Patel felt a chill at the word 'encourage'.

Dr Brenner continued. 'Give him twenty-four hours. In his note he is vague about his intentions. It is possible he might want to contact Patel again, and by then we will know more, and I'd have had more time to predict his next move.'

'You can do that?' said Chandra.

Rima said, 'What about *your* psychologists? Surely they'd have a better understanding of the Indian mind than ours?'

'We only have two,' replied Chandra, 'and they are tied up with terrorism cases. Anyway, as I said to Vijay earlier, the nature of the Indian criminal mind isn't all that different to any other criminal mind.'

'She's written a thesis about it,' said Patel.

Rima's eyebrows rose a millimetre. '*Vijay* is obviously getting an invaluable insight into Indian detective methods.'

Chandra smiled. 'You can study current Indian detective methods in your Victorian records office in the Black Museum. What we don't have in advanced technology and training we make up for in sheer numbers of moustaches and pot bellies.'

Rima bestowed a half-smile.

'So Vee-jay,' said Dr Brenner, 'my advice is to sit tight for twenty-four hours, and I'll advise you again.'

Rima said, 'Call me if there's any development.' The screen froze on Rima's blurry face and raised arm, and beside her, Dr Brenner's somewhat probing look directed at Patel. Chandra struggled to log off. Skype wouldn't quit. Then she just took hold of the laptop and snapped it shut.

'Sit tight!' she said. 'Great advice!'

'Your phone buzzed,' he said.

'Text from Rajkumar. "Press conference in one hour." She looked at him without expression. '"Bring Patel."'

Chapter Twenty-Three

Rajkumar had called the press conference in a dusty reception hall tucked away in the back of the building. Chandra's face reflected the tension in the gathered faces of Kadambri's rivals and friends. One or two women, in jeans and kurtas, had blotchy faces, eyes bleary with tears. Indian faces, he thought, so mobile, so expressive. They didn't know the meaning of the word 'reserve'. He imagined the women must all be putting themselves in Kadambri's sandals.

Rajkumar, waiting for everyone to settle, beamed a placatory smile upon both police officers and journalists. A technician tap-tapped a microphone. Was it really necessary? It wasn't that large a room. Then he saw the plethora of other microphones being connected. Good grief, television crews were setting up. This press conference would be broadcast.

He went up to Chandra, whispered, 'I hope this isn't going live.'

'I'm afraid it is,' said Chandra. 'I just had a row with him. He feels it's necessary to show we really care about getting Kadambri back alive. He cannot have the press turning against us.'

'He wants to show we care? He's treating it as an exercise in PR. Kadambri's kidnapper will be watching, too. Anything Rajkumar says might provoke him.'

Chandra muttered, 'He's expecting you to make a statement.'

'Sorry?'

Chandra pursed her lips grimly. 'Your name is on everyone's list, whether or not you wish it.'

Before Patel could reply, Rajkumar tapped the mic, signalling the press conference had started.

'At five-twenty this morning, we received a text message that a woman is the prisoner of the so-called Gentleman, who we believe to be responsible for the murder of four well-known Bengaluru women. We now have confirmation that this claim is true, and the missing woman is a respected journalist from *Indian* newspaper, Ms Kadambri.'

Kadambri's photographer mate, tears openly streaking his cheeks, put his hand up. 'Any leads at all?'

Rajkumar looked to Chandra, as though saying, 'You're the lead investigating officer, it's your territory.'

Chandra took a step forward to the microphone. 'We have police combing every street, every building in the city. Doing the best—'

'Assuming she's being kept in the city,' said one of the woman journalists.

'How do you even know she's still alive?' added another.

Chandra looked flustered. Patel knew she shared his doubts that Kadambri was still alive.

'He said he was cleansing her,' continued the second woman. 'What exactly is the meaning of this word, cleansing?'

'There is no reason to believe—'

Rajkumar stepped forward, interrupting Chandra. 'Let me handle this.' He turned his hundred-watt smile towards the gathered TV cameras bunched to the right. 'We have had experts go over the note sent this morning.'

Patel wondered when this had happened. While they were Skyping the British psychologist, Dr Brenner, was Rajkumar consulting an Indian one? Why wasn't he told? Why didn't

Chandra mention anything? He looked at her face, which wasn't giving anything away.

'We have every reason to believe Kadambri is alive and unharmed.'

An angry-looking journo raised his hand. 'Would Mr Patel answer a few questions?'

Patel tensed. Rajkumar, smile brightening, turned to him. His eyes held his, all glassy and slippery, as he said, 'I am sure Mr Patel won't object to taking some questions.'

Patel inhaled. An image flashed in his mind, unwanted, unbidden. Kadambri, framed by darkness, face beaded with sweat, flustered, waiting, her breath held.

The cameras swung to focus on his face. He exhaled. 'I'd rather not –' someone thrust a microphone up to his mouth '– comment on an ongoing investigation, especially in the circumstances. There is a real danger of prejudicing events.'

He raised his eyebrows involuntarily, loath to reveal anything at all that would twist the mind of the killer, give him ideas one way or another.

The faces of the journos looked unsatisfied and grim. They waited for more. They wanted something snappy, more worthy of a soundbite. Damned if he'd oblige. The tension hardened into something oppressive.

'Mr Patel, here,' Rajkumar said to the gathered press. 'We've been most fortunate to have him. By an enormous stroke of luck, he seems to have built some kind of rapport with this fiend known as Gentleman.' He bestowed a paternal smile upon his source of good fortune. 'It is Patel we have to thank for the fact that Miss Kadambri is still alive and well.'

Patel flinched. First unharmed, now well? Was Rajkumar an idiot, or was he in fact playing some psychological game of his own?

A glowering reporter remarked, 'Isn't it Mr Patel we have to thank, for getting Kadambri abducted in the first place?'

'Now wait a minute ...' began Rajkumar, at the same time as Patel said, 'I had no involvement ...' but Chandra's crystal voice cut through them all: 'There is no benefit from finger-pointing, or speculating about any of this. We cannot second-guess a madman's logic, and we certainly cannot hold Patel responsible for becoming interesting to this, this, creature.' She blinked.

As if she had realised something just at that moment, Chandra's eyes widened and flitted from camera to camera. Each of them feeding her image, her speech, live to millions of households across Bengaluru, including that of the 'madman', as she'd just referred to him. Her speech would be broadcast over and over till the next bit of newsworthy soundbite pushed her off the telly.

Patel had to stop her from saying anything else. He stepped up beside her. 'Well, let us do our jobs now, please. We will need to resume our search for Ms Kadambri. We will be in touch if there are any developments.'

'Or when a body is found,' muttered someone at the back of the room, low but distinct.

Chandra slipped from the room, head level, stride casual, but shaking with rage. He too was shaken up. He thought about dragging Rajkumar out by his over-starched lapels, slapping him a few times. Instead, he charged after Chandra.

Out in the corridor, he touched her shoulder. She turned, and they stood close to each other, without speaking, both lost in their own torment, when her phone buzzed.

He went to find some tea while Chandra took the call. There was a canteen two floors down. He only had to follow his nose.

A steel-and-plastic affair. There weren't many policemen

around at this time of day. All kinds of delicious fryums advertised themselves amid the usual sambar and curd lunch items. The menu was two feet long, and the print small. He got tea, ordered an omelette, procured a table. He took a sip of the strong, milky tea. How was he ever to go back to indifferent sarnies and polystyrene tea at Scotland Yard after this? His egg omelette arrived while he took a second sip of the tea. That's what the menu called it – 'egg omelette'. As expected, it bristled with chillies. He cut it into four squares and set about extracting the chillies from the first. Chandra appeared. She seemed to have recovered her composure. Briskly, she plucked a fork from the tin of cutlery on the table, speared a square of omelette and ate. She helped herself to a piece of toast, finished his tea for him. The sparkle came back into her eyes.

'The leads are pouring in. So many suspicious people and places. Locked and abandoned apartments. But nothing of use, nothing at all.'

'What kind of neighbourhoods are you focusing on?'

'The wealthy ones,' said Chandra. 'Purely because we don't have the resources to search every single household in the city.'

'I'd be surprised if the killer isn't from the same social milieu, same class, I mean, as the women,' said Patel.

'But you see, he could have servants willing to offer him their homes for his activities. He could have a safe house in a slum for all we know.'

'Is that possible?'

'We've had master–servant serial-killer duos. An Indian speciality. Admittedly, it's always the master's house where the atrocities happen. You can't sneeze in a poor man's house here in Bengaluru without the neighbours chiming "God bless you".'

Patel laughed, in spite of the circumstances, at such an English scenario in Bengaluru. Sarah always said 'Bless you' when he sneezed. An agnostic, she liked to leave God out of it. He still hadn't returned her calls.

'We need to split up,' said Chandra. 'I'll get you a car and driver. You can follow up half the leads, I'll do the rest. When one of us hits something solid, we'll regroup.'

'Sure thing.'

She patted the crumbs off her chin. 'I'll requisition a vehicle for you.'

'I'll come to reception after I make a phone call.'

When she left the canteen, he rang Sarah. The phone rang a long time and he listened to it amid the stainless-steel clatter of the canteen. Sarah did not like voicemails. She did not like leaving them, or receiving them. Sometimes she let her phone ring and ring, right next to her, if she wasn't in the mood to pick up. She didn't even look to see who was calling. Although, now, he couldn't help wondering if she had in fact seen that it was Patel, which was why she wasn't picking up.

Relieved, he was about to hang up, when the ringing stopped. A heartbeat. Then, 'Hello?' Sarah's voice, small, faraway, inexplicably cheering.

'Hey there.'

'How are you?' she said. 'I saw the news. No details. Just a line on BBC Asia. '

'Oh, honey,' he said. 'He's kidnapped this journalist. He . . .' Patel was going to say the killer was fixated on him, but he didn't want to utter the words. 'Anyway, we are looking for her. How are you?'

'I'm fine. Is this the journalist who wrote about you?'

'Yes.'

'He's keeping her hostage?'

'He hasn't made any demands.'

'That's a lot to take in. I don't know what to say.'

'Hmm.' He cast about for something to say, to change the subject. He thought of the crack in the swimming pool. 'You won't believe . . . ' he started, then stopped. It would remind her of their visit to the Turbine Hall to see the crack on the floor. They'd had one of their first rows that afternoon, and one of their worst.

Sarah spoke. 'I hope they find her before . . . well, it's awful isn't it?'

'Tell me about yourself,' he said.

Effortfully she related bits of news about their friends, a new commission, and after a pause, began telling him about a grim, brutal art film she'd seen, two violent brothers in Manchester. Then suddenly she stopped mid-sentence and took a deep breath.

'Yeah?'

'Listen.'

'Yeah?'

'When you come back, we need to think about things.'

'What things?'

'I've been kinda struggling, thinking about everything . . . '

'Excuse me, sir, Mr Patel?' He looked up. A constable, holding out his own mobile phone.

'Hang on, Sarah,' he said.

'Inspector Rima from Scotland Yard,' said the constable in a stage whisper. 'She says to get off the phone and ring her immediately.'

'Sorry, Sarah,' he said, guilty with relief. 'Got to go.'

'Oh.'

'Ring you later.'

'Sure.'

He stared at the phone, his brain struggling to process his conversation with Sarah. Did he just cut her off while she was breaking up with him?

He rang Rima.

'Patel,' said Rima. 'Listen. Alex Goldblum. He was in Bengaluru the night Sabah Khan died.'

'What?'

'He had ministerial business in Delhi till the day before. He was scheduled to fly out that evening. Instead, he caught a flight to Bengaluru. Then he took a flight in the early hours of Christmas Eve to Chennai, boarded the Chennai Heathrow BA flight later in the afternoon. Around the time you were burping Christmas pudding burps and sending me sexy texts. So he was in Bengaluru from six p.m. on Christmas Eve till six a.m. on Christmas Day.'

Patel thought hard. Things didn't add up. The idea of Goldblum as the killer was insane. 'OK, but surely he can't have anything to with the murders?'

'We haven't asked for or verified his alibis for any of them.'

'I saw him at Heathrow before I caught the flight, and the fourth murder was committed an hour before I landed.'

'Accomplice? Some brainwashed gimp, even a woman. I'm thinking of Myra Hindley.'

'That's not unknown. But usually psychopathic killers work alone.'

'You're assuming he works alone.'

'Yes.'

'You know what they say about assume?'

'What?'

'When you assume, you make an ass out of u and me.'

'I see. Anyway, right now, Kadambri is missing, Brenner's pretty sure it's not a copycat, and Goldblum is in London.'

'Ah, there you go with your assumptions again. Goldblum, at the moment, is in Goa.'

'Goa?'

'Yes, Goa. It's the winter holiday season in Westminster.'

Patel raised his eyes to the heavens. 'I thought they liked to make a show of holidaying within the country.'

'That's the summer,' said Rima. 'They have more than a few holidays, dontcha-know? Skegness is just for the photo op.'

'I got to collar him in Goa. Ask a few tough questions.'

'You're out of our jurisdiction.'

'So I can't go?'

'On the contrary. If Goldblum has anything to do with it, anything at all ... In fact, just because he was in Bengaluru on Christmas Eve and neglected to mention it.'

'Shall I say hello from you?'

'Clock him one, Patel. On the chin. I'll pick up the tab.'

'If that's an order ...'

'Don't mention it.'

He just made it to the airport as they were closing Security. Once he boarded the plane, stopped panting, arranged his limbs and kneecaps in the space provided, gulped the stale coffee and refused the extortionate plasticky pizza on offer, he spent the flight wondering how Goldblum could possibly have anything to do with the murders. Surely the office of foreign minister to Her Majesty's Government was a full-time job, and took up evenings as well as weekends? But if the man took ten foreign holidays a year – well, nine plus the one in Skegness – that implied he had free time on his hands. But a sideline in murder? Would he really have found the time to fly to India when the fancy took him, let alone choose and obsess over the women? And in India, Goldblum would stick out like a sore thumb. Someone would have seen him, the pink-coloured man on the streets of Bengaluru, stalking or drugging high-profile women who turned up dead. Maybe he did have an accomplice, a nice local who blended in with the young crowd, while the pink gargoyle lurked in his subcontinental lair. It was possible, with a stretch of the imagination. He thought of his own days. Every day he worked. He was supposed to be overworked. The police force was under enormous strain. Cuts, austerity, terrorism, expanding population, widening poverty gap, an influx of immigrants, rising hate crimes and racism. At least there were few guns in the mix. But what did he do? Dealt with homicide cases, most straightforward, routine, which meant domestic killings, from nine till six p.m. Then he went to the pub. Initially he'd done it to wind down. He'd have a drink, leave by seven, home by eight. Something quick for dinner, or a ready meal. A film or a TV show, bed, occasionally a bath or sex, even both. Weekends? He couldn't for a few minutes remember what he and Sarah did, or used to do, at weekends. Meeting friends, pub lunches, walks, Sunday roasts, visits to her parents or his, her friends or his, seeing a movie, going down the local, endless, grinding chitchat. Laundry, washing up, scrubbing that old stain from the carpet. Fucking DIY. When he sat deconstructing his 'busy life' like this, he could see that a lot of what he did through the hours and days of his life was social, not work. All the time he had was taken up by Sarah, his friends or family. Even given the workload, he had several waking hours to do as he pleased. Stalk a woman or two, teach her a lesson, cover his tracks. And the weekends. In fact, from Friday afternoon to Monday morning, he could go around the world on a killing spree and be back at his precinct nine a.m. sharp to start the working week. If he went west to east, London to Bengaluru, for example, he even saved time. It was like something out of the movie *Mr and Mrs Smith*. Smooth, sexy, easy.

And what about Dr Brenner's hypothesis that Gentleman was an Anglophile? Well, there was no greater Anglophile than a Tory minister, was there? The foreign minister, no less. When

Goldblum did the whole 'us against them' shtick, he'd put Patel squarely in the 'us' rather than the 'them' category. A couple of Englishmen against the native Indian hordes. Patel remembered even feeling absurdly grateful for being considered English, which *he was*.

Was he, indeed, about to see the serial killer, popularly known as Gentleman in the Indian press? Was Goldblum – sweaty, chubby, fish-belly-pale, teary-eyed distraught ex-husband, arse-licker of royalty – the killer of four, possibly five women?

Chapter Twenty-Four

The gauzy red curtains billowed in the damp winter breeze. Suppressing a shiver, Manu snapped the window shut. Kadambri stirred on the settee, curled her legs up to her chest. The boy watched silently from the door. He wouldn't come any closer. Manu went over to the settee, bent over the woman's face, her breath stirring the hairs on his moustache. She wore a mannish, dung-coloured khadi kurta that, when she stood, covered her flat chest and hung all the way to her knees. The white pyjama bottoms on one leg rode up to her calf, exposing curling hair on her unshaven legs. In spite of this, he felt within him the prickle of desire. Abruptly he straightened, and barked at the boy, 'Fetch the clean rag.'

He felt a more settled response towards the woman when she was gagged, propped up. Her bleary eyes struggling to open, she coughed and spluttered her way into consciousness, sounding like a dog with a chicken bone stuck in its gullet. Her medusa hair a mess, her desirability reduced along with her humanity. Just a dumb suffering animal.

She finally stopped coughing and shook her head to move her hair off her face. Her hands were bound behind her back. When her eyes focused, they widened with recognition. She doubled over, coughing and gagging once more.

Manu smiled. Already his mind was alive with ideas for this

one. Bold, beautiful. The offensive way she dressed her woman's body, the offensive way she disregarded her own gender, and yet, and yet, the potential within her. Yes, he knew what to do with her, even though it was sooner than he'd thought he would get to this stage. The ideas came in a rush and so thrilled him he wanted to discuss them with someone. The boy wasn't yet a suitable conversation partner. The wife was beneath his contempt. He eyed Kadambri, still panting and crying. Maybe the woman herself could appreciate what was on his mind. Dare he hope that she might see, share, a little part of his vision? She might even give him ideas. Kadambri was intelligent, after all, and the spark of creativity dwelled within her disgusting mind.

He removed her gag.

'You?' she said.

So she wasn't stupid. She knew him as he knew himself.

'I,' he acknowledged, 'am he.'

Dumbstruck, Kadambri stared.

'You play an instrument?' he asked.

Her eyes strayed over to the boy, who was watching her, his jaw slack. A touch of hysteria came into her eyes. It irritated him. She wasn't focusing. Perhaps he was giving her too much credit.

'Sitar? Veena?'

It took her long moments to work the question out. 'Little bit of guitar,' she said, finally.

Manu's lips thinned in disappointment. He should have known it would be something unsuitable. Enough talk with the woman. With her candid revelations of her disgusting habits, she would spoil his mood.

He reached for the chloroform and rag again when she said, whimpering and pathetic, 'Please let me go.'

'I will, once my business is concluded.'

A bit of strength came into her voice. 'What do you want from me?'

'I think the more relevant question for you is, what do you want of yourself?'

'Meaning?'

'Do you like yourself as you are?' His mouth turned down with distaste. 'Or would you like to be gloriously transformed?'

'Oh God, no,' she said, and began to whimper again.

'Come come,' he said, 'we were just beginning to have a nice little conversation. No one likes to talk to me. And I do so love a chat.'

'Please, let me go, and I'll write your story. Front page news. Without revealing who you really are.'

He put the rag down. Not a bad idea. She could write it now, send it to the paper. Tomorrow morning, when it was printed, he would transform her anyway. Manu did not hold to modern man's idea of fair play.

'Hmmm ...' he said, watching a little bit of hope seep into her eyes.

On the other hand, when the time was right, he would reveal himself to the world. The world wasn't yet ready for him.

'For a moment I was tempted there,' said Manu. 'But ... naaa.'

He stood up with the bottle and rag. Kadambri, succumbing to what was her woman's nature after all, began screaming like a fishwife.

The boy stepped into the room and slapped her cheek once, hard, taking her breath away. She turned her face from him and shrank cowering against the back of the settee. The boy giggled, enjoying the effect he produced in her.

Grinning, Manu uncapped the chloroform, poured a little on the rag, and clamped it on to the woman's face till she slackened. With the boy's help, he laid her carefully on the settee once more.

The boy stroked her swelling, reddening cheek.

'It will heal before she dies,' said Manu.

The boy nodded. He was adjusting quickly to the increased tempo. Manu felt the changes burgeoning in the boy too. Gaining confidence, finding his passion. Made him proud. But this wasn't the time for praise.

'That nature reserve you like to visit,' he said to the boy.

'Kodi Mulle, Papa.' The boy began playing with Kadambri's hair as he used to play with his sleeping mother's hair when he was a child.

'How soon can you get there and back? In the car?'

'Four, five hours.'

Manu reached into his pocket. 'Your friend will take thousands?'

Chapter Twenty-Five

Patel switched on his phone to a bombardment of messages from Chandra. He accessed voicemail, found to his relief she merely demanded to know where he'd gone. Nothing by way of new developments. He sent her a text: 'I'm in Goa checking something out. Explain later.'

Rima had given him the name of Goldblum's hotel. He hired a non-AC taxi from the airport, arrived sweating in his thick English shirt. He'd forgotten how muggy and oppressive coastal weather could be. The glum receptionist said that the minister had, indeed, checked in, but checked out within the hour. With all kinds of alarms going off in his head, Patel phoned Rima.

Rima said, 'The Konkan is where he used to go with his ex-wife, his secretary said. Did he tell them why he checked out so soon?'

'He said no problem at all with the facilities, just changed his mind, that's all.'

'Could be two reasons,' said Rima. 'One of them, I don't want to think about, even though it's my job.'

'He flew to Bengaluru?'

'Yes.'

'Other reason?'

'He checks into the same hotel as always, out of habit, but of course, it brings back memories of his ex-wife. So he checks out within the hour. Perfectly innocent.'

'I can't search all of Goa for a white man in the tourist season.'

'I'll call his secretary again.'

At Patel's request, the duty manager rang the night manager who'd checked Goldblum in and out. He came on the phone, told Patel he had personally put Goldblum in a taxi, and heard him tell the taxi driver to take him to the nearest five-star hotel.

How many five-star hotels were there in the vicinity of the Konkan? The two managers consulted each other, reached the consensus of six.

He acquired the phone numbers. The fifth rang the cherries. It was nearly ten p.m. when he arrived at the Taj Malabar.

'He's not in at the moment,' said the receptionist, glancing at the keys on the board. He could've been the twin of the Konkan's manager.

'Any idea where he could be?'

'Can't say.'

Patel showed the man his badge. 'Urgent business.'

'Sorry. Still no idea.'

Patel wondered how to proceed. A small crowd gathered. Scotland Yard, they whispered to each other. Someone said, 'Ganpati. I saw the firang talking to Ganpati.'

Patel's eyes strayed to the ubiquitous deity of hotel foyers, the copper Ganesh – or Ganpati as he was also called – in a secure cage surrounded by jasmines. A chubby bachelor, just like Mr Goldblum.

But then they produced Ganpati, who turned out to be the hotel concierge.

'That man firang,' he said, 'he want see some sights.' He

sucked on the word 'sights', a lip-smacking sound, making it mean something other than what it usually meant.

'Take me there,' said Patel.

Patel leaned on the back of the front seat, gazed at the dark, badly lit roads between the heads of the taxi driver and the concierge, Ganpati. The taxi fled the open, breezy beachfront, heading into the dark inlands on badly lit potholed roads. It was several degrees hotter than Bengaluru. The battered taxi had no air conditioning. Real India, he thought. The roads got more pockmarked, tighter, smaller, narrower, as they left tourist Goa behind.

A stillness replaced the nervous energy of the city and its inhabitants. It was just gone midnight when the taxi slowed, trundled past low, rundown, claptrap shacks veiled in darkness and stopped by the only two-storey building on that street. Patel stepped on to the street. Faint sounds of Western-style music trickled from the building. Screened blue light spilled through the gaps in the shuttered and thickly curtained windows. A small sign surrounded by a string of red lights, some of the bulbs broken: *Jamini's Dance Bar*.

'Payment?' said the driver.

'You wait.'

'I go back,' said the concierge.

He reached for his wallet, then changed his mind. 'You both wait here for me. Payment when I get back.'

'No, no,' shrilled Ganpati. 'I go back.'

'Payment first, then I will wait,' said the cabbie.

'You will wait,' said Patel. 'Then I pay you. When you take me back to the hotel.'

'I not understand,' said the cabbie. 'You pay.' He wriggled, made noises as if about to get out himself.

Ganpati spoke rapidly to the cabbie. Patel heard the words Scotland Yard and police. The cabbie looked grumpy. He said something. His tone suggested he was complaining, though Patel didn't understand the words. Making a decision without stopping to think through the consequences, Patel reached in around the cabbie's right arm and plucked the key from the ignition. He jingled it in front of the cabbie.

'Knock on the door if I'm not back within half an hour,' he said, and, ignoring the cacophony of complaints, strode to the bar.

The door to the establishment was opened by a man in a tight T-shirt and crotch-hugging jeans. He brought a hand up to smooth his waxed, incipient moustache. A chunky bracelet caught Patel's eye. With his wavy coiffed hair and a silver chain on his neck, the boy-man was a time-travelling romantic Bollywood hero from the 1980s. Any man in a whorehouse was either a punter or a pimp, and punters did not lean against the wall and say, 'May I help you?'

'Mr Goldblum,' said Patel.

'Who?'

'Englishman? Chubby? White? Where can I find him?'

The pimp shrugged, pointed both up and down the stairs visible in the gloom beyond, and just left Patel to his own devices. Patel supposed he'd simply have to go up and down the building, and search for Goldblum himself.

He went through a dank corridor, with an overabundance of gauzy curtains and incense, Britney Spears blaring though the speakers. 'Oops! . . . I Did It Again.' Thin linen matting, a clean but well-used look to everything. He imagined it was a high-class establishment. Every doorway was covered with a curtain. No doors in the house. Patel began the unsavoury task of peeping around the fabric. Youngish girls with dead eyes servicing pot-bellied, sag-breasted, middle-aged men. Mostly brown men. There was even a black man. But no white man. He returned to the hallway. He couldn't see where the pimp had gone.

Stairs went up and stairs went down. He took the stairs up and found an office. A woman sat behind a desk. She used her fingers to do her counting, an accounts ledger open in front of her.

She looked up, said, 'You want nice girl?'

She reached for a leatherbound book and threw it open. He saw photos of pouting, semi-nude women in the circle of light thrown by a low desk lamp. Patel was reminded of standing at a butcher's stall at a farmer's market, undecided. All those glowing hunks of reds and pinks, fresh dead meat. He shut the album, thrust it aside.

'I'm looking for a white man here,' he said, indicating one of the curtained-off alcoves, whose noises were drowned by Britney Spears's piercing vocals. 'Police business,' he added.

'The police are our friends,' she said. 'Owner policeman.'

Now the pimp's attitude made sense. He, Patel, looked like a policeman, part of the establishment, as far as the pimp was concerned. And it explained why the madam was sanguine, chatting with him.

'Yep.' He nodded sagely. He wouldn't let on that he was no friend of the Goan police owners.

'You wait,' she said. 'No disturb.'

Damned if he was going to wait for Goldblum while he screwed a whore. 'You,' he said, 'go and get him right now.'

'Wait,' she said, sighed dramatically, and left the room.

The Britney Spears number faded. The air filled with the sounds of unpleasant human braying. Whores faking enthusiasm. Punters getting a tad more than their money's worth. No wonder the music was turned up so loud, and no wonder the lights were so low, belying the Indian preference for bright fluorescent lighting. Without Britney, the sounds of loveless, masochistic sex would be bouncing off the brothel walls. Another song started up, 'You Drive Me Crazy', and thankfully drowned out the shrill agonies of sex once more.

The woman came back with a huge man. 'Who are you?' he said, glowering.

Patel brought out his ID.

The glowering menace on the man's face vanished as he studied the card. He grinned at Patel, impressed. 'Scotland Yard,' he said, savouring the exoticism on his tongue. 'Very nice.' He indicated the card. 'Your minister, regular customer, very good man.'

'Go, go,' the woman told Patel. 'In basement floor.'

'Take me there,' he said. He did not want to twitch any more curtains.

Reluctance in her countenance, the woman accompanied him. They went down the stairs to the basement floor. He waited at the entrance of the 'luxury suite' where Goldblum was being 'entertained', while the madam, all four foot five of her eminence, twitched aside the curtains and spoke in rapid-fire vernacular to the girl inside. He heard a whining petulance in the reply. Good Lord, he thought. How old was the whore? Madam finished her conversation abruptly, turned to Patel with a delighted waggle of her eyebrows.

'Man no good. Girl worried he will ask for money back. She is good worker. Not her mistake. What you think?'

'Tell her to scram. I need to get him out of here.'

'You go.' She gestured towards the curtain with a fuck-you attitude.

He'd read in a manual somewhere about the traits of homicidal psychopaths. Something about how they were impotent, more often than not, when it came to heterosexual encounters. There wasn't enough evidence or data to draw any conclusions about homosexual psychopaths.

He braced himself and twitched the curtain aside. Goldblum in the nude, saggy butt, rotund belly. Whatever he owned by way of family jewels under there certainly lacked both pep and presence. He turned wet, defeated eyes on Patel. Red drunk, and utterly steeped in misery.

No flicker of interest or recognition came into Goldblum's eyes. His expression of blank stupor did not change.

The whore, primping now in front of the mirror, her hair in a curly Amy Winehouse do, was impossibly gorgeous. As she adjusted her spangled costume and reapplied her kohl, she turned her youthful mouth in disdain as she said, 'Firang no use.' She shook her fingers derisively. 'I try, but he . . .' She shrugged. 'Koi faida nahi.' She turned her attention to Patel, looked him over. 'If you want, I come, you wait ten minutes.'

'Oh no,' said Patel, then it occurred to him that he was being discourteous, turning her down. 'Yes' would have been the right answer, for who could resist such promise and beauty and spangles? And with his British pounds, he was a rich man. 'No,' he repeated, as though to himself.

The madam shrugged. 'Take him,' she said. 'Go.'

Patel had to repeat himself three times before Goldblum stirred. To his relief the minister stood up.

'I hope you don't have any underage girls here?' he asked the madam as he waited for the minister to dress.

A righteous expression animated her face. 'Oh no, minimum age fifteen. This girl, very good, sixteen going to be, in fact.'

Once at the hotel, Patel marched up to Goldblum's room with his key card, leaving the minister to follow. It felt surreal, something from a farce. He, a lowly detective sergeant, having to drag the docile rat-brained, snuff-head foreign minister out of a whorehouse from inland Goa.

Patel felt the rage burn the edges of his vision so he couldn't see straight to swipe the key card. The muggy, oppressive heat of Goa fuelled him further, adding coal to a wood fire. When the light finally turned green, he stopped cursing, pushed the door open.

He marched straight to the bathroom and doused his head under the tap. He needed a cool head, literally, to handle this situation, to handle the drunk-as-a-skunk, high-as-a-kite stereotype of a politician Goldblum had turned out to be. Now a paedophile to boot.

He heard Goldblum collapse on the sofa.

The minister called to Patel, 'You want to see if there's any whisky in that fridge?'

The water trickled down Patel's nape as he emerged from the bathroom. The hotel room was three times the size of his. Goldblum slept on a bed that could sleep four. He sat in the middle of a sofa, letting himself spill to either side, engulfing all available space.

'You're busted, mate,' Patel said. 'Better sober up and answer some questions.'

Goldblum stared like a goldfish. Not entirely surprised, but infuriatingly smug.

Patel stepped up to the sofa, grabbed Goldblum's shoulders and dragged him to the bathroom, yelping. He shoved the minister into the shower stall, turned on the water.

The cold water hit Goldblum on the face. He choked and spluttered and wheezed. But he stood there without protest, his Savile Row creations soaking. In a while, a semblance of life came on to the minister's features. He stripped, soaked, soaped, rinsed. Patel left him to it, but stood by the door, struggling to contain his anger.

Goldblum towelled off and ensconced himself into a jasmine-scented dressing gown before seating himself back in his centre sofa position.

'I suppose you found out I was in Bengaluru on Christmas Eve,' said Goldblum, his voice sounding crisp again, the way it had been at Heathrow.

Patel nodded. 'Explanation?'

'Yes, by God, yes. Although it won't edify my reputation as a hard man, and it will certainly bely the stiff-upper-lip impression I've given since the divorce, how calmly I've handled it, how civilised the proceedings, etc.'

'I don't give a fuck about your stiff upper lip,' said Patel. 'Answer the question.'

'Watch your mouth, young man,' said Goldblum.

Patel looked at him disbelievingly. Was he for real? He stomped over to the fridge, got the whisky out, poured two glasses.

The minister sipped the whisky, rubbed his chin, sighed, began again. 'Thing is, I really was desperately lonely, desperately missing Sabah. In spite of appearing to be handling it well, I was not. Handling it at all well. I was terribly cut up about her leaving me. And taking up with that tennis brat so soon. And so young. And to get engaged. The worst of it, she looked happy. We weren't in touch or anything. I just followed her in the tabloids, Facebook, Twitter. Makes me cringe to admit it, but I created a fake Facebook account in the name of one of her London acquaintances. Royal acquaintance, as a matter of fact, so Sabah wouldn't dare refuse me. I pilfered a picture from the internet. Of course the woman already had a Facebook account so I simply changed one letter of her name.' Goldblum looked rather pleased with his cleverness.

'What name is this?' asked Patel, fishing out a pen and pad.

'Tallulah Jayne Spencer,' said Goldblum. 'I spelled Spencer with an "s"' instead of a "c". Sabah never noticed.'

Patel scribbled the name down.

'I kept track of her activities. I checked Facebook and Twitter accounts, her and her *fiancé's* –' he spat the word '– at breakfast, lunch and dinner, and once before bed. I was proud of my self-control at regulating my obsession this way. God, it was terrible. I took to eating more and more so I could spend longer on the accounts, in case he or she updated their status or spewed 140-character bons mots in that time. What a high when they did. Of course, I piled on the pounds. That's when the rumours about my health began to circulate. Just because I panted a little climbing up the steps of Westminster and a goddamn *Sun* journalist happened to be fiddling about nearby . . .'

'Keep to the story,' interrupted Patel.

'I was in Delhi on the twenty-third. It was agony, pure agony, having her so close in Bengaluru. Being able to do nothing about it. She tweeted about attending some local politician's benefit. Updated her Facebook status about how she stammered while hosting some celebrity game show. Then, a few hours later, she posted a picture of a badly parked car in front of her house.

'And when I went on Freddie's page there was a selfie of him and his Davis Cup teammates, thanking his sponsors, ITC Hotels, for hosting them during their winter training for two weeks. And my luck, as I was looking, a comment popped up from some fellow. "You are in Calcutta? Meet me for a drink?" Young buck replies, "Ha ha, will have to be fruit juice. Pop by any evening. Here till 2 Jan." Ah, I thought. He's missing Christmas with Sabah. Of course, she being Muslim, he being Hindu, no kids, and it being India, what did it matter about Christmas?'

Goldblum stared glumly at the carpet. Patel waited.

'At the thought of spending Christmas on my own in the UK, where everyone from Prince Harry to my bootman was holed up with their family, eating goose and playing Scrabble, it was more than I could bear. All I'd had were sympathy invitations from my Aunt Donna and Uncle Rob, and a half-hearted "do join us if you haven't got any plans won't you", from a couple of friends. I decided on a whim. It wasn't a rational decision. I rang my aunt and said, rather gleefully, that I had other plans after all, that I wasn't coming.

'I caught a flight to Bengaluru. My nerves were humming. I refused to think through my decision, however rash. What were the chances of Sabah being home? What if she wasn't in town? Well she was in town when I checked about the benefit and the parked car. She could be leaving to spend Christmas in Goa even as my flight landed. I obsessively checked social media. Not a blip. The crew got annoyed and made me switch off my phone. Anyway, the plane landed around six. I logged on to Facebook again and saw that she was at home. In fact, she'd had a hell of a time. She'd rung the police after noticing a burglar shimmying up the coconut tree by the side of the house. She shouted at him. The burglar escaped. But the chief of police himself came by to check on her. Coconut tree.' Goldblum shook his head. 'Can you believe it? I reached Sabah's house at eight. She was just—'

'Hang on,' said Patel. 'How did you find out where she lived?'

'Not hard. She gave me her address a month ago – as Tallulah, I pretended I wanted to send her an engagement present.'

'Did you send it?'

'What?'

'The present?'

'Uh, no.'

Cocksucker, thought Patel. 'Carry on,' he said.

'Well, she was shocked to see me. Not too upset. We were still on friendly terms, after all. I blubbered. She was sympathetic. She cancelled her plans for that evening. We ordered a takeaway. Have you ever tried Chinese food here? The Indians make the best Chinese. As foreign minister to Her Maj's government, I ought to know.'

'So you ate the takeaway.'

'Yes, and drank some Pepsi. No alcohol. She was Muslim about that, at least.'

'OK. Then?'

'Then nothing. I wheedled about sleeping in her bed.'

'She let you?'

'No, it was the sofa for me. Strictly no hanky-panky. She let me have a little cuddle though.'

'Then?'

'Anyway, I was more in control when I woke up. Got out of there before dawn, called one of those private cabs that come in seconds and drive at breakneck speed with the AC blasting.'

'Wait a minute. You left at dawn? She was—'

'I thought she was in the fucking bog, all right? I thought I'd sneak out before she came in and made a stink. Cos she always loved making a stink first thing in the morning. Get a man when he is down.'

He shook his head. Tears prickled his eyes. 'I thought we had a chance. Poor, silly old me. I thought I'd leave while things were good. That I'd contact her again, after the Christmas break. I was so happy. You don't know how many times I've beat myself up about it. If only I'd stayed, if only I'd checked . . . I could have just said, "Hey, you in the bog? I'm leaving, honey."'

'You were out for the count, you're insisting? Didn't hear her slip out, or hear anyone come in?'

'Nothing. Nada. Zilch. How I could've slept through whatever happened, I don't know. I wasn't even drunk. But then, I'm a heavy sleeper. You could drop a coconut on my head, it wouldn't rouse me. I mean. I'd been suffering from little sleep for so long . . . just seeing her, being enveloped once more in her scent, even briefly, had sucked me into such a contented stupor. Why didn't she wake me up? Maybe she tried to. I have nightmares where she is desperately clawing at me, trying to wake me up, and I sleep like the fucking dead. Except I'm alive, and she's . . . '

Patel waited.

'If only I'd the slightest inkling – I would've stayed awake. I would've pinched myself over and over, stapled my eyelids to my skull.'

'What time would you say you fell asleep?'

'About midnight. A dog yapped as I was drifting off and Sabah said: that stupid pommy always has a little bark at midnight. I smiled because she loved dogs. Even yapping dogs at midnight, she didn't really mind.'

'So you have no alibi from about seven p.m. on the twenty-fourth of December to five a.m. on the twenty-fifth?'

Goldblum silently shook his head.

'And you admit you were with Sabah Khan the whole time although you cannot be sure where she was between the time you fell asleep, you think it was around midnight, up until five a.m., when you woke up and called the cab?'

Goldblum nodded, eyes cast down.

'It's been established that Ms Khan was murdered between eleven and three a.m., judging by the contents of her stomach.'

'Oh, don't say that.' Goldblum put his hands on his head and groaned. 'Don't talk about her like she's a fucking cadaver.'

'Sabah Khan is dead. Murdered. And you've withheld vital information about your whereabouts that night. Information that puts you at the scene of the crime.'

Goldblum looked up from his hands, laughed outright. 'I'm a suspect now? Even the Indian police can't be dumb enough to entertain the notion that I'm the killer.'

'Even the Indian police? Be thankful you're dealing with me, Mr Goldblum. The Indian police would have you strung up and quartered, confessing to every fucking murder including that of Subhas Chandra Bose by now if they had a whiff of this.'

'You seriously believe this shite?'

Patel shrugged. 'Indians or English, we can only work with the facts. Fact is, you've lied, been caught out. You have no alibi for the whole night of the twenty-fourth. You had motive to kill Sabah. It could very well be a copycat. I'm not saying you killed all of them. Maybe just Sabah. So convenient to make it look like all the others.'

Goldblum stared speechlessly.

Patel enjoyed needling Goldblum. The police as well as psychologists on both continents had already established that Sabah's wasn't a copycat murder. Plus, if Goldblum intended to kill Sabah, why lure her into some stables where he could be spotted? Why not just do her in her own bed? After all, he was in there already. But Patel wanted to push some more buttons.

'How can you prove your innocence?'

Goldblum thought for a minute. His eyes sparked up. 'Of course,' he said, 'I bet you can't find my fingerprints at the stables.'

'Gloves,' said Patel.

'Surely there's CCTV at the stables. Isn't it part of the racecourse?'

'There is, but it's no better than a cardboard box. A fake.'

'But how on earth would I know how to put a sari on a woman?'

'You were married to an Indian woman.'

'You arrest me,' said Goldblum, 'I'll be out within hours. I have alibis for every one of those murders. And while you are resting on your laurels, he'll go and murder some other girl. And this time he'll indulge himself. Your mate. He'll do some nasty weird shit, and you'll pay, Patel. You'll fry in the media, end of career.'

Patel considered. Procedure was clear. He had to arrest Goldblum. The cocksucker was the only man with any direct link to any of the murders. The only fish in the net they had so far. But he was obviously telling the truth. Plus, he didn't know about the kidnapped Kadambri. Patel had glanced at the evening papers on the plane. News about Kadambri hadn't made it upcountry. Coverage on front pages included a political rally, a Hollywood actress's divorce, the Indian team's failure at the early stages of the T20 World Cup.

Patel made a decision. He didn't actually have the authority to decide Goldblum's innocence. He was flying by the seat of his pants, but hell, he was in India. Anything went.

'OK,' he said. 'Fuck off back to London, next flight. No more fifteen-year-old hookers.'

'Hey—' started Goldblum.

Patel pulled his good elbow right back, flexed his shoulder, twisted his fist, cracked Goldblum's jaw.

The foreign minister howled, fell to the floor, clutched his jawbone through the waggle of flesh.

'Present from Scotland Yard,' said Patel, and left the room.

Chapter Twenty-Six

Patel switched on his phone as the flight taxied in. Just the one voicemail from Chandra. Her voice flat, devoid of any emotion, as if stating a fact about something commonplace. 'They've found her.'

Following Chandra's directions, he arrived at the scene in an auto. Brigade Road was sealed off. The crowds thronged in front of the barricades, the news spread, thanks no doubt to gossiping policemen. He did not need to present his credentials. The cops manning the barricades recognised him. Of course, his fame preceded him. Famous once. Now infamous. They waved him through.

Some idiot, Rajkumar, he presumed, had allowed the press in. The fourth estate besieged him. Pelted questions, thrust microphones up to his face. One actually bumped against his jaw. Questions designed to provoke. 'Is this your fault, Sergeant Patel?' 'Do you feel you failed Kadambri?'

He moved forward silently. Ever more persistent and hysterical hacks weighed him down. 'Do you feel responsible?' 'Blood on your hands, Patel?' He was reminded of Mr Incredible, the cartoon superhero, caught in the underwater lair of his nemesis, the erstwhile IncrediBoy, now self-fashioned into Syndrome. Mr Incredible is pelted with black blobs that stick on him and grow heavier and heavier as he tries to run. Weighed down by the ballooning blobs, Mr Incredible walks, crawls then goes down on his knees and gives up. Patel knew that feeling as he fought his way to the domed building at the end of Brigade Road.

Battered but keeping his mouth shut, he made it to the second barricade outside the Opera House. The cops there raised batons to beat back the paparazzi, and he got through. Chandra waited at the entrance.

'How much do they know?' he said.

'Only what you do.'

'You've seen her?'

'Yes.' She looked down for a moment. 'It's different this time.'

Wondering what she meant, Patel stepped into the tent set up inside the barricade, placed to shield the building entrance from prying press eyes.

As he pulled on disposable gloves, his stomach flip-flopped. At the Yorkshire Dales, he had waited with the polite old man, sitting companionably at the kitchen table while the police took their time. He'd prayed, *Oh please never again*. The ugliness a human mind could devise. The twisted alleyways. And what did gender have to do with it? Having power over a weaker creature corrupted the best of men, and yet, he would have never picked *weak* as a description for Kadambri, or indeed, from what he gathered from the tabloids, Sabah Khan. That afternoon in the sleepy village of Thirsk he'd prayed, and hoped there was a God to hear his prayers and grant them.

Chandra tssked. 'The quicker the better,' she whispered. He realised he was frozen in the midst of pulling on his left glove.

Patel entered the derelict, once-grand building. Stony-faced policemen lined the entrance and the hallway inside. They all wore approximations of decontamination suits. Workmen walked past, carrying bulbs, rigging up lighting. They had to wait for the wires to be tidied.

'Why is it called the Opera House?' he asked Chandra.

'Because that is what it used to be. An old opera house. Belonged to the Raj. Then somehow or other it ended up as the property of one N. C. Ram. The man died in 1950. The government wanted to buy it for cultural preservation, or did, then, briefly. Anyway it's in some legal wrangle between relatives. No one can touch it till it's resolved and boy, wouldn't they all love to knock it down and build a multi-storey commercial complex. Real estate in Bengaluru doesn't get more prime than this.'

They were cleared to go in. Light drifted in from the unshuttered windows and from massive spotlights. Power lines had been run in through the windows, feeding from the generators outside. Row upon and row of moth-eaten red velvet seats circled a stage. All over the seats, layers of dust, decades of dust.

Upon the stage, a woman in a lab coat knelt, dusting for fingerprints. She shut her metal case with a snap that rang through the acoustically rigged auditorium. She got to her feet, pulled her heavy case with a grunt and slap-slapped away on her flip-flops, dust billowing from the rubber soles. Patel's eyes searched the stage. Nothing save the backdrop. A plastic sheet hung in front of a tantric goddess background. He could just about make out through the plastic the female figure and its fetishes, decorated in daubs of bright-coloured oil paint and flowers. Very kitsch. Not a backdrop he'd associate with an 'opera house' in the traditional sense, but he knew that art tended to cannibalise across cultures much like cuisines. He wondered why the forensics woman fingerprinted there, and turned to ask Chandra, but she had been accosted by a police officer, and was in the midst of a rapid-fire exchange unintelligible to Patel. No body on stage, nothing in the aisles or seats. But why did forensics fingerprint the backdrop?

Abandoning Chandra, he strode down the central aisle and

leapt on to the stage. Breath stopped, hand shaking, he pulled back the plastic curtain. He had thought it was a backdrop, a calendar goddess scene he knew from his school studies of the Hindu religion, and from coffee-table books about tantric goddesses. But what he faced wasn't a calendar poster or a blow-up of a Nepalese Thangka painting.

Raised up on a sort of dais, crowned, clutching instruments and fetishes, bedecked with garlands of sandalwood and surrounded by flowers, was Kadambri.

Like her sisters in death, Kadambri wore a red sari, and the hole in her forehead. That's where the similarities ended.

She'd been hoisted upright and pinned to an old cartwheel.

Concentrate on the details, he told himself. Look for clues to the killer's identity.

Chandra joined him on stage. Silently, they faced the tableau in front of them. Eventually, Patel spoke. 'What do we know about the wheel?'

Wooden, well worn, the iron axle parts rusted useless, long forgotten.

'From an old ox cart. Caretaker confirmed it's been lying here for over five decades, since the time opera had ceased and semi-professional theatre groups began putting on plays. English, Kannada, Tamil. Sivaji Ganesan played Hamlet here. All kinds of props scattered through the storeroom, prop room, in the area backstage: papier-mâché Grecian columns, ornate drapes, bicycles, all sorts.'

The wheel leaned upright against the back of the stage. Masses of purplish-red flowers lay on the velvet cloth. The cloth was faded so much it was more texture than colour. Kadambri's feet were propped on a plastic stool as if she stood on it. Tied with a piece of rope to her left forearm, a musical instrument, the tanpura, giving the illusion that she was holding it. The right arm raised, ring and middle finger bent down, presumably an attempt to indicate the goddess posture, offering blessings.

Chandra said, 'He's broken the fingers to get them to stay in that position.'

Tied to the wrist were some old palm leaves. He remembered those from renditions of ancient sages. Valmiki dictating the *Ramayana* to Lord Ganesh who scribbled it down on a palm leaf with a broken bit of his tusk, for instance. By her feet, in front of the banal plastic stool, hiding it unsuccessfully from view, he realised, was a bunched-up fluffy throw. He frowned at it. Or was it feathers?

'A dead, stuffed swan,' said Chandra. 'Clumsy job.'

Its neck flopped, the head and beak buried in its own feathers.

'We've been contacting all the water parks and nature reserves in the area, and even the neighbouring states, to see if they know anything about a missing swan.'

Patel said, 'If it's dead and stuffed, shouldn't you be looking at natural history museums? Why water parks and nature reserves?'

Chandra said, 'Pick it up and see.'

He put his hands around the feathery softness of the swan and hefted it up. It reminded him of childhood visits to petting zoos, the feel of feather and fur on alien, warm-blooded creatures. Except this one was stiff, dead.

The feathers felt soft and real, but the eyes looked funny. He realised they were dry and unreflective. Not glass. Real eyes. Dampness through the gloves. He held the swan upside down. The whiff reached him. The smell of putrefaction. He made a face as his stomach roiled. He felt the bird's underbelly. The stitches were coarse. The cotton thread was fraying. The flesh was shrinking. Straw poked out of the stitches. A thick ooze dripped, landed on his boot cap. He placed it back in front of the stool.

'How on earth did he get her up there?' Chandra said. 'It would have been tough for even a big strong man. And why is there no sign of a struggle?'

'Put the fear of God into her,' said Patel. 'He probably got her dressed and made her climb the stool, tied her up before . . .' He indicated her forehead.

So much for the elegant scene setting. Now there was no mattress or straw or pillow or riverbed to soak up the contents of the dead woman's head. Kadambri's exploded brain had dripped through her hair and along her back, dribbled down the spokes of the wheel. A puddle of congealing blood and brain matter had collected on the stage, seeped into the rotten floorboards.

Patel took a step back.

'Careful,' said Chandra. 'My foot went through over there.' She pointed to a bit of the stage floor, the hole now covered with a piece of yellow police tape.

The sight of Kadambri's bare feet upon the plastic stool was a knife through his gut. Did she plead with her killer as she stepped on to the stool? Did she promise sex, promise silence, issues threats, enumerate her big connections in the police who would hunt him down and seek revenge? Did she pretend her boyfriend would search out Gentleman and tear him limb to limb? Ah, the irony. The goddess she represented would have torn Gentleman's head from his shoulders in an instant. But Kadambri, with her hippy kurtas and cigarette habit, was all too mortal.

Chandra's voice at his shoulder. 'We're looking at what vehicles came and went in the last twenty-four hours.'

Patel saw a thin trickle of dried blood from Kadambri's dirty foot along the side of the stool. 'Did you notice this?' Patel asked Chandra. 'She must have stepped on a nail, a spike or a piece of jagged broken floorboard. Scratched her foot. Perhaps she walked barefoot in his lair. We might have some clues from forensics.'

'If only we could bring over the CSI like we brought you,' she said. 'Our Bengaluru forensics team are more like bears in woods. Wouldn't recognise their own shit if they came upon it.'

'Do it anyway.'

Chandra sighed and rolled her neck. 'I'll double check if they've taken swabs. But you know, they did once file their own fingerprints after forgetting to wear gloves. The whole team.'

Patel cracked a pained smile.

She held out her hand. In it a piece of crumpled paper. 'I was saving this for you. I'm afraid Rajkumar saw it before I did.

'Where'd you find it?'

'Clenched in Kadambri's fist.'

He uncrumpled the paper. Grey fingerprint dust blew. A torn scrap, ruled in blue lines.

'It tore while we were trying to pull it from her hand,' she said. 'But it's all there is.'

He read.

Patel. You are the only one, I fear, who can SEE.

Patel's skin turned cold, in spite of the humidity of the day, the dry heat inside the Opera House. It felt as though the killer was continuing a conversation he had started with Patel – like old friends, picking up where they'd left off the last time they'd met.

Chandra spoke. 'Probably written by Kadambri. A copy is on the way to her boyfriend for confirmation.'

'And the paper?'

'From a school notebook bought at any corner shop.'

He looked over the body once more. Kadambri's arms were tied to the spokes with ropes. A sash went around her waist and tied back around the middle of the spokes. On her forehead, slightly askew, an old tiara, gilt with fake bright gems.

'The caretaker said there were hundreds in the costume cupboards, or he could have bought it from any shop.'

The tiara was old and cracked, made of metal, not plastic. Patel was reminded of his little niece, obsessed with *Frozen*, the Disney film. Every time he saw her, she insisted on donning her Queen Elsa outfit, complete with sparkly shoes and tiara. She'd decided, at the tender age of three, that it was the only way to dress, to socialise, for going anywhere, to do anything. She needed her Elsa dress and tiara like she needed skin or hair.

They turned away from the elaborate scenario laid on stage for him. (Oh, *all this just for little old me*, a voice shrilled inside Patel. Oh, *it's too much, you shouldn't have*.)

Chandra nodded at some policewomen. They'd been waiting for Patel's inspection of Kadambri's corpse. Now they could commence the task of separating her from the cartwheel and her goddess's fetishes.

He spied a familiar figure among the police. Rajkumar. He seemed strident about something.

Chandra noticed Patel looking. 'More bad news. Rajkumar's called another press conference.'

'It's too soon.'

'Why?'

'We need to judge what information we give to the press. First consult Dr Brenner and Dr Dinesh. It might be possible to devise a press item that would provoke the killer, make him reveal something about himself.'

'You don't understand, Patel. Before you arrived, people in Bengaluru were grumbling. The rich and powerful were mildly worried that their women could be in danger from Gentleman. The morning you landed, the fourth woman was murdered. Just three days later, number five. He's speeding up. He has all the time in the world while we are drowning under all the work. We don't know where to look, so we've been looking everywhere. Rajkumar is under great stress. I've never seen the man sweat before. He needs to appease the wealthy. And the press. One of them is now a victim. They're going to tear us apart. We need the fucking PM to issue a statement expressing confidence in us. You know, Modi flew to New York to do one of his stage shows, Bollywood-style razzmatazz, yesterday, and the audience and press grilled him about our inability to catch Gentleman. The fucking NRIs think they'll be targets next. A lot of their women visit relatives in India every winter. The situation, I'm afraid, is escalating. Rajkumar depends on this press conference. He's even called the BBC and Reuters.'

'What is he hoping to achieve?'

'Self-preservation. He's been police chief for over a decade now. That's several lifetimes in this profession. He knows how to play everyone. I'm afraid you aren't going to like this.'

'Me?'

'I reckon. Perfect putz, fall guy. You take the hit when things go wrong. And when Gentleman's caught, he'll take credit. You'll drown in the shit, but he'll come up smelling like roses.'

'Fuck,' said Patel.

'Is right,' said Chandra.

Outside the Opera House, under a eucalyptus tree, serenaded by a bunch of crows perched on its branches, Rajkumar gave his statement. Every effort, sincerest condolences, sympathies with the family, difficult time, no stone unturned, promising leads, new information. Thankfully, he didn't give out the details of how Kadambri was found, the extra elements to the latest murder, but Patel knew the juicy details would make their way into all but the dourest of the newspapers. Too many people – cops, forensics, the caretaker – had seen the stage show Gentleman had arranged. Being India, any friend or cousin of a policeman had probably been to view the entertainment even before Patel's flight from Goa had landed.

Rajkumar wound his speech down and asked if anyone had any questions.

'Could you tell us what new information you have regarding the murders?'

'Well, it seems Gentleman has made a friend, our esteemed colleague who's come all the way from Scotland Yard to help us. The special bond they have is the reason he targeted poor Ms Kadambri. He was attracted to her due to the newspaper article she wrote about Mr Patel here. Gentleman seems keen on communicating with Mr Patel. In fact –' Rajkumar smiled a smile of grim distaste '– it seems he targeted Kadambri specifically to impress Mr Patel. We are working on ways to use this connection to our advantage. I hope you have the sense to not print this, yes? I'm only telling you because, as friends of Kadambri, you all deserve to know exactly what's going on, and that we are taking concrete steps to catch this, this creature that calls itself Gentleman.'

Oh boy, Patel muttered. He took a breath, but before he could release it, he found his collar grabbed by a fist.

The fist belonged to the photographer friend of Kadambri's. He didn't seem as full of bonhomie as when Patel had first met him at the tea shop.

'You did this,' said the man. Silence all around. No one took a photo. Of course. He was one of theirs. Anger on some of the watching faces. Towards Patel. 'It's sick. A bond with a perverted killer.'

'I didn't choose it.'

'What's the point of having you here, if every woman who talks to you becomes the next victim?'

'Not every woman,' said Patel.

'Oh yeah? You've been here, what, two days? How many women have you talked to?

'Three,' said Patel, his eyes straying towards where Chandra stood, her face expressionless, colourless. Was she petrified, he wondered, or perplexed? She ought to put hundreds of miles between herself and him. Instead, Chandra strode over and wrenched the photographer's hands from Patel's collar, and the next instant, he was bent double, clutching his midriff.

Rajkumar said, 'OK, I think we are letting our tempers get the better of us here.' But beneath his cross-daddy demeanour, Patel saw that Rajkumar was pleased. He'd succeeded in his plan, Patel guessed. Tomorrow's papers would hail brown-skinned firang as the new public enemy number one.

Chapter Twenty-Seven

In silence, Patel and Chandra made their way back to HQ, and marched up to an empty office.

'Where were you?' she said, shutting the door.

Patel told her about Goldblum.

She didn't interrupt once. When he finished, she didn't speak for long moments. He could see the fury building up in her. Oh dear, he thought, here we go. It was then he remembered what Goldblum had said, just before Patel punched the daylights out of him.

'Wait, before you tell me how pissed off you are, Goldblum said something important. That Rajkumar personally went to Sabah's house after she called to report a burglary attempt. Just hours before she got killed.'

He could see it took Chandra an effort to focus on his words. Visibly swallowing her anger, she said: 'So what? I know about the burglar. Probably a child or a young man sent up the tree. Standard practice – to jump on to a balcony, hoping for an unfastened door. Rajkumar going around there is no big deal. She was an important woman.'

'The other thing I've failed to mention is that Bupathy saw a man on a bicycle with a gunny sack coming back from the dam.'

'Are we so desperate,' said Chandra, 'that our attentions

are turning to the chief of police and some peasant on a bicycle? Go do some real police work, Patel.' She stalked from the room.

Patel spent the rest of the day, together with a translating constable, interviewing some of Kadambri's friends and family, plus the caretaker and others with access to the Opera House. No one knew anything, saw anything, had suspected anything.

Dumping all the useless transcripts on some poor secretary's desk, he began reviewing lists of the material from the scene, and the attached pictures. Everything could have come from the storage rooms or the prop room. Nothing seemed out of place, left accidentally. A team of forensic investigators was analysing the footprints, firstly to isolate new prints from those of the police and the caretaker, then to match them with footprints from the other crime scenes. There were a couple of promising prints right next to the stool where layers of soft powdery dust had settled to give a perfect template for someone's soles. But this wasn't a Cinderella story. They couldn't take the prints to each and every man wearing shoes in the city.

The call he expected, of course, every hour on the hour, in the midst of his fruitless flailing, was an official one. And it came just after he was brought the evening papers.

GENTLEMEN IN LOVE, read one banner headline, with a grinning Patel from his Australian cricket touring days. GO HOME, PATEL, said another, the picture of him taken at the press conference, his doubts about his own credentials, his uncertainty in this foreign place, and the horror of it all, writ plainly on his countenance. A special printing of *The Indian*, Kadambri's paper, led with an exclusive interview with Rajkumar: PATEL LED GENTLEMAN TO KADAMBRI, CLAIMS POLICE CHIEF.

He read the article.

'We are fortunate,' says Chief Superintendent Rajkumar, 'that Mr Patel has flown in all the way from London to lend us his expertise. It is possible that because of the coverage in the media, the killer known as Gentleman took a fancy to Mr Patel. A special bond, shall we say, developed, although wholly from his side. I'm sure I believe Mr Patel did not reciprocate. It is Miss Kadambri's article about Mr Patel that brought both to the attention of Gentleman. Of course, it doesn't mean that any woman associating with Mr Patel is in danger, or that this feeling of admiration for Mr Patel is reciprocated by Mr Patel. Quite the contrary, no doubt about it. But what we had thought as an advantage, this focus on Mr Patel by the killer, turns out unfortunately to be encouraging him and resulting in him speeding up. So, I'm afraid we are back to the drawing board, reviewing strategy, and of course, following up some very good leads, which, you will understand, I cannot discuss.' Mr Rajkumar refused to answer any questions about Mr Patel, but in the end, relented, and answered just one. When asked if he could provide a specific instance of Mr Patel having proved useful or necessary to the investigation, Mr Rajkumar struggled, thought long and hard, and finally said, 'Well, I cannot go into such details. At the very least his presence as a representative of the esteemed Scotland Yard boosts our average constable's morale. Plus, of course, everyone's a cricket fan.'

Patel groaned and put his head on the desk. The constable tut-tutted sympathetically. Hesitantly, she said, 'Chief Rajkumar requests your presence in his office when you finish reading the papers.'

'Did he send the papers?'

'He did.'

It was a long and dreary walk up two floors and around the winding corridors. Everyone he passed looked at him and looked away.

He entered Rajkumar's office and, before the chief could speak, said, 'I'll be leaving first thing in the morning. I do not think it is appropriate for me to still be involved in this investigation.'

'Good decision, Mr Patel. Saves me from having to spell it out for you.'

Patel turned to go, paused. 'Chandra is an excellent officer. She can directly liaise with the technical experts at Scotland Yard. I'm sure Inspector Rima Seth will ease her way. She doesn't need my help in conducting homicide investigations.'

'Thank you for the vote of confidence, Mr Patel.'

Patel nodded and walked out.

While he was snapping shut his laptop, Chandra burst in. 'Hey, take a look at this.' She opened a purple personalised Apple Mac and clicked on something.

'Chandra, I just met . . . '

'They cracked the password in minutes, can you believe it?'

'Who?'

'The police hackers. Hard at work sniffing at potential terrorists' home computers and Twitter accounts. Don't ask how I even got to know where they were holed up. Took an hour, across town. I had to promise sexual favours to three senior police officers. No. Just kidding. I said I'd hound them day and night. Didn't they see the news about the fifth fucking Gentleman killing? Anyway, the bastards took two minutes to crack the password and two more to open the encrypted, deleted sex video from Kadambri's laptop. Can you believe it? It was deleted from the trash can! Permanently deleted. And they fished it out of there like fishing out a last chip from a bag of Ruffles.'

'Chandra, I'm done here.'

'Look,' she said, and turned the laptop around to face him. There was no audio. The video quality was poor. A shaking camera. Handheld. No surprise, it was from a phone. A poor-quality phone camera. A flash of flesh. A naked man running around the room laughing. Then he turned and ran straight at the camera, collided in a blur. The phone fell on the bed and the focus worked automatically to correct itself. The ceiling fan came into view. Then the screen moved. The phone was picked up. The man made a face at the camera and smiled winningly. He moved it to show a bottom – from the curvature it appeared to be a woman's. Beyond, a head of hair lifting and thrashing on the pillow. An arm, knotted, muscular, across the woman's body, holding it down. The same arm then propped the camera a couple of feet away and slowly, excruciatingly slowly, rubbed the squirming female bottom and then gave it a stinging slap. The woman erupted at that. Something fell over the phone and covered it. After a few seconds, the phone was uncovered. Focus back on the ceiling fan. It ended.

'So that is Kadambri and her boyfriend?'

'Yes,' said Chandra. 'You see, the making of a sex video connects two of the victims. Laxmi and Kadambri.'

'But I'm the connection between Kadambri and the killer. I'm afraid it's impossible for me to be involved in this investigation.'

'We haven't checked if the other ... what? Where are you going?'

'Back to the big smoke. Just had a chat with Rajkumar. He agrees.'

'You can't go. This is the first real clue we have.'

'You're doing fine without me, Chandra.'

'Oh,' said Chandra, her voice small. 'You really are going?'

'Yep. Early-morning flight.'

'Back to your girlfriend?'

'Just back to where I belong,' he said. He zipped up his laptop and got up. 'Sorry Chandra. To leave this business unfinished.'

She shrugged. 'She is very beautiful. And she must be very worried about you getting involved . . . in this.'

He knew she meant his involvement with Gentleman, not her, Chandra. He pulled the files into his bag and was about to click it shut, but let the bag drop down, still open.

'How do you know she's beautiful?'

'I googled her,' said Chandra, her chin raised up, defiantly. 'I came across her website. I was just curious. I needed a break from the useless interviews and trawling through the phone-in leads. You won't believe what these morons mark up as viable tips to be followed up.'

Patel sat back down. 'You googled her, saw her pictures.'

'Yes, and her sculptures. Interesting.' Chandra nervously tucked her hair behind her ear. 'There must be a market for racy sculpture, no?'

'It's not . . .' he started, then stopped. 'You know, did I tell you what Goldblum said to me? He stalked Sabah Khan and her fiancé on Facebook and Twitter—'

'I wasn't stalking her.' Chandra looked horrified.

'No, let me finish. He stalked them online under a false name. That is how he found out that Freddie Bhatt had left town and that Sabah was on her own.'

'Oh yeah? Did she make a sex video with Goldblum, do you think? Probably not. The tennis star though, he's ripped.'

'You aren't listening,' snapped Patel. 'These women were all active on social media. The killer could be on their Facebook or Twitter contacts. He might have lured them in using a false ID. If you can get one of your hotshots to track down any false IDs from these women's friends lists, it might lead us to the same person. Chances are, the killer being wealthy, suave, Anglophile, he's also an internet geek. Goldblum isn't an IT expert, but he was able to easily open fake Facebook and Twitter accounts and intercept specific information about the whereabouts of Sabah and her fiancé.'

'Even my mother can do that. But to find the real identity of someone who is using various false IDs—'

Patel interrupted, 'One easy way to check is to find out which accounts have been deleted soon after the deaths of the women, and see if they lead to the same person. We need to check where the messages were coming from, IP addresses where accounts were created and so on. Existing and ex accounts.'

She sat down with a sigh. 'Patel, Indians have thousands of Facebook friends. I have no IT help at all, to trawl through all the . . .' She trailed off. 'Unless . . .'

'I'm pretty sure Scotland Yard is going to put as much distance as possible between you and them after this fucking fiasco I've created. But they might give you some pointers. Maybe, if Rima—'

'No,' said Chandra. 'There is someone with the expertise. I know him. He's just a kid but a genius.' She laughed. 'It was his Enfield Bullet you ruined, in fact.'

'The mayor's son? Or has he got another one?'

'No, he's got just the one son. He's autistic. At least I assume he is. They are a bit sensitive about him. He can behave very differently from day to day.'

'Gosh, that kid from the party?'

'He's eighteen,' said Chandra.

'He rides a Bullet. And he's a computer genius.'

'He is strange but sweet. I'll ring him and ask.'

'You better get Rajkumar's permission first, though. He's an outsider. Confidentiality and all that?'

Chandra pursed her lips. 'The mayor and Rajkumar aren't exactly great pals. He wouldn't be a fan of the idea.'

'Back-door policy.'

'Exactly.'

'Are you sure you can't get help from some grown-ups?'

'No chance. They changed the locks on the building after I left today.'

'You had keys?' He was impressed. She had keys to the top-secret building where they hacked IT systems of potential terrorists.

Chandra shrugged, dismissive of her own resourcefulness.

'What about the mayor?'

'Oh, Uncle will be glad to help. It will keep his son from sitting in the living room and obsessively picking his nose.'

Already raring to go and hunt the annals of the internet with the whizz-kid genius, she began scrolling her address book. 'I'll come and see you in London. I'm applying for an exchange programme next year.' She winked, putting the phone to her ear. 'You'll be married and bouncing babies by then.'

A feeling of horror came over Patel at the image her words conjured up.

'Well, good luck, Chandra,' he said, his tone casual.

Chapter Twenty-Eight

Patel was running low on vodka. The fifth time the same breaking news aired on BBC World, he decided he'd had enough of the American president's latest outrage and switched the telly off.

He'd come back to the hotel and rung Rima. She told him Dr Brenner agreed he had to remove himself from the picture. His bond with the killer meant any further involvement was unsustainable.

His flight to Heathrow was at nine in the morning. Time stretched in front of him with no prospect of sleep. Everyone got on with important work while he loitered fruitlessly. Somewhere the sophisticated Indian murderer of women stalked his next victim. But all that was out of his hands. He imagined sighs of relief all around. Patel off the case. If – *when* – the bastard was caught, Rajkumar could claim credit without an upstart impinging on his glory. Chandra could continue to break the law in her own inimitable fashion, without frowny-face Patel looming over her. Skinner would have the satisfaction of seeing Patel fall from grace, something he'd wanted for the last three years. Goldblum, too, would be jiggling his belly in relief, for a discredited Patel would be in no position to make accusations about his involvement with Sabah Khan on the night of her murder, or about his dalliance with underage prostitutes in Goa.

He scratched forlornly at a mosquito bite. Should've brought a book. His eye strayed towards the reading material he already had, the case files in his Billingham bag. He would have to take them back. Couldn't be arsed to return them to the Indians, and couldn't bring himself to dump them. Each case file was a document of a life snatched unfairly.

A knock on the door. A skinny Indian gofer handed him a package wordlessly, then left. He opened it and the red spilled out. He froze. Was this from his new friend? A red sari and blouse. He looked for a note. Then he remembered asking to be sent one of the saris. The relief made his knees wobble. He sat on the edge of the bed, took the material out of the package. He looked at the straight stitching on the blouse. He was reminded of his mother's blouses, which he wouldn't touch as a child. They were a fastidious family. Somehow, the idea had seeped into him that women's clothes were shameful. Traditional clothes, that is. He had no problem touching Sarah's clothes. He now realised that fact had added to the sense of discomfort when Chandra had been with him. Certainly he had been aware of the unprofessionalism of being intimate with a colleague, especially a liaising foreign one. On top of that, he was cheating on his fiancée. But the real kernel of his discomfort came from the fact that his smutty assignation was with somebody who wore a version of clothes he associated with his mother, the clothes he had considered shameful to touch as a child.

Patel rubbed his nose like he used to when he was young and in trouble for some minor prank. He admitted to himself that he was, at some level, a fucked-up individual.

He fingered the blouse, trying to come to terms with the strange tensions the garment elicited in him. He read the label. Poongi Silks. XL. He smiled, wondering if the constable had thought Patel wanted to try it on himself. He could imagine the poor fellow at the shop counter, trying to describe Patel's chest dimensions, and working out together with the shop assistant what size Patel wore. An old aunt of his came to mind, who used to accompany young brides on endless shopping trips during the wedding season. She liked to say, 'Get it bigger to be on the safe side. You can always make it smaller using a safety pin, but you can't make it any bigger, and with all the laddoos you are eating, you will be a laddoo yourself come the time for Suhaag Raat.' He laughed aloud at the memory.

He called room service for more vodka. After it arrived with the requisite half a pound of ice cubes, he made himself a stiff drink, stripped to his boxers and sat up on the bed. After a few minutes of staring into space, he switched on his laptop. He checked his emails. One from Ballistics. 'Definitely not a cattle gun. Will continue to explore options.'

He sighed. The bullet hole conundrum still in progress. After glancing through the usual round robins from work, he went on Facebook. Seventeen friend requests. His last post was in 2010. He looked through a cousin's wedding album. It'd been in Birmingham, too soon after his London posting to take a day off. He had a Saturday rota. This cousin he used to see all the time – never in a sari. There she was at her own wedding, in a red sari shot through with gold. Maximum bling. He suppressed a shudder and smiled at the thought of a gaggle of aunties pushing and pulling the material, trying to pin it on to the slender frame of his cousin. He found himself watching a YouTube tutorial on how to wear a sari.

The hotel wardrobe had a mirror stuck to the inside. He got the blouse on. Perfect fit on the arms and chest. He balled up some socks and stuffed them in where the breasts went. The sari was tricky. Three attempts, and he managed it. Spectacular was a word invented for the sight of him. Proud of his perseverance, he took a turn around the room. It was hard to walk without tripping. How did women manage it? He certainly couldn't run in a sari. He stepped closer to the mirror. Pushed his hair off his forehead. Not bad. He looked the deal, having shaved his stubble off earlier. Something missing. He took a marker pen from his laptop bag and drew a dot between his brows. Should be red, he thought. Something pinged at him again. Something about the red dot.

He rang Chandra.

'Hey,' he said.

'Hey.'

'Hey.'

'So that's it then, you're off the case.'

'It's sayanora, sister.' He smiled. He could be a sister, he thought. In his sari, bindi.

Chandra cursed. Sound of a horn blast.

'You driving somewhere?'

'Yep. To the mayor's house to see Suren. He won't pick up his mobile. And he won't come to the landline, the servant said. He can be a bit, you know . . .'

The mayor's house wasn't far. Even with the traffic. He looked at his watch. Nearly nine p.m. Patel made a decision.

'I'm coming too,' he said. 'Never did get around to thanking him for the loan of his motorbike.'

He took the sari off and rummaged in his suitcase for clean clothes, pulled out his All Saints jacket. He'd thought it was languishing behind the kitchen door in London. He shrugged it on, stepped out and took a cab. A light rain fell. The air, which had been muggy all through the day, had turned chilly. Chandra waited in her car outside the mayor's house. She stepped out as he approached.

She smiled. 'What's this?' She touched his forehead where the marker pen had left its indelible ink.

'Just an accident,' he said. 'Won't come off.'

'Looks like a . . .'

'Bindi,' Patel finished for her.

'It does.'

'I need to ask you something. Traditional Hindu women wear bindis, right?'

'Right.'

'Muslim and Christian women don't?'

'True generally, but some do.'

'You are a Hindu.'

'Yep, Sherlock.'

'Sabah wasn't. Laxmi, Anuradha and Kadambri were all Hindus.'

'That's right.'

'None of them wore bindis. You don't, either.'

'Ye-es,' said Chandra. 'Not sure why this is relevant.'

'Well, why don't you wear one?'

'Do you know many Indian women?'

'Only those from my family, but they are from Uganda and the UK.'

'Well, Patel, it is more common for modern young Indian women not to wear bindis.'

'Why?'

'It's too traditional. It doesn't suit Western-style clothing and modern thinking.'

'It's only a little dot.'

'My mother believes it covers the bit of nerve-ending that makes women vulnerable to hypnosis by nefarious individuals.' Chandra raised her eyes heavenwards. 'It is a symbol of something or other. My grandmother would simply say it is a mark of chastity, which is like a weapon for her. My mother and grandmother wear it every day. They feel naked without it. I need to separate myself from them. I'm not like them. I'm modern, equal to men and I prefer speaking in English. Plus my clothes and make-up need to be functional, not draw attention to my gender.'

'Right. Something to think about.' He turned to go towards the house.

'Wait.' Chandra's hand was on his shoulder. She kissed him full on the mouth. Raindrops on sweet lips. 'Thought I'd never see you again.'

'Well, never say never,' he said lightly.

A servant answered the door, showed them into the living room. Patel noticed Suren ensconced in a corner armchair at one end of the long room. Intent on his laptop, he didn't seem to have noticed them. The mayor and his wife both appeared after a minute.

The same servant brought them coffee. The wife, who remained nameless, after some small talk, left her husband to take charge of more serious conversation and went to supervise the procurement of snacks. The mayor's son seemed on an entirely different planet. His tongue clamped between his teeth, absorbed in his laptop screen. His eyes, when he did look up, were wide and drifting.

The mayor talked with Chandra about the investigation. She mentioned what she wanted from Suren. The boy wasn't roused even by the mention of his name, and did not apear to be following the conversation.

Hariharan spoke to Suren from across the room. 'Will you help Chandra?' The boy nodded, briefly lifting his eyes without meeting his father's. Chandra went over to him. The mayor sat on one end of a long sofa from Patel, and took a call. Suren remained in front of his laptop, Chandra kneeling beside him, talking to him in a low voice, consulting her phone from time to time.

Patel watched them for a few minutes. He wondered what Gentleman was doing at the moment. Was he on a sofa too, taking a break? He watched Suren's fingers fly over the keyboard. He became aware that the mayor had finished the call, and was studying him.

'You are leaving us, Mr Patel.'

'Afraid so,' he said, glumly.

'Unfinished business here?'

'Exactly.'

'Life for you now must be different to when you were a cricketer.'

'Oh, very.'

'Family back home happy you are going back?'

'Overjoyed.'

'Wife and kids?'

'Just a fiancée.'

'Is that so? Congratulations. Wedding all planned?'

'Ha ha.' He knew his laugh sounded feeble. 'At some point we will get to it.'

'Nice, traditional girl? If there is such a thing in your country?'

Patel twitched his lips. 'Name's Sarah. I suppose she is conventional, really, in everyday life.'

'But?'

'Sorry?'

'I'm sure there is a but?'

'Is there?'

'I'm interested, Mr Patel. It looks like Chandra will be awhile with Suren over there. We have a little time. Tell me about your Sarah.'

No one had asked him what his other half was like in a long

time. They had been together for seven years – or was it nine? His friends were her friends, and he'd never needed to present an account of her for anyone's scrutiny. Mayor Hariharan was showing an interest. Hell, he might even have some good advice.

'Well, in cricket terms, you know how when the pitch is new and dry, and the ball new, you bowl straight, the line true . . . '

'I know exactly.'

'Then the moisture creeps in, the pitch cracks, the ball's old, the reverse swing begins. Uneven bounce. I suppose I'm shifting to the batman's point of view here. As you know, I was never any good at batting.'

'The worst. But you didn't need to be good at batting.'

'Yes, more's the pity. I suppose that's the thing with relationships. Communication.'

'Donkeys might recite poetry, but we call it braying.'

'What?'

'Communication can be fixed. But to fix personality, that is hard. Again, I ask, what is this Sarah like?'

'Lovely, really.'

'She must be beautiful, no?'

'And inflexible.'

'Isn't there something in English literature about willows bending and snapping in the wind?'

'Is there?'

'Go on, about Sarah.'

Sarah. He thought about her beauty, her inflexibility, and in his mind, her skin changed texture and became glassy, like that of a porcelain doll. A sudden violence entered his head, and he thought of smashing the doll.

'Thing with Sarah,' he said, 'she is always calm. Never gets cross.' He laughed a painful little laugh. 'It can be infuriating, her reasonableness. Every time we have any trouble, she likes to sit down and talk, analyse it, like worrying a splinter in your heel with a safety pin.'

'Is she a moral woman?'

'I suppose she is.'

'What does she do?'

'She makes sculptures of women screwing.'

The mayor's eyebrows rose. 'Is this true? Who would do such a thing?'

'She's an artist. Avant-garde, provocative.'

'Very disturbing.' The mayor crinkled his brows, but Patel noticed the excitement in his eyes. The man's titillated by the idea, he thought, for all his propriety and reserve.

Hariharan's wife brought an array of snacks on a tray, plantain fryums, little coloured milk sweets.

The mayor excused himself to take another call. 'Sorry, Mr Patel. Indians do not understand the concept of work–life balance.' He moved to a sofa further off.

Suren met Patel's eyes for a moment, his eyes piercing and cold. Patel felt the ice sinking through his nerve-ends, before the man-child looked away. Patel realised this was the first eye contact he'd made. He went over and stood by Chandra's shoulder. Suren flipped through the webpages at great speed, processing or absorbing information. A lot faster than Patel could process or absorb information.

Suren suddenly stopped swishing his finger. The browser was open on a fashion piece about Laxmi. There were three images of her looking sexy beyond belief. Svelte, well-nourished skin. Glorious hair softly fluttering about her nape in layers and shades of gold, copper and black.

'These women,' leered the *enfant terrible*.

Patel began to correct him – these were images of one woman, after all – when the boy said, 'All these cows.'

He abruptly remembered the newspaper article he'd read about a police raid on a abattoir. Something about it had stuck in his teeth like a string of meat. It *was* the meat. The picture of a cow had accompanied the article, a man holding a shotgun to its head. Old fashioned. It all fitted. The women were killed like the cattle in an abattoir.

He turned to Chandra. 'If it's not a cattle gun, I cannot see what it could be.'

Chandra shrugged.

Mayor Hariharan interrupted, still on the phone, 'What's that about a cattle gun?'

'Murder weapon,' said Chandra. 'We're scratching our heads about what it could be.'

The mayor ended his call. 'Is it not a cattle gun?'

'Not any that we have on record.'

'You know, funny you mention it, but with all the abattoir raids happening in the city, I heard they are seizing all the cattle guns, the cow-murdering weapons, and keeping them somewhere at your headquarters under lock and key.'

'I didn't know this,' said Chandra.

'All sorts of them. Probably some Scotland Yard's never seen the like of.'

'Some Indian antique?' Chandra said.

Patel's pulse quickened. 'Where did you say they've got it stored?'

'Rumour is, at the police HQ.'

Chandra looked thoughtful.

'I'm not leaving,' said Patel.

'We'll go in a minute,' she said absently.

'No, I mean I'm staying.'

'Oh boy,' said Chandra. 'Let's go.'

*

They drove to HQ.

Chandra said, 'If anyone knows about where everything is, it's Sridevi.'

On the admin floor, a few women poked forlornly at keyboards.

'Chitra,' called Chandra. 'Where's Sridevi?'

'Gone home.'

'Got her number?'

Chitra shook her head. 'She lives at the bottom of the hill. Dead zone.'

Chandra cursed.

'What do you need?'

'I need to know where the cattle guns from abattoir raids are kept, and the keys.'

'Perumal will know.'

'Where can I find him?

Chitra looked at her watch. 'Ask Mumtaz.' She waggled her eyebrows.

Mumtaz at reception sent them to the little porch at the back of the building. Designated smoking area. Perumal was the lone fellow sucking on a beedi.

An hour later, they'd laid out the 257 cattle guns roughly into three categories. A couple of older ones, great big ones with air tanks. But these were rusted, defunct.

Patel said, 'Ballistics ruled out all these.'

'So it's not a cattle gun.'

'It must be, though. Something about cows and tradition and bindis. The cattle gun in the middle of the forehead, blood-red hole between the brows. Cows, goddesses.'

'We need the weapon before we write that thesis.'

Patel studied one of the air tanks. 'Have you seen that movie, *No Country for Old Men*? Javier Bardem totes one like that. Chilling.'

'It's from the seventies, no?'

'His hairstyle is. But the cattle gun's an antique.'

A low, gravelly voice from a corner said, 'That is what Rajkumar sir said.'

He'd forgotten Perumal hadn't left. Slumped in a corner in an attitude of repose, his dark eyes were tinged red in the gloom.

'What did he say?'

'When we are finding this all guns at the butcher place behind Fatehpur station. Few months ago, now. We raiding and finding these. Few very old. Rajkumar sir calling them anti-key.'

'Antique? These two here?'

'These old. But one much older. Lots of broken anti-keys but that one looking tiptop. One constable, he fooling about, pretending to execute. It wasn't working mind, but very bloody scary. Every time he pressing the lever it make popping sound. I is scared. Chief Rajkumar he take it home.'

'What?' Patel and Chandra said at the same time.

'He likes to collect strange things. Eccentric, he is. His hobby. Anything interesting we find, we take it to him for good-boy pat on head. Promotion, maybe not. To be in his good ledger. One time we got a bronze statue from a drug dealer. It Rajkumar loving. But the Bhai getting released on bail and he coming straight up in the lift and pulling Rajkumar on the collar, police chief or not. Dead mother's, he saying. Madhar-chod. Rajkumar giving back crying.' Perumal chuckled.

Patel and Chandra left Perumal to lock up, and stepped out of the HQ. 'Let's go,' said Patel, getting into Chandra's car on the driver's side.

'Where?' She shoved a bunch of things from the passenger seat on to the floor before getting in, and gave him the key. The rain still pattered.

'Rajkumar's house.'

'Are you insane? You are supposed to be on a flight to London.'

'No way, Jose.' Patel put the clutch in first gear and stepped on the gas.

'You can't be serious,' said Chandra. 'We cannot just barge into Rajkumar's house and rootle about for an antique cattle gun.'

'Why not?'

'He's the chief of police.'

'Let's check it out. Then we'll know for sure.'

'You heard Perumal. The cattle gun they found was old. It wasn't working.'

'He could have fixed it, restored it. He's had it for two years.'

'So Rajkumar is hunting himself? It's too bizarre.'

He thought of the old man in Yorkshire. Never in a million years would even a hard-nose homicide detective suspect the shuffling, bumbling, polite, friendly old man.

'Just want to follow where this goes. Follow the bread-crumbs, that's all.'

'Couldn't we just ask him?'

'And warn him off? He'll destroy whatever evidence there is.'

'We haven't got a search warrant.'

'And I'm not even meant to be here.'

Chandra pursed her lips, shook her head.

Running in to bowl, every nerve ending on fire, the ball following the arc of obliteration mapped by his mind. Stumps flying, despair in the batsman's eyes. How could he communicate to Chandra his gut feeling of being on the right track?

'You said I was here for my wonderful instinct, right? Guide you with my sixth sense?'

'Patel!'

'Ah.' He realised she'd been taking the mickey.

A blast of horn. A lorry came at them, forcing Patel to swerve and run up the pavement. He braked and the car stopped an inch from a tin shack lettered *Ram's Cycle Repairs*. The lorry sped through the gap, still blasting its horn.

'You are driving the wrong way up a one-way system.'

His heart had nearly stopped. He took a deep breath. 'Thanks for letting me know.'

'I don't believe in mumbo-jumbo like instinct. What I meant to say back then was that your presence here was completely unnecessary. That you didn't belong here. That you were useless to me.'

'I got the gist now.'

'But I was wrong. You are good at reading people, just not street signs.

'I have a theory about how much time so-called busy people can actually carve out in a week.'

'And?'

'Anyone can fit in a full time job, a few murders, and still get a good night's sleep.'

Chandra groaned.

Patel spoke softly now. 'So give me a better lead than Rajkumar's antique cattle gun?'

Chandra opened her mouth, but said nothing.

'You drive.'

They got out of the car. As he passed her coming around to the driver's side, she chuckled, and said, 'I've always wanted to piss him off.'

'It might get you fired.'

'He can't fire me.'

'Why not?'

'I won't let him.'

Patel smiled. 'Well, if you want to piss him off, this is your night.'

Chapter Twenty-Nine

Manu licked his lips. Moisture beaded his moustache. Excitement tempered with caution. He gazed at the image on his laptop screen. Pressed CONTROL + on the keyboard to enlarge it. Stared deeply into the pixelated eyes. Hazel, flecked with golden lights. He reached out to the screen, touched the face upon it. The number next to the photo taunted, tempted.

He gathered his laptop and phone, left the living room without a word to his wife and son, barely aware of their existence, mind ablaze with the images he'd seen on the website. Rapturous, erotic, filthy, a provocative, damned cesspit of womanly urges. He fought his own arousal. The shame of it.

In his private alcove, he sat in front of his deity and tried stilling his mind, gazing into the inky metal eyes before him. But his arousal increased as the images kept popping into his head. His hand crept down to the front of his trousers. Avant-garde, yes, but also elemental, tapping a nerve, touching the base of desire. Base desire, in fact. The desire that made man and woman abase body and soul before it. At the thought of all the women who oppressed him, he groaned, with hatred and desire both. They constantly undermined him by asserting themselves. Continually the creatures challenged the world as given to them, littering it with their filth, smearing their cunts all over it like dogs. He gasped as he squeezed himself too hard in trying to stopper his filthy desire. The phone number seemed to dangle in front of him, taunting. No, too dangerous. It had been a risk choosing Kadambri. So many people had seen them talking at the party. But oh so satisfying to let loose his creativity on that one. He had given his rare words of praise to the boy for the work with the swan. But this, this woman belonged in another league altogether. The whole of Scotland Yard would descend from the skies, not just some gullible sergeant. But his lovely Patel had bared his heart to Manu. His mouth curved into a little smile. Patel had made himself cosy in Manu's rag-and-bone heart. A salve, a real balm. Perhaps he would turn to Manu in his hour of crisis. Then there'd be so many opportunities to provide succour.

He slapped himself. One hard smack across his left cheek. He must be cautious. He ought not to get carried away. He had to get himself under control in order to carry out his actions dispassionately. Or he would make mistakes, be caught. What he did may be morally untouchable, but against the law of the land all the same.

He would get the boy to fetch a couple of dogs. Nobody missed those. Sure, there was some commotion in the area about the missing strays, but people were secretly relieved.

The images on the website toyed with his desire and hate.

Just a phone call. See how it went. He wouldn't commit. He'd just dip his toes in the water, wiggle the foot gently, see if the fish was the nibbling kind.

Before he could change his mind, he picked up his phone and dialled the number.

'Hello.'

Part Three

Chapter Thirty

'How many rooms?' Patel asked.

'Two bedrooms, living, kitchen. Where could he keep a collection? It's too small.'

'There's basement parking.'

'But he gets picked up and dropped off by police Bolero.'

'So four rooms plus basement. Ten minutes each room, ten extra in case of hidden panelling.'

'Hidden panelling,' repeated Chandra, looking amused.

'So twenty minutes if we split the rooms, plus ten. We need half an hour in there. How far to HQ?'

'Fifteen to twenty minutes.'

'OK, make the call.'

Chandra was already dialling.

'Krishna,' she said into the phone. 'Rajkumar sir wants to be picked up. Yeah, no. No, not in one hour. Right away. Why? Who's there? Yeah, send him.' She rang off. 'Ten minutes,' she said to Patel.

She dialled again. Patel heard four rings before it was picked up.

'Sir,' she said, 'new kidnapping. Yes, sir. Car on the way. I'll meet you at the office. I'm on the way now. Yes. Yes.' She looked at Patel. 'A note. Unconfirmed. Can't be sure. Surpriya from forensics is on the way – yes, sir.' She rang off, nodded to Patel.

They waited, didn't speak. Cars drove past. People walked, their conversations too loud in the unearthly quiet of their waiting. The city didn't sleep. Indians ate late, stayed up late. A mosque called for prayers. A drunken man shouted. His wife shouted louder.

A dog strolled past, sniffling at this and sniffing that. It stopped to rifle in a pile of garbage, settled down with a titbit. A Bolero flashed by, screeched to a halt. Twelve minutes. The driver leapt out with his mobile phone, speaking into it. He had the back door open. Down the steps dashed Rajkumar, his speed belying his bulk.

'Look how fast he moves,' said Patel. 'All that sluggishness is pretence.'

Rajkumar leapt into the back of the Bolero like an athlete in a fat-man body suit.

'That pot belly could be fake for all we know,' said Patel.

'This is too much like *DI Indrajit*, you know the Tamil movie?

'Haven't seen it.'

'Not known for its realism.'

'Touché.'

The Bolero disappeared around the corner.

'Come on,' said Patel, jumping out of the car. 'Half an hour. I'd give it twenty before Rajkumar cottons on to the trick and turns around.'

'Right-oh,' said Chandra, imitating his accent.

They ran up the stairs together. She leaned on the buzzer. A flustered-looking woman opened the door. 'Chandra,' she said.

'Sorry Mrs Rajkumar. Mr Rajkumar left something in the house and he wanted us to find it and bring it.'

'Eh? He only just left.'

'He is in a hurry to get to head office.'

'I'll find it. What is it?'

'He said you wouldn't know what it looked like. It's an antique cattle gun. Rusty and big.'

Patel had already slipped into their living room.

'He collects all this junk,' said Mrs R, a shake of her head in exasperation. 'But he keeps—'

'What's going on, Ma?' A sleep-smushed teenager emerged from a room.

Mrs Rajkumar told him. The boy said, 'But he just left, no?'

Patel and Chandra got busy. It wasn't a big apartment. Kitchen, small cupboards, fridge, freezer. Patel concentrated on the nooks and crannies. Nothing. He carried on to the living room. Dark, printed settee. TV. Behind the TV, newspapers stacked up. He felt the stack. No hollow hiding space. Behind the settee, old mosquito bats, cobwebs, a cricket bat.

He wiped the cobwebs off his forearms with a shudder, stood on a kitchen chair to look above the display cases with awards for the father and son, in work and in sports, in spelling bees. Nothing but a thick wedge of dust above the cupboards. Chandra came out of the son's room and shook her head. She had already searched the master bedroom. 'Need the loo,' she said, and nipped into the bathroom.

'How to get into the basement?' Patel asked Mrs Rajkumar, who'd been sitting on the dining chair, watching him, frowning.

'I need to call my husband and check with him.'

Chandra came out of the loo, said, 'Oh you can call him if you like, Mrs Rajkumar.' She flashed her a smile and whispered to Patel, 'There are stairs from the kitchen.'

Mrs Rajkumar jabbed numbers on her cordless. Patel looked at his watch. 'Oh shit.' They'd only been ten minutes. Which meant Rajkumar wasn't far enough away. Which meant he'd be back before they finished. Chandra stopped to rifle behind a gas cylinder.

'Hurry,' he hissed.

They raced down the stairs. Dark basement, smells of mould and damp, scattered junk. An old car rested under a Rexine cover. Flat tyres, rusted rims.

'Shit, this is old,' said Chandra. 'Ten years, at least.'

'Ten years isn't old,' said Patel, taking hold of a corner.

'In the tropics, it is.' Chandra pulled the opposite corner.

They peeled the cover off, coughing with the dust. A Fiat. He recognised its shape from 1980s Bollywood films. 'Make that thirty,' he said.

Chandra transformed her phone into a torch. 'Car's full of junk,' she said.

Patel tried the door. Locked.

'Pull harder,' she said. 'It's rusted.'

He pulled. It didn't open. He looked around with the light of his own phone. A jumble of objects in a corner. A switch by the basement door. He flipped it. The lights wouldn't come on. Some light from the streetlamps filtered through the airing grills on the side walls of the basement.

'I'll go back up and get a proper torch,' said Chandra.

'She's on the phone to Rajkumar. The son looks strong.'

'I know kung fu.' She winked.

Patel peered at the junk in the light of the phone. Plastic, metal shapes, he could not work out what was what. A broom handle he recognised, a brush attachment, a flowerpot, a bucket. It was all just junk. Commotion upstairs. Chandra came down in a patter of boot soles.

'All right?'

'Yes, got the torch. I locked the kitchen door from the outside. And got the car keys too.' She threw them to Patel.

He missed.

The keys fell to the floor, skittered under the car. He scrambled to his knees and retrieved them.

'You dropped a sitter.'

'Not a cricketer any more.' He turned the key in the car door. 'Just an old Indian copper.'

It creaked open. They pulled out some stuff.

'Goodness,' said Chandra. 'They use the car to store things.'

Photos, boxes, old toys, kitchen appliances, mixer-grinder combos his mother would recognise, another broom handle.

Pounding at the kitchen door.

'Uh-oh,' said Chandra.

A sharp crack. A square of light. Hurrying feet.

A voice incoherent with anger.

Patel and Chandra didn't look up. They rummaged in the car. Slowly, Patel stopped looking, squirmed from the car. Chandra did the same. She shook her head at him.

'Me neither,' said Patel.

They turned at last to face Rajkumar, his wife and son, plus driver. The driver looked petrified. Perhaps he knew that as a minion in the Indian bureaucracy, he would get the blame no matter what went wrong in the workings of the higher-ups.

Unused to hurrying, out of breath and brushing his dishevelled locks from his face, Rajkumar gasped, 'What is the meaning of this?'

Chapter Thirty-One

Phone wedged between ear and shoulder, Sarah poured Fairy liquid into an old yoghurt pot.

'You would like to commission? How did you say you know Vijay?'

With a glance at the clock, she grabbed a bunch of paint-brushes and swirled the paint-engorged bristles into the detergent.

'Uh huh,' she said, half listening. 'I would prefer if you wrote down your requirements in an email. Then I can give a quote, depending on complexity, time involved, materials used. Let me give you—'

She gave a small, embarrassed laugh. 'Why, thank you, yes, they are very popular with women. What kind? How do you mean? Nationality? Well London is very cosmopolitan – oh no? Their what? Values? You mean what do they cost?'

She ran the tap a bit too hard and the water splashed on her, icy cold. Biting down a curse – her New Year's resolution: stop swearing – she leant the cleaned brushes on the counter and tore a paper towel from the dispenser.

'Listen, I'm in the middle of clearing out of the studio here. Perhaps I could call you back? Your name?

'Is that with a U or a double O? And oh, have you a title for your project? Self-explanatory – oh yes? Let me write it down.'

She rummaged in her bag for a scrap of paper and pencil. 'Yes . . . yes . . . got it. Is it about yourself, then? No. All men. Sounds exciting. I love a challenge. Yes, I will call you right away. In less than an hour. Yes.'

She hung up, smiled to herself in the mirror, rubbed off the plaster dust from her forehead. Quickly walking to the door, she hung up her apron with the dozens of filthy others, picked up her coat and bag from the stand, pattered down the stairs.

'Sorry, I ran over a bit,' she said to the young man at reception. He shook his coiffure and smiled mysteriously in the middle of his artful beard. 'See you tomorrow,' she said, and strode out into the gloom, pleased at the prospect of obtaining a commission. All the way from India, too.

Sarah came within sight of the Tube station and groaned. The queue bent around the station building and stretched into Latham Road. Reduced service still, and Christmas break was long over. Fuck it, she thought. Swearing in her mind didn't count. She'd go and have a coffee, come back in half an hour when there was less of a rush. After all, she didn't have anyone to go home to. Not even a pet cat.

Looking for a cafe, she wished Vijay was with her. He'd spoken highly of her work with someone, so much so they wanted to commission her. Wow. She made a face of exaggerated surprised delight; a llama face, her niece called it. Walking on, she rejected a cafe that was too crowded. A dark-haired little child held her mother's hand, waiting for a bus. They would have one like that – dark haired, pale eyed. Blue or green eyes in her family. Vijay's were nearly hazel. A thrill went through her at the picture of a blue-eyed, black-haired child. They'd had their ups and downs like other couples, but his absence this time was bringing home to her the fact that, in spite of all the frictions, she did really love him, and wanted to start a family. She couldn't wait to tell him.

She went into a Caffè Nero, settled under a poster of old Greek men smoking fags and imbibing authentic Greek coffees. She checked her email. Of course, too soon for the chap to have sent anything. What a charming accent he had. She tried to picture him. Someone small of stature, with kind eyes and a lush voice, like that writer, Vikram Seth? She'd been to one of his readings, back in the 1990s.

What did he call it? She slipped her hand into her bag, felt around for the scrap of paper. Where had it disappeared? Odd in a way that her sculptures symbolising female sexual liberation should move him to want something to express his ideas of masculinity. Or was it odd? Perhaps it was an appropriate response. She sipped her coffee. Link yin and yang. Perhaps her female series could trigger a male series. Either way, this commission should be interesting. If it actually materialised. A lot of people made tentative enquiries, then lost interest. Or baulked at her quotes. She checked her emails again. Nothing. She looked about her. An elderly couple, all the time in the world, eating a grim-looking toastie (him) and a flapjack (her). Some university students; a woman her age, but some kind of office worker, smart coat, sensible black shoes. The woman glanced up.

Finding refuge behind her phone screen, Sarah found the cafe's free wifi. Glancing down, she saw the piece of paper stuck half under her foot. Must have drifted down without her noticing. She bent down, picked it up, read it. Sounded like an old scripture title. Some mythological text. She opened the web browser and typed 'Resurrection of Manu'.

Blog entries. A book on Amazon. She opened the link to the book. *The Teachings of Manu* by Valarmiki. Strange name. Looked like a self-published book. She went back to the search results, opened the blog, titled 'Manu's Musings'. Ah, something about the tone seemed like this was her potential customer. Yes, blog author was a Manu Purush. Eastern-sounding name. She scrolled down, skim reading, took a sip of the coffee. She read on, forgot the coffee – first the beverage, then the cup itself turning cold. She stopped skim reading, began to focus. Her cheeks stiffened, and she forgot to breathe.

Clumsily, she grabbed her phone. It slipped and cracked on the floor.

'Fuck,' she swore loudly. Everyone looked up. The elderly man tut-tutted.

The screen was cracked. She pressed buttons. It still worked. Relieved, she rang Patel.

'It's me.'

Chapter Thirty-Two

'Put him on the plane in handcuffs,' Rajkumar told the two constables.

One nodded meekly. The other, more tendentious, said, 'But, sir, who will unlock them on the other side?'

'They can get a bloody blowtorch.'

The constables glanced at each other. 'As you say, sir.'

The police car bumped across the potholes from Rajkumar's house. Patel looked back through the rear window. Chandra raised a forlorn hand.

The car turned a corner without reducing speed. He searched for a seatbelt in vain. This was it. It had all come to nothing. He must've been insane to think Rajkumar would hide a murder weapon in his own home. Surely his wife and son would have noticed it? And what about his stock of saris and blouses? They found nothing in the house or basement to make Rajkumar look the least bit like the killer. But it couldn't be just a coincidence that such an unusual murder weapon was the same thing Rajkumar had decided to keep from a raid two years ago. Unless. Unless that Perumal fellow was lying. Could it be that? Why would Perumal lie about such a thing?

Rain splashed the windows. Patel sat helplessly, waiting to be put back on the 4.15 flight to Gatwick. Chandra would be facing the music from Rajkumar. The soprano voices of the Indian singers on the radio cut right through his eardrums.

'Why whisper when you can shout?' muttered Patel.

'Eh?' said the constable next to him.

Patel ignored him, looked out of his window. The tropical rain cut visibility to zero.

His phone rang. Awkwardly he fished it out of his jacket pocket, handcuffs clinking as he transferred it from left to right hand, but the car went over a pothole, jolting the phone out of his hand. It slipped and fell to the floor, ringing shrilly somewhere in the murk below. The constable tut-tutted, brought out the handcuff key and released his hands.

'I put it back in aeroplane,' he said to Patel.

He combed the floor, found his phone. It had stopped ringing. Sarah. He hesitated over the call-back button. Why waste breath, when he would be seeing her come morning. Five hours magically disappeared during the flight west so he'd arrive sharp as a tack in London at nine a.m.

'You not call?' said the constable. For an Indian, of course, not ringing back someone who'd called was tantamount to sacrilege. Along with killing cows. Cows, cows, cows. Where was that fucking cattle gun? His phone rang again. Sarah? No. Chandra.

'Hey,' he said.

'Rajkumar has another house in Kalimpi.'

'Where?'

'Outskirts of the city. His wife let it slip. I don't think she likes him very much. He's livid. Think the house is very much off the record, if you know what I mean. I knew he had to be taking bribes. All those contractors mysteriously slipping my net. Anyway, I'm going there now. Rajkumar's suspended me for a month without pay. I have all the time in the world.'

'Be careful,' said Patel. 'You can't rely on backup now, can you?'

'I've never in my life relied on backup, Vijay Patel,' she said and rang off.

Nothing left to do but lean back and close his eyes. The phone beeped. Voicemail. Hour and a half till they reached the airport. Chandra, he thought, going rogue, not batting an eyelid. Would he dare? He didn't think so. He was no good at striking out by himself. His paths always seemed to choose him. He'd set upon one path until the hand of fate grabbed him by the scruff of his neck and set him on a different path. Ironically, as a child he'd fancied himself a sleuth like Sherlock Holmes. Bookish and lost in his own world. It was why his father signed him up to cricket lessons at the Leicester Cricket Academy. His papa had felt his son was too woolly and dreamy, all this lounging anathema to his Gujarati businessman mentality. All his relations, boys and girls, were into cricket. His coach said he had talent, took over, became a kind of surrogate parent. His bemused mother watched from the sidelines; the coach, not her, from then on deciding what he should eat, when he should sleep, train. Patel glided from club to county to country without hiccup, settling into a long and illustrious cricketing life. Then boom. Nothing. All the years of work, training, diet: for nothing. He never could bat for shit. In the abyss of apathy that followed his injury, he returned home, holed up in his room like a teenager, salved his wounds with Sherlock Holmes stories. Once again lost in his head, lounging around. His father hadn't the wherewithal to say or do anything. His mother had been the one to persuade him to sign up for the criminology degree.

Then Sarah.

'Phone beeping,' said the constable. Patel ignored him. They could leave a message.

He barely admitted it to himself nowadays that it had been her friend he'd fancied. Golden, tall, he could neither remember her name nor recall her features any more. Sarah and this friend were at the college bar. He stared. It was Sarah's head that turned.

Sarah went to the toilet, and stopped next to him on the way back. Said, 'You were staring at me?' He grinned, not knowing how to tell her the truth without insulting her. It wasn't gentlemanly. So he grinned like an idiot, Sarah bought him a drink, then another, invited him to her room. The friend, the beautiful, distant moon, lingered at the bar, smiled vaguely at them, wandered off. He saw her once or twice after that, and then never again. Finished his course, began spending nights at Sarah's, moved in. Almost as a contrast to her artistic path, he joined the detective academy, did the relevant training, exams. Ticked boxes. Got job.

And then the Dales Ripper. By then he'd lost all illusions about being some Sherlock Holmes. He detested the realities of a career in police work. Endless bloody paperwork. The numbing, labyrinthine procedures and criminal processes, the sheer idiocy of the criminals and would-be criminals he dealt with. Premeditated murders looked sexy as hell in films, but it wasn't so in real life. Husbands beating their wives to death. Putrefied blood. Pale, grey corpses. Dead people stank. Nothing remotely sexy about any of it.

They drove, swinging from side to side. Rain continued to cascade down. Patel stared at the curtain of grey. He thought of Chandra driving in this, phone pressed to her ear, rain lashing her little green car as it bumped along on the badly lit roads, swerving around highway lorries en route to Madras. Thought of her turning up at the remote, unlit house. Bad-ass rural types lurking under brollies and plastic bags. Or was it eerily quiet? 'Not a soul abroad', as Conan Doyle might put it. No neighbours, no sounds except for the clapping of the same thunder he could hear above him. The incessant drumming of the rain lulled him. His head slipped back on the seat. His eyes closed.

Chandra. He sat up with a jerk. Was she tiptoeing to the door? Would she get it open? What would she find? Nothing? Everything? He crunched his hand into a fist and banged it on the seat in front of him, startling the driver. Damn! He needed to be there with her.

'Could you let me off here, please?' he said. 'I'll make my own way to the plane.'

The officer next to him – Murugesh, his nametag read – sucked air. 'Chief Rajkumar said to put you on the plane in handcuffs, Mr Patel, sir.' He waggled his head apologetically.

Patel sighed. Chandra should be all right without his guidance. In fact, without his famous instincts to hinder her, she'd probably do just fine. The rain increased in volume until even the cop car was forced to slow down. Visibility opaque. He could not imagine Chandra slowing down. A lorry thundered past. The driver swerved, braked, honked, cursed, and then put his foot down hard on the accelerator.

Murugesh glanced at Patel, as if daring him to judge the Indian logic, as if he knew what Patel was thinking. Patel held his breath. Then, as if responding to Patel's unspoken recrimination, Murugesh said, 'If he drive fast in bad weather, other vehicles forcing to slow down. If he drive slow, others driving fast and in India, it is not safe for the slow car on a dangerous road.' Finished, he grunted, as if daring Patel to challenge him.

'Right,' said Patel.

'If you drive slow in bad light, no one notice you. That is bad, no?'

Patel shook his head. The gods danced on dead flesh and slew each other in this land. Who was he to say 'this was this' and 'that was that'?

No doubt Chandra had the same philosophy, in spite of her year in Cardiff. Perhaps she'd drive a car when she came on her exchange trip to London.

A pang as he felt the foreboding. What was she driving to? A house on the outskirts of the city.

'Stop the car,' he said.

'It's OK,' said Murugesh. 'Mani very safe driver.'

'No, no, I have to be sick. Stop the car.'

Murugesh shook his head. 'Sorry, Patel, sir. We no stopping till you getting on aeroplane.'

Mani picked up speed, as if Patel had ideas about jumping out and needed to be thwarted.

'Where's Rajkumar now?' he asked Murugesh.

'At home,' grunted Murugesh.

Rowing with his wife, thought Patel. She didn't like Rajkumar, Chandra said. Let it slip about the second house. Or did she do it on purpose? The wife could be a co-conspirator. Serial-killing husband and wife teams were well documented, were they not? What if it was a trap? The wife dropped a hint for Chandra to pick up. Chandra fell for it, hook, line and sinker. Didn't he and Chandra speculate that the murders might be the work of not a loner, but two, possibly even three people? It would seem impossible for one person to hoist the wheel up into a vertical position at the Opera House. What if Rajkumar at that very moment sped towards the second house in his Bolero? It would beat Chandra's stuttery little car hands down in any cross-country track fest. He might be, even now, lying in wait for her. Wife in the back as a lookout, relishing the prospect of skewering Chandra's pretty forehead with the bolt-and-shot cattle gun. Or was she in the kitchen, oiling and checking the bolt action and levers?

Through gritted teeth, eyes closed against the vision of death in his head, Patel said, 'Stop the car, Murugesh.'

'I'm Murugesh. Mani is driving.'

'It's very important. Assistant Commissioner Chandra is in danger.'

'Chandra madam in danger?' said Murugesh, laughing. 'She is Bruce Lee.'

'Bruce Lee died when he was thirty-two,' said Patel.

'No, sir,' piped the driver. 'He still alive in America. He did *Rush Hour* with Chris Tucker.'

'That was Jackie Chan.'

'No, Bruce Lee.'

'Just stop the car.'

'Or what, you jump out like in Bruce Lee film?'

'Pull the fuck over,' he shouted.

Both men shook their heads. Mani stepped on the gas. Lightning whipped the eastern sky. Patel's fingers curled on the door handle.

Murugesh gave a sly grin. 'Like *Rush Hour 2*, you jumping?'

Patel waited. Murugesh turned his snooty head away. Mani slowed to make a curve. Patel clicked the door open, held his breath and rolled out.

He fell hard, spun round and round. Tarmac shredded sleeve and skin. A knee scraped a jagged stone, and an ankle twisted in a way it shouldn't. His elbow bashed against a piece of iron. Iron! A drainage lid had been titled open to draw the torrential water.

Cursing, dragging and pulling his limbs along, he lurched

over the pavement on hands and knees and stumbled head first into a ditch.

Crouching there uncomfortably, he held his breath and peered out at the road.

The car braked, screeched, slid, then reversed. The two men peered out of the windows, first through the glass, then with the glass lowered. They did not step out. They put their heads out, just a peek, withdrew from the rain. He saw Mani lifting a handkerchief to wipe the drops from his forehead. He pulled the rear-view mirror around to check his hair. For an insane moment, Patel expected him to begin applying Fair and Lovely for men. They shouted at each other through the rain pattering on the metal. Mani thrust a plastic folder out through the window, leaned his head out under it, and peered straight where Patel was crouched. He frowned. He spoke to Murugesh, whose door opened an inch, and stopped. Patel waited.

Lightning cracked open the sky, followed a second later by the boom of thunder. Mani withdrew his head and his file. The car turned around. Murugesh's door swung open and he wrestled it shut again. Having done just enough to be able to say they had looked but could find no trace of the lunatic English gentleman who rolled out of their car in the heavy rain, the car U-turned in the middle of the road and left.

After making sure they weren't coming back, Patel limped to a transparent bus shelter. There he huddled, soaked to the skin, filthy and reeking of ditch water. He examined his leg, where the cut was bleeding. He tore a piece of his shirt and tied it around the wound. His right elbow hurt like hell, probably cracked. He was in no shape to be hunting a psychopath. He needed to phone Chandra and ask her to turn around immediately, or to send him a taxi and wait till he got there. Call Chandra, then call Rima. She'd know how to rustle up some contacts to help them out.

He felt his sodden trouser pocket and cursed. Empty. Where was his phone? He'd taken the call from Chandra, under Murugesh's sly, sidelong glance, trying to listen in. He'd had the phone on the left, keeping it on the far side from Murugesh. Usually he held it on the right. His left-hand shirt pocket. Yes, he'd slipped it in there after Chandra's call. But it wasn't there. All he could feel under the thin material of the sudden shirt was a cold-stiffened nipple. He searched the ditch where he'd crouched, retraced his steps through the run of rainwater swirling into the drain with eddying bits of leaves and plastic. He didn't see his phone.

He limped along the road in the rain, wondering what to do. He could catch an auto to his hotel, but that wasn't a wise move. The police could be waiting for him there. He didn't have a single phone number stored in his head, except Sarah's, but best leave her out of this.

A peeling poster on a wall. He'd seen it before. A lovelorn youth. A dancing wench. Foggy, misty background alien to the tropical land. Trees, waterfall. Impossibly dressed woman, a soaking-wet, turmeric-coloured cloth wound around her body like a quasi sari. Who on earth dressed like that? Someone had drawn a moustache on the young man's face, a cartoon maharaja's moustache. He'd passed this way before. Next to the poster was a set of traffic lights. He realised he'd seen the poster while on his way to the mayor's house. Which meant he knew where he was – at least in relation to the mayor's house. Couple of miles away. And he could work out how to get there.

Chapter Thirty-Three

Hariharan was thinking of going to bed when his phone buzzed.

Chandra. He glanced at the time. 'Hello?'

A smile arrived on his countenance as he listened. 'Don't thank me, child. I only relayed a rumour ... Suren? Yes, I'll wake him ... Is it a Mac? He can tackle any make ... A charger? Not sure. I'll ask Suren. He might have some kind of universal gadget. Address? Mmm hmm.' He rummaged for a pen at the bedside table, scrawled on his forearm. 'Got it. I'll drive him myself ... Dry clothes? You want me to bring you dry clothes? Of course.'

He hung up and rubbed a hand over his chin. Chandra gone AWOL, and illegally ferreting around in Rajkumar's suburban house. No one knew where she was. And she wanted Hariharan to bring her dry clothes. Preferably a salwar kameez, she'd said.

Hariharan went to the bathroom, splashed water on his face. Chandra, at that very moment, rummaging through Rajkumar's collection of junk. Who knew that the man was a hoarder? She'd found an old laptop. Without charge. She needed Suren to look at it, while she tackled the litter to search for a possible murder weapon, some kind of antique or cannibalised cattle gun. She needed help.

He was beset with worry over Chandra, whom he'd known since her birth. Her father was his close friend, and her mother had served him many a meal. He stilled his heart for long minutes, and thought about his options. He could do as she asked. Take the boy with him, and while he broke into the laptop and gathered evidence against Rajkumar, he would help Chandra look for the cattle gun. Rajkumar would hang. He found he did not have any feelings about Rajkumar's possible dire end.

He went to stand outside Suren's door. Silence. He turned on a small lamp in the hallway and went in to kneel by the bedside. The boy looked fast asleep. He felt a great reluctance to wake him. Suren found it difficult to sleep. It was rare indeed for him to be so deeply asleep, the cares of youth fallen away, his eyebrows unknitted, his mouth relaxed. To wake him and drag him into a complicated setting. The child needed his rest.

Leaving Suren sleeping, he went into the bathroom, looked in the mirror. Calm, collected, unswayed by the rush of his blood. He could meet Chandra alone.

Why not?

Chandra was like a daughter to him. He opened the cupboard with the jumble of unguents and toothbrushing paraphernalia. Moving aside sponges and a bottle of Listerine, he brought out a small wooden box. He would choose a terrific piece of jewellery for her lovely neck. Amma's emerald necklace.

He would leave the boy out of this one. He went to the cupboard, picked out some clothes for Chandra. His wife did not possess a salwar kameez, so a sari and matching blouse. In a colour that particularly suited her.

He strode out in the rain, clutching his car keys and Suren's backpack.

Chapter Thirty-Four

Sarah put down the phone, frustrated. She was at home. All through the long queuing into the Tube station she had repeatedly called Patel. No joy. Once underground, there was no signal of course, and she endured the mounting panic with a superhuman effort. Then as soon she emerged overground, she tried Patel again, but this time fared no better. After a minute of reluctance, she logged online and found a phone number for Patel's Scotland Yard office. She rang and asked for Inspector Rima Seth.

'She's not in at the moment. May I take a message?'

'It's about Sergeant Vijay Patel. He's in India . . .'

'Oh yes, well you might want to try Superintendent Skinner then. He's Patel's superior on this case.'

'Could you connect me, please?'

After a minute's silence a voice came on the phone.

'Skinner.'

'Mr Skinner. I think the man who Patel's been sent to catch just rang me.'

A pause. 'Hold on. Let me write this down. Tell me the details from beginning to end.'

Sarah did, and felt from the tone of Skinner as it changed, that he wasn't feeling the urgency of the situation the same way she was. Couldn't he see that this was becoming deeply personal for the investigating officer? They needed to get Patel out of there immediately. She told him as much.

At last, Skinner said, 'We will look into this. But you can set your mind at rest, miss. I've just been informed that Patel is being put on the plane back. He has been dismissed from the investigation. He will be coming home soon.'

'Oh, thank goodness.'

No sooner had she clicked off than it rang again. Unknown number. Heart thumping, wondering if it was the killer again, she said a tentative, 'Hello?'

'Sarah, It's Rima. Have you heard from Patel?'

'No I was just trying—'

'He's gone AWOL. Crazy bastard. They were going to put him on the flight back. He rolled out. Can you believe it? Rolled out of the moving car! Hello? Hello?'

'... I'm here. I don't understand. Who can I speak to over there? Patel's phone seems to be dead.'

'Yes, I'm trying to reach the assistant commissioner in charge of the case, Chandra Subramanium. I'll text you her number. You can call her to see if she knows his whereabouts. He's getting into dangerous territory there. All the Indian police are after him. After the killer, it's Patel who's public enemy number one.'

'Oh dear.'

'You just sit tight. I'll try to find out as much as I can.'

'I'm not going anywhere.'

After a few fruitless hours, Rima got off her mobile phone, found a voicemail message from Sarah. 'Hi, Rima. I'm boarding a flight to India. Tell Patel, if he rings, that I'll be at his hotel.'

Rima flicked the hair off her forehead, muttered, 'Oh shit.'

Chapter Thirty-Five

An inky darkness cloaked the mayor's mansion. Rain, hard fat bullets, lashed the stucco walls. Patel rang the bell. No answer. A faint light glowed in one of the upstairs windows, as if from a TV or computer screen.

'Hello?' he shouted up at the window. Nothing stirred.

He looked around. The Enfield Bullet slept under a tarp, beneath the Harsingar tree. The place he'd met Kadambri for the last time. Next to it the little outbuilding containing the mayor's den. The den glowed from within. Some kind of reddish lighting left on in there. Perhaps the mayor was still awake, sitting there with his thoughts. Patel was about to make his way there, when the heavy doors groaned open.

Suren, wide awake as an owl, stared beyond Patel, either at the rain or for someone else. Perhaps he expected Chandra to be accompanying him.

'Hi there,' said Patel. 'I got into some trouble nearby. Got hurt, lost my phone. Mind if I step in, dry off, make some calls? Have you got Chandra's number on your phone? Or in an address book?'

Suren shook his head but didn't speak. He stepped back, made room for Patel to come through, shut the door after him. Patel remembered there was a bathroom through the second reception room. He went to find it, leaving Suren by the door still having not uttered a word.

He wondered why they'd left the strange boy all alone. Where were the servants, the mother? He remembered how absent she'd seemed and then, suddenly, all present, like a switch had been flipped. As he looked around for a towel, the bathroom door opened. Suren stood in the doorway, naked.

'Come,' he said to Patel, spun around on his heels and skipped down the hallway.

Patel was motionless for a moment. No, he thought, I can't go after him. The mayor's son, naked, propositioning him. But it was something else. Something about this didn't seem right. He followed the boy up the stairs, footsteps a dull echo on the marble.

Suren's room was in musty darkness, except for the light from a very large computer monitor. Patel could make out posters on the wall with shadowy superhuman figures from American films. The window was swathed in drapes. Suren sat in a corner, stroking himself. Patel glanced away. A movement on the computer screen. A video playing with no sound. Patel noticed several windows open. Looked back at Suren, keeping his eyes on his face. Suren gestured towards the laptop.

Patel limped into the room and crouched at the desk. The first window showed a man and woman, having sex. His buttocks thrust between her legs splayed on either side of him. As he watched, her hand came up with a metal ruler and began to whack his right buttock.

The boy's watching porn, thought Patel. What a surprise. He made to turn away. He needed to get out the room. If anyone saw him . . .

He narrowed his eyes at the screen. The lighting was too dark for porn, the man's bottom too flabby, the angle of the camera too flush on. You couldn't see anything of the woman except her unlovely calves. The camera didn't pan and in fact, the shot was out of focus. He realised the camera was perched on a tripod or propped up on a cushion or a book. The picture quality was grainy. Probably shot on a phone camera.

Patel flung an arm on the back of a chair, willed his heart to slow down. He was watching a home sex video. Laxmi had made a home sex video. Kadambri had made a home sex video. His face felt frozen. Slowly he lifted his eyes off the laptop screen and sought Suren's. The understanding passed between them, silent but crystal clear.

Suren must have hacked into women's iCloud storage. Twisted genius. Patel knew then that if he searched the dead women's computers or phones, he'd find sex videos.

Suren had stopped stroking himself, and sat in a pose reminiscent of those marble statues of classical Greek boys.

'Did you look into the files of every prominent woman in the city?' Patel asked the boy. Suren ignored him, cast his eyes down and away.

Patel turned back to the screen. Some videos were of good quality, some poor. Some abortive. One or the other of the couple, giggling, changing their minds, turning off the camera or knocking it from the other person's hands before the action truly began. There were a few threesomes, in every case two women with one man. His leg pinged with hurt.

Movement in his peripheral vision. The boy, opening a cupboard, giggling.

Draped in some sort of cloth, he posed for Patel. Reminded him of the quasi sari worn by the heroine in the movie poster. But the colour wasn't turmeric gold. He switched on the desk lamp and twisted its neck, aiming at Suren, who recoiled from the sudden brightness like a scalded cat. The colour of the sari leapt at him. Red.

Patel stood up so fast he upended the desk. The computer

monitor crashed to the floor with the lamp, plunging them in darkness. He stumbled to the wall by the door and found the light switch. Flicked it on. The ceiling lit up fluorescent white. Suren remained where he was, his face bearing the same placid expression.

The door opened. Mrs Hariharan. She saw Suren, not Patel.

'What was that noise? I fell asleep.'

She followed Suren's gaze to Patel, and a sound like a hiccup shot out of her throat.

'Where's the mayor?' Patel said.

Mrs Hariharan dashed from the doorway.

'Papa likes you,' Suren said to him.

Everyone likes me, thought Patel, his head pounding. 'Where is your father?'

Suren unwound the sari and looked from his hard-on to Patel, a bit shy, like a new girlfriend showing her breasts.

Patel took a step back towards the door.

Suren let the material of the sari drape his hard-on and swished it around.

'I'm going to find your mother,' Patel said to him. 'You stay here and get dressed.' He winced backwards, out through the door. He made to pull it closed, when Suren burst past, screaming. He forced Patel aside, then whipped around.

'Don't tell, don't tell,' he pleaded. Eyes darting this way and that, he shoved Patel towards the stairs. Patel stumbled backwards, his knee twanging. His cut was bleeding again, his foot slipping in the blood. He stumbled back towards the marble stairs.

'Stop,' he said to Suren. 'Go back to your room.'

The sari flowed from Suren's shoulders, tangled around his legs. His hard-on sprang up from a mass of pubic hair.

Much as he flinched to touch a naked man, Patel also didn't

want to crack his skull on pink marble. He stood his ground. He hooked his good arm on the banister and used the shoulder above his injured arm to shove back. Suren stopped, shouted, 'Don't touch me.'

Patel pushed Suren from him. Suren's eyes widened in horror at the sight of Patel's fingers pressed against his chest. Suren stepped back. His feet caught up in the circling length of sari and swayed. He put out his arm and grabbed Patel by his injured elbow.

Pain shot through Patel's arm. Instinctively he punched Suren in the face with his good arm. But that entailed letting go of the banister. His foot slid on the silky sari. He fell forwards, plumb on Suren. Suren's hard-on cosied into Patel's belly. Blindly he shoved at Suren who, still reeling from the punch to his face, stumbled back, his other foot also tangling in the sari. His thighs struck the banister but his upper body kept going. He flipped over the banister and vanished from view.

A crack and a thud. Then silence. Patel looked down. Suren lay like a fashion model in a photo shoot, the red sari covering his nakedness here and there, half-covering his crotch. Blood, dark and glistening, spilled out from his cracked skull and raced along the marble floor. His head lolled at an impossible angle to the rest of his body.

Patel's knees sagged at the realisation that he'd killed an autistic teenager. Was he involved in the murders? Or did the mayor just make use of his IT skills to target the women?

A cry. Mrs Hariharan rushed in, her mobile pressed to her ear. She stopped short and the phone slipped her hand and hit the floor. Patel could hear the tinny voice on the line, its sharp, unintelligible queries.

Mrs Hariharan did not approach her son. Instead, she simply turned around and walked away.

Patel went down the stairs as fast he could manage, scooped up her phone on which a male voice still spoke shrilly.

'Hello, Mr Mayor?' he said, and the line cut off. He slipped the phone into his pocket and went after Mrs Hariharan.

He found her in the kitchen. Back to the hob, she stood, as though waiting for him to show up.

'He always said I was a good wife,' she said, and struck a match.

'Why . . . ' The words died in him.

Behind her he could see a red cylinder with the words LPG on it. Liquid petroleum gas. She must have unscrewed the pipe. Colourless, odourless gas suffused the air around them.

The match didn't light. Patel threw himself forward. Mrs Hariharan stepped neatly away. Patel fell on his injured leg, pain shooting up through his thigh.

Her sari was wet down the front. The empty can teetered on the hob. He smelled something sharp. Kerosene. She struck another match. It lit.

She paused with the lit match, her wide eyes on him. Fire reflecting in her black irises, she said, 'Run,' and dropped the lit match.

He made it to the doorway, half scrambling, half crawling. The floor was on fire behind him.

He threw a glance over his shoulder. The fire raced up the side of the LPG cylinder. Why wasn't there an explosion yet? A keening sound emerged from Mrs Hariharan. Patel couldn't bear to look at her. He limped and dragged himself to the bathroom. It seemed much further than he'd thought. He turned the taps, clumsily soaked towels under the running water. Filled a plastic bucket. Still no explosion. He had to go back and attempt to save her.

He had lugged the bucket out of the bathroom when the

explosion shook the ground from his feet. A jolt cracked through his spine as his back slammed against the doorknob. Black spots danced in his eyes. Water cascaded over him from the bucket in flight. Then nothing.

Chapter Thirty-Six

Hazard lights flashing, eyes unseeing through futile wipers on the rain-engulfed windscreen, Hariharan held the phone in his hand for a long minute, even though he had switched it off after hearing Patel's voice, taken the sim card out and slipped it into his pocket. He stared at the dead phone, as though he could watch the catastrophe unfolding in his home through it, and *will* some kind of influence over the situation.

A blast of horn stabbed his eardrums, a lorry passed inches from the fender. The car shook like a leaf in the crosswind.

He dropped the phone on to the passenger seat, turned the car around. He did not know what awaited at his house, but he needed to go there.

A blaze engulfed the front of the house. Hariharan parked the car on the front lawn and stumbled out. The flames pummelled him back and around to the side of the house. The unholy heat seared through his clothes. Throat too dry to swallow, eyes burning with the smoke, he tried to see through to anything that was living, moving, breathing, inside his inhospitable home. Nothing. He heard shouts. Neighbours. Someone ran out from the house opposite, lugging a bucket. Hariharan ducked under the Harsingar tree and peered around the trunk. Another neighbour dragged out a coil of hosepipe. Samaritans in a crisis. Commotion near a window. Some people ran to the other side of the building. Two men materialised with handkerchiefs around their mouths and noses. They would go in, either burn to death, or drag someone out, alive. Hariharan felt paralysed. He had not accounted for this. He had to act. But act how? There wasn't anyone in there he wanted to risk his life for the chance of saving. Whatever deformed, half-melted cripple was left inside would have to die.

The flames were sucking at the annex now. His painting! Miraculously, it seemed, considering the circumstances, he had a key in his pocket. And in a gesture that seemed hysterically banal, he unlocked the door. Inside, the flames were already bursting through the cotton curtains, licking at the furniture. He got the painting off the wall, but an arc of flame shot forward, its monstrous hand grappling at his chin. Pain seared his skin and he stumbled against the sofa in the dark and fell awkwardly. His knee burst through the canvas. He cursed, pushed the broken picture away towards the fire. Fuck it. He turned to go, noticed the bottle of chloroform on the shelf, grabbed it and slipped it into his pocket. He felt his way out, eyes screwed almost shut against the stinging smoke. The front of the house blazed too intense to bear looking at. More people stood in front of his car, watching, slack-jawed, to see what singed, creeping thing would emerge from the inferno.

He couldn't get to his car without a dozen people seeing him. His gaze fell on the little shed further along from the annex. The rusty old Raleigh he'd inherited from his old dead retainer was kept in there. It had been handy at the Bannerguda dam. He went to the shed and fumbled in the dark, checked air pressure. A little slack, but not too bad.

It was only when he'd cycled half a mile, climbed up the Hill View Road, passed Suren's old school and stopped at a set of traffic lights that he realised where the hand of Manu was leading him. A gentleman in need goes to a gentleman, indeed. Within minutes, the rooftop of Hotel Top End came into view, smirking at the clouds.

Hariharan pushed the bike behind a pillar supporting the foyer roof, and went in. He rang the reception bell. A sleepy woman appeared. 'The police commissioner sent me,' he said.

In Patel's room, Manu felt home among Patel's things. A red sari and blouse discarded on the floor by the bed. He picked them up, inhaled Patel's scent from the fabric. Clutching it, he curled up on the bed and began to whimper. The events of the day crowded in, overwhelmed him. He was alone now. The boy and the wife were gone. The whimpers grew more frantic then slowed, settled, and Manu slipped into welcome oblivion.

From a gruelling, restless sleep, Hariharan's eyes were pried awake by a banging door down the hotel corridor. It took him many moments to remember his circumstances. He'd been asleep for what seemed like hours in Patel's hotel bed, and the time now, late evening. He had slept for way too long.

At seven p.m. he slipped from the hotel, keeping his face averted from potential busybodies, retrieved his bicycle and pedalled to his house. The fire had been completely doused. Several policemen were standing around stiffly, a police cordon in place. He tried to get nearer without anyone noticing him, passing an empty police jeep, its windows down, the walkie-talkie crackling. He reached in, grabbed it, lurched behind a neighbour's tree and tapped into the police channel.

After several minutes of inanity from chit-chatting constables, there it was: 'Scotland Yard rang again, looking for Patel.'

'... you tell her he's alive?'

'... Is he? I thought ...'

'... University Hospital ... been brought there. Rajkumar's on his way.'

An interruption from someone. 'Rajkumar just called ... All alerts out for Chandra madam. Top priority.'

He'd heard enough. He threw the walkie-talkie back into the jeep and jumped on his bicycle once more.

Freewheeling downhill towards the hotel foyer, he was nearly clipped by an airport taxi. He put his feet down to stop himself from colliding into the back of the taxi that had abruptly come to a halt in front of him. Shaking from the no-doubt rollercoaster taxi ride, a silky-haired white woman emerged from its back.

Shoving the bike behind the pillar once more, he walked in behind the white woman. The reception desk wasn't manned. She waited, her hands on the counter, too polite to ring the bell, with a barely perceptible tremor on her fingers.

Hariharan waited a step behind. After a minute, she casually glanced around, threw a tentative smile at him.

'Sarah,' he said. She looked exactly like the photo on her website.

Her eyebrows raised in surprise.

The right words slipped out easy as pie. 'Mr Patel is on the way. Shall I take you to his room?'

'So he got my message, after all. You are?'

'Chief Constable Varma.' Hariharan smiled his avuncular smile that took away the effects produced by his burnt chin, scruffy, smoky clothes and tousled, windswept hair. He took her elbow. 'Come.'

There was a buzzing noise from somewhere deep inside her handbag.

'Oh,' she said, rummaging. She produced a phone, held it to her ear. 'Hello? ... Yes, I'm at the hotel now. Going up to see him. When?' She looked at her watch. 'OK, I doubt we'll be going anywhere. Of course we will wait for you. See you in a bit.' She put her phone back in her bag.

'Was that . . . ?'

'The Assistant Commissioner,' she said. 'I called her when I couldn't reach Vijay.'

Hariharan said, 'She is coming here?'

'Yes. On the way. Which floor is it?'

Chandra on the way. Bird in the hand, or bird in the bush? He grinned. Why not both? Indeed.

Chapter Thirty-Seven

Words swirled and pinged on Patel's consciousness. A sing-song voice at odds with the meaning of the words. 'Ankle sprain' ... 'dislocated elbow' ... 'flesh wound' ... 'severed tendon' ... The fog slowly cleared further. 'Not enough blood loss to require a transfusion. No veins have been cut.'

His eyes focused. A small man in a white coat, stethoscope around his neck. 'You'll live to fight another day, Mr Patel.'

Patel sat up on a gurney on a busy hospital ward.

'How long have I been here?'

'Not to worry, Mr Patel. You were brought in the early hours of the morning. Now it is next evening.'

The paramedic looked and spoke uncannily like his GP back home. The one who had told him to come back in six weeks if his cough was still there.

'Luckily someone recognised your face after we cleaned you up. Word has been sent.'

There were two dead people. One a woman, one a mere boy. He had no superficial injuries. Man up, Mr Patel, and don't complain.

'You will need to stay in hospital. Ah, here you have a visitor.'

Rajkumar waded through the crush of patients towards him, glowering.

'Where's Chandra?' said Patel.

'You better have a hell of an explanation, Patel.'

When Patel finished, Rajkumar stared wordlessly for a moment, then found his tongue. 'You are a damned fool. You think that I, the chief of police, am chasing myself like a dog chases its tail? And you got Chandra to suspect me and sent her off on a bloody wild goose chase. She is like a daughter to me. If she ... if anything ... Scotland Yard and Minister Goldblum won't be able to protect you.'

'Where's the mayor?'

'He's not anywhere, not even at the council building. I've sent men out.'

'What if he's got Chandra?'

'We'll keep trying her phone,' said Rajkumar. He looked at Patel without speaking, taking in his torn, sodden clothes, his stench, his weariness. 'Go back to your hotel, freshen up, Patel. I'll call if we find anything. We will be here sometime. I am unable to believe, I mean, the boy is sixteen, seventeen?'

'Older,' said Patel. 'He just seemed younger, the way they treated him.'

'Still, a boy.'

'I'll go the hotel and call you from there,' he said to Rajkumar.

The doctor tutted. 'You will need fixing up first.'

'Oh I'll bear this too,' said Patel and hobbled out of the hospital to find an auto.

Chapter Thirty-Eight

The receptionist, rubbing tiredness from his eyes, said, 'Oh Mr Patel, so many messages for you.'

Patel's heart beat faster as the man rustled the pages of his notepad. 'From last night, one from Inspector Rima, Scotland Yard. Ah, erm . . .'

'Spit it out, will you?'

'"You jackass. Pick up your phone. Super's fuming."'

'OK, carry on.'

'Another call from Rima. "Sarah can't reach you either. What are you playing at?"'

'Any others?'

'Three messages from Sarah. That she called. Nothing more the first two times, but the third time, she said to tell you, "Call me, please. I'm here."'

'"I am here"?' said Patel. 'What does that mean, "I am here"?'

'I don't know, sir.' The receptionist looked frightened. 'Last message came only one hour ago.'

Typical bloody Sarah, he thought. Why couldn't she leave a bloody clear message like everyone else?

'And last one from a Miss Chandra, sir.'

Oh thank the lord, he thought, his heart knocking against his ribs.

The receptionist frowned. 'I can't remember if I wrote it

correctly, sir. It says, "Going to airport. Meet you at hotel." Or it's, "Going to hotel. Meet you at airport." He looked up and declared, 'I am slightly unclear about this.'

'If you've written it down, how can you be unclear?'

'I ran out of ink here, and by the time I found another pen, she'd hung up.'

'Give it to me.' Patel pondered the message. Chandra would have most likely said, 'Meet you at the airport,' because he was heading there. But why would she come to the hotel first?

'Did she come here then?'

'No sir, no lady came.'

Patel turned to head towards his room.

'Oh, one last message, sir.'

'Yes?'

'Your friend Gerry.'

'Friend?'

'That's what he said, sir. Your friend Gerry. "He knows me better as G," he said.'

Ice in Patel's veins.

Gerry. G. Gentleman.

'What did he say?

'"Come and get it."'

'What?'

'"Come and get it." That's all, sir.'

'That's all?'

'He's upstairs.'

Somehow, Patel overcame his frozen nerves and ran up the stairs, ignoring the howls of protest from his broken body. His door was ajar. Patel took a deep breath, willing his heart still. Quick glance in the bathroom. Nothing. He stopped.

Chandra was slumped at the foot of the bed, blood from her stomach collecting thickly in the ribbed carpet.

He dropped beside her, tried to find a pulse.

Bending close to her face, he whispered, 'Chandra.'

She was breathing, but faintly. Her eyelids fluttered when he repeated her name, but didn't open. She wasn't conscious.

He lurched to the telephone and rang reception.

'Call an ambulance. Find a doctor at the hotel and bring him. Get a first aid kit. Hurry. AC Chandra has been stabbed. Hurry!'

He dared not move her. Helplessly he looked around, grabbed a pillow off the bed, carefully slid it under her head.

It was then that he saw the piece of paper caught between her head and shoulder, tangled up in her hair.

In upright, square writing, it said, *Patel. Rooftop.*

The receptionist rushed in.

'Ambulance on the way sir,' he said, 'and a doctor on the first floor. She's coming too.'

'When the doctor gets here, call the police,' said Patel. 'Send them to the rooftop.'

'But there's nothing on the rooftop, sir.'

'He's all about the setting,' said Patel, and walked out.

As the lift closed, he saw a woman rush past, clutching a small black case. The doctor. A breath of relief broke out from his lungs.

He ran through the empty spa and massage areas, and on to the empty swimming pool, flickering blue in the city lights and dusty starlight.

A whimper.

In the far corner of the pool, Sarah sat cross-legged on the broken floor.

Suddenly, the hurts in his body ceased, every fibre of his body grew rigid with tension. Another whimper. Sarah wasn't in a position, he could see, to appreciate the parallel between the crack on this floor and the work of art they had bickered over so many years ago at the Turbine Hall.

Slowly he edged forward. A sense of inevitability released him from fear. Of the fact that he would survive, he had no doubt. Not for him the merciful, if ignoble exit at the hands of the murderer. But how to save Sarah? How to live if she died, and how to survive Chandra's possible death?

With his arm around Sarah's waist sat Mayor Hariharan. They were like some Indian couple on the beach. But the mayor's free hand belied that image. It held a knife to Sarah's throat. She trembled like the puppy he'd once found locked out of the neighbour's house. Wriggled out through a hole in the fence, couldn't get back in, caught in the cold rain.

Hariharan appeared to have his face buried in Sarah's hair, which probably still smelled of England. Slowly he lifted his head, inhaling deeply.

'Oh there you are. Come join us, Patel.' His tone was relaxed, charming and friendly, just as it had been at the party.

'Let her go,' said Patel, sounding to himself eerily calm.

'Oh no, Mr Patel,' said Hariharan. 'She's flown a long way to meet with her fate.'

'What do you mean?'

'Your fiancée is a nice girl, Mr Patel, but the filth she produces in the name of art ... You know that I am a connoisseur, Mr Patel. I have very developed tastes in art as well as life. She is a good girl, but not yet a suitable girl for you, Mr Patel.'

'A suitable girl?'

'You must be aware, that at heart, you are an Indian gentleman, Mr Patel, no matter your upbringing, your accent, your Western point of view. I recognised in you, my dear Patel, a sympathetic mind. And we have to make sure you aren't polluted by the influence of this woman. Modern whore, prostitute. We need to create an ideal pairing for you.'

'Why did you hurt Chandra?'

'Forget Chandra. Don't talk about Chandra.' There was an edge to Hariharan's voice.

'What about your wife and son?'

'What about them?'

'They are dead.'

Hariharan took a moment to take it in. 'Ah.' His grip tightened, and Sarah shut her eyes and forced her head back from the knife.

'My wife, my son. Suren. A smart boy, really, and damned handy too. He was a great help with that swan. Did you like the stitching?'

Patel gritted his teeth and forced an even tone into his voice. 'I'd like to understand what this is all this about.'

'All this? Everything? Why, Mr Patel, I'm disappointed. I thought you of all people understood the big picture.'

Sarah cried out. Patel caught her eyes and raised his eyebrows. She quietened.

Patel wondered how long the Indian police took. In Bollywood films, they always turned up after the hero triumphed, in time only to round up the villain and his gang, and cart them off to jail.

'I am the author, Mr Patel. I cannot explain my work. It is all written for people to read and to interpret and imbibe. Imagine if after writing the *Ramayana*, Valmiki was asked to explain it.'

'I understand. But what about your wife, Mr Hariharan? Where did she fit into all this?'

'She saw and didn't see. She knew and didn't know. I tried my best with her, gently and kindly, showed her how to become my perfect companion.'

'How did you meet her?'

'Arranged marriage, you see. The romance comes last. First the bond, the trust, the developing of the girl's character to suit the husband's mindset and temperament. But then I lost her to the care and duty of her son. He is all her doing, I must say. Useful in parts. On the whole a slight disappointment. But I started noticing his peculiar habits. He takes after my father, for sure.'

Patel itched to look at his watch. 'How like your father?' How long did they bloody take? He wished he had something, a weapon, a gun, a knife, at least a pencil. His fingers inched towards his pockets.

'You are stalling me, Mr Patel. But for what? The police will never come. Even if they get their fat bellies to move into gear quickly enough, they will be stuck in traffic for hours. Rapid-response team is based in Gulamnagar. Takes one hour at least. But to answer your question, I wanted him to become a cricketer, like yourself, but he just wanted to sit on his arse, all day. And then, about the time I was mulling over my life's work, I noticed his secret glee. He is screwing the servant girl, I thought. That wouldn't do, that just wouldn't do. My father's fears were mine. I followed Suren. He had taken to hanging around the garage down the road. They had found an old cattle gun . . .'

'A cattle gun!' So he was right about that, at least. 'But—'

'Yes, an ancient, broken one. They welded it for him, modified it to fit in a tiny bolt and marble-sized shot. He found stray dogs and fed them stale bread till they became as docile as you please. I saw him in a park in Basavant Nagar. He placed the cattle gun to a dog's forehead, and the animal stood there, wagging its tail, grinning its love, and boom. I saw the dog, even as its brain exploded through the back of the skull, still wagging that tail.'

'Jesus.' Patel could see Sarah held her nerve with the greatest of efforts.

'Beautiful, in a macabre way. It occurred to me. If only

women were as loyal as dogs. And it was curious, the mark the gun made on the dog's forehead. Just a dot, really, a red dot. Like a bindi. Like on a woman.'

Patel's stomach flip-flopped. Revulsion flared within his gut. But he nodded to the mayor. 'Carry on, please.'

'I was proud of him then. For the first time, I felt affectionate towards him. Not a lost cause, after all. The bugger had some spunk in him. But what a waste of that talent, killing stray dogs. What higher purpose did that violence serve? This pursuit of some momentary, transient pleasure, like hunting and killing, or eating a burger. Then you know what I saw?'

'A higher purpose?'

'I knew you'd get it. I adapted his excellent method to create my own revolution. At the risk of sounding like a braggart, I think it will go some way to setting society right.'

Patel stared at the mayor, his throat dry.

Sarah slumped. Her eyes began closing.

'Everyone's a critic,' said the mayor. He tightened his grip on Sarah. He looked angry. 'What have you achieved in your life? Have you created anything? You were a sportsman. A failed one. Your career died. Now you are what? A policeman? Is that all you are? I am at the zenith of my political and philosophical career. Where are you?'

'I am looking at you across a cracked, empty swimming pool. In this country, they still hang people like you. Let Sarah go.'

'Oh no,' said Hariharan. 'You killed my son and wife. Fitting in a way. The gods demand sacrifices. Now I kill your cunt for you. And I already killed your other cunt. I free you, Mr Patel. Your ideal woman is a dead woman, let's face it. I free you. That is my gift. One gentleman to another. Then you can join me in my revolution.'

'You are insane.'

'Oh no, I am very sane, just misunderstood in my own time. But it's changing. Under Ramrajya, my actions will become righteous.'

Oh boy, thought Patel. They are focusing on the wrong kind of terrorist here. His left hand went into his pocket. A phone. Mrs Hariharan's.

Gripping the phone, he closed his eyes, and imagined his hand clasping a cricket ball. Beautifully rounded wood, covered in red leather. Criss-cross stitching. He was right-handed. The tendon in his right wrist snapped in two, all those years ago. No confidence in his right hand. No time to swap either. Milliseconds ticked. Left hand it had to be. Left elbow partially dislocated. He'd have to throw from his shoulder. It was going to hurt.

His eyes opened into slits as they focused on the mayor's forehead. One two three paces. Mentally he did the run. He imagined twirling the ball, thumb on seam, two fingers down. He rolled his gait, he lifted his arm – the wrong arm– and brought the hand high, curved, let go.

The pain exploded in his elbow. His scream mingled with another scream, male or female he could not tell. His vision went black. Something clattered. When his vision swam back to his brain, he saw Sarah scramble away. The mayor, on one knee, clutched his face with one hand, groped with his other hand on the pool floor. The knife balanced on the edge of the crack.

Patel lunged. The mayor was already there. His hand closed on the handle. Patel was too far away; his foot snagged on the jagged edge of the crack.

Sarah, somehow, was there. She kicked at the knife. Hariharan screamed. She must have broken a finger or two with her boot. The knife fell into the crack. Patel flung himself upon the mayor and shouted, 'Go Sarah, get help.'

She stumbled and scrabbled to the end of the pool as Patel

held down the struggling, cursing mayor, his nose and fingers all bloody.

A door slammed, distracting Patel. Hariharan twisted away and scrambled up the side of the pool. Patel lurched after him and grabbed his foot, tugged. Hariharan fell back on top of Patel. Something crunched. A bone, spectacles, phone, who knew. A thud and a searing pain in his head. He found himself bent over the crack, the mayor's knee pressing against his throat.

'Police,' came a shout. The weight lifted off him. Relief exploded in his brain as Patel rolled away from the crack and blacked out.

Epilogue

There were bunches of flowers piled high all over the room. Chandra's face, pale and wan like the reflection of the moon in a river of hospital sheets.

Patel set his Billingham bag carefully on the floor and drew the armchair close to the bed, wincing a little. Nearly mended, but a few niggles remained.

Chandra, her voice barely a whisper, said, 'Afternoon, Inspector.'

Patel grimaced, smiled. 'It's only a recommendation. They will have to meet about it first.'

'Still. Congratulations.'

'Ta.' He fiddled with the flowers on the bedside table. 'You all right?'

She nodded.

He felt the tension, coiled inside him for days, ever so slightly relax its grip.

'No one tells me anything,' said Chandra, sulkily. Days of utter helplessness had reduced her to a needy child, thirsty for information denied her. She had been in a stable condition for only two days.

'Nice room you got here.'

'My dad booked a Deluxe room, you know, where you share with someone. But they gave me a free upgrade.'

'So this is what? A Super Deluxe? Deluxe first class?'

'The Deluxe Royale.' She sniggered, and winced.

'I am sorry I put you in so much danger, Chandra.'

'Don't be silly. It wasn't your fault.'

'But it is. I was the one not picking up my girlfriend's calls.'

'You can hardly blame yourself, or blame her, for that matter. She had to call someone after failing to reach you.'

'I can blame myself.'

'Oh shush. Anyway . . . ' Chandra paled. 'I need to know why.'

'Are you sure you don't want to hear this another time?'

'Now.' She reached out and clutched his hand, the skin on her fingers, dry, papery.

Patel sighed. 'They unearthed a diary. Or scriptures of sorts. The "Manu Chapters". He saw himself as a kind of avatar, sent to set society right, correct women who went astray. He published a book, wrote a blog.'

Chandra made a weak sound of laughter. 'So what's his background? Abusive mother?'

'Father. Some journalist dug out a big scandal about his mother. She had an affair with a low-caste servant. She had been this very traditional, motherly woman, big bindi, sari, yards of flowers in her hair, the works. There are hints about it in his diary, where he cannot help but slip into the past. He was very close to his mother. Worshipped her. He witnessed her having sexual relations with this servant. He couldn't reconcile the two images of her in his head. His father was brutal. He beat discipline into him, plus his archaic views on society. Brenner reckons there's a bit of homosexual suppression there, probably in the mayor's youth. But it's conjecture. His father thought he was spending too much time with his sisters, so beat him, raised him to be a leader among men, the mayor of the city he eventually became.'

'Bloody good mayor, too,' said Chandra, sadly. 'I was fucking fond of him.'

And he stabbed you in the stomach, thought Patel. A rush of emotion into his head. He leaned across and kissed her gently on the lips.

He said, 'Don't think about anything till you have the strength.'

'What else am I to do here?'

'Read a book,' he said. 'Listen to music. Get your friends and family around you.'

'I threw them all out at lunchtime. Couldn't get a minute's peace.'

Patel glanced at the single bed pushed against the wall. 'Who's staying with you?'

'They are taking turns. So far it's been my sister and mother. My dad's sulking because I said he can't.'

'Why not?'

'He talks too much.' She smiled.

Patel gazed at her for a minute, taking in the tubes running into her wrist, her complexion, her brittle hair, her pale grey lips. 'My flight's in three hours.'

'Back to your fiancée?'

'We have a lot to discuss, but I think I'll leave London for a while.'

'Where will you go?'

'Leicester for a bit. It's the sporting capital of the world, apparently.'

'Really?'

'Yeah. I'll eat Gujarati food, sleep late.'

'Very sportsmanlike.'

'Reminds me. I got you something.'

'Not more flowers.'

'Wait.' He opened the Billingham, brought out a box. Peeled back the layers, snapped off the lid, dug out the spoon.

'Is that?'

'Bisi bele bath. Mad Dog Hot.'

Acknowledgements

Jo Bell, Sharmaine Lovegrove, for making this real

Kath Grainger, for your brilliant input and enthusiasm, and the prologue!

Nila, Brân and Lupin, for all the love and cuddles

And again, Harry Whitehead, for keeping me honest

Bringing a book from manuscript to what you are reading is a team effort.

Dialogue Books would like to thank everyone at Little, Brown who helped to publish *Cold Sun* in the UK.

Editorial
Sharmaine Lovegrove
David Bamford
Hamzah Hussein

Contracts
Amy Patrick

Sales
Andrew Cattanach
Ben Goddard
Hannah Methuen
Caitriona Row

Design
Sophie Harris
Jo Taylor

Production
Narges Nojoumi

Publicity
Millie Seaward

Marketing
Emily Moran

Copy-editing
Charlotte Chapman

Proofreading
Saxon Bullock